W. B. Yeats
and the
Secret Masters
of the
World

W. B. Yeats
and the
Secret Masters
of the
World

P. R. Jennings

Let us go forth, the tellers of tales, and seize whatever prey the heart long for, and have no fear. Everything exists, everything is true, and the earth is only a little dust under our feet.

W. B. Yeats, 1896

Peter Fludde & Partners

W. B. Yeats and the Secret Masters of the World

This book is a work of fiction. Except in the case of historical fact, representation of all characters is a product of the author's imagination. Any resemblance to actual living persons is entirely coincidental.

ISBN 978-0-9575364-1-8

Peter Fludde

Poetry makes nothing happen.

W. H. Auden

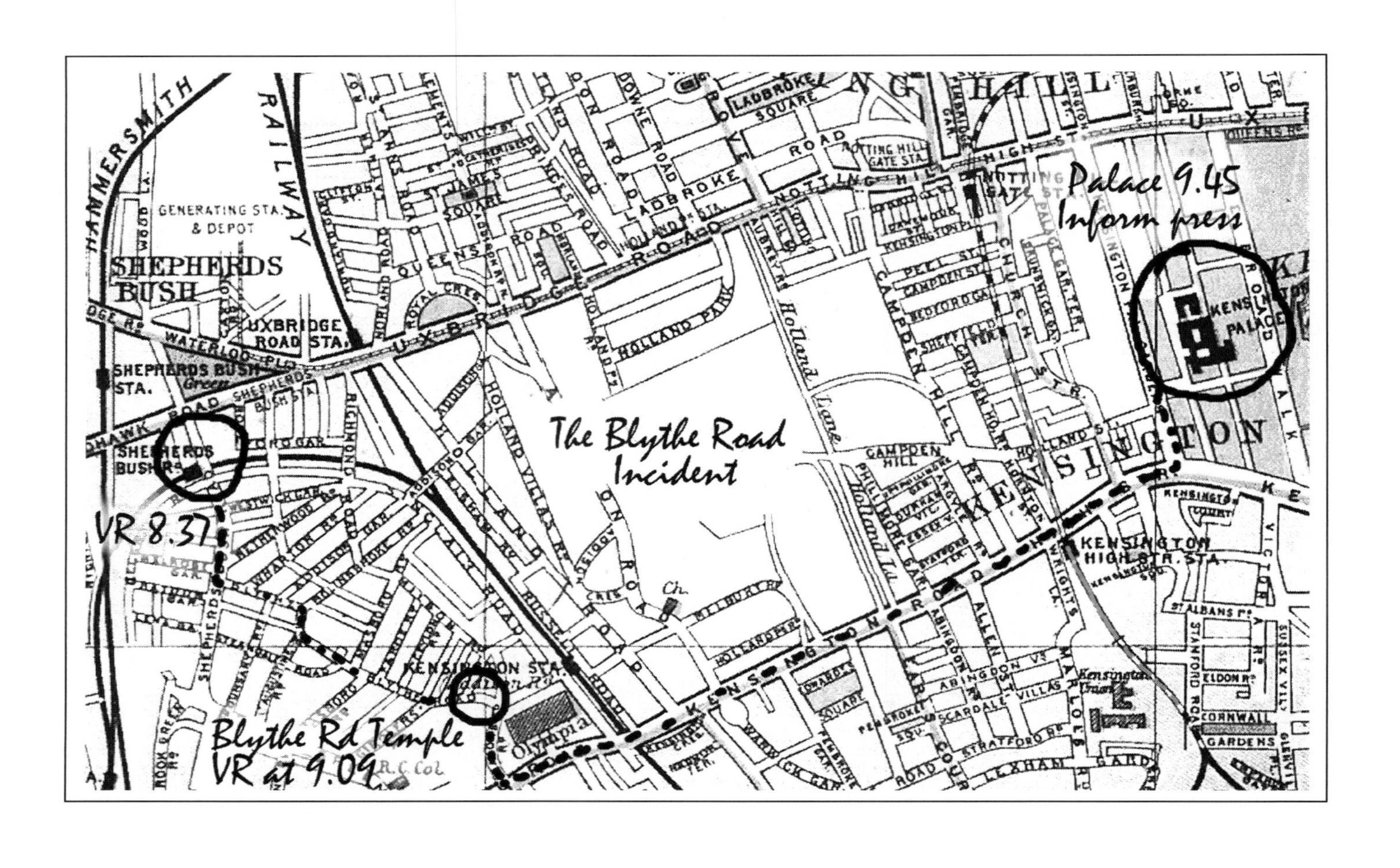
The Blythe Road Incident
Palace 9.45
Inform press
VR 8.37
Blythe Rd Temple
VR at 9.09
SHEPHERDS BUSH
GENERATING STA. & DEPOT
HAMMERSMITH
RAILWAY
UXBRIDGE ROAD STA.
SHEPHERDS BUSH STA.
KENSINGTON PALACE
KENSINGTON HIGH STR. STA.
KENSINGTON STA.
Olympia
Holland Lane
NOTTING HILL GATE STA.
LADBROKE SQUARE
HOLLAND PARK
HOLLAND VILLAS RD
CAMPDEN HILL
STANFORD ROAD
CORNWALL GARDENS

Contents

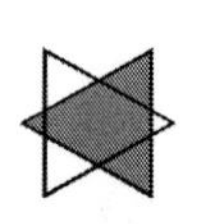

Fairies

'Mama, Mama, Willie has been talking to his little man again!'

His younger sister ran delightedly into the house in search of their mother. William Butler Yeats walked to the bottom of the garden and stayed there. He sat on a tree stump, staring darkly at nothing, imagining the future. One day... one day, there would be a great towering something, with him at the heart of it, and possibly the sound of gongs, and they would all fall back, open-mouthed, wondering. He had to forgive them, of course, because that's what you did when you were superior - forgave people who laughed at you. It troubled him how many people, especially the hard-fisted English schoolboys, he had to forgive for finding him funny. He sighed. He needed to make up a poem. Being a poet wasn't easy, but it was better than just being ridiculous. He reached for where the words came from but found a memory instead, a memory of early childhood, as clear and yet mistily-remote as the view through the penny telescope on Tower Bay Beach.

He is two years old, first-born and bright-eyed. His father generally speaks to him as if he were grown up, 'to bring the boy on', hoping his son will be more worldly-wise than himself.

'Well now Willie, what d'ye think?' John Butler Yeats says as they walk the coastal path very slowly, hand in hand, watching the red morning sun climb above Dublin Bay. 'Salmon pink or cerise? There, where the light touches the cloud-base.'

His son laughs explosively, a high gurgle. 'Ittle man,' pipes Willie. 'Funny ittle man.' The elder Yeats starts and turns pale. For a moment he thinks his two year old son is mocking his artistic sensibilities, like those philistines in Sligo. He smiles shakily when he realizes that Willie's attention is elsewhere. The relief is quickly replaced with parental concern. The little boy is staring delightedly at his own chubby outstretched palm. He is nodding and smiling.

'Willie, dear boy,' says JBY. 'What are you looking at?'

'Ittle man says you can't see him,' says his son, after cocking his head and listening for a moment. 'Or hear him.'

'Oh,' says Mr Yeats, 'of course.' He has read about this sort of thing but it is still worrying. Willie is such a sensitive boy. You have to be careful not to let things go too far. On the other hand, you must also take a child's imaginings entirely seriously. It is practically a sign of good breeding these days. It is all so hard.

'Does your little friend have a name?' he asks, getting the words out with difficulty. Both nature and nurture make him suspicious of whimsical fantasy. Believing in Fairies is what the Irish do. It is the kind of thing that makes them weak, and justifies their centuries of humiliation under Anglo-Norman common sense.

'He says you may call him Andy,' pipes the child after a few seconds.

'Oho, I expect that is because he likes to sit on your *hand*,' says his father. He watches anxiously for any reaction to the joke in his son's pale and rather earnest features, but the boy is listening again.

'Oh no, it's not. He says it's a an - a - gram. He says it's funnier 'n yours, cos you can turn it round as much as you like but it'll still take you people fifty years to see the HOW and the WHY!'

'What?' exclaims John Yeats, startled by his son's high-pitched screaming of the two words. 'Why did you shout so, Willie? You quite surprised me.'

'Cos he did, Papa. Ittle man shouted, so I did.'

'I wish I could hear him, Willie,' says his father, with a wobbly artificial smile.

The two year old boy brings his levelled palm to his own ear, his eyebrows, already darkening away from baby blondness, drawn together in concentration. I'm meant to think the little man is whispering, thinks his father. Very good. Why am I frightened?

'Ittle man says,' whispers the young Yeats, looking up intently into his father's face. 'He says, be vewy careful what you wish for.'

At the end of the garden, perched poetically on his apple tree stump, twelve year old Willie Yeats could not hear his sister Lollie any more. She had probably been intercepted by Lily, the elder of the two girls. Lily was protective, did not like to see him teased. They were close in age and the little man who appeared and spoke only to her sensitive brother had been an unquestioned part of the secret life of the very young. By the age of six Lily had known that big boys had mice and catapults, not invisible fairies. Willie Yeats knew it too. After that cliff-walk incident, his father had become terrified of encouraging his son's imagination in the wrong direction. The young Yeats had been firmly pushed towards reason and the sciences. This had not stopped the fairy from appearing to the boy, but it had made Mr Yeats less anxious, which pleased his son, who was learning to protect the brittle gaiety of his father's restless nature. He was in any case becoming more careful about sharing knowledge of his little man. People were so ready to think you were peculiar, and anyway, it was the little man himself who advised him to be cautious.

It was hard to follow the advice. The little man told him such interesting things, such as no serious artist using the word *cerise* any more. When Yeats proudly repeated this to his father, there were a few terrible days of interrogation concerning who had put the boy up to it. After that, Yeats stopped trying to talk about the little man with anyone except Lily. His younger sister could not be trusted. She had enjoyed the game at first but when she found it was not just a game to her brother, she had become angry and then scornful. She called him a big baby (she was only four at the time) but the truth was, of course, that she wanted a fairy of her own.

After Yeats turned seven, the little man's visits became less regular and far less frequent. He would be gone for a week, a month, four months, then return just when his conversation, lessons and stories were beginning to seem like the memory of an intensely imagined game.

This was the first time the little man had ever appeared to Yeats outside Ireland. The bottom of this garden in the London suburb of Hammersmith was not a fairy-friendly environment. The garden wall was raw red-brick, and the gravel pathway encircled the stumps of an ancient orchard which Mr Yeats had been advised to cut down because old fruit trees encouraged pests. The volatile artist had immediately regretted the act and for days afterwards would crunch angrily round and round the path with his fists stuck deep in his jacket pockets muttering Damn Damn Damn. After that, his children saw the end of the garden as cursed ground, a place of doom and shame.

The Fairy sat on the next apple-tree stump. It did not look well, seemed distracted. Yeats would remember it, wouldn't he? Yes, it was going away for a while. Something about bodies and clocks. It would be back, when it was time. Until then, be sure and not forget his lesson. What lesson?

They found Willie Yeats pale and cold, asleep in the long grass which had sprung up in the old orchard since the gardener was dismissed. It looked as if it had grown around the sleeping boy. They could not wake him at first and when they did he wept as if his heart was breaking. He was in bed for a week, and then he went back to school. When his form master was reading to them from The Faerie Queene, Yeats put a hand up in his serious rather middle-aged way, as if to offer a point of information. When the master looked at him, he slowly put his hand down again. 'I am sorry Sir, I have forgot what it was.'

And he really had.

He loved his sister Lily because he knew she loved him. It would be many years before he dared love anyone else. It would be exactly the same number of years, months, days, hours, minutes and seconds before he saw the Fairy again.

February, 1899

Twenty-two years further down the timeline, and one hour away by the London, Brighton and South Coast railway, William Thomas Horton, artist, visionary and mystic counsellor to anyone who would listen, placed a little round brass lamp in the centre of the circle he had drawn in pink chalk on his living room floor. He took great care not to scuff the pentacle and other symbols drawn within the circle's wobbly perimeter. His hands were shaking and the flame quivered, a single angel dancing on an oily pin. The shadows it cast were coal black and they all moved at once, like a crowd of faceless demons watching a tennis match. The biggest and blackest of the shadows was his own. It loomed over him, massive and menacing, not at all the friendly companion of daytime. He kept glancing at it and sometimes, when it was behind his back, he had to twist right round to see what it was doing. You probably understand.

It was difficult to hold the spell-book open while he worked. He really needed an assistant for this sort of thing, but Horton was not the kind of man with lots of broad-minded friends who would be up for supernatural experiments, and the only other people he could have called upon, well, he did not want the purity of his scepticism tainted by any crass belief.

It had all been so exciting at first. Yeats was obviously going to be a Great Poet and it had been an immense stroke of luck to be able to call him a friend. From wondering whether you were any good, to seeing your stuff in a flash magazine, was an amazingly easy step with Yeats behind you, tall dark and intense and so impressively sure that he was right. Knowing Yeats, someone else who thought the world was upside down, with all the important stuff at the bottom and stupid time-wasting delusions like money and business at the top - it felt like being in the Bible, finding someone who really believed in what people were supposed to believe in but generally didn't, so your whole life changed.

They both saw England from the outside, like foreigners, Yeats because of the Anglo-Irish thing, Horton because he had been born in Bruges, and spoke French until the age of ten; but even if he had been a native of Essex, a man like Horton would never belong anywhere; not strong enough to lead and too proud to follow, he was osmotically drawn to Yeats, a weak solution to a stronger one. The thing about Yeats... the thing about Yeats was he made you feel so damned important, as if you and he were the only two people in the world to share the Great Secret.

Horton had tried to believe in magic, he really had. He was the kind of man who threw himself wholly into the interests of his latest acquaintance: not in the spirit of competition, of course - it was a kind of flattery, an attempt to please, to fit in. Yeats and the Golden Dawn: the whole thing was so ready-made and right for him. An atmosphere so-to-speak musky, attractively strange, hung around its people and their rituals. They all seemed to have money, or know how to get it. Must be the magic. Except they didn't seem to do much magic. Lots of dressing up and chanting, but you were always being told 'not yet' or 'the time is not propitious'.

If ever a magician deserved to get something back for his efforts, thought Horton, it must be W. B. Yeats, but the great man never had much luck - unless you counted things like premonitory dreams, elusive smells and odd coincidences which weren't that odd when you really thought about it. He felt both a fraternal sympathy and a pleasing sensation of superiority: Yeats earnestly pursued magic and got absolutely nowhere; he, Horton, had allowed himself to be lectured on magic and secret masters while suspecting it was really all self-deceiving piffle and probably wicked as well. For him there was only one Master, and He made no secret of his location in the human heart.

Nevertheless, the failure of this impulsive experiment would make a good story at the next of Yeats' Monday evening gatherings. He would casually drop into the conversation that he had done the ritual (Yeats had told him not to, *warned* him not to, for God's sake!), done it exactly right and according to the book which they did not know he had. He then imagined how he would tell the knowing little circle that it had not worked. He would say something like, '... and all I got out of it was back-ache!' and everyone would laugh. They might even remember his name next time.

He squatted by the lamp and sat down clumsily, cross-legged and straight-backed. He held the book up at arm's length, made a false start, cleared his throat and then spoke the words printed in thick black letters, oddly fat and close-packed, in two columns on the knife-cut linen wove pages. 'Veni O Spiritu Tenebrae, in nominibus quinque gradus vitae, Adenax, Gwanon, Thumin, Uracil, Sitoz.' Horton felt less nervous when the first words were out. He did not feel such an idiot now, just resigned to three more pages of this hocus-pocus stuff before he could legitimately declare victory over superstition. He drew in his breath to begin the next words of the incantation and then gasped, choking as the two actions wrestled in his wind-pipe. Something like thick black smoke was pouring from the knot-hole, the one which had always reminded him of a skull, on the bared floorboards exposed by the rolled-back Chinese rug. The desperate thought came to him that some spilled oil had somehow caught fire and he stood up awkwardly in the little protected space at the centre of the circle, lost his balance and kicked the lamp, which went out. Now it was completely dark.

'Now it is completely dark,' someone said.

It was sixty yards to The Ploughman's Rest and Horton was still accelerating when he hit the swing doors like a demonic blast. Two old men playing dominoes looked up, startled, until they saw who it was. Just Mr Horton in one of his existential panics; there was no harm in him, no harm in him at all.

After half an hour in the tobacco-hazy heat and noise of the public bar, Horton felt better and rather ashamed. He went back sheepishly to inspect the wreckage of the ritual in his living room, which in the gaslight told an embarrassing story of frightened blundering and ignominious flight. Where he thought the smoky presence had been, there was nothing - not a dent or a stain on the varnished floorboards. He turned the gas up, retrieved the lamp, mopped up the spilled oil and dried the boards, then spread the rug and set a cheerful little fire crackling in the grate. He straightened up, smiling at himself in the mantelpiece mirror.

'Not going mad then.'

'Of course not,' his reflection said.

Several hours south and across the English Channel, Horton's admired friend and patron W. B. Yeats, thirty-four years old, is catching the boat-train at Paris Gare du Nord, chin dug into a swathe of scarf, hands stuck deep into the side pockets of his high-collared traveling coat. The long black skirts of the close-woven woollen coat whip around his legs as a cold gust finds its way into and through the echoing iron forest of the station concourse. France always gets him down. The country robs him of his main weapon, language, and with the language his voice, and with the voice his always-fragile confidence.

What was the French for 'gone'? Passé? Disparu said it better. Disappeared, vanished, his hopes of marrying the love of his life or even, frankly, getting into bed with her. Maud. Maud Gonne. All gone. What made it worse was, she had said It again: 'Don't be silly, Willie.' She knew how much it annoyed him, and always pretended she didn't.

'You should be grateful,' she had said, 'that I don't say "yes". Think of all those wonderful poems you wouldn't be able to write if you weren't miserable. Anyway,' she had continued, reaching up her white arm to swat a fly on the ceiling, 'if you think you're miserable now... I'm not even sure I want men.'

Like several other anti-sex women he knew, Yeats reflected, who had consoled him with the same confession, Maud had given it a pretty good go to make sure – only not with him. It wasn't fair. He was perfectly prepared to be rejected after the event. Sometimes there was the tiniest glimmer, the mere shape or shadow of a thought in his mind that it would be a lot easier *not* to love Maud Gonne, with her shallow enthusiasm for the latest cause, her liking for violence and violent men and her unspeakably smelly collection, which went everywhere with her, of caged and unhappy birds.

He thought of Wilde then, and felt ashamed. Poor Oscar Wilde, also tamed and caged, holed up in a dingy room at the Hôtel d'Alsace, exiled by the Tory establishment for being clever, for being Irish and for being right about them. Yeats had gone on to visit him after the last futile hour at Maud's with a relief that dared not speak its name.

Oscar Wilde now seemed so much older than Yeats, more than the actual ten years' difference. His fall from grace, trial and imprisonment had marked the heavy features like blight across a familiar Irish hillside. Wilde's brilliant conversation in London and Dublin had once silenced the young poet, but now the exile spoke slowly and with long melancholy pauses, in which he let his face fall into tragic troughs and creases and stared sightlessly like an old warrior into the past. News from London, Dublin gossip, stimulated a courteous pretence of interest; there was only one thing which had re-animated Wilde's dark heavy-lidded eyes and brought a smile to his sensuously large lips, and it was something which worried and embarrassed Yeats.

Towards the end of the uncomfortable visit, Wilde became more and more agitated and then revealed, in an urgent half-whisper, that he had a beautiful companion, 'a lovely little man,' he said. 'No, not him. I mean here, with me, in these rooms.' Wilde beckoned Yeats nearer and the tall poet dutifully but with guilty reluctance leaned his long body over on the cold hard Parisian settee so that the tight leather creaked. 'I can honestly tell you,' Wilde had murmured, at uncomfortably close range, 'that without my beautiful little man to keep me company, I think I should have gone completely mad.'

Yeats had muttered something about discretion – even now – a new scandal – but Wilde cut through him. 'No, no, no,' he had whispered fiercely, the sunken eyes feverishly bright. 'You don't understand. This little man is here all the time. He is here now. He is standing by your elbow.' And the exiled dramatist had focused his eyes on empty space, laughing and weeping, until Yeats wept too, and took his leave.

On Platform 5 of Paris Gare du Nord, Yeats was going over and over the scene: Wilde, staring at nothing and talking fondly of his invisible little friend. There was all the sadness of a noble mind o'erthrown, but there was something in Yeats' memory trying to get his attention, a shape in the corner of the mind's eye like a small figure waving, which disappeared if he tried to look at it directly. Wilde's behaviour disturbed Yeats because it was familiar, with the unsettling quality of last night's dream suddenly remembered in broad daylight.

All things considered, Yeats was relieved to see the Boulogne train reversing in, sliding very quietly around the long curve of the platform. The first carriage passed him, in its maroon, black and gold livery, dripping from a sudden downpour that was still hammering on the station's high roof. Clack-clack, clack-clack, the big wheels slowed, the second carriage passed, the third, the fourth… and the fifth drew to a gentle stop, offering its wrought iron steps and handrail to him.

Five again. A shape made itself in his mind. Four points in a square with a fifth point in the middle: the Quincunx. He was seeing fives everywhere. Aware of the fine line between observation and obsession, Yeats deliberately chose the seventh carriage back from the engine and settled into the corner of an empty compartment. It was not the season for cross-channel holidays and there were very few passengers. He was glad to have the compartment to himself because he needed to think. He rested his blue stubbly cheek against the coarse tobacco-smelling cloth of the high-backed seat, and thought about Macgregor Mathers.

43 rue Ribéra, Ahathoor Temple Number 7 and home of the Chief and co-founder of the Golden Dawn, had been his third and last call in Paris, there to meet with Samuel Liddell MacGregor Mathers, Compte de Glenstrae, and Mina, or Moina, his wife: *he* was the scion of an ancient Highland dynasty, priest-kings of a kind, fiercely yet tenderly guarding the mysteries of a noble Celtic heritage; *she* was the sister of the brilliant Henri Bergson, one of the greatest minds in nineteenth century France. Bergson argued that analysing our corkscrew passage through space-time using vocabulary adapted to crossing rivers and dodging landslides in Ice Age Europe might explain some of the philosophical and logical problems which philosophers and logicians made whole careers out of solving. This simple and apparently sound remark made him a great many enemies.

Mina, as clever as her brother Henri, was the practical one; from her own mystical insights she developed a working ritual, a magical ladder which could raise the adept to a direct knowledge and experience of the All. She was kind, darkly attractive, affectionate and forgiving; she let her husband call her Moina because it sounded more Scottish, and she did not question the reality of his noble ancestry because he himself was real and his mind was noble, and she loved him for it.

Sam Mathers was a dreamer and she wanted him to have his dream. Together they presided as Imperator and Praemonstratrix over the Parisian Temple of the Golden Dawn, subsidised by Mina's great friend Annie Horniman, the tea-heiress and patroness of the arts. Miss Horniman did not approve of Mathers and felt guilty about encouraging him. She had found him employment in her father's library and had introduced him to Mina Bergson. *He* thought she was envious of his magical knowledge and power; *she* thought he was ungrateful and weak.

Yeats had visited them in Paris in an attempt to repair the rift. The poet was all for the independence of the creative mind, but considered that in his feud with Miss Horniman, Mathers was not only biting the hand which fed him but going for the arm as well.

'Willie me boy,' said Mathers when he and his wife greeted Yeats at the imposing entrance of their suburban villa. 'May a thousand blessings light on your head.'

'And on yours,' replied Yeats politely.

'And may the earth currents flow strongly up your Tree of Life,' said his wife Moina earnestly, squeezing Yeats' upper arm.

Yeats opened his mouth, thought for a moment, and closed it again. 'Thank you,' he said and smiled awkwardly. The Mathers had a way of outbidding any of your counter-culture behaviour before you had really got going.

'Enochian Chess?' said Mathers, taking Yeats into his pleasant high-ceilinged study, overlooking a garden and the surrounding houses, elegant and tall, which gave Ahathoor Temple No. 7 its useful privacy.

'Paris is like a permanent Royal Ascot,' Yeats said as he pretended to take in the view from the window, 'so many self-confident people.' He was trying to think of a way of refusing Mathers' offer which would not hurt his feelings.

Enochian Chess was a game invented by William Westcott, co-founder of the Golden Dawn, which Mathers, according to his own account, perfected. It was a game for four people, playing in pairs. Each player controlled a full set of chess pieces, advancing from one of the four points of the compass under the colours of the four elements. The complex rules were based on Dr Dee's angel magick: certain sequences of moves invoked spirits, and some were considered too dangerous to be made by a beginner.

Mathers had never been beaten but tended to win by default, as his opponents usually gave up after about a dozen moves, tired of being told in deeply condescending tones that 'Nothing obvious is correct' and 'the only Right Move is the one not made', and then seeing him slam his most powerful piece down on theirs with the artless aggression of a ten year-old. Another reason for Mathers' invincibility was his custom of playing with an invisible spirit partner. When four players were not available, a participant might play both of his side's positions to make up the number, but Mathers claimed to have a supernatural companion that made this unnecessary. He would shade his eyes and squint at the empty chair opposite, frown and nod a few times as if receiving complicated instructions, then lean forward and move his unseen partner's piece for him. This would unsettle even the most determined opponents. It was also annoying to be told, 'Ssh, my spirit partner is thinking.'

All this flashed through Yeats' mind as he hesitated, unwilling to say yes, unable to say no. Blessedly, Mathers seemed less manically pressing than usual.

'They're… watching me, you know,' he said, moving to Yeats' side at the window.

'My God!' said Yeats, peering through the net curtain, deliverance from the dreaded game energizing his agreement. 'I believe you're right. There, in the narrow entrance. There are two men in bowler hats, looking straight at us.'

'I don't mean... humans,' said Mathers, turning to Yeats and staring hypnotically. *How does he get his pupils to contract like that?* thought Yeats. With an effort of will he broke away and sat down, determined to slow the onset of Mathers' usual headache-inducing intensity.

'I have had… company,' said Mathers, lowering the gas on the staring-eye treatment while he pursued Yeats across the room and then turning it up again when he was sitting opposite him.

I wish he wouldn't always do that, thought Yeats. The little pause that said, 'You are to take the next thing I say as coded language, metaphor or euphemism because a) I am sworn to secrecy about what I really mean or b) you are too far beneath my level of initiation to understand the truth, even if I were to make it known to you, which I won't.' Even a possibly forgiveable 'c) We both know what I mean but you never know who's listening,' was still annoying when someone did it all the time.

'They are… in the house,' said Mathers. 'They are… here… now.'

'What?' said Yeats, too startled to resent the mannerism. First Oscar Wilde and now Mathers, talking of invisible companions! Then he saw that Mathers was only being Mathers. Someone who was really seeing fairies would not affect such a conscious pose of mystery. Yeats knew the right signs - bright-eyed excitement, a restless impatience with the ordinary or else, perhaps, the remote contentment of someone who is never lonely. Memory stirred. Fairies. A chasm was opening up at his feet and he felt dizzy.

Moina Mathers appeared in the study doorway. 'Would you like… a cup of tea?' she said in a deep hollow voice, and smiled at Yeats over her husband's thinning sandy-haired head. He thought about that smile all the way back to London, the smile, women - and something else: his carriage was designated, in gilt-edged black letters, against all logic or observation, Numéro Cinq of thirteen and his end compartment was the fifth of five and the corner seat into which he had thrown himself heedlessly was identified in a faded hand-painted number on the wooden panel above and behind the high back: *5*

Meanwhile, back in the capital of Britain and its Empire, Alexander Snelgrove, editor and part-owner of the Kensington Mercury, was struggling to put the next day's paper to bed.

As a newspaperman for thirty three years, ten of them in Fleet Street, Snelgrove was a stickler for accuracy, not truth. He knew truth was something that usually emerged years after the event when the dust had settled, sometimes never; but accuracy was something any sharp eye could recognize. Even now, in semi-retirement, a 'short' column would torture him for twenty four hours, until the next edition came from the press like a papery balm to sooth the irritation.

Snelgrove had a particular phobia about white space. A packed front page filled his heart with the pride and pleasure of a king fondly reviewing his model army. Empty space was the nightmare, and empty space was looming. An advertisement for false teeth - 'Genuinely indistinguishable from the real thing' - had been withdrawn at the last moment on a tip-off that they *were* the genuine thing, and obtained in a genuinely illegal and really unpleasant way.

'What have we got, Micky?' he said, without taking his eyes from the paste-up proof sheet he held in his spatulate ink-stained fingers. Micky was his assistant and in charge of the reserves. These were current stories considered too trivial, dull, strange or unverifiable for normal printing but useful in an emergency. Micky flipped a large forelock of oily black hair back from his pimply forehead, sniffed adenoidally and read off the headings, shuffling through the stack of stories with the ease of a card-sharp:

'Ice on Serpentine, Fairies in Balham, Odd Lights in Finchley Road, Spiritualists Upset in Maidenhead, Intoxicated Vicar "Sees Gnomes"...'

'Seems to be a bit of a theme going on in the reserves, Micky,' said the editor, still not taking his eyes off the paste-up sheet. It was a superstition. If he looked up, there would be Nothing To Print. There would be White Space.

'It's all about fairies,' Micky muttered resentfully riffling the stack again and muttering to himself, 'or spirits and such.'

'How about Ice on Serpentine?' said Snelgrove. 'That's not fairies.'

'Hyde Park Warden Cobb,' read Micky in his glotal monotone, 'has volunteered to swear before two witnesses that he saw crowds of Little People skating and dancing on the Serpentine which although it was a warm day had the appearance of being covered in ice of a peculiar blue-green tint which made him, Warden Cobb, "feel all funny". Warden Cobb is to lose his employment.'

'Quite right too, by the sound of it,' said Snelgrove, primly. He was starting to sweat though. Where was the Story, the filler? You couldn't go with any of these. It was all about fairies, not real life. He felt faint.

'Fairies,' he said, clenching his fist on the stub of his square-sectioned Grey Knotts pencil. 'Fairies are silly season. You can't fill with fairies in February. I don't believe in fairies. I don't. I don't.'

'Mr Snelgrove?' said Micky, trying to draw the editor's attention and at the same time check where the door was. 'Mr Snelgrove, there's a...'

'There's a what?' said Alexander Snelgrove, turning his head, and his eyes were the bolting eyes of a March hare.

'Nothing,' said Micky, from the doorway. 'There's nothing on your shoulder.'

A few miles away across night-time London there was a man who knew he had something on his shoulders. Guarding the Prime Minister was no light matter to Sergeant Jim 'Duckman' Platimer. The big policeman would be pleased to reach the end of another shift without an attack from mad Irish bombers.

On this particular night he had been looking forward to the end of his duty from the moment it began: the puddles had iced over at sunset and now, with Big Ben clanging out midnight, the temperature was still falling. The only way to keep the circulation going was to do a deep knees-bend every minute or so. Platimer shivered under his thick cape and blew on his cupped hands, his breath condensing cold and wet on his moustache. The action prompted a thought and he smiled, proud of the knowledge that even on such a night, his fellow-volunteers in the Society would be busy in the streets.

The Society was the Society of the Church Penitentiary for the Reclamation of Fallen Women. Sergeant Platimer had helped a number of fallen women back to respectability, some of them more than once, and always in the name of the Society's founder, and his hero, William Ewart Gladstone, the Grand Old Man. Platimer unconsciously brushed a finger through his large side-whiskers, remembering. Number 10 was looking a bit run down these days but when the GOM was there – such times! You could say what you liked about Gladstone (and plenty did), he hadn't been too proud to share it round.

This thought brought Platimer's mind back to the present and he glanced up at the grand Portland stone frontage behind him. Lord Salisbury, the current Prime Minister, preferred the more impressive accommodation opposite Number 10, the Admiralty Building. He was in there now, working late to keep the Empire's enemies at bay. And Sergeant Platimer was at his side, or not far off. The posting should be a fillip to his career - whatever that was - he imagined something pillar-box red glued to his record. He needed the encouragement. People, other coppers in particular, could be so hurtful.

The expression on Sergeant Platimer's face abruptly changed from contentment to deep gloom and two cold drops fell like tears from the ends of his moustache.

He appreciated a joke as much as anyone, but for the life of him he could not see why the knowing old hands of the Downing Street detail had burdened him with the nickname 'Duckbill', rapidly altered to 'The Duckman' when he complained. Platimer. Platypus. It wasn't funny. It wasn't fair. It preyed on his mind so much that his wife no longer suggested riverside walks. Duckman! As the twelfth deep chime rang out, he wrinkled his large, inward-curving Platimer nose and pensively drew in the wide upper-lip with pronounced over-bite which he had got from his mum: no, he just couldn't see it. The whole world was on his back. And now this.

It had started with a movement, sensed rather than seen, at the extreme edge of vision: a colourful moth, perhaps, or something more leggy like a cranefly, dipping and rising just above head height. It would have puzzled a naturalist; but even Sergeant Platimer, who thought nature was something which only happened in the countryside, knew that not many rainbow-winged insects were likely to be hovering above your head, glowing, on a frosty February night in Downing Street. His eyes agreed, and told him what he was seeing. His mind had not quite had time to catch up with his eyes when the dark intruder appeared from the night and Sergeant Platimer's first encounter began.

'Do you believe in fairies?'

The dark figure stood in front of him as if it had just asked for the time of day. Irish dynamiters didn't act like this. Or did they? How could you tell with the Irish? They were all mad, even the ones who looked all right, but this one, in the electric moonlight of the Downing Street lamps, didn't look like anything except cloaked, hatted and undersized. The angle of the hat suggested a certain attitude. Platimer leaned forward, warily, for a better look.

The cove was not obviously a threat, it was just that you couldn't see any face beneath the wide brim of that floppy hat – the electric light did cast such very deep shadows. He was probably a homeless vagrant, one of the thousands who lived, briefly, on the streets. But what was a vagrant doing in Downing Street at midnight? Drunk, probably. This could look bad if he did not end it at once. He might not get that fillip – certainly not a nice red one.

'Shove off, will you?' said Sergeant Platimer, straightening up with an official sniff. 'Nearest kip is up Piccadilly way.'

The slight figure remained strangely still; his sort were usually shifting from foot to foot. The unseen face under the hat-brim was beginning to affect Platimer's nerves: he didn't like its expression.

'Do you believe in fairies? That's the third time.'

The voice was patient, with an odd regional burr and an overlay of something dangerously like mockery: it had been a long day, and Duckman Platimer had had quite enough.

'Nah, I don't believe in fairies,' the police sergeant said, 'but I do believe in this here big truncheon, which I am now a-drawing, and I do believe also…'

But the Platimer creed remained unfinished. The following day, his report to a rapidly convened Committee of Enquiry aroused hurtful laughter when, helmet clenched under a quivering arm, he dutifully responded to their question *And what is the last thing you remember?* because the last thing he remembered, before everything went swimmy, were the words 'That's a pity,' spoken right in his ear but also somehow from very, very far away.

What he did not tell the smirking toffs on the Committee, and only dared whisper to his drowsy wife in the warm underworld of blanket and eiderdown, was the first thing he saw.

'Don't be daft,' said Mrs Platimer, drawing her troubled husband to her, 'there's no such thing as fairies, so you can't have seen one.'

*

Fairies. Arthur Conan Doyle looked out of his study window and tapped his front teeth with the blunt end of a pencil, thinking hard. His elbows rested on either side of an open manuscript book. On its first page, otherwise unmarked, he had written *Arthur Conan Doyle. Conan Doyle. Arthur Doyle. Sir Arthur Doyle. Lord Conan D…*

A few months from his fortieth birthday, able to sell pretty much anything he felt like writing, and the creator of Sherlock Holmes had dried up. It's what comes, he said to himself, from getting involved with politics, even in a good cause. Public life quenched the creative fire. The story-urge was there, but there was no inspiration. Nothing. Or maybe - he had something for a moment - there would be a boy, a wizard's orphan, ignorant of his magical destiny. He would be in the power of spiteful guardians, and then, a fairy... oh damn and blast, he was just remembering Cinderella.

He had been very keen to help when they first approached him but he might have thought twice if he had known how it would affect his professional life. He sighed. He was in too deep now. He was doing something for them next week, yet another talk on Our Lost American Colonies. At least it would not require any original thinking.

Rat-a-tat-tat. The postman was knocking at the door. Doyle ignored it. Tap, tap, tippety-tap went the pencil on his teeth. Rat-a-tat-tat went the postman.

The blank page stared at Doyle, and he stared back. Now the postman had stopped knocking at the door. He was kicking it, and shouting, 'Let me out! Please let me out!'

With a sigh, Doyle pushed his chair back and went to a narrow door, shut and locked, in the corner near the fireplace.

'If I let you out,' said Doyle calmly and clearly, 'you must promise not to do it again.'

A voice, muffled by solid oak, said, 'I won't do it again.'

'I want to hear what you're not going to do again,' said the author, patiently.

'I'm not going to hide in this cupboard to find out whether you are really Sherlock Holmes.'

'Or...?'

'Dr Watson.'

'Or?'

'Or to see whether Sherlock Holmes secretly lives here with you.'

'Or...?

'Visits you.'

'Or...?'

'To prove you are Professor Moriarty and keeping Sherlock Holmes prisoner.'

'Hmm,' said Doyle, 'well, we'll see.' And he turned the long-barrelled brass key and opened the door. 'Come on then, Patrick,' he said.

In the large windowless store-room, otherwise empty except for a few tea-chests from the Doyles' last move, stood a sharp-nosed man of middle height in the smart brass-buttoned uniform of the General Post Office. His peaked cap was under his arm, a big brown hessian bag half-full of letters at his feet. He put the cap back on his head of curly hair (hair rather bushy at the sides so that it projected well beyond the cap rim and spoiled the institutional effect), slung the bag over his shoulder and shuffled out. Doyle shut the cupboard door and turned to speak to the postman. He wasn't there. He was over by Doyle's desk.

'Now then, Pat,' said Doyle. 'I really do wish there was something for you to see.'

The postman grinned engagingly and shouldered his sack again. He had the demeanour of a loyal and much-loved family dog with a known weakness for sausages.

'Away with you,' said Doyle, 'and I hope you haven't disturbed Mrs Doyle.'

'Never in a thousand years,' said the postman. 'Is Mrs Doyle...?'

'No, no better,' said Doyle. 'Now, off you go.'

The postman hitched the heavy bag of letters higher on his shoulders and turned to leave.

'I do miss him, you know,' he said. 'Is he ever coming back?'

'No, I'm afraid not,' said Doyle. 'He rests in peace at the foot of the Reichenbach Falls.'

'Couldn't Dr Watson...'

'No!' snapped Doyle.

The postman left by the study door, and Doyle went back to his desk and began to think about plots again. A bony hand silently appeared in front of his face, making him jump so violently that he nearly knocked over his cut-glass inkwell.

'Almost forgot,' said the postman. 'Letter for you.'

'Thank you, Pat,' said Doyle. Frowning like a schoolmaster, he watched the postman through the door, along the hall, and out. Only when he heard the back door slam did he return to his desk, smiling. He had often considered complaining about Patrick, but the man's cheerful eccentricity called to something in himself.

Doyle was still smiling as he slit the envelope open with a bold surgeonly flourish. Inside was a letter on a single sheet of paper. The poor handwriting did not bode well; nor did the first line. Doyle's smile faded as he laid the envelope aside and began reading:

Dear Mr Doyle,

I hope you are well. Please could you ask Mr Sherlock Holmes to look into how our Fanny has taken up with Black Magishuns and Forengers. Fanny is a Sweet and Innocent girl and Handsome with it but she has changed since she has met Mr Crowley and I fear he is an evil Influence on her and puts Ideas into her head. I am but a poor laboring man but maybe Mr Holmes will take this on gratis and for nothing like he does sometimes when it is a case of Unusual Intrest with several Unique Features, which this one defnitly has, our Fanny being as I say the most Beautiful Young creature in the world or at least this part of London, and seeing as it involves Dark Powers which we wot not of which the offishul police would scoff at.

Yours in hope, Eli Smith

PS You will find Them at 36 Blythe Road this Monday coming. I have followed Her there but more I dare not do.

PPS Mr Crowley said he would put a Curse on me if I was boring about it and Asked Questions but this does not count does it?

As he read, Doyle's face went through a series of expressions: weary recognition, kindly contempt, a preparatory hardening and then – after a moment during which fate hung suspended – genuine interest: 'Our Fanny has taken up with Black Magishuns and Forengers…' Intriguing – and at least it wasn't about America.

The reference to magicians reminded him of the Golden Dawn, that mysterious society which Pullen Burry had tried to get him to join last year. And 36 Blythe Road sounded familiar. But they weren't black magicians, were they? Were they? And what about this man who could inspire fear by threatening to lay a curse on someone? In London? In 1899? Doyle wanted to believe it with all his heart. He placed the letter on his big walnut-veneered desk, to one side of the inset rectangle of green leather, and smoothed it several times with a hand like a hairy spade. He then took a sheet of note-paper from the desk drawer, placed it neatly on top of the nearly virginal writing book, uncapped his beautiful Waterman fountain pen with a flourish and, in his large, clear and somewhat boyish hand, began to write.

Arthur Conan Doyle received a great many letters from the simple or outright mad who, like his postman, believed, or wanted to believe, that his fictional detective really existed. As usual, his correspondent, was politely if briefly informed that Sherlock Holmes would sadly be engaged elsewhere and unable to take the case, but then there came a pause in the smooth progress of the iridium-tipped gold pen-nib, during which Doyle gazed out of the window with a happy gleam in his eyes, imagining 'the most Beautiful Young creature in the world' in need of rescue by a sensible chap with some boxing skills and a large British Army-issue revolver, never used but often aimed, in his bottom desk drawer. The marbled-red Waterman pen moved again across the notepaper, lustrous royal blue ink flowed and Eli Smith was informed that on this occasion, on this very rare occasion, Mr Doyle himself could be persuaded to take an interest in the case.

Conan Doyle reached for an envelope, looked guiltily over his shoulder, put his reply inside the envelope and stuck it down. His pen nib hovered and withdrew.

'Idiot,' he muttered. 'He hasn't put his address.'

Again Doyle glanced over his shoulder, afflicted by the feeling that someone was watching. He laid his useless reply aside and picked up the other letter.

'I would really like to know where you live, Mr Smith,' he said, knowing it to be a lie, that it was not the letter's author who had aroused his curiosity. To distract himself from guilty but exciting thoughts, he tried to recover the thread of his ideas for a supernatural story, but was soon staring unseeing out of the window again.

What Doyle wanted was not fairies, but Fanny.

Magicians

'Two thousand four hundred and forty-one, two thousand four hundred and forty-two...'

Back in London, Yeats had thrown himself into magic. It kept other things out of his mind. Now he was counting paces as he walked. When he reached his destination, the Isis-Urania Temple of the Hermetic Order of the Golden Dawn, he would apply numerological analysis to the total. There would be a significance in this journey, and it would reveal itself in the number of his footsteps. He could have taken a cab, and worked with the cab number and the date, but the horse is a creature of wind and fire, not water and earth; the magical sympathies would work better through the downward thrust of the soles of his feet meeting the upward round of the great mother in her stony London skirts.

As a magician, Yeats knew that everything is connected to everything else throughout space and time. He walked with Lully and Agrippa. Merlin was his spiritual father, and a lot more reliable than his earthly one. He knew a hundred different Words of Command and the proper way to address a demon of the Third Level. He laughed out loud, feeling sure that today there were in his face no marks of weakness, marks of woe; he wished that Blake were still alive so that he could surprise the older poet in the act of being disappointed with the mind-manacled London commuters. There would have been a meeting of eyes, pagan sorcerer to Christian cabalist, a moment of recognition, a grave nod exchanged (Yeats' head dipped at the thought) and they would have passed on, equal but different, strong towers both, self-possessed.

'Yes thank you madam, I am perfectly all right,' he said. The three small East End women, up to town for the day, were wearing big hats decorated with fruit and feathers. They had life-hardened faces, but they looked at Yeats kindly. 'Only we thought you'd been took peculiar.'

Three thousand one hundred and nine, three thousand one hundred and ten... he must remember to be nice to Miss Horniman and to watch out for Aleister Crowley. Yeats suddenly found himself noticing the cold acid sting of the London air, and how grim everything looked under the low roof of fog. *It is thicker, and darker, down by the river.* Now where had that thought come from?

Three thousand six hundred. Three thousand six hundred and one... and into Hyde Park. Yeats stepped out with more energy as he reached the gravel path which followed the north bank of the Serpentine, enjoying the crunchy give underfoot. Past the Royal Humane Society's Receiving House for drowned swimmers and soon afterwards his footsteps were resounding on the bridge which marked the beginning of Kensington Gardens. Across the bridge, and a few hundred paces brought him to the Round Pond, where he stopped to breathe the fresher air which came off the water.

Yeats shut his eyes and imagined Coole Park in Sligo, with its swans and Lady Augusta Gregory's soup, opened them and still saw swans. There were five of them (five again!) floating placidly in the dark water, very white against the tendrils of grey mist, and being fed by two children, a boy and a girl, twins, in the charge of a uniformed nursemaid.

The nursemaid, young and pretty, glanced at him and smiled. Yeats looked quickly away in case she thought he had been staring and she made a face at him instead. The children threw the last of their bread all at once and began playing a game, clapping small clean hands in time to a riddling rhyme which Yeats had never heard before and yet was teasingly familiar.

'This is the truth, I tell no lie
A thing you need to know
Low is just the same as high
And high the same as low
Lots and lots come from the one
The one that's hard to find,
Though kindled by the moon and sun
And carried in the wind,
It grows upon the good old earth
It makes us all we are
And all in all is what it's worth
When fed upon a star.'

The children chanted their rhyme with serious little faces and then turned and looked at Yeats as if studying its effect. Yeats smiled vaguely and quickly walked on.

On. Six thousand one hundred and two, six thousand one hundred and three… the trouble with Crowley was…

Something flew across his path and made him blink and start back. It was too early for butterflies. There had been the fleeting impression of a solid body and colourful wings but when he turned his head to follow its line of flight, there was nothing to be seen but bare branches and a fat grey pigeon which looked as if it had never taken wing in its life. The poet shook his head and walked on with his long-legged and slightly bobbing gait.

'Six thousand one hundred and four,' Yeats whispered to himself. 'Six thousand one hundred…'

He felt odd. Something had just happened to him – but what? Again he sensed that movement near his eye but when he turned there was nothing except, maybe, just for a second, the fading image of a small compact body like a bumble bee hovering; but bumble bees did not fly around in February, did they? Maybe English ones did. Sligo suddenly felt a long way away.

'... and five.' The poet walked on. His heart was beating too quickly and he would be glad to get out of the park, which felt strange today. Marks of weakness, marks of woe were back on his face, he was sure. It would be a relief to be amongst the magicians at the Isis-Urania Temple of the Golden Dawn, where you could get a nice cup of tea.

The park would not let him go so easily. There was something happening at the West Gate, where the foot and road ways came together and swept out into the main Kensington Road. A hansom cab had come to an untidy standstill at the end of two deep furrows in the gravel. A larger and heavier private carriage, black, with unusually small windows, had been driven across its path. There was no sign of the cab driver.

A blue-uniformed soldier, tall, tanned and moustached, stood by the open door of the hansom cab, his pillbox hat cockily aslant. There was a leather satchel slung over his shoulder. His posture was relaxed, his eyes steady, but one hand was kept firmly on the satchel strap. The driver and two passengers from the private carriage were lined up aggressively, staring at the soldier. He looked back calmly, smiling slightly, but still that strong hand gripped the satchel strap. Suddenly one of the three, straight-faced and swarthy under a brown bowler hat, walked forward, slapped contemptuously at the soldier's face and tried to pull the satchel from his shoulder. The soldier swayed away from the slap and punched the brown man on the point of his jaw, making him sit down, hard. Yeats stood there with his mouth open and his heart pounding, thinking *I am watching someone being brave. This is what it looks like.*

Then the other two men attacked the soldier. One of them received a lightning straight-armed shove under the nose with the base of the soldier's palm which took him right off his feet. Yeats gasped. It was a warrior's skill, a hero's move, the salmon-leap of Cuchullain. Then the third man, grey haired and canny, stepped in and punched the soldier in the face with a professional boxer's force and accuracy. He still got a kick to the belly that drove him back but the soldier now looked dazed, supporting himself with his free hand on the carriage door-frame.

Yeats felt a powerful urge to help. He imagined going to stand beside the soldier and saying loudly and clearly, *I am no fighter but three against one is wrong.* And then the poet's endlessly shaping mind imagined one of the attackers producing a knife and driving it with casual skill into his heart ('death would have been almost instantaneous') while the soldier looked on in uncomprehending and not particularly grateful surprise. So W. B. Yeats stood, wrestling with his fears, and did nothing.

The other two attackers were on their feet again, making as if to rush the soldier while the third crept round behind him. Then, seeing the crowd of onlookers growing and hearing the word 'police', the three abruptly returned to their carriage. The grey-haired man took the reins, the other two jumped in, a brown hand pulled the door shut, and they were gone.

The hail of gravel created by the departing carriage pattered and stilled; the cloud of dust dispersed, taking all the drama with it. A fine-featured middle-aged woman, in the elaborate black dress of a fashionable widow, bustled forward and fussed over the soldier, loudly declaring how shameful it was and how she would have dearly liked to help him had she been a man. At this point the widow, the twenty-or-so people who had drifted up during the incident including the nursemaid and the two children, a park attendant and a stray dog all looked at Yeats.

Six thousand four hundred and ninety-one, six thousand four hundred and ninety-two… ti-tumpty-tumpty-tumpty-tumpty-TUM… a gloomy king watches the last of the Nine Heroes of Erinn die of shame, in dreary Irish rain, and the wind… what does the wind do? What did it do last time? Soughs over the dry bones of dead warriors. Is that sows or sogs? Suffs? Rattles the warrior bones. Rattles the dead bones. Rattles the bones of the dead. Six thousand eight hundred and fifty-five, six thousand eight hundred and fifty-six… the dead men rattle their bones and dance. The hour of the Fool is at hand. But what about the coward?

*

Agent 42 straightened up and put the leather-covered wire cord back in her overcoat pocket, still breathing hard from the unexpectedly determined resistance put up by the Target. She sucked in a strand of yellow London fog and coughed helplessly for a few seconds when the acrid vapour stung her throat. She straightened up, tensing, as two figures suddenly appeared out of the fog, feeling their way along the new Thames Embankment wall. She had heard no footsteps, sensed nothing. A voice came out of the murk: 'Don' breeve, darlin, that's the trick!' The other one laughed hoarsely, then the fog swallowed them and the tap and crunch of their hobnailed boots died away. In a cold rage at herself, Agent 42 stirred the body with the toe of her shoe. She would have to do better or They would not trust her with the serious work. This one was only a journalist; her sister's murderers would be harder to reach, let alone kill. Now there were voices again but these were the ones in her head: *Patience*, the voices said, *your time will come.*

She suppressed another cough, bent down and rolled the body to a gap in the Embankment parapet. She listened intently for a moment (no point in looking) then shoved it over the edge. She remembered the Thames tide at exactly the same moment that she heard the unwatery splat as the body hit river mud. Another mistake. She drew in her breath to curse again but had to cough instead, her eyes streaming. Damn the fog, but the returning flood would float the corpse off and wash it far downriver before it lifted.

Then up from the waterline thirty feet below came a groan and wet sucking noises as someone detached himself groggily from the soft grey Thames mud. At the same moment she heard people approaching along the Embankment. Agent 42 stamped her foot and walked away, furious. It wasn't fair. Human beings were so easy to hurt but so hard to kill. This was her second failure since being recruited, by a man she knew only as Elijah, to execute the enemies of freedom. Had something made her ease the tension on the throttling loop, as she sensed the last spark of life preparing to leave the limp body of her victim? No one had shown such compassion in her sister's last moments.

Angry and ashamed, Agent 42 resolved that there would be no mistake with her third target, an important one, the Irish literary enthusiast. 'He will be at the Cheshire Cheese eating house,' her controller had said. 'You will find him showing off amongst his cronies. Do it where it will be noticed, but don't get caught. He'll be no trouble. He's a poet, a dreamer and a physical coward.'

*

Walk, count, don't think.

Yeats' destination, 36 Blythe Road was one of a row of solid suburban houses, each with businesses at ground level and three floors of private accommodation above, the uppermost in the attic. It was thought by some at the time and has certainly been said since, that Number 36 Blythe Road was an odd, if not embarrassingly ordinary place to locate the headquarters of the greatest magical order of the modern era. True, it was discreet. Yeats and many of his colleagues appreciated being able to slip in and out of the unassuming house without feeling conspicuous; uninformed people often failed to understand the difference between applied transcendentalism and devil worship.

36 Blythe Road – notwithstanding the generous support of Miss Horniman, the tea heiress and clairvoyant – was also cheap. And it had another attraction: the Vault. Constructed by Mathers himself, the Vault of Christian Rosenkreutz was a holy of holies reserved for the members of the secretive Second Order. Although it consisted of Golden Dawn members, met in the Society's premises and ran the Society, it was effectively an entirely separate organization.

Macgregor Mathers had started it when the Outer Order became too numerous, and the neophytes too pushy, too knowing; the Chief of a magical society needed a mysterious Other to lend him weight; and the trouble with teaching was that you did yourself out of a job. New mysteries were required and Mathers had supplied them. Great and terrible indeed were the secret mysteries of the Vault, surrounded by Moina's artwork, to her husband's design and intended to recreate the tomb of Christian Rosenkreutz, mythical founder of the Order of the Rosy Cross, the Rosicrucians.

Nothing stays secret for ever, sometimes not even for long, especially when modern magicians are involved. The real mystery lay beyond the Vault: no one, not even the head of the order, Samuel Liddell MacGregor Mathers, the Comte de Glenstrae himself, knew why it was so important that their meetings should be held at Number 36 Blythe Road. Only the king of the fairies knew that.

Still counting, Yeats turned into Blythe Road. A horse-drawn lorry had drawn up outside Number 36, home of the Golden Dawn's London Temple, and two flat-capped men, in shirt-sleeves despite the chilly day, were sliding a wire-bound wooden case down a rough board and into the building's basement.

Pog ma hone, and wasn't that Horton too, hanging around and waiting for him while pretending to be interested in Crossley's Carpentry at Number 34? The visionary mystic looked agitated. Yeats began to insert mild obscenities between the numbers, black eyebrows drawing together. This was hardly the discreet arrival that Blythe Road usually offered.

'Wait!' he said sharply, as the wooden case teetered on the cusp of its splintery slide down the delivery men's plank. 'Let me see that.'

The deal wood case, the size and proportions of a milk crate, was stencilled YEATS LONDON, on top and at each end. It was heavily wired in doubled strands, four across, two along, twisted, cinched tight then expertly knotted and crimped. There was no indication of the contents. It would be hell to undo.

'There you are, Mr Yeats,' said the smaller of the two delivery men, whose enormous grey cloth cap made him look like a human-mushroom hybrid, 'Just sign this if you please.'

Yeats scanned the flimsy blue delivery form and made an odd little noise in his throat that was the inadvertent vocalization of the deep groan which he uttered inside. The crate came from 43 rue Ribéra, Ahathoor Temple Number 7 of the Golden Dawn in Paris, but had been paid for, Yeats guessed, by the love of his life, Maud Gonne. She had drawn 'their' sign in one corner of the form: a cheeky boy with a wide grin, eyes upturned in an affectation of innocence and a cap turned awry on his tousled head. Maud had been shown how to draw this by one of her childhood friends. Yeats had the feeling that she did it because she had heard about intimacy. It always made him feel slightly sick.

Briefly a member of the London Temple, Maud had retained a condescending interest in the Society; Yeats suspected she encouraged his commitment to the Golden Dawn to distract him from his other, less convenient, passion for her.

'Ceremonial candles,' Yeats read out loud. 'I can't sign this. It refers to one hundred items.'

Another mushroom man thrust his floppy-capped head and shoulders out of the delivery window in the basement.

'Any more?' he said.

'Coming down,' said the chief mushroom. 'Last one.'

Yeats stooped and peered into the dim interior of the basement, where a large pyramid of wire-bound boxes was revealed. A hundred crates! What could Maud possibly think he would do with that many magic candles? And who had let the delivery men into the basement?

'You know, you should look after that document,' said Horton to the delivery man as Yeats scribbled a signature. 'It will be valuable in years to come.' The man acknowledged this with a noncommittal grunt and a tug on the peak of his cap, an action that might have been meant as deference but certainly hid his face. The last crate went down, his mate in the basement shot out of the delivery hatch and scampered like a baboon up the inclined plank, pulled it after him, used it to shut the tin door over the hatch, chucked it up into the wagon and swung himself up after it. The wagon rumbled off, the iron-shod feet of the two great shire horses slithering and sparking on Blythe Road's hard little cobbles.

Yeats' frown came back. 'Odd,' he said. 'Very odd.'

'Listen,' said Horton, 'I must tell you. Something disturbing happened to me last night.'

'Ssh, wait, Horton,' said Yeats, as he went the last few paces to the doorstep of Number 36. 'Nine thousand six hundred and fifty-one, nine thousand six hundred and fifty-two, nine thousand six hundred and fifty-three.' The poet turned his dark eyes and strong pale face to the London sky, calculating, lips moving. He reached his result, put it from his mind, and turned his attention wholly on his friend.

'Now then,' he said, taking Horton's elbow and drawing him towards the street door of the Golden Dawn, 'let me see if I can remember - you have dreamed again of a tall, dark, pale-featured man journeying in pursuit of strange lights which he can never quite reach. A lovely half-naked girl follows him with her arms outstretched, weeping…'

Two women with identical ankle-length high-buttoned dresses and severe hair-styles turned simultaneously and gave Yeats, and then Horton, a long hard look.

'A lovely *symbolic* half-naked girl,' said Horton with harsh emphasis, turning his back to the women and moving closer to Yeats. 'Yes. In my dream, as always, she follows you, and from inside you there comes a great knocking and a voice which says, My son, my son, open unto me and I will give thee light.'

'Horton, dear Horton, if your drawings were as fine as your visions...,' Yeats began, then stopped and decided to take another line. Horton was so volatile, so on the edge, one had to be careful. 'I know you fear for me,' Yeats said, 'and I appreciate your concern, believe me. I recognize that inner voice of which you speak. It says different things to me. Can't you accept that?'

Horton, who was unusual in being tall enough to look Yeats in the eye, did so for a good few seconds, with an expression of slightly unhinged benevolence. 'Just be sure,' he whispered hoarsely, 'when you hear such a voice, that you know who or what it comes from. I tell you, something peculiar happened last night when I was trying a ritual…' The sentence was never completed. Horton froze like a startled rabbit as a dead-white hand fell upon his shoulder and a pale face appeared silently in the shade of the brick entry like an ominous planet rising.

'Crowley,' Horton croaked through dry lips, with a bad imitation of self confidence.

Aleister Crowley smiled wolfishly for Horton but he was looking at Yeats. 'Gentlemen,' he said, 'I killed a man today.'

Yeats stared back at Crowley. Challenge prickled in the air. 'You killed his spirit,' said Yeats, 'of course.'

'Is there any other way to kill a man?' said Crowley, his intense eyes boring into Yeats' at close range, his voice deep and sonorous in the confines of the brick arch.

'Well, yes,' said Horton, now very red and annoyed at being caught in the crossfire of egos. 'You could shoot him, cut his head off, strangle him, in fact you could, you know, actually kill him instead of coming out with damn stupid...' Horton tailed off, because Crowley was obviously not listening to him – not hearing would be more accurate, just staring unfocused as if reading something on the bricks behind him. Crowley's fleshy lips moved and in light conversational tones he said,

'It will come back. It knows where you live now.'

Then the big pale face cleared, the eyes focused and he looked from Yeats to Horton: 'What?' he said.

'What?' said Yeats, startled.

'What did you mean?' said Horton in a high strangled voice.

'When?'

'Now. You said it would come back.'

'No I didn't. You were just inciting me to commit murder.'

'Me? I...no...' spluttered Horton, but Crowley shouldered him aside and threw the door open. 'Come,' he intoned, 'let us go up.'

'You coming up?' said Yeats to Horton.

' I - I'm not a member any more.'

'Come as my guest,' said Yeats firmly.

They followed Crowley as led the way up the steep stairs to the Golden Dawn's meeting room, his long black cloak brushing the bare treads.

'If that was anyone else,' thought Yeats, 'it would snag on a nail. Why am I letting him lead?' Crowley, only admitted into the outer circle of the Society a year ago, was getting far too powerful, and with unnatural speed. It was very troubling to the regular members. The man was obviously a magician.

A number of other distracting thoughts revolved in the poet's ever-working mind as he climbed the stairs. The magic number derived from the nine thousand six hundred and fifty-three paces he had taken today from his home to the Golden Dawn was nine plus six plus five plus three, twenty-three, which yielded two plus three: five, again! The quincunx was following him. What did it mean?

Another mystery: the delivery man had addressed him confidently, even familiarly, as 'Mr Yeats' when asking him to sign for the candles, although Yeats had never seen him or his wagon in Blythe Road before.

The poet was concerned too about Horton, who had gone as white as a sheet when Crowley had come out with that silly 'it knows where you live' stuff.

And he ought to find out what *Pog ma hone* meant.

*

The Intelligence Department at the rear of the Admiralty Building in Downing Street looked from the outside like the offices of a moderately successful biscuit manufacturer. On the top floor, behind cheap decorative brickwork and cosmetic turrets, sat a small man with sandy hair and a moon face, complete with craters left by childhood smallpox. He sat alone, on two cushions and a swivelly chair with surprising arms, behind a desk with a surface area approaching that of a small tennis court. He spread his short-fingered much be-ringed hands to either side and pressed down on the desk-top as if restraining it from taking flight. 'Yes,' he said, emphasizing and prolonging the word, like someone who knows a *hell* of a lot and doesn't know where to begin the exposure of someone else's naivety. 'Ye-e-esss. The Irish Question. Ha!'

There was a scratching at the door; it opened after a nervous pause and a long blue chin and pointed nose came into view, followed by the rest of a black-suited and high-collared clerk. 'Oh, I am sorry, Sir Cuthbert,' he said. 'I heard you shout. I thought…'

'Tube!' shouted the sandy-haired man at the desk, head back, eyes shut and face screwed up like a saint enduring the hot tongs.

'Oh… yes, of course.' The clerk scuttled out, closing the door behind him, carefully. A moment later a shrill whistle sounded and the man behind the desk, Sir Cuthbert Dangermouse (pronounced Dormers) slowly and methodically removed a brass and rubber bung from one of a great nest of similar horned tubes which sprouted like a bouquet engineered by Isembard Kingdom Brunel, and spoke into it.

'Yes?' he said distractedly, pulling some documents towards him as he did so.

'It's O'Hara, sir.'

'What is?'

There was the slightest pause at the other end of the speaking tube as someone's brain changed gear. 'I was just in there sir.'

Sir Cuthbert signed his name at the foot of a paper marked Topmost Secret. His signature was illegible, or rather it was legible but looked exactly like *Clangers*

'What matter? Forget something?'

Another pause, slightly longer, then: 'No sir, sorry to bother you sir.'

'Well, try not to tube me unless it's important eh?' said Sir Cuthbert, and shoved the stopper back in while his secretary's words of apology, tinny and hollow, were still spilling from the horn.

The whistle went again almost immediately, making Sir Cuthbert drop his dip pen, which splattered ink on Topmost Secret. He removed the speaking-tube stopper and held the slightly prosthetic-looking horn to his ear. 'Yes?' he snapped, drying the ink with a telegram. The telegram had MOST URGENT printed all the way around the edges, creating a nice floral effect.

'Sir Campbell MacMack is here to see you sir.'

'Well bring him in, for God's sake man,' shouted Sir Cuthbert, 'What are you tubing me for?'

The door opened immediately and O'Hara stood aside for a big fat man dressed from top to toe in brown tweeds, complete with a brown tweed fisherman's hat and brown leather boots which laced halfway up his legs and into which his trousers were tucked, creating a jodphur-like effect and giving him hips like a neolithic fertility goddess.

'What ho, Dangermouse!' boomed the newcomer, striding forward with his fat red hand extended.

'Dormers,' said Sir Cuthbert levelly, coming round his desk and taking MacMack's hand, 'it's pronounced "Dormers" '.

'I know, I know,' said MacMack, 'couldn't resist it. Schooldays, y'know. Seems like yesterday.'

'Well it wasn't,' said Sir Cuthbert, flapping his hand crossly for his secretary to go. 'It was fifty years ago, and it damn well feels like it sometimes.'

He gave his visitor a drink, sat him down and regained his own seat behind the desk in the spring-loaded swivelly chair with patent castors and surprising arms.

'Remember the Head, old Swisher Pervis?' said Sir Campbell. 'Now there was a character!'

Sir Cuthbert sat bolt upright on his cushions, looking at his glass. 'A character,' he murmured, 'yes, he certainly went his own way. It's why my face is covered in these scars. Pervis thought using bovine serum to inoculate against the smallpox was an abomination against nature, so he got his good friend the school doctor to administer the real thing.' Sir Cuthbert held up his hand, with thumb and first finger wide apart. 'Just there,' he said, 'I felt a strange pang when they cut it. As if my body knew. The first pustules appeared within days.'

MacMack sipped at his whisky and looked at him, blue eyes cold under bushy white brows. 'It's Salisbury,' he said. 'He wants an answer.'

Little Sir Cuthbert leaned back on his chair, then rapidly forward again as his cushions threatened to slip. 'Ah yes,' he said, spreading his hands palm-down on the shiny desk-top. 'Ye-e-esss. The Irish Question. Ha!'

The speaking tube whistled shrilly, completely spoiling the effect. MacMack sank another large glass of single malt and looked on with intelligent interest as Sir Cuthbert barked 'What?' into the horn, held it to his ear then snapped 'No, I am perfectly all right,' and hung and stoppered the instrument with a loud *pock!*

'The answer to the Irish Question is perfectly clear, as our current Prime Minister well knows,' said Sir Cuthbert, rather red in the face. Somewhere behind that face a decent man was drowning. 'The trouble is that every few years…'

'The Irish change the question,' said MacMack. 'It's no longer amusing, if it ever was. Together with the Sudan business, Russia going mad, Germany strutting, India still seething and ready for another go…'

'You know the Germans have been talking to them?'

'Yes.'

'Well so have the Irish.'

'Hmm.' Campbell MacMack chewed the nail of his ring finger and stared at the coal scuttle, a picture of worry. 'Look here, Cuth,' he said after a few moments. 'You're Head of Special Intelligence.'

'Well spotted,' said Sir Cuthbert.

'Lord Salisbury,' said MacMack, now staring at the carpet and ploughing on, 'wants Ireland cleared up. Finished, and on his watch. It's his last go as PM and he wants a settlement that will last…'

'Until he's sold his memoirs?' said Sir Cuthbert, stretching for the decanter then topping up MacMack's glass and his own.

MacMack watched Sir Cuthbert's small freckled hands, busy with stopper and carafe. The watching eyes, once intensely blue, were now milky with age, fading like his generation. His gaze still fixed on the little security chief's hands, he murmured,

'Philo Maynebeam is pushing to get involved.'

He said it very quietly. No one further than a few feet away could have heard.

'If we don't do something, they will anyway,' he added, hardly doing more than push each syllable just beyond his lips, which showed pink and rather wet through his overhanging ginger moustache

'Maynebeam,' said Sir Cuthbert, just as quietly. 'Not his real name you know. Not even British. No one knows where he came from, and I mean no one. Might as well be a time traveller, or a Russian. Don't know how he gets away with it. And wherever he goes, odd things happen.'

'Oh?' said MacMack.

Each man was looking at the other with a curiously similar expression: weighing up a friend's capacity to absorb more worry.

'Someone got in to Admiralty House last night,' said Sir Cuthbert at last, 'Straight past the police guard.'

'Who was it?' said MacMack with a sigh.

'We don't know.'

'Won't talk?'

'It's not like that. He is not in custody. Got clean away. Walked into the PM's office, and half an hour later just walked out again, apparently. No one can quite remember what he looked like even though everyone agrees someone was there.'

'What about the policeman?'

'He was found asleep on the doorstep.'

'And the Prime Minister?'

'At his desk - also asleep.' Sir Cuthbert Dangermouse steepled his short fingers and propped his large triangular nose on the thick tips, and closed his eyes as if at the suggestion of the word.

'Is it happening again?' said MacMack.

'Looks like it,' said Sir Cuthbert, opening his eyes.

'I thought we'd seen the last of that. After Kaspar Hauser...'

'Apparently not,' said Sir Cuthbert, sliding down off the swivelly chair. He walked about restlessly behind his desk. Only the golden curls on top of his head were visible to MacMack, moving to and fro like an unusual target at a fairground rifle range.

'What can be done about them?' said MacMack, losing something of his carefully cultivated heavy calm. 'What kind of intelligence service can fight an enemy which doesn't – which cannot - officially exist?'

'Maybe an intelligence service which also cannot officially exist,' muttered Sir Cuthbert Dangermouse, out of sight and pacing.

MacMack looked up sharply, and half rose in order to see the face of the other man, otherwise hidden behind the enormous Civil Service desk. After looking down at him silently for a few seconds, MacMack just said, quietly 'The PM expects action. On Ireland, I mean. He doesn't talk about the other business.

'Seriously, Dormers,' he said, raising his voice, as if for an unseen audience, 'Salisbury wants – we all want – a proper answer to the Irish Question.' Then, lowering his voice again: 'If you and I don't find one, somebody else will, and there will be no room for people like us, who keep things just about civilized. All the talk around the PM is of a Solution for Ireland.'

'A final solution?' said little Sir Cuthbert, climbing carefully back on to his chair, accompanied by an ascending arpeggio of spongs and twangs; like everything else in the Department, the chair was getting old and the surprising arms could go off with no warning.

'A final solution,' said MacMack. 'It's a telling phrase. Not one for the public of course. Sounds a bit…'

'Inhuman?' said Sir Cuthbert Dangermouse. He turned his patently dangerous chair and looked out of the window, touching his fingertips to his scarred cheek as he said:

'You can tell Salisbury – or Maynebeam if you like – that the Irish matter is in hand. A man called Yeats is going to answer everybody's needs.'

*

At the top of the stairs to the Golden Dawn's Great Meeting Room, Aleister Crowley met an obstruction, forcing Yeats and Horton to queue on the narrow treads behind him. The obstruction was Miss Horniman, the tea-heiress and seer. Crowley attempted to walk through her but she straightened her arms at her sides, clenched her small red fists, closed her eyes and declaimed: 'None shall enter the gates of instruction without he be clean of mind and pure of heart.' Crowley looked down from his superior height as if gathering immense forces. 'I think it's pure of soul and clean of heart' he said mildly.

'Well,' said Miss Horniman, opening her brown button eyes with a snap, 'that *definitely* rules you out – Crowley!' The Second Order initiates behind her murmured and nodded cautiously, not sure who was going to win and so reluctant to take sides – in the majority of cases this was actually the most magicianly thing about them.

Crowley's eyes turned upwards in his head until only the whites were visible. His fleshy lips moved as he muttered inaudible words. Miss Horniman herself seemed unable to speak, her face turning an ever-darker shade of pink. Yeats and Horton followed like obedient coal trucks behind their engine as Crowley advanced on Miss Horniman, picked her up at the elbows and set her to one side like someone shifting a hat-stand from A to B.

'You're not Second Order any more,' whispered Crowley in her ear. 'Mathers has expelled you. I know.'

Then Miss Horniman at last began to sputter but her moment had gone and the watching horseshoe of members broke up, satisfied if not entirely happy with the outcome. The Golden Dawn had no provision for banning dangerously powerful magicians, since that was what the members secretly believed themselves to be, or hoped to become; but if there had been anything of that kind in the rules, Crowley, they were sure, would have been exactly the type to be kept out.

As soon as they were able to set foot in the meeting room, Yeats and Horton were descended-on by Miss Horniman, the tea-heiress and socialite. She had quickly climbed back on the dented bicycle of her dignity like someone who had done it before. 'Willie!' she said, 'and Mr Horton too! I'm so pleased.' She grasped their hands and pulled them quite violently towards her. 'It's going to be a good one today,' she whispered loudly, just for them and anyone else in the same room. 'We've got Madame Lauderdale.'

Yeats sniffed and looked into the middle distance. His lordly brow wrinkled. Who the hell was Madame Lauderdale?

'She's the best automatic writer in town,' said Miss Horniman, hardly missing a beat. 'We're going to use the Egyptian Annexe. She likes the feeling of a good crowd around her and we're a bit thin this afternoon, though there is a new member someone brought along, a girl - who wants to meet you, apparently.' A desire to meet Yeats, Miss Horniman seemed to say, was inexplicable, even suspect, in a young woman; Yeats, especially after Paris, saw it quite differently. He furtively cast an eye over the crowd, but could not see any unfamiliar faces. A little bell tinkled and conversation died away. 'We shall commence!' cried Florence Farr quickly, the Chief Adept in Anglia of the Golden Dawn just beating Annie Horniman to the announcement.

The small high-ceilinged side-room in which Madame Lauderdale was to contact the spirits was meant to call Ancient Egypt to mind, with deep blue walls round which a broad white band had been painted and filled with painstakingly-copied hieroglyphs – Moina Mathers' work again. Everyone squashed in, the men, a minority amongst the twittering females, standing out like fir trees in a vineyard. No one, however, stood out more than Madame Lauderdale.

The automatic writer was five feet tall and not much less wide, with a broad brow, deep-set eyes and a great tangled mass of iron-grey hair which rested like an oversized helmet on her powerful shoulders. Her accent was that of England's North West, but it was well known that her father had been a colonel in the Irish Republican Army during its ill-fated 1866 invasion of Canada, clumsily betrayed by their embarrassed American allies on receipt of £15,000,000 from the British government. The Irish were joined in their doomed attack on Canada by a tribe of native Americans and a regiment of freed African slaves. Both groups must have recognized, with poignant romantic empathy, the desperate gamble of an oppressed nation. Madame Lauderdale's mother, so her publicity claimed, had been an Indian squaw, a chief's daughter, who had nursed the Irish colonel back to health after a meaningless skirmish had left him badly wounded. Amazingly, apart from a forgiveable artistic licence regarding Madame Lauderdale's mother, who had been a theatrical agent in Liverpool, this was all true. It was the kind of thing that happened at that time.

Madame Lauderdale sat at a rickety green-baize card table, with Miss Horniman, the tea-heiress and sponsor of the arts, standing with a hand on the well-padded Lauderdale shoulder. After an outbreak of officious shushing, silence fell.

'We will begin,' said Miss Horniman. 'Madame Lauderdale, are you ready?' The helmet of iron-grey hair nodded with massive gravity, half a second after the large head: 'I shall attempt to make contact with my Control, Ackroyd,' she said. She fixed her gaze straight ahead, which meant staring at the middle button of Aleister Crowley's waistcoat, he being the kind of man who would always unthinkingly shove his way to the front of any audience. If the competition consisted of females half his size, then so much the easier. Yeats had been piloted by Miss Horniman to a place of honour beside the medium; poor Horton had to make do at the back.

'He is here,' said Madame Lauderdale at once, her voice high, ceremonial. Anticipatory murmurs rose and were stilled. The automatic writer jumped a little as if she had received a small but startling electric shock, then bent over the card table like a keen examination candidate receiving permission to start. She wrote for a few seconds, rapidly and with firm strokes which made the table sway, stabbed the page with a full stop and leaned back with a sigh. 'What does he say?' she said. 'I never read out Ackroyd's communications meself, you know. Too spiritually draining.'

'It says,' said Miss Horniman, 'Ackroyd welcome white folk from other side. I have been here before. This is a strange dream indeed, and seems to mean more than it says.'

'Ackroyd often gets muddled,' explained Madame Lauderdale, who looked a tad confused herself. 'Sometimes he forgets he is a Red Indian, and talks in the oddest ways. But you get used to it. Now, does anyone have any questions for him?'

'Do all human souls enjoy an after-life?' came a harsh female voice from the back. Madame Lauderdale faced front, jumped again but as if the voltage had been turned down a bit, and wrote: *Yes, all who die pass over. Who are these dim figures?*

'Is this magical Society set upon the right path?' That was Horton. There was a stifled groan at his question and a great deal of cross female fidgeting: Horton's reaction against the Golden Dawn was well known and he had long passed the point of being an interesting case for retrieval or romance. As Yeats' guest he was beyond direct criticism, but - well!

Madame Lauderdale seemed unaware of the emotional currents running and set herself to write with hardly any wriggling or eye-widening at all. *The wise deer know there are many ways through forest.*

Christ that looks like Yeats. Miss Horniman read this out and looked up quizzically at the poet, whose arm she still kept pressed fiercely to her side. 'Well, Willie,' she said, 'go on, he seems to know you're here. Ask something.' Yeats was not looking at the medium, or her writing. He was studying Madame Lauderdale's face and it was several seconds before he responded, in the rapid deep-toned speech that so impressed the Golden Dawn ladies: 'Is there a correspondence, above and below?'

Madame Lauderdale's spirit control seemed a bit stuck over this one. *Yes,* came the answer eventually, *but not like your correspondence. All is different here.*

Yeats frowned and wrinkled his upper lip as if he had tried sucking a lemon. 'If all is different there,' he said, 'then there is no correspondence. How do you make sense of that?'

The Golden Dawn sensed a crisis and there was dead silence in the Egyptian Annexe, not entirely untarnished by spiteful glee. Madame Lauderdale's great grey helmet of hair dipped slowly over the page, her pen came down reluctantly on the paper. *White man see much, but not all. I have a message for you, from someone dear to your heart.* Miss Horniman, who had read the words out, and Florence Farr who was standing back rather from the crowd, both gave Yeats exactly the same worried glance. The poet drew himself up and looked over everyone's heads, expressionless.

'Oh?' he said icily, 'and who is that, indeed?'

The pen hovered, was put down and there was a loud and startling scrape as Madame Lauderdale's chair was pushed clumsily back. The medium stood up and her head turned repeatedly from side to side like an outnumbered ironclad's gun turret.

'No, no, no,' she muttered gruffly. 'This won't do, Peter old chap.'

The questing motion of Madame Lauderdale's head stopped as if the guns had settled on a target. She was looking at Aleister Crowley. Then she opened her mouth (and she had a very big mouth indeed) and screamed, one long rasping shriek. Everyone drew back in alarm and there was suddenly clear space around the medium and Crowley, who stared down at her unmoved, as if this kind of thing happened to him every day. She took two lurching steps towards him. 'This is real, isn't it?' she said huskily, in the same male voice. Then, as if her strings had been cut, she crumpled and fell in a heap amongst the Nile lotuses painted on the floor.

The meeting of the Golden Dawn reached a premature end with the collapse of Madame Lauderdale, despite her rapid recovery and demonstration that two or three glasses of strong wine would indeed set her right. Little knots of members began to emerge from the door of Number 36, talking animatedly as they dispersed on foot or into cabs and horse-buses. Yeats and Horton left rather later than most, the poet waiting near the head of the stairs for Horton, who was delayed by some secret business with the medium. As Yeats listened politely to Miss Horniman, the tea-heiress and flirt, something was pushed into his hand and pressed against the palm for a second. 'Notice this,' the pressure said. By the time he turned he only saw, receding down the stairwell, long hair and a slim female back, achingly perfect in a close-fitting powder-blue coat.

'And you will go to Dublin soon, Mr Yeats?' said Miss Horniman, 'I believe your eye there, and voice, are all that is keeping the new theatre alive.'

'For the present, maybe,' said Yeats absently, finding it hard to focus on Miss Horniman's wistful energy. He had not even seen the new girl's face. How could a back be so expressive? It had said, 'I want to see you again, and I *know* you will want to see me.' How did they do it? Who was she?

Horton appeared, looking much brighter than he had been. His interview with Madame Lauderdale seemed to have done him good. Yeats detached himself from Miss Horniman who as always, her brown button eyes wide, seemed on the point of saying something as they parted, and followed Horton down the stairs to the street, where he hailed a cab.

When the old black hansom had trundled out of sight, a small quick-moving man in a dark green rain-cape and deer-stalker hat appeared on the far pavement. He crossed the road and stood looking up at the Golden Dawn's first-floor windows. He then walked off at speed towards Olympia, pursuing a young woman in a powder-blue coat.

Some twenty yards further along from where the man in the rain-cape and deerstalker had emerged, a big bulky fellow in a tweed overcoat and with his face almost completely covered in the windings of a long Edinburgh University scarf stepped from the doorway in which he had been lurking and looked up and down the road with a studied carelessness which would instantly have aroused the suspicions of a child of three. He then set off, with the brisk athletic tread of a confident sportsman, after the man in the deer-stalker and cape. The game was afoot, and Conan Doyle was on its trail.

Horton and Yeats were sharing the cab back to the poet's rooms in St Pancras. Both side windows were down, despite the evening chill: not only did the interior smell of damp and decay, one of the lamps had gone out, leaving the wick to smoulder and give off nauseating fumes. The harsh rumble of the wheels was very loud and the sharp draught of cold air made Horton gasp whenever the cab turned. He had been glad to accept Yeats' offer of a few nights' lodging. The poet's rooms were convenient for the British Museum, where he was reading for the commentary on a series of visionary drawings commissioned by Yeats' London editor, Arthur Symons, largely on the poet's authority and insistence. As usual, gratitude stirred up Horton's pride like a tide running against the wind, making him pompous and prickly.

'I entertain grave doubts, as you know,' said Horton, bracing himself against the swaying of the ancient top-heavy hackney carriage, 'about the whole spiritualism fad. What we saw tonight left me no more confident.'

Yeats was tempted to say that the grave doubts would soon tire of Horton's entertainment. He imagined himself repeating this to Wilde, and felt guilty. *There is only one thing worse than not being funny, which is being funny at the expense of a trusting and sensitive friend.* In any case, Wilde would just correct Yeats on some point of grammar and then talk about himself non-stop for two hours over a tiny cup of thick gritty coffee at the Deux Magots. Thinking about Paris reminded Yeats of other things and for the next few minutes the drumming of iron-rimmed wheels and the clop-clop of hooves were the only sounds, until Horton said, in a different tone of voice: 'I think it's wrong to play on people's feelings, don't you?'

Yeats chewed a knuckle and looked out into the London evening. The carriage had halted for a moment near a gang of labourers working on some emergency of applied utilitarianism, and the light of the flares revealed the strong lines of the poet's face with a subtle force which Horton, quick-eyed and observant in the darkness on his side of the cab, knew he could never reproduce with his pencil.

'Maud's turned me down again,' Yeats said. 'It's final this time. I won't ask again.'

'I am sorry to hear that,' said Horton.

'No you're not. I know what you think of her.'

'There is nothing wrong with one-sided love,' said Horton, 'when it *is* love.'

'And you know about all that, do you?' said Yeats, and was immediately sorry when he saw his friend flinch. 'Look, it frees me, d'ye see? I feel lighter. In any case I'll never stop loving her, never love another as I do her. We're going to be spiritual lovers, that's all.'

'Well, I think that's a rather fine idea,' said Horton, with the eager sincerity which made him likeable despite his unattractive longing for fame. Yeats felt a sudden desire to offer his sensitive and unhappy friend something from the crowded table of his social life. 'I'm dining at the Cheshire Cheese,' he said, raising his voice as the cab lurched forward again. 'It's not a Rhymers night, but Shaw will probably be there. Why don't you come?'

'Oh, I don't think so, thank you,' said Horton quickly. 'The Reading Room's open till late tonight, and there's so much I need to check for my Commentary. I am not like you, I find it hard to carry it all in my head.'

Yeats felt relieved. Bernard Shaw would not respect Horton's intellect, or warm to the artist's eccentric dogmatism; and there was another reason not to want Horton there – meeting with the blue-coated young woman, which his naïve friend might think sat oddly with the speech about loving Maud Gonne for ever. Yeats himself felt perfectly at ease. He was damned if he was going to abuse himself into another depression. *Do what thou wilt is the whole of the law.* Furtively holding it away from Horton, he looked again at the card which the new girl had slipped to him. It announced The United Jamaica Sugar Company, giving addresses in Kingston and London, but on the back, in a bold clear hand, was scribbled 'Tonight at nine, the Cheshire Cheese'. It was amazing: by sheer chance the girl in the blue coat had suggested meeting somewhere that was practically his second home in London! And the leading mind of his nation wandered innocently off on the theme of happy coincidences and the possibility of bed with fireworks and smiles instead of worry and guilt.

Do what thou wilt…

Decisions

The interior of Major General Kitchener's campaign tent was artfully designed and furnished to look like a boy's bedroom. There were rosy-cheeked soldiers all over his quilt and the matching pillows. The heavy furniture, including his very solid bed that it took four burly native servants to move, was the plain and hard-wearing stuff suitable for a growing lad. His well-brushed uniform hung ready for an early start and there was a night-light burning on the dresser. Propped up at the foot of the bed there was a large painting of himself, staring face-front, eyes bulging with zeal, in a dress uniform derived from three different regiments. Above his painted self, a banner was in the act of unfurling, caught by an artistic breeze blowing across the top of the canvas. On the banner were the words 'My Country Needs Me.' Outside the tent, things chirruped and whirred in the velvety black night of Sudan but Kitchener lay on his back beneath his soldier-quilt, deep in the sleep of untroubled conscience, and the bedcovers rose and fell like the hide of a dozing kraken.

There was nothing squatting beside the bed, projecting a pale shape like a negative shadow on the candle-lit canvas of the tent wall. Nothing should have a shadow like that, and it did. The dark form leaned gently forward and bent its head down to the sleeping general's ear. Shadowy lips moved; Kitchener's lips moved. After a while, the shadow-man straightened up and stood, with head lowered, apparently gazing down at the unconscious human, before fading away like a sigh.

*

'Peep!'

Sir Cuthbert Dangermouse took the stopper out of the speaking tube and set his ear to it.

'Sir Campbell MacMack,' said O'Hara, his secretary, from the outer office. 'Needs to speak to you on the secure tube, when you're alone. I told him to call in ten minutes.'

Sir Cuthbert made an indeterminate noise into the tube, which sounded more like 'merry hell' than not, and replaced the bung.

Some minutes later – 'Parp!'

The tube was the old black one, dating back to the days when the Secret Intelligence Service was a department of the Royal Navy. The Service still trusted the speaking tube more than the newly-installed telephone, as being a known technology working on obvious principles. MacMack's voice from the other end sounded different - smaller, older.

'What I was saying – about doing something before someone else did? It's more than ever important, Dormers. And it's down to you now. Don't rely on me. I'm getting out of the game. They've... just count me out, all right?'

Sir Cuthbert replaced the speaking-tube horn, pulled the whisky bottle towards him, picked it up, looked at it for a long time, then put it down again. Out of the game – there was only one way out of the game that MacMack was in. He thought of MacMack's wife and family, with grandchildren now, a family that had welcomed him, little Sir Cuthbert, wifeless and childless, summer after summer, to their beautiful Scottish estate. He picked up the bottle. He put down the bottle. He snatched the battered workaday tube which communicated with the outside office and blew hard into the whistle. He blew again, and again, but O'Hara did not reply.

This was because O'Hara was some distance away in a small service room, hardly more than a cupboard. Speaking tubes ran through and around the room like spaghetti or Peruvian vines. One of the tubes, black-painted and dusty, but armoured like a steel python for its run through the service room, had been nevertheless pierced and the hole filled with a short length of brass pipe. The pipe ended in something which looked like a stethoscope, with a screw end and two flexible hoses each terminating in a metal ear piece.

There was someone else in the Tube Room with O'Hara, sharing the stethoscope, a sparely-built graceful old man with white hair and wise eyes, slightly dandified with his green coat and yellow silk scarf. He removed his ear-piece, straightened up and watched O'Hara take out the listening device and screw a small plug of black-painted metal back into the hole.

'You have done well,' the white-haired man said to O'Hara. 'I must report this to the Really United Irishmen. If a man of MacMack's type is scared, it must mean something very bad for Ireland. You are sure Sir

Cuthbert suspects nothing? They will hang you if anyone betrays you.'

'He seems to suspect everything, which comes to the same thing,' said the blue-chinned secretary in his usual gloomy manner; but there was a spark of ironic intelligence in the deepset eyes under the hearth-brush eyebrows. 'Does it matter what he suspects? If you mean, does he know anyone was listening, then no.'

'You will be rewarded,' said the visitor, after a long look into O'Hara's lugubrious face, 'with the triumph of our enlightened ideas over English stupidity and Irish ignorance. One Ireland!'

'One Ireland,' said O'Hara, with all the fiery enthusiasm of someone consenting to an unpleasant but life-saving procedure.

'Come,' said the other, seeking to lift his agent's spirits, 'the Sign,' and they shook hands with their thumbs rigidly extended like the pricked ears of a startled donkey.

The white-haired man, whom O'Hara knew simply as Aengus, climbed the narrow back stairs which led to the broader corridors and brighter lights of government offices. He paused at a turn in the stairs and put his hand to his hair, touched his face at several points, put his yellow scarf in his pocket, took off the green coat and turned it inside out. Thirty seconds later, a dark-haired man in the prime of his life, trim and athletic, soberly dressed in Civil Service black, emerged at the top of the stairs and Philo Maynebeam made his way quickly to the office of Lord Salisbury, the Prime Minister.

Back at his desk, O'Hara sifted papers thoughtfully. Peep. Peep. Peep. From the inner office he heard one of Sir Cuthbert's speaking tubes demanding attention. The secretary froze, papers spilling unnoticed from his hand. '…if anyone betrays you.'

The other side of the pale oak door, Sir Cuthbert Dangermouse's posture and expression were strangely similar to O'Hara's. He stood staring out of the window, ignoring the flaring ebony horn, as if hoping it would give up.

Pe – e – e –p: like the Chief Eunuch with urgent news for the Caliph, the big tube was going to pipe for attention until it was delivered. Slowly, moving as if his knees hurt him, Sir Cuthbert sat down in his swivelly chair and carefully, precisely, lifted the business-end of the speaking tube, the Special, which went All The Way There, off its cradle.

'Yes,' he said into the horn, 'I'm listening,' and put it to his ear.

*

'So, gentleman, that's the plan.'

Kitchener had been whisked from the Sudan, spirited past the watchful journalists of the American agencies, steamered by warship to Portsmouth, England, and whisked again, by special train, to Royston in Hertfordshire. He had assaulted every available humanoid on the way, including Stoker Meadows of HMS Exquisite, who got a lifetime of free beer from 'Bet you a pint I was under Kitchener in the navy.'

There, as midnight rang out over the market town, with a cordon of policemen keeping late walkers out of the high street, Kitchener had entered a small green door under a certain archway, descended some time-worn and slightly winding steps, and joined a number of other men in an underground chamber, tall, round and narrowing towards the top - bottle-shaped in fact. There were mysterious signs carved and otherwise marked all over the time and smoke-yellowed walls and a low stone step or bench all around the circumference at floor-level. This had been, in the thirteenth century, the secret chapel and storehouse of the Baldock Knights Templar; now, at the end of the nineteenth, it was one of a dozen chosen meeting-places of the twelve men who controlled the British Empire.

One of the policemen in the street above was Jim 'Duckman' Platimer. After the embarrassing Downing Street incident he had expected demotion, even dismissal, but to his amazement someone high up had given him a pay rise and a week's special posting to this sleepy Hertfordshire town. The therapeutic peace and quiet had so far made up for absence from home; but now the Royston church clock was sounding midnight and the ponderous chimes brought back memories of 'the night he had seen the Fairy'. Sergeant Platimer shivered, despite the thickness of his coarse woollen uniform. Thank goodness all he had to look after tonight were the proceedings of this antiquarian society – goodness knows what they had against quares, poor little buggers. Hold on though, someone hadn't got the message:

'Oi, you there,' shouted Sergeant Platimer. A slight figure in hat and cloak, was sauntering past him towards the forbidden archway. 'Now then,' said Platimer, 'you can't…oh!'

The dark figure had stopped and turned, the jaunty angle of the broad-brimmed hat suddenly and horribly familiar. Sergeant Platimer approached using the policeman's walk – unhurried, dignified but most importantly allowing plenty of time to see what you were getting into.

To see; but see what? The figure was all outline, your eyes filling in the details because they had to be there, didn't they? The back of his neck cold and prickling with fear, Platimer peered into the shadow where the face should be. He started to wonder whether there was anything there at all. Nothing could look like that, and it did.

And nothing spoke to him. It said: 'Have you changed your mind about fairies?'

Deep down below street level, directly beneath where a policeman was thinking very hard, the secret society of The Twelve Worthy Englishmen was sitting around the circumference of the Royston Cave. The Twelfth Worthy eased his backside into a more comfortable position on the low stone shelf which ran around the base of the Knights Templar's underground chapel. He was trying his best to look wise and mysterious, while gloating like an excited schoolboy at being on the inside at last. He had replaced the original Number Twelve, who had decided to leave the Saxonian Order after finding out what it was for. Sadly his Lordship had suffered a fatal head injury before he could do so. Technically it was a neck injury, the aristocratic head with its distinguished white hair being found relatively undamaged several yards from the body. His old regimental sword appeared to have gone off while he was cleaning it.

Before being made a Worthy, the new Number Twelve already had an inherited title, a top post in the Civil Service and a large income derived from land rents and investments. All these were so well and good, but there must, he had always felt, be something more. He had become a collector of secret facts, a connoisseur of *what was really going on.* He loved to interrupt some show-off's dinner-party riff with remarks beginning 'You do realize…'

You do realize, he would say, that truth is not only the first casualty of war but is generally strangled at birth. If you want to find out what is going on, he would add, look at the day's newspaper, reverse or ignore the sense of all official statements on the front page and then carefully scan the other pages for small stories of death, disgrace and dispute. The inside pages, that's where they bury the truth. The big picture, cut up like a jig-saw – they relied on the public being too lazy to put it together.

'But why publish anything at all,' the show-off objected one evening (it was at an embassy), 'if They are really so much in control?'

'Ah, now, there you have it,' and Number Twelve's knowing head oscillated sorrowfully at the world's innocence. 'I believe They have a sense of humour. I think They enjoy being in plain sight yet invisible.'

'Sounds like the Rosicrucians,' someone said.

He was a quiet man with observant eyes, seated at the less influential end of the table, speaking for the first time that anyone could remember, and so larger personalities had jumped in and loudly changed the subject.

It was two days later that They contacted him. Possibly. He was fairly sure it was Them. Fairly sure.

They had made him wait, made him sweat for a while – a hint here, an invitation there, then had come the test. 'The thing is,' his distinguished visitor had said, 'some of us want to go into northern Sudan, but we need a jolly good reason. Can you think of one?'

'Protecting the Suez canal? Curbing French ambitions? A warning to the Mahdists?' he had offered.

'Excellent,' said his visitor. 'Make it happen, will you?'

'Er – which one?'

'Oh, it doesn't matter. We just need about a year for the excavation.'

'Excavation?' he said, but the door of the Foreign Office was already closing behind his visitor's natty grey-suited form.

The adventure went ahead, with the predictable results of using machine guns against men armed with spears.

'Well done,' his visitor said exactly a year, to the day, later.

'Did you find what you were looking for, Sir?' he said nervously.

'No,' said his visitor.

'I'm sorry,' he said, thinking of the slaughter at Ferkeh and the terrible reprisals against the allied tribes.

'You misunderstand,' said the very distinguished visitor, flicking cigar ash onto the carpet. 'The excavation was not intended to find anything.'

'Ah,' he had said, nodding wisely, then, 'What?'

Like the other eleven Worthies, Number Twelve was wearing evening dress and a rather stylish black mask. There were two men who were not wearing masks. One was Sir Cuthbert Dangermouse, sitting quietly and almost unnoticed on the first of the stone steps, nursing his briefcase like a plum pudding. The other man without a mask occupied a wood and canvas field chair in the centre of the roughly circular floorspace. He was in the uniform of a major general in the British Army and had the ruddy brown face, big moustaches and twinkly eyes of a Victorian adventurer who knew his moment had come. He was Baron Kitchener of Khartoum.

'If I understand you correctly…' said the First Worthy. 'Actually, Kitchener, I'm not sure I do. Run us through it again, will you?'

'This is just how it came to me,' said Kitchener. 'Might need a bit of work.' He cleared his throat, threw his head back, stuck a clenched fist against his chest and began:

'If we stop flirting with Hansi Boer. If we hunt and kill him like the pest he is; if we destroy his crops and burn his dwellings and cut him off from any outside help; if we seize his females and his offspring, cage and make them see our point of view; if we can do this though the liberals are bleating, yet seem responsive to their bleating too, then we'll get the Boers' land and everything that's in it and - what is more - the world will know that England's got its balls back.'

'And he says this came to him in a dream,' thought the Seventh Worthy, 'I wonder what his nightmares are like.'

'Thank you, Kitchener,' said Number One, the worthiest of the Twelve Worthies, 'I would like to call now on the expert advice of Two.'

The Second Worthy, a trim, and graceful personage, stood up. It might have been a trick of the light down there in the Templars' cave, but his shadow seemed to move slightly after he did.

'Did you see that?' said the nearest Worthy to his neighbour.

'No.'

'Neither did I.'

'Major General Kitchener,' said the Second Worthy, 'we feel that you have come up with an excellent plan but *we don't think it goes far enough* we don't think it goes far enough.'

'Odd echo you get in here,' muttered one masked Worthy to another. 'You get it before the words.'

'What's he talking about?' whispered another, 'not murdering the women and kiddies, surely.'

'Not far enough,' went on Worthy Two, with an expressive turn of the head towards the whisperer, 'in every respect. Why stop at the Transvaal? If this strategy works, and it will, let's go for the big one. Gentlemen,

you have an answer at last to the Irish question

you have an answer at last to the Irish question. We will need a new word for this approach to territorial control.

Genocide.

Genocide. You can see it as a spring cleaning of the human race.'

Afterwards the Twelve Worthies of the Empire had filed back up the winding stair, some of them loosening collars, letting their breath out and generally doing what people do when they get out of somewhere they don't want to be. Why meet in a tiny underground cell then? It is a fact (and there are more facts in this book than you probably think) that powerful people seek romance and meaning in their lives just like everyone else. The Templars had once been the unseen movers and shapers of their world, so their modern day equivalents wanted to feed off the energies still clinging to their ancient places. And, they thought, it's not as if anyone is around to object.

Little Sir Cuthbert Dangermouse alone suspected that this might not be true. Although his quick mind had been restlessly at work all through the proceedings, his equally sharp eyes had had little to do for several hours but study the strange graffiti on the yellowed walls. Higher and higher he had followed the enigmatic words and symbols, upwards and upwards in a spiral until his eagle eyes under enormous fierce eyebrows spotted the tiniest difference in reflected light, such as might occur when an eyeball shifted from left to right, and he knew beyond any doubt that from high up on the circular wall of the Templar chapel, through spy holes all but invisible from floor-level, someone was watching, someone was listening.

Like any good chief of intelligence, he had no intention of sharing this knowledge with anyone until he had extracted every ounce of personal advantage from it. If he was right in a theory derived from certain longstanding interests and far-reaching enquiries, the watchers at the spyholes had every right to be there, and to object to this invasion of their Temple Chapel. He would have to make contact with them, if they were really coming back; but that was for the indeterminate future. There was someone else to whom he had to talk, urgently. He had heard sufficient, waited long enough.

It was time to talk to the Colonel.

*

The Cheshire Cheese public house stood in a quiet tributary of the river of carriages and people which was Fleet Street, just yards from the hurrying crowds and clattering hooves but almost untouched by their noise. Just now, however, it was generating its own: in a large upper room the poet W. B. Yeats and George Bernard Shaw, playwright and critic, were arguing loudly about the Gaelic Revival. Shaw was including it with fairies as something in which he did not believe. At the window-rattling height of the debate, which perhaps only another Irishman would have realized was not the prelude to murder, a man looked in and stared hard at them, saying nothing. He had the scar-thickened features of a boxer, a head as hairless as an egg, and was dressed entirely in black – black overcoat, black muffler and black gloves.

'It's the referee!' shouted Shaw.

'Hush, man,' said Yeats, who always feared violence in public houses.

The man in black surveyed the room, taking in the facing pairs of high-backed benches, each with its mug-ringed table, saw that Yeats and Shaw were alone, and went out again. A young woman appeared in the doorway with a speed that suggested she had been waiting with foot-tapping impatience; yet she stood there for a moment, lit by the gas light beside the door, giving Yeats time to look at her. It was the new girl at the Golden Dawn meeting; she was wearing the same blue coat but now he saw her face for the first time.

A woman in an upstairs room Yeats thought, looking for an opening line, *...fine dark eyes ...arch of those brows ...Troy, no not Helen,* *something real, warmer.* The poet admiringly took in her slim well-made shoulders, and how straight she stood; he was less pleased by Bernard Shaw's murmured, 'I say! Tally ho!'

Yeats stood up and from the pocket of his bottle-green velvet jacket took the visiting card which had been pressed into his palm at the Golden Dawn séance.

'Miss... Tough-guide?' he said, articulating carefully, with one eye on the words and the other on the graceful form before him and, with will-power newly gained from certain rituals, not touching his hand nervously to his flowing blue silk cravat. Self-possession was nearly his.

'Too good,' declared the girl in the doorway, confusing him for a moment. 'It's pronounced Toogood. And it actually says 'Mrs' if you look more carefully, 'Mrs Stephanie Toughguid'. I am pleased to meet you, Willie Yeets.'

'Yates,' the poet replied, meeting her aristocratic confidence with his own hard gemlike artist's passion, 'It's pronounced Yates. And use of the Willie is reserved for friends.'

'Is it indeed?' she said, looking quickly down but not quickly enough to hide a strange dancing light in her eyes. He had the sense that she was holding back some powerful impulse. Crowley, for all his bullying affectations, was right: there are sex-magickal currents in the etheric ocean. He could feel them flowing strongly, bringing this young woman into his life. On her behalf, he silently recited the protective formula for strangers meeting unknowingly with a powerful adept.

Mrs Toughguid looked up again, full into his face, her eyes now wide and serious, and said, 'Really, I am so pleased you are here. I must speak with you, and this seemed the best way.' She crossed the floor to him, her dove-grey skirt rustling, her button boots loud on the bare boards. 'They are always watching,' she whispered, so close that he could feel her warm breath upon his neck.

It was one of those moments in which time seems to stop and one sees and hears with unusual clarity. It was also one of those moments, Yeats found, when one's body is overtaken by a certain feeling, as if the servants of a great house were throwing heavy curtains open and removing dust-sheets from the furniture ahead of the master's long-awaited return from some pilgrimage involving extreme abstinence. He observed himself noticing that Stephanie Toughguid's long hair, which he had thought was plain brown, had red glints in it. Her eyelashes were black as soot and her dark brown eyes tilted up at the outer corners in a way which somehow made it hard to breathe. Her mouth, above a firm chin, was wide with a humorous curl. She had the grace of the willow trees at Knockdrum, the fire of the Hag of Taoghaire, she ...

'I'm Shaw,' said the playwright, appearing annoyingly at Yeats' elbow.

'So am I,' said Mrs Toughguid promptly, with just one quick and straight-faced look at the red-haired writer, and then, with more charm, 'Would you mind? I desire a few moments with Mr Yeats, alone.'

'Oh,' said Bernard Shaw, the hopeful twinkle fading in his eye. 'Oh well. I'll leave you to it then.' He paused in the doorway and for a moment his eyes met the poet's. The expression on his satyr's face above the bristling orange beard said something unfamiliar to William Butler Yeats. It said, 'You lucky swine.'

Mrs Toughguid shut the door after the disappointed playwright as if she were in her own house and not the stronghold of writers who intended to dominate English and Irish literature and thought for decades to come. Yeats felt he ought to say something, but found himself watching her instead.

She moved like - something about dancing, something Spanish, no, better, a Minoan dancer. Light-footed, quick and carelessly graceful. *The careless grace old Minos saw...*

An amused smile warned Yeats that he was staring and he motioned to the young woman to sit down. His arm seemed to have turned to lead and his fingers into a cluster of uncooked sausages.

It reminded him of the time he seconded McGregor Mathers in a magical duel. Mathers' opponent claimed to be a master magician from the Russian court and the Golden Dawn's champion had secretly feared for his life. One of Yeats' arms had gone completely numb as a result of the conjurors' supernatural blasts – an inconvenience, as it was his task to hold Mathers' heavy Highland-weave cloak for the three hours it took the mages to settle for a draw, neither having been able to produce the slightest effect on the other – such, they agreed, was the power of their protective amulets and talismans. Shaw had said it was just the usual Golden Dawn shit. Yeats wished he would not say things like that, or at least say 'shite' in the Irish way.

Just now he wished that he had a talisman to protect him from himself. He avoided Stephanie Toughguid's eyes and tried to imagine what a confident man might say to break the ice. He was drowning in his own silence, rejecting gambits with increasing desperation, when a white-aproned waiter came in. Behind him, through the doorway, Yeats glimpsed the man in black, bulky, impassive and unmistakeably on duty.

The waiter was a stick-thin and long-haired young man. 'What will you be having?' he said to Stephanie Toughguid, leaning all over her and ignoring Yeats.

'Absinthe,' she said, 'and Mr Yeats will have the same. Bring a bottle, water and glasses.'

The waiter seemed about to object and she cut in with 'I know you keep some for Giovanni. He is a friend of mine. Do you understand?'

Whether it was the tone of voice or the name Giovanni, the long-haired waiter's supply of suggestive arrogance was abruptly turned off. He closed his mouth, looked at Mrs Toughguid, glanced at Yeats, and went out.

The young woman and the poet sat facing each other across the narrow table. Yeats felt very conscious that they were alone together. Still searching desperately for something to say, he recalled that it was she who had wanted to meet him. He tipped his head back slightly to look more masterful, and his hat fell off. She looked thoughtfully at him without speaking, the dancing light back in her eyes. He felt his heart sink. It was going to be Maud Gonne all over again. No sex, just another bloody poem.

The room was getting smaller and Yeats was feeling faint by the time the waiter came back, with a tall bottle, a jug of water and two glasses on a tray; when he left, Yeats noticed how carefully he closed the door behind him. Stephanie Toughguid took off her own hat, a little round silver-cloth cap which she wore on the back of her head, and reached for the bottle at the same time as Yeats, so that their hands touched.

'I see you are unconventional,' he said, withdrawing his hand. 'A new woman?'

'Is that what you want?' she said, not looking at him, concentrating instead on adding cold water, very slowly, to the small amount of clear green spirit which she had poured into each glass. Suddenly she raised her eyes to his and the contrast between her teasing words and the gentle warmth of her expression pierced his heart like

Dhlaichaoiliochiadan's Lance of the Three Sorrows.

'You know,' she said, with that mischievous spark in her dark eyes again, 'speaking of convention, some people would say that it was not exactly right and proper for me to be sitting here with an older man who writes about love quite as much as you do.'

Yeats knew he was expected to respond to this challenge, and he felt faint again. It was the same when he dined with Oscar Wilde, or when the Dublin mob shouted his name, or when he discovered what really excited Maud Gonne: in the face of expectations of valour an icy fear gripped him. He froze.

Something as ancient as life seemed for an instant to look out through the girl's eyes. This moment, it seemed to be saying, on this moment rests something tremendous. Speak! Speak! *It is the tragedy of time,* he said in his mind, preparing the right words to dramatize and distance himself from another failure of nerve, *imprisoned here in this older self, peering from my high tower through the memory-barred windows of my eyes at the inaccessible theatre of a younger world. At you.*

The words which actually came out of his mouth were, 'Do we care what people think, Mrs Toughguid?'

Yeats was amazed and excited. He had done something brave. He had not run away from opportunity. The universe seemed to sway like a train changing tracks; the girl's dark eyes were speaking an invitation which made his heart pound but she only said, 'Please call me Stephanie.'

'Call me Willie,' he said, his accent thickening and the daring of Erinn upon him.

'I believe I have,' she said, holding up her glass is if to salute the occasion.

'I'm sorry?' Yeats was not listening. There was that half-seen movement again, this time on the bracket of the gas-globe above Stephanie Toughguid. You could almost think that the round knob on top had a face. In fact, you could almost believe that a tiny... that a very small... that *a little man* was sitting astride the bracket, two thumbs raised, and grinning down in approval.

Yeats quickly wrenched his shocked gaze away when Stephanie began to turn in her seat to see what he was looking at, and when he stole another glance, there was no little man to be seen. Anyway, it was so much better to notice how Stephanie's hair swayed when she moved, how the curve of her waist met the gentle rise of her breast...

'Now, Willie Yeats,' she said, squeezing his hand to get his attention, 'what do you know about the revolution?'

*

Sir Campbell MacMack sat alone in his study at his house in Box Hill. He was drinking a glass of whisky very slowly, as if there would never be another, making every sip last, keeping the pleasantly mordant fluid on his tongue, pressing it against his palate, only reluctantly letting it trickle down. His eyes were closed. He was reliving scenes from his life, memories growing like soda bubbles from the complex flavours of bracken-brown Highland stream water, the earthy tang of malted barley, the holiday associations of peat smoke, all on top of a substratum of dark oak barrels so impregnated with ancient spirits that the wooden staves were effectively immortal.

Dark oak also covered every inch of the study walls and ceiling. Around the whisky drinker's feet a rich red rug made a warm island in a cold expanse of highly-polished floorboards. Black night pressed against the window panes; the curtains were undrawn, the gas was turned down to no more than candle brightness. Scores of animal heads displayed on the panelled walls, stag, boar, ibex and a melancholy rhinoceros, seemed to gaze down at Sir Campbell MacMack with weary empathy. Although we bear you no vengeful ill will, they seemed to say, we cannot deny that it is interesting to see you in your covert, exhausted and waiting for the hunter.

Sir Campbell held his whisky glass up as if reading his future in its amber glow, and said, 'How long have you been there?'

'For the last twenty minutes or so,' said someone in the shadows of the deep bay window. In daytime it afforded a pleasant view, from the first floor, of an ancient rose garden. It was locked; so was the door. Even the chimney was secured with a steel grid.

'You're very good,' said Sir Campbell.

'I will remember and value those words. You are alone?'

'Of course. My wife and children are in Scotland and the servants are being treated to a night out.'

'You didn't send them all.'

'Oh. Is Compton dead?'

'I'm afraid so.'

'He was very good too. I'm sorry. I'm not worth the pointless death of a man like Compton but he simply wouldn't go. Are you here to kill me?'

'I will if you try to use the pistol you are holding under that cushion.' The speaker in the shadows came forward and leaned with casual grace against one roly-poly end of the big sofa

'So it *is* you,' said Sir Campbell, bringing out his hand, and the gun it held. 'At least I was right about that, although, come to mention it, you don't seem to be armed.'

'Oh, I don't need to be,' said the intruder. 'You'll do it to yourself. Just look at my hands as I make this sign, and this, and now – see? – that closes it. Can you feel something?'

'Yes,' whispered Sir Campbell, sitting up very straight. His face had gone white and he was sweating. 'What have you done, you devil?'

'Another compliment, Sir Campbell? Well, I'll be going now. No, don't get up. I doubt that you can anyway.'

Sir Campbell looked at his own left arm in confusion. It was refusing to bring the heavy revolver up and the gun dangled in his limp fingers.

'You people really should have listened to Mr Yeats and his friends,' said the man at the window, which was wide open.

But Sir Campbell MacMack was no longer listening to anyone.

*

'Revolution?' Yeats said, immediately on his guard and glancing at the door. 'I know it's a dangerous subject.'

'Willie,' she said, 'I only meant the theory that everything is always changing, that everything revolves, it is all – a revolution. Would you feel endangered discussing that?' Again that half-shy, half challenging look, the voice so quiet and slow it seemed about to disappear, yet fascinated, like a bead of honey dripping from a spoon, so you wanted to catch it, to put your lips to it and taste it, to…

'I will talk about anything you like,' he said, more emphatically than he intended, stung by her words.

'It is not I who wishes to talk with you. I am only a messenger,' she said. 'Oh, I wanted to meet the author of "The Celtic Twilight" of course, and so I asked for the job, but there are some people, very wise and knowledgeable people, who wish urgently to communicate with you on certain matters, of enormous significance. They could not make contact directly. They must act secretly. You are the only man in Europe who will understand what they have to say.'

'Who are these wise and knowledgeable men?' he said, trying to conceal his emotion. 'I can already begin to guess at what they want to discuss.' Yeats' long hands clenched with excitement: even though his occult studies were far from complete it had naturally been recognized that he was on the path of the Higher Magic. Could this be the call he had been expecting from the Secret Masters in Nepal?

'You understand,' Stephanie said, leaning forward so that her long hair, some strands braided, swung forward and framed her face, 'there is a hidden tradition which cannot be publicly acknowledged. A group, a very small group of initiates, has kept this tradition alive. They wish to speak with you.'

'But you,' he said, 'as a woman…'

'The secret tradition cares nothing for sex,' she said, leaning still closer so that her hair touched his forehead and tickled his nose. 'They said I must tell you a word. I must whisper it in your ear. They said you would recognize it. It is magical.'

And it was. She put one hand softly on the back of his neck to draw him even nearer and breathed the word into his ear, her lips so close that he felt them as they parted and came together, and the little puff of breath of the last syllable.

'Well?' she said, leaning back, 'shall we be off?'

Yeats' lifelong caution slammed into action before he could stop it. 'Tonight? I don't know, I... er... I need to think, to prepare.' He had also suddenly remembered that Horton was staying with him and did not have a key.

'Then tomorrow,' she said, standing up and giving him another card, warm from her glove. 'Come to that address, and meet with the person named below it'

'I will,' Yeats replied, putting the card in his pocket, 'I shall be there,' and so began his adventure with Stephanie Toughguid, and the Secret Masters of the World.

He had absolutely no idea what she whispered in his ear.

Outside the Cheshire Cheese inn, the fog seemed even thicker - solid enough to cut up and put in a cake-tin, reflected Agent 42. She put the image firmly out of her mind. It was the kind of thing her sister would have said. There was to be no more of that now. Agent 42. She wondered what the other forty one agents were like. Perhaps the right question was what they *had been* like. She shivered.

She was standing just inside the deep shadow of a narrow unlighted alley almost opposite the tavern's entrance. A few minutes' work earlier in the day had shown her that the alley was the perfect place for an assassination, running between high blind brick walls to an insurance office with an aged watchman nodding in the foyer. Agent 42 turned her long sinuous back to the road and a sulphur match flared, cupped in her hand and shielded too by her hair, which spread like a glossy cape over her wide shoulders. In the light of the flickering yellow flame she studied a photograph, a tin-type. There was a caption carefully written in white paint along the lower edge: 'Mr W. B. Yeats, the Poet, addressing the People of Dublin'. It was a clear picture by the standards of the day but someone's arm, raised in enthusiasm or protest, had cut across the lower half of the poet's face, leaving only an impression of unusual height, intense eyes and a strong growth of dark hair. No matter. How many tall and opinionated Anglo-Irish writers were going to be holding forth in a London eating house at exactly nine thirty on a Monday evening?

The match burned down and Clarissa Jane Laurel put the tin-type away, pushed her thick blonde hair back and walked with a confident brisk step towards the Cheshire Cheese; the door opened and closed quickly behind her, briefly releasing a cloud of beer-fumes, laughter and yellow gaslight which the vast London fog absorbed like an old, old sinner receiving a stolen sixpence.

When Yeats came down from the upper room, knocking sawdust off his boots with sharp backward kicks on the stair treads, the first thing he saw in the public bar was Bernard Shaw making a fool of himself with a woman. 'He just can't stand any competition,' thought Yeats indulgently, 'so he's gone and grabbed the first shawl he sees.'

The woman was coldly beautiful. She was tall and blonde, narrow in the waist and wide-shouldered, a Juno in a long green coat, with a black fur collar fastened tight to the throat: it was hard to work out who had picked up whom, but Shaw did not look as if he cared. He seemed much the worse, strangely, for a bottle of his favourite non-alcoholic beverage. 'Oi'm a BEER teetotaller,' he brayed, making newcomers to the Cheshire Cheese public bar jump and regulars grimace and put the hands over their eyes or, in some cases, their ears, 'NOT an ELDERFLOWER teetotaller!'

'Yes, very good, Shaw,' Yeats said, approaching and laying a hand firmly on one hairy tweed elbow and pulling the self-exiled Irishman down into his seat. 'What are you drinking? Are you sure it's just elderflower cordial?'

'Now listen,' said Shaw, suddenly and rather odiously intimate, 'you have said it yourself - the worst thing about some men is that when they are not drunk...'

'They are sober? It's obvious just at this moment that a man may be drunk on other things than alcohol,' he said, then cursed himself as he saw GBS winding up for another rendering of 'Oi'm a BEER teetotaller...' but the playwright subsided and instead let out an almighty belch.

'Oops,' he said, 'some more *wind* amongst the *reeds* for you. Is it on sale yet, your latest collection?'

'Will be, very shortly,' said Yeats, very shortly.

'Oh well,' said Shaw, with another gusty burp, 'better out than in, eh?' His yellow teeth grinned knowingly through his beard, which was encrusted with dried gobbets of vegetable soup. 'Where's your nice little friend?'

'You're doing the cause of Ireland no good by this performance,' Yeats said, one embarrassed eye on the other patrons.

'The cause of Ireland!' Shaw laughed and slapped the table edge, making glasses chink and bottles sway. 'What is the cause of Ireland? There's a good Christmas riddle for the Countess Kathleen ni Hooligan. If Ireland didn't exist, Willie my boy, you'd have to invent it and by God you have!'

'I thought you didn't believe in God,' Yeats said, feeling himself beaten down as ever by Shaw's diabolic energy.

'No more I do – nor your Ireland neither, as well you know,' said Shaw. He pulled Yeats closer, making the poet struggle to hide his distaste. 'I'm off now,' whispered Shaw loudly, with a spinach-flecked grin and suggestive wink.

'Where?'

'You see my lovely companion there?' Shaw said, leering up into Yeats' face.

'No,' said Yeats, truthfully, for where the beautiful blonde Juno had been, there was now an empty chair and a glass with one sip taken out of it.

'Oh,' said Shaw, standing up very suddenly and swaying a little, 'she's gone over already. She must be really keen. I'll be seeing you.'

'Wait!' said Yeats, and stepped quickly after the tweed-suited Shaw. The arrogant red-bearded vegetarian was not the type to inspire protectiveness in other men, especially his friends, but this was something well beyond Shaw's usual outrageous attention-seeking. How could anyone get drunk on elderflower cordial? It was almost as if someone had put something in it!

Yeats was even more concerned when, once outside in the sharp fog-laden London air, Shaw shook off his attempt to steer him safely along the lane that led to the bright lights of Fleet Street, instead lurching towards the alleyway opposite the Cheshire Cheese. It looked evil, an ominous embrasure in the soot-blackened brickwork, with barely room for two people to walk abreast, but Shaw went straight in, the fog-heavy darkness closing around him after just two paces. Dreading some embarrassment but also fearing for a fellow-countryman, Yeats hovered at the alley's entrance, reluctant to be a party to whatever sordid arrangement the playwright might be making. Instead he heard Shaw cry out in what sounded like physical pain, and shout, 'Yeats? No! I'm George Bernard Shaw, GBS, you know? How could you possibly confuse me with that soggy length of sentimental string?'

Shaw exited the alley at speed, shoving past Yeats with, 'I don't believe it! Another one for you!' and a harsh laugh that came out like a curse. This was repeated as he turned the corner into Fleet Street and then there was nothing but silence, fog and darkness.

Yeats remained where he was, just beyond the light that leaked from the Cheshire Cheese. His encounter with Stephanie Toughguid had left him buzzing with life, his senses sharpened. Somebody in the alley sniffed. Again. A woman was crying quietly, miserably in the dark.

Yeats walked very slowly just inside the deep shadow of the canyon-like alley. 'Hello?' he called quietly, then louder: 'Hello?'

Snif. Snif. A hiccuping breath. *Something is wrong here.* The words rang in his mind so clearly that he jumped. It was as if someone had spoken them straight into his ear. *Be careful.*

The tall poet took another step into the dark, and another. The impenetrable dark of the alley engulfed him and all around he sensed blackened bricks and stonework that knew little of the sun. A pale blob appeared out of the darkness and then receded again. 'Are you all right?' said Yeats, peering ahead into impenetrable blackness. 'Did you want me?'

A second passed. Three seconds.

'Yes,' said a voice from behind him. Something went round his throat and was drawn tight. Yeats' hands went instinctively to his neck but before they got there the pressure on his windpipe and powerful drag backwards and downwards suddenly ceased. He straightened and reeled around, gasping and flailing. An enormous black figure was outlined for a moment in the alley mouth. There was a struggle in the darkness. He heard a woman cry out. He tried to intervene and was fended off with an arm that felt like a thick iron bar.

Yeats lost his balance, groped for support and finding nothing, fell. His cheek hit gritty uneven ground, and he lay momentarily dazed. There was an instant in which nothing made sense. He saw Bernard Shaw's bearded face from below, looking shocked, his mouth making a perfect 'O'; then the inexplicable vision disappeared as if blown away and was replaced by wheels, locked and skidding, in the luminous rectangle defined by the alley's mouth. He heard his name called, sharp and urgent, and he leapt up wildly in response like a string-puppet controlled by a child; he would always know that voice now, even if he lived for a thousand years and never heard it again. It belonged to Stephanie Toughguid.

'Willie, get in here, now! No, leave that,' she shouted, when he hesitated and looked back into the alley. 'It's you they're after. Now, get in!'

The carriage leapt forward with amazing speed as Yeats stumbled up the step and he half fell across the lap of the only occupant. After an embarrassing moment when his cheek was pressed into the meeting-place of two long slender legs, he righted himself and saw Stephanie staring ahead with a strangely intense gaze. Thinking her offended he sought for something to say. 'It's all right,' he said, although he was himself slightly appalled at how quickly the Fleet Street buildings on either side seemed to be flowing past and out of sight, 'I am sure the driver knows what he is doing.'

'What driver?' said Stephanie, still keeping her dark eyes, slightly narrowed now in concentration, fixed straight ahead as if studying every movement of madly galloping horses, which must be galloping, now Yeats came to think about it, with velvet shoes on.

'Is there something wrong with the horses?' he said, trying to keep his voice level in order not to increase her alarm.

This time she did look at him, just with the merest sideways shift of her eyes, which were then immediately directed forward again in that fixed stare which he found so worrying.

'What horses?' she said.

Surprises

Now when Cuchullain of the knotty fist saw the warriors of the West descending like the snowflakes of fimbulwinter he uttered the Great Cry of Connaught and clashed his spear Laoinche upon the bronze-bound rim of his shield Buthochaire – he did not yell 'Oh my god, my god, my god!' and shut his eyes, as Willie Yeats did when he looked through the front window of the speeding carriage. His vision had always been weak but even a blurred impression of the view ahead was too much, a tunnel of light walled with unforgiving brick and iron into which, with a rush of air and strange high-pitched whine, the horseless vehicle was hurtling headlong.

There was a strange feeling of falling forward. Everything was happening too quickly. Horse-bus, wagon and cab, were there, here and gone before the poet's brain could do anything with the threat of their approach. The tendrils of fog were thinning but they still streamed past like the grey spools of fate reeling the strange vehicle and its occupants onto the bobbins of doom.

'Close your mouth,' said Stephanie, 'or you'll catch a fly in it,' and she shifted her dark almond eyes just enough to the left for the poet to see that now-familiar glint of laughter.

'In heaven's name, what is this thing?' Yeats shouted, although the machine was in fact so quiet he had no need to raise his voice.

'An electric carriage,' Stephanie said, still with that odd forward-looking intensity which he could now understand. 'And at thirty miles per hour I need to concentrate. My employers will be cross with me if I wrap it round a lamp post.'

Now he looked, tearing his eyes with difficulty from the fascinating and ever-changing view of impending death, he realized that one of Stephanie's slim gloved hands was resting lightly on the circumference of a leather-bound wheel with spokes and shaft of shining brass, the other on a brass lever, both instruments emerging from a wide curved panel of highly-polished wood which ran beneath the forward-looking window which screened them from the wind of their terrifying progress. She, a woman, was controlling this electric monster! Yeats felt the same thrill of admiration as when beautiful beech-high Maud once stood up to speak at a political rally and a little fat man in the front row fell backwards off his chair in his attempt to look her in the face.

'Where are you taking me?' he said, directing his own gaze firmly forward in case he distracted his driver.

'To the Secret Masters, of course. It's not safe to go home tonight.'

'Not safe?' Yeats cried, ready to stand on his dignity, and then, for almost the first time in his life, laughing at himself instead: 'And this is safe, is it? Careering through the streets at – what did you say? Thirty miles in the hour? That's as fast as a steam train!'

'Not quite, and it's safer than what lay ahead of you back there,' said Stephanie calmly. 'If Igor had not stopped it...'

'The man in black? What is he to you?'

He was ashamed to see Stephanie's lips twitch in a half-smile at the question.

'Igor is - good at encouraging people to behave nicely, that's all,' she said. 'He and I, we both work for the same man.'

'The one I am to see? The Secret Master?'

The electric carriage took a corner with a sickening swoop and Yeats felt himself sliding along the bench seat towards Stephanie. He grabbed the nearest handhold and braced himself against the inexorable force like a man resisting the pull of destiny's whirling wheel.

'OK, you can let go of me now,' said Stephanie as the carriage straightened up.

'Oh, sorry,' Yeats said. 'You know, if there was some sort of belt attached to this seat...Oh-kay? That's what Americans say. Is that what you are? And is this an American machine?'

'No, and no,' she said. 'I am not an American and this car is entirely British – designed and built by Thomas Parker of Liverpool.'

'Then how do you come to be driving it? Does Mr Parker know?'

Stephanie did laugh then, properly, head thrown back and eyes closed, and the electric car imitated a snake for a moment, motor whining and relays clicking and clunking as she reduced speed to regain control.

'What's so funny?' said Yeats.

'You – you've still got your hat on,' said Stephanie, glancing at him with a smile. 'After all that.'

'Why, so I have!' said Yeats, and laughed too. 'You know,' he said, 'This is – that's to say, I'm looking forward to meeting your employer.'

'Well, that's good, because we have arrived,' said Stephanie as they shot through a narrow gateway which loomed up out of the murk so quickly that Yeats did not even have time to flinch. The wheels crunched on gravel and then everything went dark.

'What... what is this place,' said Yeats, trying to keep his voice steady.

'We call it a garage,' said Stephanie. 'Wait there and I'll let you out.'

In the road, after the rush and blaze of the Parker automobile, the stillness reasserted itself. Moisture gathered on bare branches and drip-drip-dripped in big fat drops onto last year's leaves, each drop landing with a crisp smack. The fog seemed to sigh and give way to the night all at once. A dome of stars hung over the city. The stars were hard and bright, saving their twinkle for children in the country. It grew much colder.

Opposite the neo-gothic archway through which the electric car had passed, a figure appeared from behind the silvery-mottled trunk of a plane tree. He was a heavily-built man, made all the larger by a thick overcoat and muffled to the eyes with an Edinburgh University scarf.

Doyle calculated his next move. He estimated the height of the wall and evergreen hedge which screened the property, divided it by the emptiness of the street times *Fanny* times *handsome*, and two minutes later he had got over the wall, squeezed through the evergreen barrier and was amongst the outer trees of a large spinney, looking at the back of the biggest private house he had ever seen.

Stephanie led Yeats out of the garage and along a pale gravel path through twiggy trees which threatened to snag his hat from his head. It was very dark under the trees and he had to follow her by the swish-swish of her long skirt and the slightly luminous cloud of her condensing breath. They left the shadowed path and there was a brief impression of an extensive garden bounded by great elms and beeches before they arrived at the little side-door of a large building, its presence dimly-felt in the darkness rather than seen.

Inside it was pleasantly warm after the dank chill of the February night. Yeats found himself in what was obviously a back hallway, stone-flagged, vaulted, a pleasantly utilitarian place where muddy boots could be slipped off and wet things hung up. There was a narrow flight of heavily-varnished and uncarpeted stairs leading to the next floor.

'I'll take your things and you should go straight up. He will want to see you,' she said.

'He? Is it… I mean, are you…?' said Yeats, who had become more and more certain during the last few minutes that he would shortly have to endure another man's claim on Stephanie's slow secret smile with the little dimples at the corners.

'My husband?' said Stephanie, pausing as she hung up the poet's cloak and broad-brimmed hat. She suddenly turned, her hair swirling, crossed the three paces between them and stood, very close, looking with warmly amused eyes into Yeats' face as she had done earlier that evening in the Cheshire Cheese. 'Mr Toughguid is ancient history,' she said. 'I keep him around for convenience. In fact he's more useful now than he ever was when we were together. Yes,' she said, brushing invisible lint off Yeats' shoulder and unaware, he hoped, that the touch of her fingers through several layers of clothing made every single one of his body-hairs stand to attention, 'you could say Toughguid's name was the best thing about him. Now, go on up. You will find them on the first floor. There is no other door.'

Upstairs was a surprise. At the head of the stairs a pair of heavy green cloth-covered doors opened onto a different world. As he set out along a broad bannistered gallery, Yeats found his shoes sinking silently into thick midnight-blue carpet. Artfully concealed lighting awoke golden glints in the frames of the many pictures on the richly-embossed crimson-papered wall to his right – and what pictures! He thought he recognized a Poussin allegory but when he stopped and looked more closely the subject was strange to him, a pair of human figures, or perhaps gods or spirits, standing like guards on either side of - a cave mouth? A tomb? Further along there were other pictures which he immediately saw were alchemical and magical, although he could not read their meaning.

Yeats became aware of the murmur of voices and that he had been hearing them for some time. His progress slowed and stopped; from his deep side pocket he took the second card which Stephanie had given him. What he saw, written, not printed, on the otherwise blank rectangle of pasteboard, made him bite his lip and frown: *Kensington Palace (West entrance) Ask for Colonel Madriver.*

Kensington Palace! He passed it every time he walked to Blythe Road. Arrival in the dark, at speed, had made everything look different.

But no one had lived at the old palace for years and it was well known that the state rooms were derelict. Someone must have worked with magical speed and secrecy to produce this enchanted luxury.

The rest of the instruction kept the frown in place. How the hell would this one be pronounced? de Mad-river? de Mad-driver? He decided on 'mah-dreever' as a credible and fairly inoffensive guess. *Ask for Colonel Madriver.* But he wouldn't have to now, would he? All the while Yeats knew in his heart that he was just postponing the meeting with the Secret Masters; he straightened his back, tugged creases out of his bottle-green velvet jacket, adjusted his large blue silk bow tie and continued towards the sound of voices.

It was coming from another pair of doors at the end of the gallery, one of which was ajar. The poet hesitated, one hand on the brass door handle, the old familiar feeling, a sick dread of everything, flooding back from wherever it had temporarily been driven by desire. He willed himself to hold his head up, and whispered, 'I will not give in to it!' He was about to meet one of the Secret Masters of the World. The inside knowledge for which he longed, the potent insights and grand secrets which might make him interesting to Maud Gonne, were perhaps just the other side of this threshold. Why was it, then, that the only thought in his mind was of a pair of dark eyes and braided brown hair with russet tints?

Yeats smiled, as widely and unaffectedly as the boy he had once been, and stepped forward, unafraid.

'Hello, Yeats.'

The tall Anglo-Irishman halted with the speed of someone who feels the ice cracking underfoot. In an instant his universe had re-shaped itself, with monstrous results.

'Crowley?'

*

Not very far away, Arthur Conan Doyle, with the exaggerated care of a surgeon operating in boxing-gloves for a bet, parted the evergreen branches of the spinney and surveyed the house beyond, the window recesses starkly shadowed in the moonlight like empty eye-sockets. It had been absolutely quiet in the garden since the electric carriage had arrived. Even the trees seemed to have stopped dripping. He felt an overwhelming desire to have a look at the wonderful machine which had come silent and glittering in the night like an emblem of hope from the coming century. He justified the risk with the thought that everything was relevant until you knew what you were dealing with – a line he could have used in a Sherlock Holmes, if he hadn't sworn never to write another word about the great bloody detective.

Doyle was just about to shoulder his way out of the dew-damp greenery when he stopped dead, eyes wide, scalp crawling. Something was there. He shrank back, stifling a cry. Black magicians!

On the moonlit lawn a weird shape was moving. It was man-sized but two wings hung from its shoulders and in the silver-grey light a terrible beak stuck out from its head. The apparition was quick-marching to and fro like a sentry on cocaine, and chittering to itself as it went.

'Fool. Coward. Why didn't you? I can't. Just knock. You never know. Dammit, dammit.' The words receded with a slight Doppler effect, then came back. 'Faint heart never won... And it's not as if…'

Doyle drew back into the shrubbery but his weight came down on a fallen branch still dry from the previous summer and it cracked like a breaking bone. The demon-penguin uttered a strangled yelp and ran straight for the shrubbery just as the creator of Sherlock Holmes burst from his hiding place; they met with the kind of beefy thud Doyle had not heard since he played in goal for Portsmouth.

At close quarters the demon seemed much smaller and more manlike, the wings and beak an illusion created by a flapping cape and the jutting peak of a deerstalker hat. The two men rolled apart and stood up and at precisely the same moment, in exactly the same well-judged tone of educated confidence, each said: 'I am a well-known author and I can explain everything.'

The line of uncertainty between Yeats and Crowley was the base of a triangle. Crowley was not alone. There was another person in the room. Yeats experienced an unplaceable feeling of having met him before. He was a slightly-built but very erect man in his fifties, pink-cheeked and clear-eyed, with a neat moustache and pepper-and-salt grey hair well-brushed back over his temples. His black three-piece suit suggested law or medicine but he carried himself like a military man who was used to command. He was standing by a richly ornamented rosewood desk with his hand on the lid of a small brass-bound mahogany box as if he had been in the act of closing it. Crowley had been sitting in one of two deep-winged armchairs by the great iron-cowled fire. He stood up when Yeats walked in, and the poet saw in the big pale features something unfamiliar, which he could not place. As soon as the man with a military bearing spoke, Yeats realized what it was: the domineering Crowley was not the master here.

'Come in, Yeats. I am sorry we have had to rush things somewhat. I understand there was a little difficulty?'

'Apparently someone wants me dead.'

'You don't seem too bothered about it,' said the spruce grey-haired man, casually closing the box and advancing on Yeats with his hand extended.

'If you knew Ireland, you would be less surprised.'

'Ah, now, I didn't say I was surprised,' said the other man, gripping Yeats' hand briefly. 'I am Antony Maurier.'

'Why is Crowley here, Mr… I beg your pardon?' said Yeats.

'*Maurier*,' said the dapper rosy-cheeked man. 'People often get it wrong - and it's "Colonel", and "Sir Antony", actually, but I don't insist on the latter.

'Ah, well then, Colonel, I insist on knowing what this man is doing here before proceeding further.'

'Perhaps, like you, he seeks information,' said the Colonel, keeping his clear grey eyes fixed on Yeats' dark ones.

'It was knowledge, not information which Mrs Toughguid…'

The self-revealing words died on his lips. This was awful. The golden haze which had hung over him since about 8.30 pm at the Cheshire Cheese was blowing away like mountain mist revealing a stomach-churning gulf of embarrassment at his feet. Crisis. Stick to what you know. Run away!

'Sir Antony,' he mumbled, avoiding his eye, 'I must go. This was a mistake. I cannot think why...'

'Mr Yeats,' said the Colonel, 'we brought you here for reasons of the utmost gravity. You are more important than perhaps you realize.'

Anyone who knew W. B. Yeats might well have rolled on the floor laughing at this point, and even the poet had the grace to look askance at the sober pink-faced Colonel.

'Hmm, maybe, but…' and his eyes shifted betrayingly to Crowley.

'Is knowledge diluted by being shared?' said the Colonel.

'Perhaps it is only the sharing of privilege that Mr Yeats resents.' The acid comment came from between the deep wings of Crowley's armchair.

'Steady, Aleister,' said the Colonel, keeping his grey eyes on Yeats, not looking at him so much as watching him.

'Colonel…,' Yeats began, then hesitated.

'Madriver,' supplied the Colonel brightly.

'Colonel,' said Yeats, moving closer and lowering his voice. 'Your… operative… made reference to a certain tradition, to (he was now whispering) secret masters… she led me to understand…'

'Then she did not mis-lead you. Please sit down now and let me give you something to drink.'

'Anything,' said Yeats absently, then, remembering, 'no, have you any absinthe?'

'Oho, then I see Queen Mab has been with you,' said the Colonel, surprising Yeats by a knowing wink, meant for Crowley. 'Don Eduardo, a drink, please, for Mr Yeats.'

Yeats, in the act of sitting in the armchair facing Crowley across the great iron-hooded fireplace, realized with astonishment that there had been a fourth man in the room all along, in plain view but so completely quiet and still that he had been invisible until invoked by name.

Don Eduardo was a smoky brown colour like something hung up in the rafters to cure over a long winter, but you had the feeling that there were not many winters where Don Eduardo came from. His forest-dark eyes looked out from mahogany brown features and his hair was blue-black. On his head was a strange felt cap, burnt orange in colour, with two wattles of cloth hanging down at each side. He wore a long cotton gown, striped vertically in many shades of green, with close-fitting wool underneath encasing his arms and legs; his horny feet were bare. Don Eduardo did not seem talkative but his sad, wise eyes, deep-set in a network of wrinkles, never left Yeats' face as he solemnly handed the poet a tumbler containing a dark fluid which the poet did not recognize; the aroma too was unfamiliar, pleasantly earthy and vegetable, like an unwashed potato.

'Is this absinthe?' Yeats said. 'It looks different.'

'Absinthe changes colour when you take it with water, which is what you should do if you want to live long enough to enjoy your royalties,' said the Colonel. 'Now then, drink up and listen.' He moved to a red leather couch which faced and warmly reflected the firelight, but remained standing, leaning lightly on the couch back, like an orator at a lectern.

'I am in a sense a secret master,' said the Colonel, 'but more accurately a master of secrets. There is someone like me in every country, and always has been, since the first hero fought his way to the top of the first tribe and then wondered how to stay there. We learned early on to recognize key players in the theatre of the world, people who are the focus of energies and forces which might destroy or save their nations, even humanity at large. You, Mr Yeats, are one such. You already have some power and knowledge of your own. We will help you to attain more knowledge than you can dream of. In return, you will spend the rest of your life helping in our Great Work, to prepare the public for a new age and new thinking. The linear age, dominated by the Western vision of Creation, Redemption and Apocalypse, of a beginning, middle and end - this age has almost run its course: it is time for an alternative vision, of the circle and the gyre. The New Age needs its prophet. It has chosen you. You have the capacity for vision, the genius with words, the artistic soul, to carry out the wishes of my superiors, the Secret Masters of the World, keepers of the ancient flame of true knowledge and wisdom; through you, they will shape the next two thousand years.'

Yeats swallowed his drink in a few absent-minded gulps. It did not taste of excitement and adventure as in the Cheshire Cheese, but there was probably a reason for that, a reason in a little round silver-cloth hat. He was thinking hard. Not about the Colonel's words, which broadly confirmed his own view of himself. He was thinking about Secret Masters. Now it came to it, he realized that he had never actually believed in Madame Blavatsky's Secret Masters in Nepal, or anyone else's for that matter. Maybe McGregor Mathers' contacts in Germany maybe... possibly... When it came to it, the idea of secret masters only worked at a distance. From close up, they were just masters, and W. B. Yeats wasn't keen on being anyone's slave.

Only half listening to the Colonel's disappointingly familiar manifesto for spiritual revolution, he studied the man's ruddy firelit face. Where had he seen it before? The knowledge was at the edge of his conscious memory and slipped away as he grasped at it. In any case, something odd was happening to Colonel Sir Antony Madriver. He seemed to be shrinking and at the same time getting closer. Yeats clearly heard him say, in his precise military tones, 'Two can asseverate pastures, stew underhand.'

The poet good-humouredly wanted to tell the Colonel that it was nice of him to do tricks and talk nonsense to amuse him and make him feel at home. He supposed this was how it was in army messes with distinguished guests. There would probably be paper hats and games later on. Yes, Yeats was desperately keen to say something warmly appreciative to the Colonel, but when he opened his mouth to speak his lips felt like two bicycle brake blocks jammed shut by rust. Although Sir Antony was so far away, Yeats could see his face quite clearly, those cold grey eyes looking at him in detached appraisal. Then from miles and miles away he heard the Colonel say, 'Get his feet, Crowley.'

Yeats watched calmly as they got hold of the man in the armchair by shoulders and ankles and awkwardly (because he was a big lanky fellow) laid him on the couch, on his back.

What an interesting ceiling. The plaster mouldings chased each other round and round, round and round and round...

...and then there were snakes. With them came the sensation of suffocating size, or proximity, or both. Yeats felt that he himself was unbearably small. A great scaled trunk began to pass slowly across his vision, lower right to upper left, midnight black and sun yellow, the interlaced colours gorgeous, heraldic and full of a meaning which just escaped him. The serpent's motion was stately, regal and inevitable, and there was another snake, crossing the path of the first diagonally towards upper right. This double motion seemed to last for a geological age. All the time there was a feeling of sinking deeper and deeper into - something. Then there was only night and then, with a suddenness which left his stomach behind, he was in a room, brightly-lit. There were people there. He never saw their faces. They did not seem surprised to see him. Some of the people showed him a picture. It was of a long stick or wand, with two snakes intertwined along its length.

'What do you see?' they said.

'A Caduceus,' Yeats, an educated man, said at once, 'the wand of Hermes.'

'No,' they said, 'you are not looking at it hard enough.'

So Yeats looked again at the snakes and the wand, which now looked more like a rope.

'What do you see?'

Yeats was also a poet, so he chose his words more carefully.

'I see unity of opposites, harmony of contraries circling each other while each progresses, making vortices in space and time, gyres.'

'Still,' they said, 'look harder.'

Now Yeats was also a magician and so having looked again, he said, 'I see two ribbon-like structures, equidistant from each other, spiralling around a mutual core which, now I look at it carefully, only seems to exist because my mind tells me it should. The core is only there because the ribbons must gyrate around something, the gyres are only there because that centre calls them into being.'

'Not enough,' said the people. 'Look harder.'

But Yeats, because he was a genius, stopped looking so hard, and sent his mind to where it knew everything, and said: 'I see nothing. There is nothing there at all.'

'Well done,' they said, 'have a banana.'

Yeats was just about to bite into the perfectly ripe banana when the room and people vanished and he found himself looking into the vortex, interlocking spirals, double gyres, mutually interpenetrating, moving in an endless slightly sickening dance, round and round, round and round...

'...round and round and round....' Yeats opened his eyes and found himself looking into Don Eduardo's expressionless mahogany face. 'Good you not eat there,' said Don Eduardo. A long brown hand was extended. It held a cup. 'Here, drink. Only water.' Yeats propped himself on an elbow and drank the water gratefully, then sank back on the couch. The room was dark and the fire had burned low.

'You sleep now,' said Don Eduardo, throwing a blanket over the poet. Yeats obediently closed his eyes and slept without dreaming.

And woke with a start. He could sense that it was very early in the morning. His mind felt clear and strong, his body languorously rested. He stretched as he lay until his joints cracked, feeling more alive than he had for years. Only then did he realize what had woken him up:

someone had slipped under the blanket and was lying beside him on the couch. Someone warm and slender with her back to him and the soles of her bare feet pressed against his leg. Hardly daring to breathe, Yeats raised himself on one elbow to look at her face.

Stephanie.

*

With cold-eyed patience and a kind of affection, Agent 42 lay in bed waiting for Bernard Shaw to finish whatever he was doing in her bathroom. She had lived alone since the death - the murder, the execution - of her sister by the British police, but if any man had a claim on her now, this clever Irish mountain of egotism was at the head of the field. Maybe not that clever. He had saved her from the Man in Black last night in the alley where she waited to assassinate the turncoat poet, Yeats. She had been shown a hundred different ways to kill, but none of them worked when a human gorilla was calmly squeezing your life out through your ears. Shaw's clumsy gallantry had saved her. He had come back, moved by some guilty sense of Yeats' peril, his inexpertly windmilling fists eventually embarrassing the Man in Black into releasing his hold on her neck. The massive bald head had loomed over her for a moment, then receded into the foggy night, but not before Bernard Shaw had been knocked to the ground with all the hesitation and time-consuming drama of a blacksmith hammering home the last rivet of the day.

She didn't kill Shaw. Finishing him off might have been tidier, but the voices had spoken to her. *Let him take you home.* This was dangerous for her but far more dangerous for Shaw; Agent 42 knew that if They were using him, he would now be on borrowed time anyway. Agent 42 suddenly wanted to give herself to him. At least there would be one thing he would not regret later.

She sat up in the bed, naked under the white lace coverlet, and ran her hands up and through her long pale-blonde hair, then shook it loose until the shining cascade swirled and fell soft and heavy around her bare shoulders. She exercised her arms, stretching them above her head. Shaw came in from the bathroom and stood there looking at her.

'Bloody hell,' he said, loosening the cord on his dressing gown.

'You've got ten minutes,' said Agent 42.

As Shaw climbed aboard, he found himself unable to follow his usual script. 'You little minx' just didn't work with this one, while 'you dangerous valkyrie', notwithstanding silken fair skin and eyes like twin crystal models of Planet Cornflower, while more accurate, would just put him off. He looked at the bedhead for inspiration. The agent formerly known as Clarissa Jane Laurel looked at the ceiling. There were places to go, people to kill. William Butler Yeats was still alive. If this red-bearded satyr had told the truth, he was going to bring Yeats to a perfect killing ground. *Do it where it will be noticed.* The thought energized her and she suddenly clamped her long legs around Bernard Shaw, forcing him to give up his search for a good line and just concentrate on keeping up.

And at some point he'd better tell her about his wife.

Maybe some other time.

*

'All right, I was following her,' said Thomas Hardy, trying to extract a bit of twig caught in his large moustache. 'So were you, it seems.'

'Ah, yes, but,' said Doyle, 'My reason is perfectly defensible.'

'Oh?' said Hardy. The twig removed, he whiffled his moustaches, left, right, and twirled them fiercely back into trim. 'Satisfy the curiosity of an ageing man please – your perfectly defensible reason for being here would be…?'

'Actually,' said Doyle, rather stiffly, 'I was responding to a letter from one Elijah Smith begging me to save an innocent and beautiful young Englishwoman, Fanny, from the clutches of a gang of black magicians… and foreigners!'

Hardy was still laughing helplessly as the furious Doyle dragged him, quite roughly, deeper into the trees, where he collapsed, still squeaking and writhing, tears streaming down his cheeks.

'Oh – oh – oh – Doyle, that is the funniest, the funniest – oh, I'm sorry - a letter, really?' gasped Hardy at last, 'you really got a letter that said all that? Suddenly, life is worth living again. In a world where you can get letters like that, anything can happen.'

'It's no laughing matter, you know,' said Doyle. 'Someone is in danger.'

'I completely agree,' said Hardy carefully, controlling his response with a deep quavering breath. 'This girl, Fanny, according to you, and to my own observation, has confidently penetrated a gathering of upper class fantasists and struck up cordial relations with at least two of them, both of imposing appearance, and conveyed one, by means of a machine straight out of Mr Wells' scientific romances, to a notable residence in one of the most expensive areas of the capital, and it is now half-past eleven at night and they show no signs of emerging. I put it to you that Fanny, if that is her name, may be young and beautiful but is probably not innocent. Frankly, Doyle, after what I have seen, I would say it is the black magicians and foreigners who need to watch out.'

'Hmm, well, you may have a point,' said Doyle, peering carefully out of the leaves that gave them cover in the bright moonlight, 'although perhaps it's a little cynical.'

From the darkness of the spinney, the walls of the great house beyond the lawn looked in the starlight like a smooth pale expanse of chalk cliff, broken at intervals by dark rectangular caves. Because he was still annoyed with Hardy for laughing at him, Doyle said, without looking round,

'Do you often follow attractive young women?'

'Yes,' said Hardy. Then Doyle did turn around. He could not see Hardy at all, yet his voice was still there. He had disappeared in the night wood with the ease of a wild creature. Doyle, superstitious and mystically inclined, felt a chill run down his spine. Then he realized that Hardy was simply below his eye-line, a few feet away, sitting with his back against a soft-barked redwood tree, on the dry residue of numberless summers, and looking straight at him.

'I do, actually,' said Hardy's voice in the darkness. 'In the last few years it has become, I have to say, a rather bad habit. Things are difficult at home, you know, and one does so long for... contact. Trouble is, I can never think what to say to 'em.'

Doyle looked down carefully at the Dorset man, trying to see the expression on the pale blob of his face. 'But surely, Hardy, you, the author of Tess and all those passionate – I mean to say…'

'And you, Doyle, creator of a brilliantly clever and successful detective?'

'Hmm. I take your point. You were my chief suspect.'

'Well, well,' said Hardy consolingly, 'you have made some progress, within your limitations.'

'Limitations!' exclaimed Doyle. 'I suppose you know better.'

A shaft of silvery moonlight penetrated the screen of branches and evergreen leaves, dramatically lighting one side of Hardy's face.

'Know?' he said, his voice deepening. 'What does anyone know? But I say that the young woman you know as Fanny was born into one class, raised in another; that her innocence was abused when she came of age by a seducer who lost interest once he saw experience cloud those bright youthful orbs. Now she pursues a dangerous path, a single slip on which would be fatal to her situation, always faithful in her fashion to that one good man who might renew her stolen hopes, and yet habituated to the excitement of worldly affairs and dreading the manacles of an orthodox liaison.'

'Oh now really, Holmes...er...Hardy!' exclaimed Doyle, 'that's too much. Unless you yourself...?'

'Sadly no,' said Hardy, 'I only follow 'em. Saw her on a station platform. She smiled at me so sweetly through the carriage window. Decided I'd do something about it this time, so I jumped off at the last minute. The station staff were helpful and, well – I tracked her down.'

'Oh,' said Doyle, nodding wisely, as one big-game man to another, 'sort of like stalking then.'

Hardy gave him what used to be called, in old-fashioned times, an old-fashioned look.

'No,' he said, 'not like stalking, thank you - just a very slow approach. This is the end of the nineteenth century, you know, not the twentieth. We're late Victorians, not - not Greater-Americans or whatever we're all going to be by then.'

He stood up suddenly. 'That ground's cold. Well, at least we know where she is.'

'Do we?' said Doyle, a dangerous glitter in his eye. 'Doubtless you're on the right track about her. You have left out one thing though.'

'Really?' said Hardy. 'Only one?'

'Yes,' said Doyle, 'but it is quite important.'

At this, more in response to Doyle's tone than his words, the Dorset poachers in Hardy's genes narrowed their eyes and considered possible escape routes. He pulled down the sideflaps of his deer-stalker with the small deft movements of a mouse cleaning its ears. 'Oh yes?' he said casually. 'What's that then?'

'Do you know where you are?' said Doyle.

'Course I do. Lundun,' said Hardy, the urban sophisticate.

'And, um, which particular bit of London is this then?'

Hardy thought for a moment. 'Kensington?'

'Well done. Any idea which part of Kensington?'

'Well,' said Hardy expansively, 'obviously a part with great big houses and lots of rich people.' (He said rich people with the salivating disapproval with which some might have said fallen women.)

'Yes indeed,' said Doyle. 'And would you like to hazard a guess at which particular rich *royal* person owns this garden, that house and lots and – ooh - lots of other stuff as well, like India, Canada, Australia...?'

After that, it was not hard for Doyle to find the quickest way out. All he had to do was follow the rocket trail of broken branches and crushed weeds which Hardy left behind him.

*

It was the morning of the next day. Stephanie sat at one end of the settee with her long legs tucked under her, writing in a notebook. She was wearing a blue silk dressing-gown over white cotton pyjamas and to Yeats, reclining lazily with his back against the other end of the settee, she was utterly beautiful. 'Just to look at her makes me complete,' he thought to himself. Were all clichés true, and sufficient? Was poetic invention no more than a poor replacement for the wonderful experiences it pretended to describe? She was all in all to him. He would die for her. He was ten feet tall. He was in love.

'The Colonel will be in soon,' Stephanie murmured.

'Oh yes?' said W. B. Yeats, grinning like an idiot.

'I mean in, as in "in this room", she said, shutting the notebook, 'it is his office, after all.'

She stood up, shook her long hair out and put it up with a few deft movements of her hands. All the other women Yeats had ever known would have needed half an hour at the dressing table. An ache began in his chest and moved downwards. It was like falling. She was so attractive to him that the effect was very like an illness, very like fear.

Eight o'clock rang sweetly from an absurdly small gilt clock on the mantelpiece above the iron-cowled fireplace. Very soon afterwards there came a loud 'Good morning' to someone out in the corridor, a rattle of the doorhandle and then the dapper figure, tweed-suited today, of Colonel Sir Antony Madriver strode into the room. 'Morning Yeats,' he said crisply, placing a bundle of documents on the desk beneath the great many-paned window, 'morning, Your Highness.'

Yeats shot an astonished look at Stephanie. She smiled, a tired smile which had been used before. I'll explain later, her eyes said, and she slipped out of the room, her bare feet silent on the thick carpet.

'Feeling all right?' said the Colonel. 'Sorry to impose on you last night. Couldn't wait, you see. Things are moving too quickly. We took care of your friend, by the way.'

'Horton!' exclaimed Yeats. 'I clean forgot. What did you...?'

'He received a message - in your hand I'm afraid, sorry about that, but we are a secret intelligence agency – to say you'd been called away overnight, and inviting him to lodge, at your publisher's expense, with your housekeeper's friend, who would appreciate the custom.'

'You obviously understand Horton very well,' said Yeats. 'But would it not have been simpler to arrange for Mrs Old to let him in?'

'Simpler, yes,' said the Colonel, 'but not safe for your friend. He already lives on the fringes of the other world, and he knows you. That's quite enough to make him interesting to your – and our - enemies without staying at your address overnight, and unprotected.'

'Unprotected? By whom?'

'By you, of course,' said the Colonel. 'Now - you'll find a bathroom, through there. Make yourself free of everything. It's on the nation. Join us downstairs for breakfast in half an hour. Somebody will show you where.'

Steam. Yeats luxuriated in the kind of hot cascade unknown in the decaying castles of the Anglo-Irish ascendancy. It was an enormous and luxurious bathroom, fit for a... *your highness*? Sorchaid na cruichean! What was going on?

Secrets

'It's a kind of war, you see... no, that will give you entirely the wrong idea.'

A young soldier-servant in a scarlet uniform had shown Yeats to a large room on the second floor of the palace. Daffodil-hued sunshine slanted in through tall diamond-latticed windows, hosts of dust angels hovering in its beams. A bare expanse of polished floorboard reminded the poet of certain agonies experienced in provincial ball-rooms. Here, however, there were no circling couples; a table and chairs stood within comfortable distance of a spitting newly-laid fire, the fireplace huge and lintelled with a mighty oak beam.

Sitting at the octagonal table were the Colonel, Don Eduardo and two other men unknown to Yeats. No Crowley, which pleased the poet in a way he could not identify, until he realized that this morning he was completely without his usual nervousness. He no longer feared Crowley, he just didn't like him. He probed his own feelings, like someone searching with the tip of his tongue for the aching tooth. Nothing. Where the fear had always been, the fear of everything, there was nothing except a healing scar. Life rushed upwards through every vein until even the thick black hair on his head seemed to stir and lift, and he laughed out loud.

The expression of one of the two strangers, a sun-tanned European with close-cropped white hair, showed his surprise and then his lively hazel eyes grew a hundred crinkles at the corners, and he smiled broadly as he stood up and thrust out a hand across the table. Yeats thought he looked active and tough, but worn from much hard use like one of his Uncle George Pollexfen's treasured antique shotguns. He was introduced as Colin Angenent. The other man, Yeats realized with surprise, was the young soldier he had seen fighting off an attack in Kensington Park. One eye-socket was purple and the eye itself bloodshot. Last night the Colonel's face had seemed familiar and Yeats was not at all surprised to hear Madriver say:

'My son, Lieutenant Damien Madriver. Had a spot of bother in the Park, hence the shiner. It was in a good cause. He was courier for a very important letter - this one - which our enemies failed to obtain.'

'I know - about the fight, that is,' said Yeats, and immediately wished he had not. 'I mean,' he stammered, 'I saw you. I saw how it went. I'm - I'm sorry.' He did not need to explain.

'All our couriers,' said the Colonel, 'of whom Damien is not the least capable, possess weapons and techniques which could have killed or incapacitated twice as many as tried to get possession of this letter yesterday. The use of such things attracts attention. It was his duty to delay doing so until or unless things got far more out of hand. If you or anyone had intervened, he would have been forced to act, you might have been injured and that, believe me, would have very much complicated the discreet way we go about our business.'

'Ah, yes, well,' said the greatest poet since Shakespeare, and was very glad of the rattle of crockery and smell of coffee at the door.

'It's not a war,' said the Colonel half an hour later, 'because if we fought we would be on both sides. Now, where to start...'

'Let me,' said Stephanie, who had come in just at that moment. She was wearing a plain grey woollen dress and her newly-brushed hair shone. Yeats' heart turned over twice. 'You dreamed last night,' she said taking the empty seat next to the Colonel, opposite Yeats. 'You dreamed,' she said again, lowering her voice and speaking only for him, 'I *know* you dreamed last night. And what you dreamed about. You saw snakes or serpents, twisted, intertwined. You were taken to a place, and there were people. They showed you things. They taught you things.'

Yeats cursed himself as he felt the blush rise. 'You were - I mean - was I talking...?'

'No,' said the Colonel, 'and you were watched first by Don Eduardo and *then* by...' a slight shift of the grey eyes under fierce brows, answered by an almost imperceptible lateral sway of the long shining hair, '...by Mrs Toughguid.'

'It is how it is done,' said Colin Angenent, 'with the cup of the gods. A friend must watch over you.' Don Eduardo inclined his head. 'It is how it is done,' he said, very quietly, and Yeats saw that Don Eduardo was the authority in this matter.

'What did you give me?' said Yeats, no stranger to the magic mushroom and hash-cake.

'A decoction of a certain Peruvian vine,' said the Colonel, 'potent but safe in the hands of an expert. Yours, I am pleased to say, was prepared by Don Eduardo Nejedeka here, who is a shaman from Peru.

The reason we know what you saw in your dream-vision is that it is what he and other initiates to the ayawaska ritual have been seeing for the last two years. Under his careful supervision, all of us here have also had the same experience. I hope you will understand and forgive the deception. It was the quickest way to convince you.'

'Shaman,' said Yeats, frowning at the table as if something in his memory were written there. 'I have heard the word. It is in origin Siberian, and refers to a visionary magician and healer. Is he then the secret master I came here to meet?'

'No,' said the Colonel, 'although he is a master of the spirit world, a great man of his nation, the Witoto people of Northern Peru. Colin, please.'

'Mr Yeats,' began Colin Angenent, and then stopped as if searching for the right words. His hazel eyes gleamed in his pleasant life-worn features with the same intensity that Yeats had seen in Stephanie's face. The thought came to the poet that this was a secret society. But what secret were they sharing, apart from a drug-inspired vision? What knowledge or cause could create that look of transcendent excitement?

'For many years stories have been coming out of South America,' said Angenent, sure now of his line, 'strange but convincing accounts regarding the abilities of their wise men, or spirit-healers – shaman if you will. Personally I don't like the word, which is highly specific to the Northern Asian peoples, but there is not really an alternative, as there is nobody in our own culture quite like them.'

'Let us say rather that there hasn't been up till now,' said the Colonel with a glance at Yeats.

'Some who lived amongst the Peruvian tribes,' Colin Angenent continued, 'told stories of flying men, of commerce with the ancient spirits of their race, and with strange half-human, half-animal beings which became their teachers.'

'Do you yourself speak,' asked Yeats, 'as a student of the human, or the superhuman?'

Angenent looked hard at Yeats for a moment and then smiled, the wrinkles around his eyes deepening, and two vertical lines appearing like slashed wounds from cheekbone to chin either side of his mouth.

'After my discussions with Don Eduardo, I am not sure there is much difference,' he said. 'For what it's worth, I used to be – still am, technically - a Roman Catholic priest. By secular training, and profession, I am a physiological chemist, specializing in inheritance.'

'I see,' said Yeats, with a serious frown, 'I see.' Then he looked up and grinned. 'Actually, I don't,' he said, embracing his incomprehension along with the rest of the world. He had discovered a powerful drug when Stephanie smiled at him, and it wasn't the Peruvian vine.

Angenent grinned back, not fully understanding Yeats' mood but liking it. 'In scientific studies,' he said, 'the most reliable observations are those made in ignorance.'

Yeats nodded, approving a principle which seemed to have something of Hermetic logic in it.

'I mean there can be no possibility of bias or prejudice,' said Angenent, 'when the observer reports data without knowing its significance to a third party - is, as one might say, blind to the implications. In their visionary journeys Don Eduardo and his colleagues were repeatedly seeing something, always the same thing, which they did not understand. A missionary priest, Father Michael Gomez, picked up on it, and thought it was worth letting me know. We had been in the same year at Downside, then at Oxford, and shared an amateur interest in palaeontology, the study of the far distant past, deep time. We had been corresponding on the subject for some years. In recent months, I had been keeping him up to date on a curious discovery in Europe. Then in September last year, Father Gomez sent me a letter, a long letter, in which he described the beliefs and practices of the Amazonian tribes and the role of their shaman, the wise man, the priest. I believe that the Church thought my friend was getting a bit too interested in the native religion, as they saw it. He must have been on the point of being recalled when he wrote. The letter ended with something beyond the merely extraordinary, which was inexplicably bound up with the subject of our correspondence for months past. I at once wrote back urgently requesting more information. I won't deny that I was also writing as an agent of IBI.' He pronounced the acronym as 'ibby', as in the Latin for *there*.

'Mr Yeats,' broke in the Colonel, 'does not yet know about IBI.'

'Oh,' said Angenent, momentarily at a loss. 'Well, in time, I suppose.' Yeats saw Angenent glance at the Colonel and a look exchanged. There was disagreement there, even disapproval. However,

Angenent returned to his subject with the same quiet clarity:

'Well then, let's just say that our colleague Don Eduardo was not in fact the only odd line of communication that seemed to have been opened up to the strange country the other side of consciousness, but – as the Colonel reminds me - I am getting too far ahead. The fact is, that within a few days of sending his letter, Father Gomez was dead.'

'You suggest there was a connection? Foul play of some kind?' said Yeats.

'He died,' said Angenent grimly, 'of a condition unknown to science. His ability to fight infection – necessary to existence in this world - simply collapsed. To put it another way, it was as if his body had been persuaded to kill itself. Those charged with his care were reluctant to talk about it. One hinted to me of demons.'

'Well,' said Yeats, 'local superstition I suppose...'

'Michael Gomez died in the care of some rather well-educated Catholics, of European descent' said Angenent, matter-of-factly. 'It was a terrible experience for them; for poor Gomez it must have been a blessed relief when the end came. In any case, I decided I had to go out there myself, if only to make certain arrangements. I was also commissioned to make contact with those, like Don Eduardo, who had reported back from the other side of the veil that divides our reality from what is beyond. What I did not know was that Don Eduardo was making the opposite journey, under an obligation of his own. I believe we actually crossed in mid-Atlantic.'

'What was it that Gomez reported?' said Yeats. 'What was the thing beyond the extraordinary?'

'You already know,' said Angenent. After a while, Yeats said, 'You mean my dream. I saw nothing there out of the ordinary – I mean, out of the ordinary for dreams.'

'Do you really mean that?'

Another pause.

'No. It was real. More real than real. Something else. I can't quite capture its quality in words; a sensation for which there is no name. And there were interwoven spirals, gyres, in complementary relationship, equal and opposite, separate but also one. I remember that it all depended on how one looked at it. That's what they wanted me to say – I mean, see. It's strange – the sum of what I experienced in the dream has left a shape, a symbol, in my mind, which I cannot remember at any point actually seeing.'

'Even you,' said Angenent, 'trained in magical thinking and practice, have looked but not seen, apprehended but not comprehended. This is because you have encountered something which cannot exist, something which brought Don Eduardo to us, and killed Gomez.'

Yeats did not know why, but his heart started pounding at the words. 'Can you please explain so that I can understand?'

'I shall try,' said Angenent, 'though, God knows, we do not fully understand what is happening ourselves. Have you heard of Altamira? No? Well, I am not surprised in a way, although for some of us it is like a man admitting he has never heard of the Sistine Chapel – no, do not be offended, you would have been a very young man in 1880, when Sautuola published his discoveries.

'His full name was Marcelino Sanz de Sautuola, and he was an amateur archaeologist of small but solid reputation in Spain. He loved to explore any caves on his own estate and on one such expedition he discovered cave paintings, of the most sensational realism and skill, not on any wall but above him, on the cavern-roof. Certain French academics did not like a Spaniard stealing their thunder, especially with cave art found in Spain. Until then, pre-historic Frenchmen had ruled the roost, and their modern descendants had made a good living from them. These French palaeontologists set out to discredit Signor Sautuola, a modest and unworldly scholar, completely open to their scurrilous attacks – he was even naïve enough to admit that it was his eight year old daughter who first noticed the paintings. The French Academicians accused him of forgery, lies and profiteering, and it killed him. And you know, these academic assassins never even visited Altamira themselves.'

'It is a tragic story. I am pleased that you honour this... Sautuola?' said Yeats. 'One man, in heroic battle against a whole culture – that is the history of true progress in the world.'

'I hope to do more than honour Signior Sautuola in private,' said Angenent, with a tight smile. 'New discoveries are cutting the ground from under the feet of the French with every month that passes.'

'Why so?'

'We are now finding cave art under ancient sedimentary layers, more than twenty thousand years old. The forgery smear is useless against such evidence, and with the loss of that weapon the French will have to surrender.'

'Then you have won an important battle.'

'So we are meant to believe.'

There were several seconds of silence. Yeats saw Angenent glance at the Colonel before he carried on speaking. 'Two years ago, I – we – came to believe that the attack on Sautuola over the Altamira paintings was not a matter of petty academic spite. In fact we thought it was not about the paintings at all, but something else which Sautuola found. Something no one knew about.'

'Sautuola concealed it? That doesn't sound right.'

'No, he did not conceal it. He did not know he had found it.'

'Something he missed.'

'No, it was in plain view.'

'Then why did he not realize he had found it.'

'Because he could not see it.'

'But you said it was in plain view.'

'Sautuola could not see it because, like the vision you had but cannot name, it could not exist. Humans have learned not to see what cannot be.'

Yeats shivered. He had always been abnormally sensitive to atmosphere and mood, and the room seemed to have darkened at Angenent's words.

'Before I met and spoke at length with Don Eduardo,' continued Angenent, 'it was only a theory. What I learned from him and have subsequently experienced has convinced me. The French attacks on Sautuola were merely a delaying tactic. Someone was buying time.

'What could be that important?'

'A secret which could destroy the world.'

'Then it should be kept secret. The risk to humankind...'

'He did not say destroy the planet,' broke in the Colonel. 'If Sautuola's discovery were generally known, it could indeed destroy the world, our world. The web of power and privilege with its origin in pre-history; the layers and layers of experience hardening into materialistic dogma; the assumptions, beliefs and narratives which give spurious shape and meaning to the lives of the ignorant masses: there may be a secret which could utterly change this knowledge-world, the noosphere, for ever. Would that necessarily be a bad thing?'

Yeats thought, drawing down his black brows. The others stayed absolutely silent, giving him time. 'No,' he said, 'not necessarily. You must realize...,' and he hesitated, suddenly shy.

'That you are trying to do just that? Yes, you are known for your serious interest in the other side of the Veil, and its inhabitants, the beings known as fairies – it is the reason you are here. We think something or someone is trying to reach out to us from that place, the world of the fairies. We also think you are the only man in Europe capable of accepting and comprehending what that thing might be and, most importantly, communicating with it.'

Yeats thought of Wilde. He thought of Synge. He even thought of Shaw. He would give heaven and earth for a fraction of their ease with language. The fountain fluency of Synge at his best. The unanswerable stiletto of Shaw's critical analysis. The crystalline geometries of Wilde's perfect dialogues.

W. B. Yeats was just the man you got in to talk to the fairies.

The poet lifted his head, and set the mask of composed intelligence in place. 'What is this thing found in the Altamira cave that is so dangerous that it could destroy our world?' he said. The Colonel looked to left and right, fixed his grey eyes intently on Yeats like a lynx about to spring, and said, 'This.'

With his eyes all the time on Yeats' face, the Colonel dipped an index finger in his cup, picked up a fat black bead of coffee on the tip and drew something on the polished surface of the walnut table. Yeats stared at it, his blood running cold for a moment, although his racing heart felt as if it would burst out of his chest. The liquid figure was only there for a moment before a sweep of the military man's small capable hand turned it into an evaporating smear. Yeats slowly lifted his eyes as if it cost a major effort of strength and will. His mouth opened, framing a protest, but Angenent cut across, anticipating his objection: 'It was buried under several feet of sediments, undisturbed for at least 35,000 years. It's not modern – it's not even ancient – there's no word for how old it is.'

Yeats stuck his hands in the deep side pockets of his green velvet jacket and leaned back in his chair with an affectation of relaxedness, but his set pale features revealed his shock. 'The Church isn't going to like it,' he said.

'The Church!' exclaimed Stephanie. 'They won't even be first in the queue. The intellectual establishment of every civilized nation is going to implode.'

'The Jews will take it personally,' said the Colonel reflectively, 'and the Ottomans will think it's a Zionist conspiracy.'

'Everybody will think it's somebody else's conspiracy,' said Stephanie.

'There's going to be trouble,' said Yeats.

'There's going to be war,' said Angenent.

'Yes, there is,' said the Colonel, and held up the letter he had been reading, the one defended in Kensington Gardens by his son at the cost of a badly-bruised face. 'It will be in the Transvaal and at the latest October this year. The game has begun and the Boers will be the first piece to be removed from the board.'

'The Boers? Why them?' said Yeats. 'What has that to do with...?' and he waved his hand at the spot on the table where the symbol had been drawn.

'Britain wants the gold and diamonds that the Boers control – and overland access to North Africa, but that's a side issue to what's coming. The Masters of the Empire have been amassing a gigantic war-chest for some time now, far beyond what is needed to crush the Boers. We think we know why, but even that's almost a side issue. There is something else driving the Empire's policy, and we think it is simply using the Boer situation to test its own power before embarking on a project on so vast a scale of evil and destruction that its effects will be felt beyond the terrestrial sphere.'

'Something else?' said Yeats, his voice cracking a little. 'Beyond the terrestrial?' As secret societies went, this one was almost too much of a good thing. Then with an effort of will he controlled his excitement. 'You are right,' he said, levelly, looking into Angenent's face, 'in thinking me a sincere student of fairy lore. I have traced the history and character of the good folk in story and song for many years. And I - I believe in them. However, I have absolutely no reason, just here and now, to believe in *you*. You have given me a drug, I have had a peculiar dream, I sense honesty in this group, and...' He did not look at Stephanie but something like a warm pulse beat so strongly in the space between them that it seemed to shake the air. 'Even so,' he said, 'I need to know more. You are an amateur pal... palaeo...'

'Palaeontologist,' said Angenent.

'Palaeontologist,' said Yeats with dignity, 'but your profession is a scientific one, a physiological chemist I think you said?'

'Yes.'

'I think you are an alchemist.'

Yeats saw Angenent tense. He instinctively liked and respected the hard-bitten adventurer and was not proud of scoring the hit.

'How did you know?' said the Colonel quietly.

Yeats did not know how he knew. This sort of thing had happened frequently in his childhood. He knew things, about people, their lives, their thoughts and their feelings; he sometimes saw with an absolute certainty what was going to happen in the immediate future. He was quite old before he realized that this was unusual. Curiously, it was after this realization that he lost the ability altogether. As an adult he could recapture the feeling, but not the event; he remembered a bubbly sense of privilege, a gift they called it, without knowing how true that was – it was a gift, a special present which came to him undeserved, unexpected, never demanded, the gift of knowing. 'Something tells me,' people say, but never think to ask what; but Yeats had really felt the presence of a something, and it was hovering within the dark borders of his memory now, teetering on the edge of his mind, extending a tentative shoe *and coming into the light.*

'Yeats? Mr Yeats?' The Colonel was gently trying to get his attention. Don Eduardo was looking at him, his deep eyes filled with kindness and curiosity. Angenent had recovered from his momentary shock and Stephanie was sitting up alert, poised and watching everybody.

'I was - am - indeed an alchemist,' said Angenent. 'As it happens I am also a well-published professional scientist and teacher. You can look me up if you like.'

'No, I meant nothing by it,' said Yeats. 'I can see how it could be dangerous for you to be so identified, but for myself the true pursuit of the Great Work is no shame.'

'If you understand the true pursuit of the Great Work, then know this: it is why I went to South America,' said Angenent.

Yeats made as if to speak, but did not. Even in this company, initiates if ever there were any, he was reluctant to discuss what he knew about the secret goal of alchemy. He changed the subject instead:

‘As to physical transactions between the Fairy world and this one, you may be wrong to think me credulous.’

‘We know you’re not,’ said Stephanie. ‘You once wrote that you don’t believe in fairies of the English kind, who are just like beautiful little humans, “romantic bubbles from Provence” I think is how you put it, and, if the Colonel will forgive me, for our safety and yours it is very important that you do not believe in such things.’

‘Mrs Toughguid, you of all people need no authority from me to speak of these matters,’ said the Colonel drily. ‘You are in any case quite right. I suspect that it would take more than Irish milk left on the doorstep to satisfy the beings who are trying to break through into our world.’

Angenent stood up suddenly, like a man used to action who has been sitting still for too long. He strode to the marble fireplace, kicked a log into flame, walked back and propped himself straight-armed against the back of his chair.

‘Mr Yeats,’ he said, ‘I have been many things in my time. I have explained that I am not a palaeontologist, except as an enthusiast. I am a specialist in human generational inheritance, a science which Bateson at Cambridge is now calling genetics. Along with Bateson, Langstrom and Xaves were amongst the leading men in the field. I say “were” because Langstrom and Xaves are both dead, murdered we think, although there was not a scrap of evidence pointing at anyone and even the method is unclear. They both died suddenly, exactly like Gomez, from a sudden massive change in their physiological chemistry – as if something had given their bodies instructions to stop living.’

After a brief but telling silence, Angenent resumed: ‘Despite the mystery of the method, the motive can be inferred from the fact that they were both prepared to meet with Don Eduardo, and did so, while Bateson was not – and did not. Don Eduardo seems to have been directed to me as a very poor fourth choice.’

‘Directed to you?’ said Yeats, ‘but I thought…’

‘Indeed,’ said Angenent. ‘It is not I that explored the unknown. It was Don Eduardo Nejedeka, who had never before set foot outside his people’s forty square mile territory in the Peruvian forest, who is the explorer. He is an heroic adventurer and England is more strange to him than the Moon.’

They all looked at Don Eduardo. The wide-set dark eyes glittered above the long straight nose. Then the wide lips curved upwards in an unexpectedly sweet smile. 'I like the gas lamps,' he said, in a voice as gentle as the wind which ripples the shallows and sets the willow fronds nodding.

'What directed you to this country and to those people?' said Yeats with a roughness of speech in stark contrast to his usual careful courtesy. There was a kinship between him and the South American shaman, and there are tensions and rivalries in families. The Irish poet-scholar was both attracted and repelled by a dark excitement that the foreign magician carried with him. They were at an edge, a faultline between two historical continents. The earthquake was coming and manners did not matter.

Don Eduardo did not reply or even seem to hear, but looked steadily into Yeats' eyes, darkness meeting darkness somewhere high over the South Atlantic. Yeats held the shaman's midnight gaze, quite untroubled. He felt on familiar ground. This was the kind of 'magical' staring competition that went on all the time at the Golden Dawn. The society was full of amateur sorcerers fixing each other with glittering eyes. For anyone with a slight natural squint, like Yeats, it was child's-play. A second after forming this thought, he felt the full force of his error. Don Eduardo was the real thing and he was dangerous.

For the Colonel, Angenent and Stephanie it was a silent and invisible contest. They were only aware that Yeats and the South American shaman quietly looked at each other for about thirty seconds; for Yeats it was much, much longer. He felt as if every room of his mental house were being gently invaded, the ornaments handled, the titles of his books read and the sock drawer of memory turned over. His mind was being expertly burgled and he felt his personality draining away into the green shade of a million year-old forest canopy.

With an enormous effort the Anglo-Irish magician gathered his defences and forced his mind to visualize the shrine of the Celtic Mysteries which he used as his magical locus. He made a platonic solid appear in the mid-air of his imagination, then rotated it in all the dimensions. He positioned the many-sided artefact in each sphere of the Sephirotic tree in ascending sequence, then descending. By the time he reached Netsah for the second time, the pressure on the inside of his forehead and temples had eased and his heart was beating with its normal rhythm. The Peruvian shaman went on smiling his gentle smile and the calm eyes did not blink, but he slowly and gravely inclined his head, as one professional to another, and the pressure lifted.

A log shifted in the grate and a flurry of sparks shot up the chimney.

'Well done Yeats,' said the Colonel. 'You might be interested to know that Crowley failed that test. Couldn't endure it. Surprised us.'

'Was that why you needed me? To replace Crowley?'

Yeats asked the question of the Colonel but he was looking at Stephanie Toughguid. The Colonel obviously sensed something and remained silent.

'Yes,' said Stephanie clearly and carefully, 'that is why we needed you.'

Hating himself but unable to stop the words coming out, Yeats said, 'And has my induction followed Crowley's in every respect?'

Stephanie stood up and walked out of the room, her back very straight.

Breath.

Breath.

Angenent, carefully expressionless, pushed his chair back and followed her out; he did not look at Yeats. Some seconds later, the Colonel's son followed him. The Colonel went to stand and look out of one of the tall windows, hands clasped behind him like Napoleon in exile. Don Eduardo sat still, amusedly observant, an anthropologist studying his own kind in the mirror of a foreign tribe.

'You ought to know,' said the Colonel apparently to the trees outside, 'that Stephanie can trace her descent from the most ancient European nobility, and she herself bears an illustrious name. It is also only through an accident of history and his own sense of honour that her father is not head of state in his native land. All that is by the way, I suppose. What you really need to understand is that as far as I know – and believe me that is a very long way indeed – there has been no man in her life since she came to London.'

The Colonel walked briskly to the door; Yeats looked at the suddenly-interesting wood grain in the table. 'Oh,' said the Colonel, one hand on the door handle, 'when you want to leave this room, ring first, or a guard may shoot you – the Queen's coming to see the restored apartments and her people are a bit jumpy.'

'Only the dance,' said Don Eduardo, reaching across the table to lay a hand like a comfortable old glove on Yeats' inert forearm. 'Only the dance. I bring her back for you?'

'Oh?' said the poet, dully. 'How is that then?'

The door opened and Stephanie came in. In a no-nonsense way she walked up to where Yeats sat at the table in front of the great fireplace and did something which unutterably appalled him: she knelt submissively at his side, her arms hanging loosely down and her head lowered so that he could see the tender unprotected nape of her neck. Her silence and posture enraged him. A red anger beginning in his belly filled Yeats in a second and he glared at the shaman. 'What have you done?' he shouted in fury, then, mastering himself, more consideringly, chanted,

'Mind before eyes,
Spirit before mind,
Heart before all.
No more!'

The shaman went on smiling his gentle smile and the calm eyes did not blink, but he slowly and gravely inclined his head, just once. A log shifted in the grate and a flurry of sparks shot up the chimney.

'Well done Yeats,' said the Colonel. 'You might be interested to know that Crowley failed that test. Went completely under. Surprised us.'

Yeats put his hands flat on the table and breathed in deeply. It had been some sort of hypnotism, although that seemed too weak a word for what he had experienced. Angenent, the Colonel, his son Damien and Stephanie Toughguid were in the seats from which they had never moved, watching him. Yeats risked a look at Stephanie. Could she know or guess what he had said within his trance?

'Was that why…?' The stupid words had already formed in his mind without conscious thought, and his blood ran cold. He closed his mouth, cleared his throat and made himself sit upright. He set his features in an indifferent mask and said lightly, 'Crowley – well, he lacks experience.'

The words set the others smiling broadly, especially Stephanie, and there was a feeling in the air of the room like an oppressive weight being lifted. It even seemed brighter. It was like being passed fit for service, it was like the moment you knew you had got the job. 'Exactly so,' said the Colonel, 'exactly so! Did you get all that, about Lady Stephanie, I mean? Did Don Eduardo really communicate it?'

'European royalty? Illustrious name?' said Yeats experimentally.

'That's right,' said the Colonel. 'It was Her Highness' idea. You had to be told of course, and it was an interesting test.'

'Of what?' said Yeats sharply.

'Of Don Eduardo's claims,' said the Colonel. 'They were somewhat out of the ordinary.'

'Out of the ordinary!' exclaimed Yeats. 'I have never seen anything like it!'

'Oh, but we have,' said the Colonel. 'The Templars learned mind-magic from the Arabs, and I believe they got it from the Indians, and who or what they got it from, goodness knows . We just hadn't met any adepts from the New World. Are you all right? We never had the slightest doubt as to the strength of *your* mind, you know.'

Yeats breathed in, and put the mask of assurance back on his face. It was getting easier.

'Yes, thank you,' he said. 'At least I know now that I'll be shot if I start running around without telling anyone.'

'Who told you that?'

'Don Eduardo... well, you did, in a way... when I was... while Don Eduardo...'

'Interesting. Did he – I - tell you about the Queen's coming here?'

'Of course.'

'No "of course" about it! Don Eduardo hadn't been told – shouldn't have known. Now that *is* interesting.' And he gave the innocently smiling South American shaman a long hard look.

Yeats also watched the shaman. The sense of kinship was strengthened now by mutual respect. 'May I ask you again,' he said to the Witoto seer, 'who or what made you come here?'

'I fly, up into spirit land, speak to animal-gods,' said Don Eduardo in his soft smoky voice. 'They ansiosos, much ansiosos. Never see gods afraid before. They say something bad to happen. They say "Go. You cannot stop it. Others can. Find them." '

'Did they tell you where to go. A sign perhaps?'

'Yes. They say 'Go to Guillermo Bate-son of Cam-bridge in

Inglaterra.'

'Oh. Useful gods these,' said Yeats. 'Very - er - practical. What had this Bateson to offer?'

'Authority,' said Angenent, taking his cue from the South American's closed mouth and folded hands. 'Bateson's a leading man in human generational research. This suggests that whatever has frightened Don Eduardo's gods is linked to our heredity, the germ plasm, the secret code which makes us what we are. And there is external evidence that this is the case. Before he died, or was murdered, Xaves was able to make some notes, which have come to me. Believe me, he took Don Eduardo entirely seriously. That alone confirms the importance of Don Eduardo's mission, even if we did not know he was directed here by higher beings.'

'But which higher beings?' said Yeats. 'I can think of some higher beings I wouldn't trust to choose my wallpaper, let alone save the world.' He was remembering Horton's pale and intensely-concerned features and the Brighton mystic's attempt to warn him. 'Just be sure when you hear such a voice, that you know who or what it comes from.' He should have found out what Horton had meant. Messages could come in many forms. But Angenent was speaking, breaking in on the poet's thoughts.

'Yeats is right, you know, Tony. You never know what you're dealing with. We of all people should recognize that. But Yeats,' said Angenent, 'the instruction to Don Eduardo tied in with my own researches, in a completely unforeseen way. Let me explain.

'The fact about human inheritance is that we can see what it does, but still don't know how. We don't know what the mechanism is. If you like, we can see the conjuror's trick , but we don't know how he does it. But more than that, we don't know what drives that mechanism – we can't find the conjuror. Since Darwin we thought we'd seen the last of God. But it's looking as if we'll have to apologize and ask him to come back. It's the first principle thing, the prime mover. We can't even imagine it - it is like trying to study the back of your own head.'

'That's easy,' said Yeats. 'Surely you just get someone else to have a look for you.'

The Colonel looked at Angenent, with a frosty smile. 'I told you,' it seemed to say.

Angenent smiled his own tight smile, the vertical slashes appearing briefly either side of his thin lips, and continued:

'It seems to be all about division within the cell nucleus, but even the best microscopes cannot resolve down to the detail needed to see what is going on at the chemical level so we're stuck with empiricism – they're even beginning to look at Mendel's work again, and take Darwin's gemmules seriously.'

'Gemmules?' said Yeats.

'Scraps of stuff carrying the architectural drawings for you. Darwin theorized that they migrate to the reproductive organs and are passed on by sexual intercourse.

The trouble with Mendel's statistical method,' Angenent continued, 'is that it can suggest rules for inheritance but can't tell you who's giving the orders or what's carrying them out. Without actually being able to see what's going on, it's all about insights like Darwin's, prompted by informed imagination, and that is where I think we have made some progress but also encountered a difficulty.

'Through long study and practice in alchemy, I saw strong connections between ancient alchemical symbols and the direction that current genetic research is taking, but had no means of making my insights useful in any way that would not instantly discredit me with those I sought to help. Since Gomez's letter, I am absolutely convinced, the alchemical Great Work, the perfection of humanity, is connected with the Peruvian shamans' vision. As I think you know, the Alchemists do not seek mineral gold, but the golden perfection of the human, to create a being effectively immortal, of a godlike understanding and with powers which we would think divine.'

Yeats eyes went to left and right. This was top secret stuff, but the others did not seem particularly surprised. Oh well. He wanted to kiss Stephanie's nose. Angenent continued.

'It is well-known, or rather assumed, that the Alchemists' quest has failed. However, some of us are beginning to think that the idea of the Great Work did not in fact have its origin in Alchemy, which was in many respects just a way for Ancient Egyptians to make gold go further. We think...' and Angenent paused, glancing again at the Colonel, as if to draw energy from those steely eyes and frosty brows to say something difficult, 'we think it possible, even probable, that the project of perfecting humankind is very old indeed, far older even than the ancient Egyptians who were the first to practice alchemy in the quest for immortality. We think it is not… it is not…,' Angenent faltered.

'It is not a human project,' said the Colonel.

The silence that followed the impossible words threatened to go on for ever. It was Yeats who finally broke it:

'Where do the fairies come in?'

'It is not a human project,' repeated the Colonel, looking hard at Yeats.

'Oh. I see,' said the poet, making a wry face. 'Well, that is I don't, quite. You seem to be saying that it's the fairies who are trying to perfect the human race!'

'A strange idea?' said the Colonel. 'Of course. But think for a moment of all those stories of changelings and abduction. To what end other than improvement of the stock can one ascribe them?'

'But whose stock?' said Yeats. 'Even accepting the premise, which I do not absolutely admit, such stories suggest it was the fairies who were trying to bring in human blood to improve their own line, not the other way round.'

'How can we know the truth behind the accounts of confused or frightened people?' said Angenent. 'As an initiate, would you recommend that an amateur should undertake the interior journey past the Guardians? And – always supposing he survived - would you be surprised if he didn't understand what he had seen?'

'Interior,' said Yeats, leaning forward, his black eyebrows drawn together in concentration. 'Then you think the fairies are somehow inside us?'

'According to the ancients, the universe is inside us,' said Angenent, smiling again as if he had seen something in Yeats that both amused and pleased him. 'The fact is, that language itself is the wrong tool to describe super-reality. As a late nineteenth century scientist it pains me to say so, but the cosmos actually is greater – infinitely greater - than the sum of its parts.'

'Well, what next?' said Yeats after another thought-filled silence. 'You have called me in, but what am I to do? There are aspects to this which are beyond the merely supernatural, and beyond me, you should realize that.'

'The extranatural,' said Angenent, 'is what we say. And it is very much your subject, judging from your published work on fairies and the magical tradition.'

'Inheritance, fairies and dynamite,' said the Colonel cheerfully. 'The last one is my business at the moment. Angenent and yourself are the experts on the other two. They're all linked, but at the moment we don't see the how and why. That's what you're for.'

'How and why,' murmured Yeats dreamily. 'I have heard that.' For almost the first time Don Eduardo, the Peruvian shaman, looked at Yeats without the Amazonian mist clouding his thoughts, the glitter in his narrowed eyes on the surface and not guarded deep within. Yeats' reverie had aroused his professional interest. The shaman's expression was that of a top Harley Street surgeon coming across a nifty bit of knife-work on a visit to a native healer.

'Yes, I have heard those words,' said Yeats, almost chanting in the abstraction of his mind, 'a long time ago. I feel suddenly that the memory relates to all this. I had a kind of lesson, from… from someone. This person said that the name "Andy" will tell us how and why. "Turn it round to see the how and the why".'

'It might be a riddle,' said the Colonel immediately. 'Break the name down into AND plus Y. "Turning" the AND gives you DNA, which would be the "how", and leaves you with the puzzle of the "why" .'

'What does that mean?' said Yeats.

'Haven't the foggiest,' said the Colonel. 'Angenent?'

'DNA,' said the biological chemist. 'If it's an acronym, its not one I recognize. In my line, NA might be nucleic acid. Friedrich Miescher published something on nuclein thirty years ago, and Richard Altmann's recently taken it further.'

'Why nucleic acid?' said the Colonel. "NA" could be anything, even in the laboratory – *nitric* acid for example.'

'Actually,' said Angenent slowly, 'nucleic acid is an excellent candidate for the god in the machine: the "how", if not the "why".'

But not for fifty years. Like everything else his little man had said, the words were there in Yeats' memory. Had they been part of the lesson? Should he mention it? The poet let his head drop in thought and instantly cried out and jumped to his feet, making his heavy chair fall over backwards with a very loud bang on the unforgiving Kensington Palace floorboards.

‘Oh, I am so sorry,’ he said. ‘I just… I have just remembered something important, an appointment. I fear I must go.’

The Colonel regarded Yeats with a quizzical expression, then said, ‘Very well. Take no unnecessary risks but try to live your normal life. There has been one attempt, there could be others. However, you are under the protection of IBI now. You will be relatively safe while that remains the case. Be ready for Fairy communication. We think they will contact you now that you have spoken with us. Some sort of message. We don’t know how. It may be quite subtle, so be on the look-out. If a message comes, please contact Miss Toughguid through your society. Contact her in any case after forty-eight hours. You can also leave a note for “Giovanni” at the Cheshire Cheese if you want to meet. It will always arrive here inside the hour. Do not try to use any other means of communication with us. Goodbye, for now. I am sure Miss Toughguid will drive you wherever you want to go.’

‘Wait until we’re outside,’ muttered Yeats from the corner of his mouth as he walked the length of the great room, keeping ahead of Stephanie so that she could not see his front; and the Fairy ducked back into the breast pocket of the poet’s dark green velvet coat.

Yeats was escorted to a little courtyard which gave onto the street through a highly ornamented brick archway, in which Stephanie shortly appeared, not in the Parker electric automobile, but on the driver’s box-seat of a smart little one horse brougham. Yeats climbed up beside her and surprised her by immediately asking to be dropped off, not at home, but only a few hundred yards away, at the West Gate of Kensington Gardens. She thought for a moment, glanced at him consideringly, and then guided the carriage through the heavy oncoming traffic to the roadside, with no more than a caressing pressure on the reins, a sway from the waist and the subtle dip of a shoulder. Yeats watched her drive away back towards Kensington Palace with a feeling he had never experienced in his life before. He had tried loving other women but it had just made him miserable. Stephanie only had to move, turn her head, push a strand of hair away from her eyes, and he felt

happy.

'So it *was* you,' said Yeats, swinging off the path by the Round Pond and into the shade of some tall rhododendrons, where he could talk to his coat pocket without attracting attention. 'I saw you astride that gaslight bracket, at the Cheshire Cheese!'

'It was,' said the Fairy, beaming indulgently and resting its sharp elbows on the rim of Yeats' breast pocket, looking like someone enjoying the morning air from an upstairs window. 'You did!'

Yeats felt strange. Words rose up in his throat, rather childish words: he wanted to complain about the lonely years, and he wanted to weep. Instead he said coldly, 'After so long. Why now?'

'It was time.'

Yeats did not answer. The February-ragged lawns were still dewy though it was well past midday. Everywhere, lively clumps of daffodil leaves were poking through the turf and amongst them the crocuses were out, egg white and yolk yellow, while the sky was the fresh blue of an ageing Winter looking his best for Spring. The westering sun was beginning to gleam through the rowan trees around the Pond, where a mist was already rising. The cusp of the turning year, its stillness and the chilly light, the sharp smell of the air and the distant cry of children seemed to add up to something past melancholy.

'That colour again,' said Yeats quietly. 'Always out of the corner of my eye.'

'Glas,' said the Fairy. 'It was how the Old Peoples saw the world. Many things were glas. Glas was the colour of air. Distant hills were sometimes glas. The seagull's cry was glas. Glas was a sign of the sad undying ones. It was the colour of…'

'Love?' said Yeats, 'I know. It is the colour of the feeling in my heart when I think of her.'

'It has the same effect upon all humans who share the true British – er – germ plasm (There was that tiny pause which Yeats later knew meant a consultation with the Others.) The remnant of the Old Peoples have learned, or been forced, to say "blue" or "green" nowadays. Some of them can still see the true glas but most cannot. Some feel a great joy, others a sharp sorrow, without being able to explain why. It is their sensory apparatus trying to represent something for which they no longer have a name.'

'But I can see it,' said Yeats.

'You have something unusual,' said the Fairy, 'only seen in a particular line of mortals every few generations. The True Sight of the Poet's Eye.'

'Very kind of you, I'm sure.' Being called perceptive aroused immediate suspicion in a writer like Yeats.

'I don't think you understand. I'm not congratulating you on having a feeling for character,' the Fairy said, along with thousands of English Literature students. 'The True Sight of the Poet's Eye allows you to see past surfaces.'

'So True Sight means I can see things as they really are?'

'No. It means that you see things as they really aren't.'

'How is that helpful?'

'Who said it was helpful?'

'Well then, how is it desirable?'

'I refer you to the answer I gave a short time ago.'

'So if True Sight is not helpful or desirable, what is the point?'

'Are you a poet?'

'Yes.'

'Well, then.'

Silence

'Well, I can still only glimpse it,' said Yeats eventually. 'Glas, I mean. I wish that I could see it properly for longer than a second.'

'Wishes,' said the Fairy, and looked away. After a moment, still looking away, it said, 'I'll make you a prophecy. If you ever see the colour glas like that, it will not be with your own eyes.'

'How can that be?' said Yeats. 'How can I see anything except with my own eyes?'

But the Fairy was gone.

Messages

Rested and heroically breakfasted at the generous hands of Mrs Old's friend, Josie Biggs, Horton was renewing his attack on superstition. The séance at the Golden Dawn had restored his old certainty that they were all wrong, even - or especially – W. B. Yeats. They were deluding themselves or they were being deceived. The smoky presence and intimately terrifying voice of the living room ritual had been nothing but his finely-poised creative intellect yielding to suggestion. Magic and spiritualism did not work, because they *should* not work. Nevertheless, one had to be sure.

In his view the best subject for an experiment in automatic writing was someone without the education or motive to make things up. Mrs Biggs, his overnight landlady, was ideal. She was far from stupid but her ignorance of the world seemed so complete that even the sensitive and mild Horton had given way to the temptation of exploring its extent, discovering over scrambled eggs and toast that conversation with Mrs Biggs tended towards the kind of infinite recursion familiar to cosmologists and politicians under pressure:

'Better news today, Mrs Biggs.'

'Oh? Why's that then?'

'Peace talks with the Boers.'

'Who're they then?'

'Dutch folk. Live in Southern Africa.'

'Where's that then?'

etc. etc., Horton surrendering before they got to First Cause and Prime Mover and 'Who's He then?'

By the time breakfast was over, Horton had decided that Mrs Biggs' fact-proof mental bunker was exactly what he needed. He was quite confident that insulation from any glimmer of an idea about what automatic writing was (What's that then?) or what it signified (What's it for then?) or indeed, probably, what automatic meant (What's that about then?) guaranteed failure and therefore success for his experiment. This time there would be no mistake. *Automatic writing, under properly rigorous conditions, would not work.*

Madame Lauderdale had obviously been putting on an act at last night's séance, especially with that unconvincing faint at the end. When

Horton suggested as much to her outright, she had only looked blank and pretended not to hear him. It made him feel almost sorry for them all, especially Yeats.

In Mrs Biggs' crowded front parlour, a kind of donkey sanctuary for tired flowery furniture, Horton sat his landlady down with several sheets of his foolscap note-paper in front of her and a pen in her plump little fist. Her legs did not quite reach the floor and she wriggled forward like a child getting comfy for a test in composition.

'Shall I write the date?' she said.

'No, Mrs Biggs, that won't be... yes, actually that's a very sensible idea,' said Horton, looking at her suspiciously. Had he misjudged her? However, seeing her carefully write the wrong date in large curly letters, with her tongue pinkly copying every flourish, he relaxed; she was perfect.

'Now then,' he said, 'Mrs Biggs, I want you to just empty your mind and...'

She was writing, had reached the end of the first line, three lines, five, her small fat hand moving rapidly in smooth rastering sweeps to and fro across the ruled sheet.

'Mrs Biggs,' whispered Horton, 'Mrs Biggs?'

'Yuss?' she said, looking up.

'Do you feel... that is, how *do* you feel Mrs Biggs?'

'Quite well, fanks.'

'Oh well, carry on then.'

Horton stared. For at no point in their brief exchange had Mrs Biggs' hand and pen stopped moving and producing those lines of writing - neat, well-formed and perfectly regular writing. 'Not possible,' Horton whispered to himself, 'just not possible.'

On and on she went, down and down the page, only lacking a little metallic 'ting' at the end of each line to complete the mechanical effect. She reached for another sheet, without looking, down went the pen and on she wrote. Finally, when Horton was near to pulling the last sheet from under her hand, Mrs Biggs stopped writing and laid the pen aside.

'Well, I'm sorry, Mr Horton,' she said.

'Why's that, Mrs Biggs?'

'Well, I've sat here for ages and not done any – eek!' She had looked down at the slew of written pages. 'Who did all that then?' she said, staring suspiciously at Horton.

'Er… you did?' said Horton, nervous of her reaction.

'I did?' said Mrs Biggs, clutching at her clunky necklace and reddening throat. He saw panic forming in the wide blue eyes.

'Well, it might have been, probably was... um… technically it was, yes must have been, a spirit control,' said Horton, quickly deciding that scepticism was not what his landlady needed at that moment. 'Mrs Biggs, are you… are you sure…? Yes, yes, of course you are,' he said. 'Yes, I think there is no doubt that it was…uh…a spirit control.'

'What's that then?'

'Um… a dead person, communicating through you?'

There was a pause.

'Oh, that's all right then. Can't bear a mystery, me.'

Horton rather liked them, but at a safe distance – in First Century Palestine, for example. At the moment, Mrs Biggs' thought-processes were the biggest mystery on his horizon, but there were others, ominously stacking up like thunderheads on a sultry summer's day.

'Oh, right, yes,' he said, 'thank you very much, Mrs Biggs'

Mrs Biggs sniffed. 'Wasn't nuffin, just a nice sit-down,' she said, kicking her short but unsettlingly well-shaped legs as she pushed herself upright. She went through into the kitchen and begun noisily to sing hymns and bash plates together.

Horton sat and looked at the pages of writing for some time, reluctant to touch them, because then the questions would start. At last he sighed, pulled the top sheet towards him, and began to read. He frowned at the writing, peered at it closely, threw it down, stood up, looked for a long time towards the sound of hobgoblins and foul fiends being defied to the accompaniment of sturdy white china clashing in the sud, stuffed the written sheet in his pocket, grabbed his hat and strode out of the room. This was too much for him. W. T. Horton needed advice.

So there was indeed a message waiting for Yeats when he climbed the stairs to his flat. It was a folded note, slipped behind the green baize-backed lattice of wire diamonds beside his door:

Come to 14 Bedford Place at once.

H.

If the nice thing about Tom Horton was his total lack of guile, one of the best things about Willie Yeats was an unthinking generosity with his time – he never had a great deal of money. It simply did not occur to Horton that his busy friend would not drop everything to respond to his unexplained summons; but the Irish mage seemed preoccupied when he arrived on Mrs Biggs' Portland stone doorstep, speaking to the beaming landlady with his habitual grave courtesy but with his mind clearly elsewhere. In the high-ceilinged front hall Horton glanced nervously at his powerful friend, trying to read his mood.

'It was good of you to come,' he said tentatively; those black brows could look so severe when pulled right down like that.

'It's no trouble,' said Yeats absently. 'Glad to see you, after... Can't stay though. A lot going on and – and - I'm needed in Dublin, d'ye see? And there're other things.' Yes, he was strangely wrapped up in himself, even by his own Olympian standards, hardly seeming aware of his friend, and Horton had an unusual opportunity to study the poet.

He saw a tall, dark-featured man, youthful but no longer young, his face taking on the firm lines which would stay there now until death. The broad hat, dark cloak and flowing tie said 'this man is a poet' to an extent which would have been ridiculous in someone else – someone who, for example, was not. Horton thought how much worse life would be without someone like Yeats to talk to, about Mrs Biggs and about everything else. Because another nice thing about Yeats was that you could tell him a goblin was stealing your shoes every night and he would take you completely seriously. This meant that you had to be very careful what you told him. It was also why so many people, men and women both, ended up loving him.

When Horton began to describe his experiment in automatic writing, Yeats at first seemed only politely interested but when he was shown the sheets of the landlady's writing, he leaned forward with an exclamation of surprise.

'When did she write this?' he said, looking at Horton, with great intensity.

'Just this morning,' said Horton, and Yeats looked up with wild surmise, biting his full lower lip until the blood nearly came.

'It doesn't make sense,' he said, half to himself, 'yet it must be from Them, it must!'

On every one of Mrs Biggs' carefully written pages, he saw this:

W B Y	*T C T*	*T A T*	*W B Y*
T T C	*T C C*	*T A C*	*T G C*
T T A	*T C A*	*T A A*	*T G A*
T T G	*T C G*	*T A G*	*T G G*
C T T	*C C T*	*C A T*	*C G T*
C T C	*C C C*	*C A C*	*C G C*
C T A	*C C A*	*C A A*	*C G A*
C T G	*W B Y*	*W B Y*	*C G G*
A T T	*W B Y*	*W B Y*	*A G T*
A T C	*A C C*	*A A C*	*A G C*
A T A	*A C A*	*A A A*	*A G A*
A T G	*A C G*	*A A G*	*A G G*
G T T	*G C T*	*G A T*	*G G T*
G T C	*G C C*	*G A C*	*G G C*
G T A	*G C A*	*G A A*	*G G A*
W B Y	*G C G*	*G A G*	*W B Y*

'I thought it was gibberish until I noticed your initials,' said Horton. 'Then I… I wondered if it might be a kind of code,'

'Now why would the spirit world bother with code?' murmured Yeats, absently dismissive, then loud in his memory Angenent's words at Kensington Palace came back to him: *Whatever had frightened the South American gods was linked to our heredity, the unknown agent in the germ plasm, the secret code which makes us what we are.*

His initials within the block of letter-groups made a quincunx: four elements conjuring a fifth at their centre, the element of elements, pattern of patterns, maker of makers. There was something there, he could almost see it, a principle, perhaps The Principle, but Horton was asking him something.

'Do you like crumpets?'

The three of them, Horton, Yeats and Mrs Biggs, nearly filled the flowery front parlour of the guest-house. Yeats, who had proposed an immediate return to the writing table with himself as scrutineer, kept rather behind Horton, who stood, leaning forward intently, behind Mrs Biggs, who sat, untroubled by the attention, stolidly contemplating a pile of blank foolscap paper, a pen, a pink pen-wipe, some pink blotting paper and an open bottle of ink, blue.

'We shall begin,' said Yeats, rather more loudly than was strictly necessary in the tiny over-furnished room, 'with an orientation question, to calibrate the – um – instrument. Are we…' but Mrs Biggs hand had moved to pen, pen to paper, and had already written and relaxed before the poet said, '...alone?'

Horton thrust his thin face further forward, pale, handsome but marked by years of mysticism and constipation. '*No*,' he read from the writing formed by his landlady's cheerfully ignorant pen, '*we are always with you*. It is a different hand this time,' he hissed over his shoulder to Yeats.

'Extraordinary,' murmured the poet, excitement breaking through his mask of calm. He pushed his pince-nez more firmly onto the bridge of his nose and clamped his heavy black brows onto the frame. 'Tell us, please,' he said, 'who you are?'

There was a pause, during which Mrs Biggs looked as if she were compiling a shopping-list in her head. Then her hand moved again, with life and purpose of its own, like a small pet being given a run on the table. Horton followed the developing words, some of them emphasized by double strokes of the nib, with a deepening frown:

I am *who you are is who* ***I am***
Who you are is who I am you are
Who is who ***I am*** *is who you are*
You are who you are is who is who
I am *who you are is who* ***I am***

He looked uncertainly back at Yeats, whose face was glowing with occult speculation. 'The Quincunx, again!' said the poet. He too was frowning fiercely, his pince-nez glasses bending under the pressure of thought. 'Who is it? What does it mean?'

'Wait, there's more coming,' said Horton, stooping over the moving pen once more. The words were coming hesitantly now, with a long pause after every line:

Prepare to meet thy doom.
Cheer up it might never happen.
That'll be one and four, please.
The end is nigh.
God save the Queen!

Horton looked up at Yeats, helpless, owl-eyed, but the poet-magician himself was puzzled. The silly words teetered on the threshold of relevance.

'There are of course,' he said hesitantly, 'all kinds of beings in the spirit world.' Then he drew himself up and grasped his own lapels as if they were the rip-cords of a life-saving egotism.

'I am William Yeats, Second Order Adeptus of the Most Secret Ruby and Gold. I know the ancient colour of the star Sirius. I know who was not there to see no one in the Tomb. I know the secret name of the Earth. If you have a message for me, I command that it be delivered.'

Mrs Biggs immediately rose from her chair. This was more surprising than it sounds, because she lifted off vertically without visible effort and hung gently in mid-air, bobbing very slightly up and down in some unseen etheric ground-swell. Horton looked panic at Yeats, seeking guidance, but the great magician was almost equally thrown – this was the kind of thing you only heard about. You defended it passionately from the unbelief of cynics like Bernard Shaw, but when it actually happened, there was the feeling of deep, deep wrongness, either with the universe, or you. He noted with dispassionate interest that his mind and memory would not cooperate with his eyes and ears. He experienced the strange sensation of his brain deciding to forget the strange sight of a levitating woman even while it was still happening. Was this why so many accounts of the marvellous were confused, self-contradictory and unconvincing?

Yeats mastered his wandering mind, stared resolutely up at Mrs Biggs, and addressed her in the resounding tones he would have used on hecklers in the Abbey Theatre:

'I command you, if you have a message for me, speak!'

From behind them there came a low, amused female voice: 'All right, you don't have to shout.'

Yeats and Horton both jumped, Mrs Biggs, retaining her glassy-eyed expression of general benevolence, just rotated slowly on her own axis like a piece of mid-Atlantic jetsam subject to the Coriolis effect, but one way or another they all turned to face the unknown presence: silhouetted against the parlour window, the outline of her extravagant costume in strange sympathy with the flounces and furbelows of the curtaining, stood the Fairy Queen.

Horton collapsed into an armchair with a squeak, suffering from supernatural overload. Yeats stood his ground. He squinted against the window light, trying to see a face under the knife-sharp knots and re-entrants of the filigree tiara. He opened his mouth to conjure, but the Queen forestalled him:

'I haven't got long,' she said, 'He's trying to keep me out. Listen

Yeats – no, wait…' and Mrs Biggs fell, dead-weight, into Horton's lap, like a very ripe planet, and stayed there. They were both fast asleep and the Queen had become more than a silhouette. Her costume was richly embroidered, there were sparkling gems in her frizzed auburn hair and her face was a pale oval.

'Sorry, can't sustain it for more than one,' said the Queen, glancing at the unconscious pair. 'Anyway, the message is for you, Yeats, just you. *Something very bad is going to happen and it must be stopped.* We fairies cannot do it by ourselves. We can only act upon the physical world if a human is involved, a human who believes in us. The more belief, the more power we have.'

'A rational choice of the irrational,' Yeats murmured, on the move; he was changing the angle his line of sight made with the window, trying to get a better view of the Queen. As soon as he moved, she turned with him like a compass needle swinging to follow a magnet. 'At their back is hollow ugliness, like a rotten tree,' he whispered to himself.

'That is an old slander,' said the Queen, 'and it's not why you can only see me from the front. Fact is, you're not seeing me at all. I'm doing the seeing for you, and three dimensional detail is hard work, let me tell you.'

'There is something wrong about this,' said Yeats to himself. Why did the Queen of the Fairies look so much like an inferior portrait of Queen Elizabeth I? Why did she sound like Mrs Biggs? He reached out blindly and took hold of the first object he found, which happened to be a ceramic quince topping a heaped bowl of imitation fruit.

'Don't!' cried the Queen. 'You need to know…'

Yeats lobbed the quince, underarm, at the Fairy Queen. There was a crack, a screech and something went by and through him at speed, making him close his eyes and gasp as if he had been hit by a blast of frosty air. When he opened his eyes, he had broken a vase, of the Queen there was no trace and Horton was waking up with a fully-aroused Mrs Biggs on his knee.

With the Colonel's warning – and resources - in mind, Yeats pressed Horton to stay at Mrs Biggs' guest house for as long as he liked. Knowing that the mystic's nerves would trouble him after what had happened, he also suggested that Horton should sit up with Mrs Biggs in case there were any more phenomena, and to look after the dear lady, of course. Both his sensitive friend and the landlady seemed to like the idea and Yeats left behind him a happy commotion of sandwiches, eiderdowns and writing equipment as Mrs Biggs' front parlour was turned into an all-night observation room. Yeats was relieved. He needed the refuge of his own home, and solitude. He needed some time to think about fairies and the fact that everyone who had much to do with them seemed to end up insane.

*

'When - did you find out that - we were blundering around - in Queen Victoria's back garden - for God's sake?'

Even through his violent gasps for breath, Thomas Hardy sounded more aggrieved, Doyle thought, than any chap ought to sound having been rescued by another chap from severe embarrassment.

'Calm down,' he said, 'and breathe.'

They were safely locked and bolted behind the door of Hardy's Hammersmith Road apartment. It was a little place he kept, Hardy said, 'just in case'. He did not explain in case of what, but Doyle rather thought he knew. Poor man. Must be desperate. Women didn't like that. Doyle had a brotherly impulse to put Hardy right, but restrained it. He had bigger responsibilities; Hardy would have to manage. He was better off than Doyle if he could afford to keep a bijou flat going in West London.

The accommodation was small, just a bed-sitting room really, with only the bathroom separate, and was made to feel even smaller by a large double bed with gorgeous red silk counterpane that took up a great deal of the living space and irresistibly suggested the phrase whore's boudoir. Hardy was lying flat on his back on it now, wheezing. He had tried to sprint all the way there, nearly the entire length of the Hammersmith Road, but Doyle had hailed a cab and paid the driver to run Hardy down like a New Forest pony at branding time.

'Whad'ya mean, calm down?' Hardy panted, propping himself up on one elbow and pouring himself an eye-watering amount of gin from a shelf above the room's one table. It was within arm's reach; everything was within arm's reach.

'I was on the point of knocking at the door of Kensington Palace and asking my sovereign if I could make love to her damned secretary, or whatever else this wretched young woman turns out to be. Never, never again will I wonder what would have happened if I had done something about a pretty girl smiling at me. Now, I know!'

He took a swig of gin.

'And another thing – jumping out like that in the dark, you were in line for a Dorset Hello.'

Doyle sized up the little novelist's weight and strength and put on his most earnestly serious face:

'Well I was lucky indeed,' he said, 'whatever a Dorset Hello might be, to have been spared it.'

Hardy looked intently up at Doyle; his shrewd eyes, level and clear above the rim of the glass, were oddly in contrast with his panicky behaviour.

'Hmm,' he said. 'Well, we'll say no more about it.'

Suddenly he leaped off the bed, startling Doyle, and from a shallow cupboard by the door took out a violin and a bow; the violin was battle-scarred and the bow had half the horse-hairs broken and flying loose, but Hardy tore through a country dance tune with terrific energy and speed.

'I didn't realize you needed upper-body strength to play the violin,' shouted Doyle, bobbing and weaving like a boxer to avoid the jabbing bow-end.

'Fiddle,' shouted Hardy, reaching the final triumphant bar. He tossed the violin and bow aside.

'I'm sorry?' said Doyle.

'Not violin,' said Hardy, breathing heavily again but with his composure back, 'it's the fiddle, down our way. Violin's what the posh folk play. So, what were *you* doing in Queen Victoria's back garden at midnight?'

'I told you. I have reason to believe that the girl you are – interested in – is in some sort of trouble, with some pretty unpleasant people.'

'Why not tell the police?'

'My relations with the police are messed up by Sherlock-bloody-Holmes, like everything else. Besides …'

Doyle's eyes met Hardy's and an understanding crossed the gap.

'What was all that about in the garden?' said Doyle, bridging a pause more revealing than he liked. 'Faithful to the one good man, and so on. Am I right to take the letter seriously?'

'Yes,' said Hardy, putting his glass down, the gin hardly touched. 'I see a young man, artistic and sensitive though a bit simple, in love with a girl of his own type but doomed to watch helplessly as she gives herself to a laughing lordling, no, make that a cynical aristocrat with connections so high that he may snap his fingers at common morality and natural justice. She is snatched out of reach of her true love, like a butterfly whirled up from its native heath by a capricious breeze. The disprized swain, helpless, with no crime to report save that against the human heart, resorts to the only action his romantic literary tastes suggest.'

'Writing for help to a non-existent dead detective,' said Doyle heavily. 'I suppose you did say he was a simpleton.'

'True love is the simplest thing,' said Hardy, 'it's marriage that's so fucking complicated, pardon my French. No, her lover waits disconsolate in their home town, pursuing some grim but necessary trade – chiselling tombstones perhaps – waiting for her light step in the lane and the click of the garden gate, every day a fresh Calvary.'

'Bit strong,' said Doyle, looking at the ceiling with his eyes closed, 'and fresh is wrong anyway.'

'Strike out the Calvary reference,' said Hardy at once. 'His hopes rising and setting with the great orb that shone dispassionately on all players in this ancient drama, hopes as illusory as the solar movement which inspired them.'

'Hm,' said Doyle. 'Better. Not sure about inspired. So what do we do?'

'Oh, it's we now, is it? No, wait, I have it. It is she, trapped in some squalid urban seraglio to wait upon the whims of her debauched master, it is she who writes the letter!'

'Hang on,' said Doyle. 'You mean the letter came from the girl herself?'

'Yes. It is a cry for help from a young woman who is not only handsome but astute as well.'

'Why go to all that trouble?' said Doyle, a puzzled frown crinkling his big honest brow. 'Why not just ask me straight out?'

'Ah, that's just it!' crowed Hardy, waving his arms and pacing quickly back and forth, as far as he could in the five square feet of free floor space. 'Had she written to you in her own person saying "I am a highly attractive young woman in danger of being seduced into goodness knows what by a criminal mastermind working with a bunch of conjurors and you're the only man in London who can save me", would you have believed it for one second?'

Doyle opened his mouth to give the only truthful answer, which was 'Yes, like a shot', but Hardy was ploughing on.

'No, of course not,' he said, not noticing Doyle's expression. 'You were drawn to Blythe Road by the very woman you sought to protect.'

'All right. All right, I was drawn there.' (And so were you, my friend, if it comes to that, thought Doyle, and by the same girl.)

'But there's still the puzzle of why she did not give you her address.'

'Wouldn't I have feared embarrassment, suspected a trap?' said Doyle. 'I am a public figure, you know.'

'Hmm, maybe,' said Hardy, 'no - I have it – she was ashamed at her condition. Kept for his pleasure in some overcrowded tenement by her bored seducer…'

'Under the watchful eye of an evil conniving old crone,' put in Doyle.

'Yes, that's good, conniving old crone is good,' said Hardy excitedly. 'Her seducer, having cast aside all pretence of respect, visits her twice a week to rake the last glowing embers from her grate.'

'Yes, yes, I get the picture,' said Doyle, eyeing the door nervously.

'So,' said Hardy, more quietly, 'if we knew where your letter came from, we would find Fanny, confound the magicians and restore her to her despairing swain!'

Doyle and Hardy looked at each other, thirty nine and fifty nine, two dangerous ages. Their eyes shone. Writing had been like this, once, while you still owned your characters. Then the public started pushing you around. You gained a readership. They said they loved you, then they started telling you what to write – and what not to. You couldn't do what you liked, and doing what you liked was the whole point of being a writer.

Conan Doyle tapped a finger on his front teeth reflectively for a moment then said, 'Look here, Hardy, I'm staying in town tonight, 'cos I'm giving a talk tomorrow, the Royal Opera, 7.30, which I think will interest you. Afterwards you can come back with me to Hindhead so that we can concentrate properly on this Fanny business.'

Hardy studied Doyle with disconcertingly bright eyes which always seemed just on the point of crinkling in a smile, but never did.

'Assuredly,' he said, '7.30, Royal Opera.'

'Well, that's decided then,' said Doyle. 'We both want to get to the bottom of this girl, so we may as well work together.'

Hardy grinned at this more than Doyle thought the remark deserved, but he was not displeased: the way Dorset's notorious pessimist had cheered up over the Fanny mystery made you want to keep it going. However, there was something about the sharp-eyed novelist's sudden arrival in his life at this particular moment that he did not quite trust; he was beginning to feel that he had told him too much. Better, then, to keep Hardy where he could see him. All things considered, Arthur Conan Doyle left for his home in Hindhead feeling that he had been rather clever.

*

Number 18 was on the left of Woburn Buildings, going towards King's Cross. The cab dropped Yeats off at the front steps, right beside the blind match-seller who spent most days standing there like a monument to perseverance, under one of the tall plane trees which in summer rustled their leaves against the windows of Yeats' bedroom. The old man sold matches and shoe laces from a wooden tray which looked too heavy, considering old men, and blindness. Yeats had never seen anyone buy anything from the tray. Mind you, he had never bought anything himself, not from any failure of charity but because the old man did not seem the slightest bit interested in selling either matches or laces. Yeats wondered what he was doing there at that time of night. Perhaps he was unaware that darkness had fallen. The poet tactfully decided not to mention it.

'Good evening to you,' he said.

'Mldrpyip,' said the blind match-seller politely, inclining his grizzled head nearly but not quite in the poet's direction. His thick blue spectacles did not completely conceal his eyes, which looked enormous and not at all blind.

To the right of Number 18's front door, near the bell-pull, was a small brass plate, engraved with a name which might have been 'Yeats', but wasn't. The first letter of the name looked odd. This was because the brass plate had originally arrived from the engravers inscribed 'Teats', a result of the poet's careless handwriting. The mistake went unnoticed for several weeks, and unreported by delighted tradesmen and kindly friends for several weeks more. Correction was cheaper than replacement and so, while the word on the plate no longer unequivocally suggested bursting udders at milking time, it did not entirely fail to do so either. Yeats paused as always, looked at the plate, pursed his lips and muttered, 'It doesn't matter.'

Inside, the front hall was very dark. The landlord's wife, Mrs Old, who looked after the poet's household needs, must have forgotten to light the single lamp at the turn of the stairs. For some reason the Colonel's words came back to him as he fumbled for a match on the shallow high shelf where a box was normally kept: 'They will try to contact you.' The word *they* could be troubling in the dark, Yeats found. A match, he needed a match. With trembling hands he wrenched the front door open again.

'Thought you might want this, Mr Yeats,' said the blind match-seller, rattling a match-box. He was standing right on the step, as if he had been waiting for the door to open. 'No charge,' he said. 'Finding the right match for Mr Yeats is what it's all about, d'ye see? D'ye see?' And the match-seller pushed the box into Yeats' hand then turned and shuffled away, laughing, into the night. His stick could be heard tapping against the kerb for a few seconds and then the sound abruptly stopped.

'Have you a fairy message for me?' Yeats shouted into the dark. Above him, in the next house, a sash window shot up with a rattle and two seconds later closed with a bang. Yeats sat down on the doorstep and rested his chin on his hands, hoping that what had been shouted at him from the window was not a message from the Fairies. He got to his feet again. The stone step was very cold and, introspection while standing up being more difficult, Yeats went back inside the shadowy hallway, lit the gas, and started to climb the creaking stairs which led, with one turn, up to his first floor living quarters. Halfway up, he staggered, off balance. For a moment he had been in two places at once. Through the gloomy stairwell he had momentarily seen the twin snakes of his vision, twining around a common centre, gyring like a hawk, dizzying against a blinding sky. He grabbed the banister rail and the world righted itself. He checked back – the hash-pills at Henley's place? The absinthe? The Peruvian vine? He should have recycled everything by now. Maybe getting a concentrated dose of life was the problem.

The lit gas revealed two pale rectangles, a letter and a card, slipped under the wire lattice of the green baize letter board outside his door. Again the Colonel's words 'They will contact you' resounded absurdly in his mind. He put the card in his pocket and looked at the envelope. Even in the dim yellow gas light of the stairwell there was no mistaking the large erratic hand and purple ink. It was from the love of his life, Maud Gonne. He felt strangely reluctant to take the letter into his flat unopened and so read it standing up in the doorway.

'Willie,' he read, 'the important F work I do here means you are not missed in the body. My dreaming self has known you, however. You came to me last night and we kissed. There was a star between our lips and you stood back from me and said, "Tavistock in the 3.30" '

Yeats held the letter at arm's length, frowning, his black eyebrows meeting in a cross vee. Then his red lips twitched, his face screwed up and he roared with laughter until Mr Old shot out in the lobby and craned his grey head around the stair-bend to see what the matter was. 'Nothing,' Yeats called down cheerfully, 'nothing at all.' The image of Stephanie's bright eyes and wide smile crackled through his brain like the forest-fire which clears the dead wood and brings new life, and just for a moment everything was *glas*.

The first thing he did when he entered his apartment was to lift the frosted glass globe on the bracket beside the door and put a match to the gas. The second thing was to have a cautious look behind the big black bookcase which screened the entrance to the kitchen. No goblins, no boggarts, no fairies. Thank God. He had had enough for one day. Now then, what he needed was a nice cup of tea. He lit the kindling laid ready in the tiny kitchen grate, added some small pieces of coal, and after the usual faceful of smoke, expertly created enough flame to get his tiny copper kettle singing. He put the tea leaves into a muslin strainer and poured the boiling water through and straight into his favourite cup, which had Views of Sligo hand-painted all the way round. He carried the rattling cup and saucer through to drink his tea in comfort at the table which Mrs Old had laid for his evening meal.

Yeats was in the act of raising the tea cup to his lips when his eyes crossed and he put the cup down so hard it cracked the saucer and shot a gout of Darjeeling Breakfast onto his shirt front. From the cup came a sound, half bubble, half buzz, as if a very large wasp were drowning there. It stopped. He stood up and poked at the cup handle with his spoon. The buzzing returned, grew louder, and a tiny pair of hands gripped the cup's rim. A fairy, his Fairy, hauled itself up and over the gold-banded lip and fell, soaked wings hanging limp down his back, slap into the brimming saucer, where it began to thrash and fizz again. The poet watched for a moment, then got the bowl of his tea-spoon under the three and a half inch-long body and scooped the Fairy out of the saucer and onto the table, where it lay quite still at the centre of an expanding brown stain. He wondered what to do, and reflected on the ironies of scale. His human-sized fingers could not loosen the Fairy's collar or follow the Humane Society's advice for resuscitating the apparently drowned without the risk of crushing the thimble-sized rib cage. Still, you had to try.

Before Yeats' giant finger-tips could touch its soaking clothes, the Fairy suddenly came to life and sat up with a loud 'Hands off!' It staggered to its feet, shook itself, wrung tea out of its jerkin and irritably extended its wings. They vibrated, whirring, and as they dried, shimmered. The Fairy cleared its throat and spat, creating a tiny extra stain on the snowy linen cloth.

'That was a fine trick to play on Her Majesty,' said the Fairy, wagging a finger the length of a melon seed up at Yeats' chin. It had dried itself out and was leaning in a relaxed pose against the gilt porcelain stem of Yeats' tea-cup handle.

'Well, no matter now,' it said. 'We think you need a bit more time to acclimatize. We were rushing you somewhat. So, you'll get me for a while. I expect you'll be wanting...'

'Three wishes?' said Yeats, frowning down at the Fairy with a derisory curl of his lip. 'You always said they would be bad for me.'

'Answers to some questions, I was going to say. You're an intellectual. You can see the corrosive effect of unbounded potential on a finite mind. So, you want answers, not wishes!'

'Very well,' said the poet. The Yeats forehead creased and the two black slashes of his brows came together. The Fairy planted its feet aggressively a full three quarters of an inch apart and folded its arms and lowered its head as if bracing for a hurricane.

'Why appear in my tea cup?' asked Yeats, in the manner of sending one over to get the range.

'Not my choice,' said the Fairy promptly. 'I was waiting for you behind that book-case, but you were too clever for your own god, I mean good. Or do I? Anyhow, I had to turn up somewhere you weren't expecting. It's a kind of ancient tradition, sort of, class of thing.'

'Perverse narrative logic,' said Yeats. 'An ancient fairy tradition. Hmm. Very well, here's another question. Exactly how ancient are the Fairy Folk?'

'Exactly fifty-two thousand, four hundred and thirty-two years, six months, twenty-two days and seven minutes,' replied the Fairy instantly.

'You're very precise.'

'I only had to read it off from your... from the length of your...' The fairy had lost its poise. It seemed embarrassed.

'From my what?' said Yeats, feeling molested. Then inspiration came from where the perfect last lines lived, somewhere at the back of his head: 'Is this to do with the age of the human race?'

The fairy, which had been avoiding his eyes, looked up, put its hands on its hips and roared with laughter. Yeats stared. The Fairy pushed its bag-hat back, blew out its cheeks and gazed up at him in affectionate twinkly-eyed admiration. Yeats went on staring, unimpressed, so the Fairy deflated and just said, 'Yes. It is to do with that. And you, Sir Yeats, are not the slowest in the race.'

'Is there magic?' said Yeats.

'You're seriously asking a three and a half inch tall humanoid that materialized in your teacup whether there's magic?'

Yeats just nodded calmly, but his mouth was dry.

'Define magic,' said the Fairy, sitting down cross-legged like Guru Chaterjee. Yeats sat down too.

'Magic is human will enacted or projected through knowledge of nature,' Yeats said.

'Steam engine,' said the Fairy.

'Human will enacted through knowledge of immaterial or super-refined nature.'

'Hmm,' said the Fairy. 'Shame you don't know about radio.'

'What?'

'Never mind. Hypnotism. Electricity. Magnetism.'

Yeats drew a deep breath and let it out loudly. 'Human will enacted through the magician's raising himself by mental training into sympathetic resonance with higher beings.'

'Better,' said the Fairy, 'but then where do you put me?'

Yeats flicked the dregs of his tea out of the cup, up-ended it and brought it smartly down over the tiny cross-legged figure. 'There!' he said. After a few seconds he raised the rim slightly and peeked underneath. Nothing. He let it down and the upside-down cup immediately began to move jerkily across the table-cloth. Yeats lifted the cup away and recoiled when he saw an enormous black beetle waving saw-toothed pincers at him. He instinctively brought the cup back down but his hand went on moving through the table, which first became translucent and then was not there at all. Air was rushing past his ears, both of which hurt. Yeats looked down, simply because there was so much of it - down, that is. Everywhere is down when you are hundreds of feet above the ground. Emerald green fields and hillsides were flowing past beneath him. He was flying. As soon as he realized this, he also became aware that for some moments past his arms had been flapping like wings. He had been turned into a bird! He looked to his left and right, expecting to see eagle feathers, a hawk's brindled pinions perhaps - something pretty noble anyway. Instead he saw only a pair of long arms with knobbly elbows and not much muscle. He screamed: he had been turned into a Yeats!

One of his ears suddenly hurt a lot more than the other. The Fairy was standing between the poet's shoulder blades, holding strings attached to his pierced ear-lobes. It was jerking the right-hand string and making the sort of encouraging noises which grooms and jockeys use. A convulsion of rage shot through Yeats.

'I am not bloody putting up with this!' he shouted. He twisted in mid-air to get at his tormentor, and fell off his chair. He stood up, wary and shaking. He was still in his front room. The cup on the tea-spattered cloth was still spinning slowly on its side where he had dropped it. The clock completed its tick. His pulse and breathing returned to something like normal; but the Fairy was staring at him with round eyes and a half-smile. It looked surprised but pleased.

'All right,' Yeats said, 'perhaps I was wrong.'

'I didn't say you were wrong,' said the Fairy, not looking at the poet, 'but there's one tiny flaw in your thinking.'

'Oh?' said Yeats, his heart sinking. 'And what's that?' He was beginning to understand why peasants were frightened of fairies.

'This "will" you mentioned,' said the Fairy, ostentatiously gouging invisible grime out of its tiny finger nails, 'that's definitely important, no doubt about it. The will of the higher being creates a sympathetic resonance with the mind of the magician.'

'No, no, you mean the opposite,' said Yeats.

The Fairy probed a cuticle that would have tested a microscope.

'A tiny flaw,' it said, suddenly looking up with hard bright eyes.

A cold wind blowing from somewhere north of reason made Yeats' heart contract and he remembered the frosty breath in Mrs Biggs' parlour. It was not an attack on the senses. You could not stand your ground when the ground you stood on was taken away. If it was not the magician's will... if it was the will of the higher being… he felt dizzy with realized fear. It was not like recoiling from the beetle. It felt more like Arabella Flatley putting him straight about his chances of kissing her. This made him think of Stephanie and his nerve came back. With it came the memory of what the Colonel had said about Fairy abduction of mortals. Improving the stock – but on which side? Who was in charge? He put the question to one side: plenty of time to be terrified later.

'There's something that always bothered me,' he said to the Fairy, his voice very nearly steady. 'Long ago, when we were talking in my father's garden, just before you went away, I suddenly realized that you spoke like the stable boy at Merville who made me fight him and then told me stories of Irish heroes. And at the same moment I knew where you came from, d'ye see?' said Yeats, bending down to the Fairy's eye-level.

'Oh yeah?' said the Fairy belligerently, but with a look of uncertainty.

'Yes,' said Yeats. 'I recognized you from Richard Doyle's picture book 'In Fairyland', which my uncle George gave to me. You were the Fairy who follows just after the King in the great procession on page 16. I looked at that picture for weeks afterwards, until I had forgotten why. I even looked at it through a magnifying glass but all I found out was what paper was made of.'

The Fairy got to its feet, held up its forefinger, opened its mouth, shut it again and lowered the finger. 'Where does anything come from, have you thought about that?' it muttered.

'It's all in the mind then,' said Yeats.

'No,' said the Fairy, walking across empty air and climbing

companionably onto the poet's arm, sitting across Yeats' wrist, propped up on its arms and with its long legs extended relaxedly.

'Not the mind. The mind's in the mind. Anything you experience, including the illusion you have a mind, and that there's a you to do the having, comes from us.'

'And where do you come from?'

The Fairy's lips moved up at the corners with an inward little smile and something briefly tugged at Yeats' heart and was gone before he could analyse it.

'How far?' Yeats insisted, carefully lifting his forearm, and thus the Fairy, closer to his face. 'Is it another plane of being? Utterly different from the human?'

The Fairy did not reply. Its eyebrows were raised in two dark arches, its eyes closed, its pink lips pursed in thought, and Yeats realized something odd: since the days when he had recognized the Fairy as one of Richard Doyle's creations, its appearance had changed. It was still teasingly familiar, but in quite a different way: it no longer embodied a mid-Victorian illustrator's idea of comic mischief; it was taller, leaner, even gawky, with a different face under the shapeless hat, paler, longer, more intense. You couldn't say it was strange; perhaps it was normal for fairies to change the way they looked if you changed the way *you* looked.

Unaware or careless of Yeats' scrutiny, the Fairy continued to sit very still with its eyes wide open, expressionless; its lips might have been very slightly moving but it was hard to tell. Yeats thought he could hear a very faint sound, like a tiny choir humming a tune backwards, coming from the empty air around it. After a few seconds of this the Fairy opened its eyes and focused them on Yeats. 'The answer to your question of how far we are from you,' it said, with a small satisfied nod to itself, 'is a variable locus in a one-dimensional array one hundred and twenty-five thousand million miles in length. It was not an easy calculation, let me tell you. There was a dispute over the result.'

'What do you mean?'

'Some of us - er - fairies thought you being dead was a better result if you were going to demand calculations like that, but most of us were more forgiving and just did the iterative adding-up.'

'I don't understand the answer anyway,' said Yeats.

The Fairy seemed to lose patience. 'We come from far away, but also no distance at all,' it said, 'can you solve that?' Before Yeats could say anything, his Fairy snapped its fingers and vanished with a cracker-snap and smell of spent matches.

The clock on the mantelpiece chimed six times. Yeats came to himself with a start.

What a vivid dream! Then it occurred to him that if he had dreamed the Fairy then he might have dreamed Stephanie too - and he very much did not want her to be a dream. He dug frantically into his pocket for the card she had given him at the Golden Dawn and his fingers closed on the cardboard rectangle as if it would save his life. He took it out to read again and smile foolishly over the message, imagining Stephanie's slender fingers writing it.

'Yeats,' he read, 'you fake Irish bladder of pernishus wind, come with me to the Royal Opra tonite if you arnt a cowerd.'

Magic! Evil magic: a memento of a delightful meeting with a lovely woman transformed into a blackmailing invitation to a dreadful evening with George Bernard Shaw. The note was unsigned, but the spelling was clearly Shaw's, part of his characteristically arrogant one-man campaign to reform English orthography. The gesture was wasted on Yeats, who could not spell anyway. He tossed the card aside, groped desperately within his deep pocket, found another card and was filled with relief to see 'Tonight at nine, the Cheshire Cheese' in Stephanie's bold handwriting, each loop exuberantly racing out from the line then hurrying back to form the next letter. He smiled, remembering the sparkling life and upward tilt of those dark eyes. Then he realized that if Stephanie existed then so must the fairy who seemed inextricably bound up with their meeting. He felt tired; he needed time to think.

Someone was thumping at the street door below. Soon afterwards, Mrs Old's voice floated up the stairwell. Yeats could not hear the words, but whatever she had said was quickly out of date, as Yeats' own door was violently thrown open (he rarely locked it) and even as he reached for the poker, believing that They had arrived, Bernard Shaw's beady eyes and offensive beard were upon him.

'Well? Are you coming?' brayed Shaw. 'You're not going to let a little, ha-ha, frac-arse like last night keep you in? We owe it to ourselves to get out there again. Ah, you needn't feel bad. There's no disgrace in running away.'

When Yeats hesitated, Shaw preened himself, stroking wrongways through his coarse red beard with the palm of his hand, releasing a cloud of dried vegetable matter, and repeated, with meaningful emphasis, that it was only sensible to run away from danger - 'And I've the bruised knuckles and lump on the head to prove it, me boy.'

So of course Yeats had to go.

Upstairs in his small bedroom, with Shaw waiting below and charming Mrs Old so that, Yeats knew, she would be hard to please for weeks, Yeats dressed gloomily for the theatre. He just hoped Shaw had invited someone else who would share the load.

Soon his tall figure, made more imposing by an enormous wide-brimmed hat and the cloak flapping in his slipstream, was to be seen proceeding towards the West End, accompanied by, if not exactly in company with, George Bernard Shaw, critic, playwright and bounder.

Four hundred and fifty four, four hundred and fifty… five.

Murders

Yeats liked the Royal Opera's hesitantly grand architecture but was not enjoying the show. Doyle's laboured and sentimental performance did nothing for him at all, except to awaken patriotic nostalgia for the political discourse of Dublin – the personal insults, foaming rage, verbal diarrhoea and podium humping which kept a man interested.

Even had Doyle's well-meant propaganda been able to hold his attention, there was a constant distraction from Yeats' left. It was obvious that Bernard Shaw disliked the speaker – not so much his views, or even his style, just Doyle – and he heckled continuously and inventively until an embarrassed old usher warned the gentleman that a policeman would be fetched as there were ladies present. After that, Shaw apparently regarded honour as satisfied, and restricted himself, for Yeats' sole benefit, to a constant flow of 'Cor', 'I say', 'Phwoar' and 'Look at that one in the balcony'.

Yeats ignored all this, until his annoying red-bearded companion started making signals to someone in the boxes above.

'Shaw,' he whispered behind his hand, 'they're all man-hating blue-stockings, these political women. Believe me. You'd be wasting your time.'

Shaw leered at him knowingly. 'You know, Willie me boy,' he said, 'I detect the true note of sincerity in that remark but, you see, it depends how you ask.'

Forestalling any response (which, Yeats felt, might well include a punch in the face) Bernard Shaw stood up and edged his way out along the row, leaving a wake of crushed toes and elbowed heads behind him. He could be seen heading purposefully for the balcony stairs, and Yeats settled gratefully back in his seat. His relief was short-lived. After five minutes Shaw side-stepped his way back along the still-simmering row and sat down carefully, without a word and with his yellow-trousered legs carefully apart. He was, unfortunately, soon back on form, muttering stories, too close to Yeats' ear, about what he had once got up to with a chorus-girl or guesswork concerning the stamina of the little minx in the ticket-booth.

Something was not quite right though, Yeats thought. Not quite right, that is, in a way different from the usual not-quite-rightness that followed George Bernard Shaw around like the smell of damp Irish tweed. The feeling of being more alive, the magical strangeness of everything in the last two days, had sharpened the poet's already acute senses. Yeats thought again about the attack two nights ago, and the Colonel's warning about taking unnecessary risks. It wasn't a risk, surely, to attend a public lecture? In that case, why, in this English temple to mediocrity, with Arthur Conan Doyle expounding imperial daydreams in his safe avuncular style, did he feel that strange thrill, half excitement, half fear, which had never left him since meeting Stephanie Toughguid? Thoughts of Stephanie kept the Yeats mind happily elsewhere for a few minutes, until something else started nagging at him: the Fairy's riddling reference to its origin 'far away and no distance at all.' Maybe it was about Space and Time, the kind of thing Trenchard and his Royal Society friends talked about.

In fact Yeats spent much of his time with such paradoxes in his magical studies. To someone who would respond to the proposition that *the ineffable inexpressible emerges as a perfect zero that is at the same time a duality of equal opposites the tension between which creates a spiritual realm that only touches our universe at its lowest point* with 'Of course', the Fairy's riddle was not by any means at the top of the difficulty scale. What is no distance from us? We are. What contains the infinite? We do.

Yeats turned ideas over in his mind, while Doyle, up on the stage behind his lectern, patiently explained the necessity for a trans-Atlantic alliance much as a nutritionist might take a sceptical audience through the value of roughage in the diet.

'They are part of us!' Yeats suddenly said, very loudly. He came out of his reverie to find himself standing up, everyone in the audience looking at him, Doyle paused in mid-sentence and Shaw pulling him down by his coat.

'Part of us indeed!' said Doyle, peering over his lowered glasses to see who had called out. 'Thank you, my lanky friend. It is my thesis in a nut-shell. The so-called Americans are actually our fellow Britons, divided from us only by a quantity of salt water.'

When Doyle entered the second hour of his talk like a man just getting into his stride, the chairman stood up - so quickly that his chair went over backwards - and declared very loudly that time had vanquished them. Doyle grumpily shuffled his notes together, pointedly ignoring the chairman's conventional speech of thanks, and strode off into the wings. As the second round of thin applause petered out, Yeats stood up, more than ready to follow the subdued audience already hurrying out of the Royal Opera House. He guessed, correctly, that many had come to see, if not Sherlock Holmes, then the famous detective's Dr Watson: they wanted tobacco-filled Persian slippers and crimes solved in time for the Christmas pudding, not a middle-aged medic with a bee in his bonnet about Our American Cousins and Hands Across The Sea.

'Oh, there's no hurry, is there?' said Shaw, staying put in his seat. Yeats sat back down, unable to get out without climbing over Shaw's gimpy legs in their loud yellow check trousers, which the red-bearded socialist was resting on the back of the seat in front. 'May as well let the rush die down,' said Shaw. Yeats looked over his shoulder. They were bunching in the aisles, but...

'It's hardly a rush,' he said. The suspicion that his cynical compatriot was up to something had come back more strongly; and when Shaw asked, with an offensively artificial flash of his teeth, how the Irish National Theatre was shaping up, the suspicion turned into certainty. They sat there as the auditorium emptied and Yeats, never less than a gentleman, dutifully talked about the Abbey Theatre project in Dublin until Shaw yawned, stretched, looked at the large fob watch which he drew from his waistcoat pocket, said it was time to go - and dropped the watch.

'I thought we were waiting for the audience to disperse,' said Yeats.

'Well, now, Willie me boy,' said Shaw into the dusty red carpet, groping for the fob-watch under the seat in front. 'I've got a little commission going on backstage, here, you know?' He surfaced, clutching his watch, which he made a performance of examining, avoiding Yeats' eye.

'Meester Shaw?' A young woman approached them, with a vivid scarlet mouth and eye-lashes so black with mascara that she resembled a startled bush-baby. 'Meester Shaw, ze critic?'

'That's me!' cried Shaw, springing literally into action with three joyous bounds over the seats in front. 'Toodle-oo, Yeats,' he said over his shoulder, 'can't keep the French ballet waiting.'

Yeats smiled and watched Shaw and the girl go up the steps to the backstage door, the great critic's hand already straying towards his companion's waist. So that was all! He should have known. Yeats breathed in deeply, stretched his tall frame and loped up the carpeted aisle to the lobby. He was delayed there by an earnest woman with a book under her arm, who wanted to wish him luck with his Irish enterprise. 'America, our friend across the sea,' she said, in an accent which he placed as Dublin within a mile of the Castle. 'Mr Doyle talks a great deal of sense, I'm sure you'd agree, Mr Yeats.'

In fact he did not. He knew that the United States was full of Irishmen with no love of the British, many of them in government; but he evaded the question politely, signed the woman's book and finally escaped through one of the narrow doors in the Opera's massive Doric frontage. The first thing he saw outside the theatre entrance was Stephanie in another man's arms.

Now it is said that when Cuchullain of the iron grasp found golden-haired Emer playing strip-chess with several off-duty warriors of the Red Hand...

...no, none of that. Yeats straightened up and set his face into the Mask of Confidence. He walked forward and he said, loudly and distinctly, 'Good evening, Mrs Toughguid. Were you here for the lecture?'

Stephanie had been laughing and her face was pink in the chill late-February wind. A cold gust funnelling down Bow Street caught her long hair where it escaped the round knitted hat on the back of her head and blew some strands across her face. She pushed them away, irritably Yeats thought. She did not smile. She would not even meet his eye, but looked past him. He thought, forcing the shield of words into existence inside his mind: This is me being rejected. Spurned, perhaps – easier to rhyme. Look at me not caring. How cold it is. Despite everything he could do, despite everything he had learned, despite his new self-possession, a trembling started in his head and neck and began to spread to his whole body.

Then Stephanie ducked out of the other man's embrace, took two quick steps towards Yeats, slipped her arm inside his and clamped his elbow to her side, so tightly he could feel her warmth through her coat. The man with whom she had been flirting ignored her as if she had ceased to exist and looked only at Yeats, with a coldly amused smile. He had young eyes but was older than the poet, grizzled and grey but wide-shouldered and narrow in the waist, like an old athlete still in training and always ready for one more game. The skirts of his long leather coat were cut away in front for horse-riding. He wore an orange tawny muffler and his mud-splattered boots had once been expensive. His pale blue eyes, twinkling as if at some private joke in which Yeats had a leading role, maintained a challenging stare. A tiny little bell, as alarm bells went no more than a silvery tinkle behind more immediate sensations of anger, shame and fear, started to ring in Yeats' magician's mind. Words came into his mind too. *He is willing me to do something; or he is willing me not to do something. No matter how it looks, this is not about Stephanie.*

The other man raised his head slightly, an arrogant 'Well?' of nose and chin. The poet began to say something and found himself facing in the opposite direction. Stephanie was three quarters his height and not two thirds of his weight, but just by leaning on him with her hip and turning with his arm still clamped under hers she forced him to choose between following her round or falling over. It was like one of those Japanese fighting techniques Barton-Wright was promoting so hard at his new club in Shaftesbury Avenue, except that a young woman like Stephanie couldn't possibly know about things like that, could she?

Another woman, about six feet away, was staring fixedly at them, expressionless. She had a mass of corn-coloured hair and the body of a goddess, the kind of goddess known for an interest in agricultural production and usually seen with a fruit and vegetable dispenser clearly too small for the job. Her eyes were startlingly blue and she should have been what Yeats' younger brother Jack would have called a stunner, but there was something wrong with her face, an absence. Yeats had seen that golden hair, abundant figure and lifeless expression before, in the Cheshire Cheese at Bernard Shaw's table. He put his hand to his throat, where he could still feel the inexorable pressure of a leather-covered wire.

This divine form was the human face of one of the Colonel's elusive *theys* and Yeats studied her with no thought except to understand. The goddess's hand was inside her half-buttoned coat as if she had halted in the middle of some action. Stephanie moved a little forward, so that she was partially screening Yeats. The fair-haired woman pursed her lips crossly. Stephanie put her head slightly on one side. Yeats could not see her dark almond eyes but he could sense the challenge they were directing at the other woman. Then he realized that he was looking into the muzzle of a gun. He had not seen the blonde woman move, but there it was in her black-gloved hands, a short-barrelled revolver aimed precisely at the knot in his blue silk tie.

You are under the protection of IBI. You will be relatively safe. Although the gun was pointing at him – especially because it was pointing at *him*, a man of many and sometimes violent words who could not hurt a fly without agonizing over it for the rest of the day, Yeats still felt relatively safe, even while advancing bravely on the weapon and turning his head to Stephanie to warn her, in case (being female) she had not noticed that it was a…

When the shot came it did not sound particularly dangerous - more of a pop than a bang, 'Like a disappointing champagne cork,' said one witness later. Yeats had other things to think about than finding the right simile, as he was in free fall. When he lurched forward with ignorant valour and an instant before the blonde woman's black-gloved finger had tightened on the trigger, Stephanie, her arm still in his, had bent forward as if she had spotted a sovereign on the pavement. Before Yeats could ask her what she was doing, the world turned upside down. Stephanie, with some further trick of the secret Japanese art, had thrown him off his feet and into the air.

It brought back a long-buried childhood memory of being swung violently over the head of an exuberant uncle. However, the little Willie Yeats who had trotted beside his father on their coastline walks was now six foot five inches tall and had recently put on a lot of weight, much of it muscle, as a result of Lady Gregory's soup, French dumb-bell exercises and strenuous walks against Sligo's Atlantean winds. It was fourteen stone of Anglo-Irishman that went up, and further up, head down and heels high.

In fact Stephanie's throw sent Yeats so high that he had time to notice that his shoe-lace was undone and that the sky was unusually clear – surely that was the North Star wheeling majestically above him? Below him, really, as he was upside down; so it really was a case of 'as above, so below'. That might work in a poem. Correspondence. He hadn't done much on that. Hadn't done much *of* that, correspondence, in the sense of epistolary letters that is, he owed them all over the…

To see what happened when Agent 42 fired her gun, it will be necessary to slow time right down, because for the extranatural beings involved, a clock-tick takes the same time as the ponderous fall of a two-hundred foot sequoia.

The poet is at the top of his parabola, head lower than his feet, hat gone and black hair flying but his features composed, observant. You feel that someone in his position should look more concerned but people have been thinking that about Yeats all his life and it has not changed him yet. However, the small figure balancing easily on his right shoulder, surfer-style, looks worried enough for both of them.

A few feet away, Stephanie stands, poised and alert, on this timescale completely still. A sculptor would want to go at once to his studio before he forgot the curve of her neck and shoulder; a painter would feel compelled to draw the perfectly asymmetrical arc of each eyebrow on the air with his finger-tip.

Two tiny white hands appear from Stephanie's hair and push the strands cautiously apart. A fairy emerges and stands on her shoulder, watching the flying Yeats and his passenger with the benignly inscrutable expression of an ecologically aware pacifist required to attend a military air display. With his dark eyes and black brows, Stephanie's fairy is strikingly similar to Yeats. Long pale fingers (comparatively long – they measure about three millimetres) rake through the thick black hair in a nervous gesture which has more to do with suppressed creative energy than anxiety.

As the moment draws out, Stephanie's fairy lowers his eyes, looking past his airborne human counterpart, the mortal man of which he is the image in Stephanie's heart, and focuses on the bystanders beyond. They are all frozen in attitudes of surprise, mouths open, fingers pointing, arms reaching for partners in offering or seeking protection – all except one: man-shaped but rather small for a human adult, cloaked and hatted, it is made of darkness.

The dark figure nods affably at Stephanie's fairy, who instantly wilts, its chin dropping to its chest, its coal-black hair turning white. With a tremendous effort, the stricken fairy gathers itself, lifts its head and walks boldly towards the shadow man, across what to mortals is empty air. Its route takes it under the suspended Yeats, to whom it pays no more attention than a commuter walking in the shade of a fly-over.

Stephanie's little man is tall, for a fairy, and he draws himself up to his full height, his frosted hair and pallid skin now in deadly contrast to the rich plum red of his long-skirted coat.

'You are in violation of the Code,' he says in ringing tones; but the last word turns into a cough.

'*You* are in violation of the Plan,' is the response from the shadow.

Instantly the fairies' timescale and the human converge. Stephanie's fairy shrinks to a fading dot, like the spark of a spent rocket. Yeats stops imitating a solution to cross-town traffic problems and falls heavily to the ground, right through the failing glim which is Stephanie's dying fairy. For an instant, poet and fairy occupy the same space at the same time.

The dark figure's air of assurance wavers – just a nuance in the angle of the black hat. Something has happened that was not in the Plan. The fairy that its master the King considers such a threat has been destroyed, which was in the Plan; but it has not gone quietly, which was not. The dark figure lifts its head as if reaching a decision, turns to its left and disappears. The mortals in the vicinity feel suddenly warmer.

Wham! Yeats landed, unbraced, full length and dreaming, on the dourly unsympathetic London pavement. The breath was knocked out of his lungs so thoroughly that he could not even groan. After a while he got himself laboriously onto all fours, then to his knees, then, slowly and cautiously, to his feet. An unkind observer might have had thoughts of the careful, increasingly surprising and in the end magnificent unfolding of a giraffe getting up in the morning.

Yeats did not usually feel self-pity but he was distantly surprised not to find a sympathetic hand extended to the writer of The Lake Isle Of Innisfree in the act of arising. In fact the impact with the pavement had dazed him so that nothing seemed quite real, or to apply to him. He thought he felt Stephanie's body still pressed close against his arm but when he looked he saw only a tear in his coat sleeve and in the shirt beneath, through which a length of his pale hairy forearm showed, badly bruised and weeping blood. For a moment London revolved around him, then his senses came back with a cold shock as he took in what was happening. A crowd had gathered around someone lying prone on the pavement. There were calls for a doctor. He reeled forward, trying to shove people out of the way. His head hurt when he moved but he did not care. A voice, rising into panic, was saying Stephanie's name, over and over again. It was his. He saw a splash of crimson and something orange tawny between the stooping backs and shoulders, and was confused. She had not been wearing such colours. Had they thrown a gaudy blanket over her? He could not move his arms. Someone was holding them and looking into his face, shouting, 'It's not her, it's not her.'

It was Aleister Crowley holding Yeats' arms, shouting into Yeats' face.

'Come away,' Crowley said, no longer shouting. 'You must come away.' He sounded almost kind.

Crowley led Yeats a few yards down the street from the front of the Royal Opera House and then the poet resisted.

'Where's Stephanie?' he said. 'We must not leave her here.'

Crowley looked at Yeats with something as near to sympathy as you will ever see in the eyes of a field agent during working hours.

'I had a straight choice. Protect her, or you.'

'Good God man, then why did you choose me?'

'She ordered me to.'

'Why on earth would she do that?'

Crowley said nothing, just looked at him.

'Where is she?' mumbled Yeats, dropping his own eyes, ashamed. 'What has happened to her?'

'I don't know. I saw her go. That's all.'

At this, Yeats tried like a wild man to evade Crowley's restraining arm and run in search of Stephanie. People began to look at them.

Crowley pulled Yeats close to him and said, 'Listen to me very carefully.'

Elsewhere, there was a dialogue. It was an unusual conversation, by human standards. Each word was produced by slight variations in the charge, spin, colour and orientation of sub-atomic material that would require a quemadmodum theory to explain away – mere quantum would not even get you started. There were, nevertheless, two voices. Even though the medium of exchange was as different from mortal speech as the twinkling of sunlight on a broad rippling river is different from sparks laboriously struck from flint and steel, one of the voices was unquestionably masculine, the other indisputably feminine. This is a not completely misleading representation of what was said:

'So you have attacked his female,' said Titania to Oberon. 'By setting the Bucca Dhu on her fairy.'

'What did you expect me to do?' said the King.

'Perhaps to reason more deeply,' said Titania.

'Reason,' said Oberon. 'Humans are slowing the evolution of their own species. The strong are not efficiently killing the weak. The Plan will change that. Yeats by himself can only delay the Plan during his lifetime. The light paths suggest the effects of Yeats pairing with his true love could last a thousand years, a thousand years of dribbling milk and water, peace and love. Therefore the mortal woman Stephanie must not love Yeats. Therefore the sequence you call her birth fairy must be deleted.'

'Deleted,' said Titania. 'You know, that word says so much about you.'

'A word can say nothing,' said Oberon. 'Words are servants, not masters.'

'What are we but words?' said Titania.

'We were the first,' said Oberon loftily. 'We were in the Beginning. We were the Word, the Master Word.'

'But whose words made us?' murmured Titania, half to herself.

'We made ourselves,' said Oberon, 'or we grew fully-formed from the prima materia. I've told you before.'

'Yes, you have,' said Titania. 'You know that Yeats is important to me too?'

'Of course,' said Oberon. 'He is yours. Have him. His useless dabblings in our world do not concern me now.'

Titania observed an almost undetectable phase-gap in the next-generation expression of the sequence of sequences. In terms more familiar to the human race, she sensed that her consort Oberon, the King, was lying.

Arthur Conan Doyle was glad he had brought Hardy. The Royal Opera House was an unusually grand setting for one of his special lectures on Anglo-American relations and he felt the unsuccess of the evening especially keenly. The required atmosphere of manly common sense had been lacking; too many women, probably. The Our American Friends people behind the scenes were fulsome of course, but they would not look him in the eye. The Society's secretary, who had chaired the meeting, kept mentioning the size of Doyle's fee and how *completely* happy they were to pay it. Doyle did not personally care much about manners, but it grated. He found himself wanting to get away; he found Thomas Hardy sitting on a high stool at a tiny backstage servery, watching everyone and everything in his birdlike way.

'Come on Hardy,' Doyle said, 'these people may want to be friends of the Americans, but they're not getting very far with me.'

Angrily looking for the stage door and the crowded anonymity of the street, and with the uncomplaining Hardy in tow, Doyle set off through the labyrinth of narrow passageways behind the stage. He strode determinedly past a row of dressing room doors, some half open, from which spilled the chatter and laughter of women, rounded a corner and found himself face to face with Bernard Shaw.

'Doyle.'

'Shaw.'

'So I'm a lapdog of the Tory racial imperialists, am I?'

'Come now, Doyle, all's fair in love and war you know,' said Shaw uneasily. Doyle seemed bigger and more dangerous in the cramped corridor.

'Well, we're not fighting over a woman, and I'm all for peace, not war, as you very well know. Anyway,' said Doyle, 'I didn't actually mind you shouting out all the time. At least it meant somebody was listening. It baffles me that such a sound idea as a British-American alliance is not taken more seriously. Honestly, I think most of that lot tonight had come out of curiosity to see whether I looked like that wretched Sidney Paget drawing in the Strand magazine. Where's your friend, that big tall chap? He seemed to latch on all right.'

Hardy was watching Shaw, and saw a strange convulsion ran through the shrewishly-intelligent features, and the bearded mouth trying to say something which the playwright's brain apparently wanted to suppress. Words eventually emerged from Shaw's hair-shrouded lips, haltingly at first and then in a rush, as if he was getting them out while he could. The Irishman moved nearer to the Scot:

'You know - Doyle – there is always somebody – somewhere –

taking everything seriously. I mean really seriously. It just doesn't get told to the masses.' Shaw was whispering now, had half-turned his long back to exclude Hardy, the Englishman. 'Go carefully,' he said, 'that's all. Don't trust the Saxon too far. In fact, don't trust him at all.'

'Are you warning me off my American work?' said Doyle loudly and Shaw recoiled from his intimate posture like a toy on a spring. He shrugged his shoulders, brushed his red beard forward under his chain and pushed past them towards the dressing rooms.

Doyle set off again and Hardy followed, not without a wistful backward glance. He caught Doyle up at the stage door, to the sound of Shaw's: 'Oops. Sorry. Don't worry girls, I'm a drama critic, seen it all before,' until a door closed to the sound of cheerful squeals and what sounded like the beginnings of a party.

Doyle and Hardy avoided looking at each other.

'I don't think Shaw's himself at all,' said Doyle. Hardy, calculating his own chances of becoming a drama critic, did not agree. He suspected that Shaw was at that moment being very much himself.

'I wasn't referring to that,' said Doyle, jerking his thumb towards the dressing rooms. 'I mean he seemed frightened.'

'Arrogant toss-manger,' said Hardy, 'but something's got to 'un all right.'

Being ignored or side-lined often had this effect on Hardy's fragile sense of self-importance. Rural expressions swarmed around his ego like protective antibodies.

The two authors emerged from the Royal Opera's stage door into unexpected activity. People were running, people were shouting.

'The odd thing,' said Hardy, still in country mode, 'is that some of 'em is running one way…'

'…and the rest are running the other,' said Doyle. 'If these are running from, why are the others running to?'

'Summat bad has happened,' said Hardy. 'To-ers are gossips and gawpers, from-ers are decent sensible folk with a healthy respect for the law. Well, I knows what *I* am.'

'I'm inclined to agree with you,' said Doyle. 'The last thing I feel like tonight is any more public exposure.'

'There he is!' someone shouted. 'Mr Doyle! Mr Doyle!'

A tall man in evening dress, the kind of man for whom the word aplomb might have been invented, was running hard down the side street towards them, chin tucked in, coat held close to his body with one arm, the other arm raised high and waving.

'Thank goodness I caught you, Mr Doyle,' he said arriving, chest heaving from unaccustomed effort. 'I am Irving Fawls, the Under-Manager. There has been an incident at the front of the theatre. A casualty, I'm afraid. Would you..? Could you..?'

'Well, I... Of course,' said Doyle in his hearty public voice, but with an expressive sidelong glint of the eye for Hardy. 'Lead on, lead on do!'

'Where I come from,' muttered Hardy, as he tried to keep up with Walsh and Doyle's long strides, 'no sensible countryman would dream of doing this. There'll be a perleece-mun, mark my words.'

'I don't mind policemen,' said Doyle grimly out of the corner of his mouth, steaming along with his chin out, 'as long as they've never heard of Sherlock-bloody-Holmes.'

As Hardy reluctantly followed Doyle round the corner into Bow Street, he felt as if they were making their entrance in a play and had slightly missed their cue. There was the audience, a small expectant crowd gathered around the brightly-lit front of the Opera House. There were the actors, standing frozen in various attitudes of alert interest around the dramatic centrepiece, which was a man's body stretched out on the pavement, completely still and lying in a ragged patch of red. A large black police van drawn up at the kerb provided the dramatic backdrop.

Standing over the body's head was a pink-cheeked middle-aged man in top hat, pale scarf and perfectly-cut overcoat, in Hardy's eyes the uniform of wealth. At the body's feet was his perlice-mun, who must have been at the lower limit of the Metropolitan force's size requirements; even his helmet was too big for him. Both of them looked up expectantly as Doyle stepped into the lighted area.

'Thank heavens, it's Sir Arthur Conan Doyle,' said the top-hatted man loudly. There was scattered applause from the bystanders and 'Look out, Sherlock's arrived!' someone shouted from the back.

The top-hatted man flashed his teeth at Doyle. 'Hello Doyle,' he said. 'Nicholas Capehorn. I was at your lecture. Sorry about this, but there are some matters on which a mere High Court judge cannot pronounce, and as you were here... '

Doyle gave Hardy a significant look. 'Good evening, Sir Nicholas,' he said. 'May I introduce my esteemed guest Mr Thomas Hardy?'

Capehorn looked down his nose at Hardy with an expression of puzzled distaste and made a vague blaring noise that ended on a questioning note.

'Thomas Hardy,' Doyle said with more emphasis, 'author of Far From The Madding Crowd, Tess of the D'Urbervilles and other much-loved modern classics.'

'Who's the stiff?' said Hardy.

'No one knows,' snapped Capehorn, with an irritable motion of his hand as if brushing away a troublesome insect. 'It's not important now. He needs to be removed, quickly. We need a medical say-so before we can do that. It's a stroke of luck you were on hand, Doyle. I am sure, as *a fully trained general practitioner*, you know what to do.'

Capehorn had the confident tones of the ruling class and he was using them to full advantage, speaking very much louder than necessary and annoying Doyle by looking past him at the crowd. He seemed to be enjoying himself.

Doyle sighed, not without, Hardy detected, the dark pleasure of being in demand.

'Well, now, let's see,' said Doyle. 'Give me some room, will you?' He stooped over the body on the pavement and took a pencil from his breast pocket.

'Wot's ee doing then?' said a voice from the crowd.

'Goin ter draw on is vast hegperience, I spect' said the same voice that had greeted him as 'Sherlock'. This got a laugh from the audience, including Hardy (behind his hand), which Doyle fortunately did not seem to notice.

He used the pencil to move the ends of the recumbent man's orange-tawny scarf to right and left, exposing the bloody shirt-front. Then he bent and put his ear close to the man's mouth for a few moments, looked closely at the open and staring eyes and lastly put two straight fingers on the side of his neck. He then surprised and delighted everyone by getting right down to street level and crawling along for a bit with his eyes close to the pavement, then bounding several feet forward on all fours with a triumphant cry. An eerie sigh of satisfaction went up from the crowd, and another ripple of applause.

The creator of Sherlock Holmes stood up and froze, in profile, with his chin cupped in his hand. The spectators fell completely silent. A child spoke up and was quickly hushed. Doyle came to life, spun on his axis and advanced on Nicholas Capehorn with one finger raised.

'This man,' said Doyle, 'is dead.'

A cry came from someone in the watching crowd and Hardy had a fleeting impression of a fair head, uncovered and bowed in grief. Then there was a swirling movement, like the eddy left in a stream when a fish darts away, and he could see the blonde head no more.

'Good! Right!' exclaimed the top-hatted Capehorn, 'Constable, come on, into the van with him.'

Within seconds, the body had been carried into the tall police van, Capehorn and the undersized policeman had climbed in after it, and the van was trundling rapidly away, escorted for the first twenty yards by yelling street urchins, idiots who will follow anything, barking dogs and a few journalists. Only a splash of red on the pavement said that anything at all had taken place.

While everyone watched the police van, Thomas Hardy casually bent down and extended the tip of his forefinger towards the middle of the crimson patch. Before he could touch it, if that was his intention, a bucket of water was shot over the red stain, followed by a big broom head which threatened to knock Hardy off his feet.

'Sorry guv!' The blue-overalled man had appeared from the Royal Opera's entrance and made short work of sweeping all traces of the incident from the pavement and into the gutter. Behind and above him, standing proprietorially in the narrow entrance was a man in long-tailed evening dress and old-fashioned stiff collar: Irving Fawls, the Opera's under-manager. He stared coldly at Hardy until the workman had finished.

'You'll know me again,' said Hardy.

'Oh, we know you very well already, Mr Hardy,' said Irving Fawls. 'Mind how you go now.'

Clarissa Jane Laurel, Elijah Smith's agent number 42, stood gazing vacantly at her unmade bed. She was shaking. How had it happened? She had killed, not just a wrong man but *the* wrong man. It was not William Butler Yeats, the enemy of freedom, but her controller, the man who had become like a father to her, a very bad father, who was left lying, a dead thing with its head in a puddle, on the dirty London pavement.

It had been foolish of Elijah to flirt with that high class tart. He had obviously been showing off, for her. It had distracted him and disturbed her, and now he was dead, killed by a freakish mistake. She knew, bitterly torturing herself with the disloyalty, that Elijah Smith, arch anarchist, plotter against the corrupt social order, should have known better; it was inexplicable. He would have been merciless if anyone else in his shadow army had behaved so recklessly.

Clarissa had observed how the thin young woman moved, as precisely as a seamstress's needle, teasing Smith, controlling Yeats; she smiled without humour – the stupid scribbler probably thought the woman cared about him. Now, she thought, I know what professionalism in this secret trade looks like, and I know that I shall never have it. She found herself remembering the terrible grip of the black-clad man in the alley. Goose pimples rose on her bare arms, for she had not yet changed out of the evening dress she had worn to the lecture.

She had killed her saviour and protector and she was still in shock. The accident had happened in an instant but it had seemed to unfold slowly. In her memory she saw the man Yeats, tall, stooping slightly, with unexpectedly gentle eyes; he did not look like an enemy of freedom, but that was probably what made him so dangerous. She had raised the gun. She had hesitated (those dark sensitive eyes), the thin woman with silly braids in her long brown hair had led the poet in a tight circle with the light confident steps of a dancer and then, just as she fired the gun, Yeats was thrown flat on his back, and she found herself looking straight at Elijah Smith.

She would never be able to forget the look on Elijah's face. As her finger had tightened on the trigger, as the gun's mechanism reached the point of no return, as the hammer was actually descending to strike the charge in the brass cap which would send the lead bullet speeding towards its unintended target – Elijah had smiled, right into her eyes, like a man wholly confident that he would live forever.

She had seen his body react to the impact as the bullet hit him square in the chest. He had looked down, quite calmly, as if to see what had happened, then raised his eyes to hers, with the expression she knew so well, thinking, planning, looking for the way out. Then time started again, the expression went out of Smith's handsome face, and he had dropped limply to the ground.

Her own head drooped tiredly as if in sympathy with the memory, then was raised again by a visible act of will. She rolled the close-fitting blue silk dress halfway down her body and when it stuck at her hips, gave up and slumped onto her dressing table stool. For the first time since her sister's death at the hands of the British police, Clarissa Jane Laurel wept, head defiantly up, breasts shaking as she sobbed, her whole body swept by the passion of her grief, and cursed with beauty.

She had nothing left to lose. She was completely alone, with just her shadow on the wall for company.

'*Yes, you are completely alone*,' it said. '*You have nothing left to lose. This is what you must do.*'

*

'Funny,' said Hardy.

There was nothing obviously amusing to provoke the remark and Doyle ignored it. Until then it had been a conversation-free journey, Hardy immersed in his thoughts, Doyle looking at his own reflection in the darkened carriage window. There were more lights appearing now beyond the smut-streaked glass, amongst the sighing pines and furze of the Surrey uplands, as the late-night train puffed laboriously up the last mile of incline before Hindhead station.

'Funny,' said Hardy again.

'Well, what?' said Doyle, biting at last. 'What's funny?'

'The way they just stood there looking at the body and letting a crowd gather. If I was a theatre manager I'd want a dead 'un out of the way double quick.'

'Procedure,' said Doyle shortly, peering out of the window at nothing. 'As Capehorn said. He's a High Court judge, so I suppose he ought to know.'

'Well that's odd in itself,' said Hardy. 'A top legal authority and a police wagon just happening along. Seems too convenient to be true.'

'Convenient?' said Doyle, turning to face Hardy. 'What are you getting at?'

'Maybe nothing,' said Hardy, 'but it's also funny that Capehorn was so keen to get you involved. That manager ran like a hare to find us.'

'Well,' said Doyle, frowning, 'it's a bit peculiar, I grant you. But a man had been shot, he was dead, you can't get round it. Seems a bit disrespectful to make a mystery out of it.'

'I suppose so,' said Hardy. 'If he was dead.'

'What? I examined him,' said Doyle. 'You saw me. No pulse, not breathing and covered in blood from a bullet wound near the heart. He was dead all right.'

'Yes,' said Hardy calmly, 'he should have been dead.'

The atmosphere in the stuffy little compartment seemed to chill.

'I've seen death,' said Hardy, 'more than I want. In the country you see a lot of corpses, human and animal. You take a dead badger, and a dead human, there's something in common. The spirit of life gone, leaving the dead vessel behind, quite limp and super-still. Well, I could have sworn that our friend on the paving, Mr Orange Tawny, still had the spark of life strong in him. It's a kind of busy glow, an I'm-just-about-to-move look. I can see it. That's all. The whole thing seemed funny, and he didn't look dead. Not to me.'

'Oh,' said Doyle. He gathered his overcoat around him and pulled down the window by its strap. He was the sort of man who gets up long before the station. 'Well, I think he was. You said there were two things. What's the other one?'

'Why,' said Hardy, 'if you don't want idiots to think you are Sherlock Holmes, do you go and do a Holmes the next chance you get? All that crawling and leaping.'

'Looking for my cuff-link. It fell off while I was examining the body. And Capehorn can't be an idiot,' said Doyle primly, 'he's a judge. And I'm not tame. Now, come on,' he said as the train rolled sleepily to a halt by the empty platform, 'it's uphill from the station but I think you'll like the house.'

*

It wouldn't leave him alone. Ever since that night in Downing Street Sergeant Platimer's mind, waking and sleeping, had been disturbed. The temporary posting to Royston, and the second meeting with the Dark Man had made it a great deal worse: once could be explained as a funny moment, a turn; twice was a condition, or worse, it could just be real.

Do you believe in fairies? He heard the question in the dripping of a tap, the creak of a door, and slept with the light on. Like someone with a medical history who wants a medical future, he had felt a compulsion to find out as much as possible about his condition, about being bothered, pursued and tormented twenty four hours a day by the fairy folk.

His wife's knowledge of fairy tradition - she'd been a Dorset girl before coming up to London in circumstances she would never discuss – did not correspond with his experience. He had no hair to tangle, no stockings to tear, but if he had, he would have welcomed that sort of fairy with relief, milk or a large glass of gin if that was their taste.

He wanted to know about bad fairies, frightening fairies. The stories, pictures and pantomimes agreed that they were mischievous, but in small ways, small things – basically, they were small; except, perhaps, their king and queen. There was nothing about wanting to pee yourself at the thought of them. There was nothing about fairies that turned into near-mansize shadow men and back again; and so his restless searching had taken him to strange new places, like the Wimbledon public library, which he had never before entered in all its twelve years of existence.

'Fairies? You'll find something in that corner section.'

He had found something. As he got to where the librarian pointed, a book had been pushed out from the other side of the shelves and had fallen with a slap right at his feet. He had picked it up, expecting The Working Man's Fairy Encyclopaedia, but it was just a load of stories about mad Irish peasants by somebody called Yeast, or something; but then, as he made to put the book back, from out of the dark gap it had occupied, a sharp little whisper came: 'Well, do you?'

So that was the end of his researches in the library.

It affected his wife. Mrs Platimer had never had much time for fairies, angels and that sort of thing. For her, the supernatural and the spiritual side of life had first been an aspect of school and then the law of the land, neither of which had been very nice to her; if there was an afterlife they probably wouldn't let people like her near the best bits. Jesus might well be good above all other, which was very nice for Him, but being good when you were an attractive girl in a village like

Great Swyving had the unattainable mythic quality of other playground fantasies like being an Oxford Professor or a fine lady with a coach-and-pear. So she had ended up in London without much faith in fairies or anything else you could not eat, wear or spend.

She had been a ruined maid, but now she was one of Mr Gladstone's reclaimed women.

Platimer's obvious desperation concentrated her mind, which was much better than it needed to be to beat the dirt out of soapy clothing with a stick. She was also deeply loyal to her husband and wanted to help. As he would not directly share his fairy research with her, she made her own arrangements and participated in his project by attending the Spiritualist meetings which took place two streets away in a metal-roofed municipal hall. You never knew, she might pick up something to ease her husband's distress. If people want to know about love, they should look at the constant determined devotion of a woman to a difficult husband over the course of a lifetime.

For night after night she sat stolidly in the front row of the spiritualist meetings, while the tin roof pattered with rain, echoed in sympathy with the sound of adults weeping like children, or resounded with the glad cries of those whose relations made contact to tell them not to worry and check the gas-tap.

'Is there anyone here called Tom?'

'Someone here has recently lost someone dear to them.'

'There is a little child. He – or she? – is smiling.'

Yes. Yes.

Yes. Thank you.

Thank you.

The meetings were led by Mr Lewis Carisbrooke. He had a small but real gift, sensing and responding to the emotions and circumstances of his flock and bringing much consolation and happiness thereby. Carisbrooke believed himself to be as honest as anyone else in the same line, and he did not feel comfortable with the way the nice-looking but rather crushed woman in the front row stared at him hopefully and never said anything. He asked his wife to make some discreet enquiries.

Mrs Carisbrooke, regarded by the congregation as slightly disgraceful in keeping her grey hair long upon her shoulders rather than coiled out of sight under a hat, was accustomed to this role. She was in fact the one with all the supernatural knowledge, training and abilities. In the country she would have been a hedge witch; she lived in London: she was a kerb witch.

So it was that after the next meeting Mrs Carisbrooke sat down cosily next to Mrs Platimer and, after a few minutes' quiet talk, sent her on her way armed with hope and the name and address of someone who knew about fairies.

*

It was Wednesday and Doyle's wife Louise would be out all day. She was ill, unlikely to get better, but still able to enjoy her midweek routine of an early start, a morning's shopping and lunch at the ivy-covered White Hart in Farnham with Doyle's sister, Lottie. Doyle was still asleep when they left at eight but Hardy, keeping country hours and up with the pale late-February sun, had breakfasted with the women, enjoying himself immensely – he loved talking to intelligent females, and they loved him.

After the ladies left, still laughing, and with no sign of Doyle, Hardy amused himself with a professional survey of the house from top to bottom, inside and out, tapping beams, stamping on boards, checking for worm in the attic and damp in the cellar. He eventually decided the structure was sound, although the soffets could do with a coat or two of paint. After that he spent the time mooching around, peeking inside cupboards and drawers and talking to the servants.

Doyle, meanwhile, lay in bed drowsily following the Dorset author's progress around the house and wondering in a half-dreaming state whether some wild creature had 'got in'. Eventually he woke up properly and jumped guiltily out of bed. It wasn't on, he told himself fiercely, hopping around with one trouser-leg flapping, not on at all, to invite a chap to stay and make him get up by himself.

He rushed downstairs unshaved and was told by his unusually cheerful young maid that 'the gen'mun vister was in the garding'.

'Sorry, sorry, sorry!' Doyle said, advancing across the wet lawn to where Hardy was standing, notebook and pencil in hand, down by the garden's tall beech hedge. The little novelist seemed to be staring fixedly at the gossamer webs which hung, like fairy hammocks, amongst the brown rattling leaves.

Impressed by something faunlike in Hardy's alert stillness, Doyle took care to tread lightly as he approached.

'What is it? A bird?' he whispered.

'No. It's next door,' said Hardy. 'They're fighting.'

'Oh for goodness sake!'

'Nothing one makes up oneself has that tang of real life,' said Hardy, still writing notes as Doyle hustled him away from the hedge. 'Other couples' arguments are morally improving, they are cathartic. And like a good tragedy, they leave one feeling determined not to do the same. Of course, one does...'

Doyle, still keeping a tight grip on Hardy's elbow, steered him through the french windows into his study and shoved him into an armchair.

'Now,' he said briskly, pouring coffee, 'sit there and drink that while I arrange for some cold beef sandwiches. The newspaper's there too if you want it.'

Doyle was soon back, shaved and pink, preceded by a young maid almost hidden behind a tray and the mountain of sandwiches upon it. She laid the tray in front of Hardy like a temple maiden depositing an offering, with a noticeable wiggly movement, Doyle thought, and a broad smile which he did not know she had. He looked down at Hardy consideringly, as the maid undulated out of the room, still smiling.

'You've made a conquest there,' said Doyle, experimentally. Hardy ignored him.

'Read this,' he said, and handed Doyle the front page of the Times.

'Nation To Celebrate Queen's Eightieth Birthday?'

'No.'

Doyle shook the creases out and tried again.

'London Chamber of Commerce Says Kruger Must See Reason'?

'Nope. Further down, in the "Stop Press" box.'

Doyle sat down, adjusted his spectacles, spread the crackling newspaper out over his knee, doubled it and peered at the foot of the close-printed columns. There he found a smudgy heavily-inked late item:

MURDER IN BOW STREET

At ten o'clock last night a man was shot dead outside the Royal Opera House in the presence of large numbers of people. An unusual circumstance is that the murdered man was pronounced dead by none other than Mr Arthur Conan Doyle, a qualified medical doctor and the celebrated creator of Sherlock Holmes. Sir Philo Maynebeam, who had been attending a lecture delivered by Mr Doyle, named the deceased as one Elijah Smith, already known to the police for dishonest and violent dealings. It is supposed that his murder was related to some rivalry or grudge within his nefarious trade and that there is little prospect of identifying far less detaining his anonymous executioner. Sir Philo gave it as his opinion that the unknown assailant may with some justice be regarded as having done no more than anticipate the formal enactment of the law. He did not anticipate that an arrest would be sought with any vigour by a grateful public.

'Good Lord!' exclaimed Doyle. 'Good heavens above!' He looked pale.

'I know,' said Hardy. 'Elijah Smith! The man who wrote to you about Fanny being in danger. What an amazing coincidence!'

'It's not that,' said Doyle, completely missing Hardy's sarcasm, 'They've got the name wrong. It says "Philo Maynebeam". Doesn't mention Capehorn at all.'

'So? Newspapers are always making mistakes.'

'This isn't just any mistake. Maynebeam knows me. He is very highly placed. It was his office that asked me to help them, meaning the country, on a few occasions. It is extraordinary that he should be present and not make himself known to me.'

'Then he probably wasn't there and it's just a mistake. After all, you didn't see him.'

Doyle scuffed his knee with the flat of hand, a characteristic gesture of his when he was embarrassed or uncertain. 'Fact is, I've never actually met him. It isn't an official employment and they urged discretion about the connection. Said it might even be - that is, safest to keep quiet about it. I have only ever met his representative, a Scots chap, name of Campbell MacMack. Very decent sort, and obviously high up behind the scenes…' Doyle's voice had sunk lower and lower, as if he were thrown into doubt by his own words.

'What sort of help?' said Hardy.

'Oh, you know.'

'No, I don't actually. '

'Well, things like that talk I did last night, actually. It was Maynebeam who wrote to me initially, to see if I were interested. Since then, every so often, I get a note from his people, usually last minute but very courteous, suggesting I might like to talk to some group or other.'

'Always about America?'

'Yes. You see, I believe…'

'Sometimes at private meetings?'

'Well, yes, as it happens, but how did you …?'

'Paid handsomely?'

'Well, I never asked for much, but…'

'Whoever you've been working for, chummy,' said Hardy, throwing himself back in his chair and extending his small wiry legs, 'I bet it's not the elected government. This has got Conspiracy written all over it.'

'Don't be daft. And don't call me chummy,' said Doyle, not liking Hardy's expression, which was one that Hardy had worked on in his shaving mirror while suffering from writer's block. He called it Knowing Peasant and it involved tipping your head back, half-lowering the eyelids and curling the upper lip whilst looking down your nose.

'You don't think it's a bit strange?' said Hardy, maintaining Knowing Peasant. 'You get called in at random to play doctors and detectives on a West End street and find that you have a connection with several people there, including the dead man. Isn't that just slightly odd?'

'Maynebeam,' said Doyle, 'is a close personal friend of the Prime Minister.'

Hardy just looked at him, this time doing Shrewd Peasant, which was a lot like Knowing Peasant but with more squinting. Doyle's words had been slapped down like the winning trump at a village whist drive but the eyes in the big honest face were looking out uncertainly across a darkling plain.

Helpers

Someone whispered, quietly but with bell-like clarity, into Sergeant Jim Platimer's big gnarly right ear. 'She needs your help.' He was shaving, getting ready for his early shift, and the cut-throat razor almost lived up to its name. He had only just got over the shock and was dabbing at where he had taken a slice off his jowl when it happened again. 'She needs your help.' Low and clear, right into the ear-hole.

Over breakfast tea and kippers, it happened again. 'She needs your help.' The tea spilled and the kippers hit the floor and still he couldn't turn his head quickly enough, but this time there was the definite impression that the empty air above his shoulder had only a moment before held something in it. It happened again while his wife, in her old red silk dressing gown, was running the clothes brush over his uniform while he stood like a patient cart-horse being re-shod.

'She needs your help.'

His wife had not noticed anything and had to say so several times, with increasing emphasis and pitch. It happened again as he bicycled to the police station, fainter yet but just as clear, like a tiny drop of coloured ink in a crystal goblet of pure water. One shiny black size twelve boot was on the worn stone step of the station when he finally gave in, declared himself unwell, and went home.

For the rest of that day Jim Platimer was morose and silent. He sat in his armchair like a defeated king on his useless throne, drinking tea when it was given to him, efficiently eating food when it was put in front of him but refusing conversation or even the playful affection which had always been a sure route to his old self. After eight hours of this and with evening coming on, that strong considering look came into his wife's eyes, the look that says 'so, it's up to me'.

'Jim,' she said, 'if you want some help, I think I know...'

'Never,' said her husband, rising from his armchair with bloodshot eyes, 'never say that again... *I* don't need anyone's help. I'm a man I am, a strong one an all.'

He burst into tears. His wife left the room.

The morning of March 1st was bright and clear, with a hint of spring sweetness carried in a warming wind. The red brick and cream terraced houses of Wimbledon seemed to blink in the sunlight. Wednesdays were Platimer's Sundays, due to his working weekend shifts. It meant he could sleep late, and he needed to; it had been a difficult night. Another voice had joined the first, mercifully not tormenting with 'She needs your help', but repeating itself none the less. In the depths of the night the new voice whispered its words in a strange low tone. It even seemed to silence the old voice, which had sounded piqued before it finally shut up. In the small hours Platimer had woken his wife. Surely she must have heard? Bleary and dazed she said no, she hadn't heard anything. Where once, before Platimer's haunting took him over, she would have held him in her arms, now she had turned aside again and slept, as if his misery were now beyond her reach. After a while, the new voice had begun again.

Platimer, drawn and pallid in the light of the new day, stumped to the bathroom, mechanically lathered up his face for shaving, waiting for the voice. His hands were shaking. Nothing. He waited two minutes more. Nothing. Slowly and carefully he let his breath out in a tentative sigh of relief. Perhaps it was going to leave him alone today. He looked in the mirror and recoiled with a cry which brought his wife running. Words had appeared on the mirror; they were the words he had been hearing throughout the night:

Miss Cracknull 36 Blithe Road can help about fairies

'It's writing now,' he said in a voice almost strangled by desperation. 'All last night it was saying it, and now it's writing it.'

'Writing where, dear?' said Mrs Platimer, going close to the mirror but looking past it. 'You mean there on the window do you?'

'That's nothing,' snapped Platimer, irritably expert in his own torment, 'that's just where the steam's condensed and dribbled. I mean there, there on the ...'

Only it wasn't. The words had gone, the mirror was clear and contained only Sergeant Platimer's big red face and round eyes.

'Come and have a cup of tea, when you've shaved, dear,' said his wife kindly. She had hardly left the room when the same strange low voice that had spoken to him in the night said, 'Miss Cracknell, 36 Blythe Road, can help with fairies.' It was a soothing voice, even a caring voice, quite different from the sharp little voice that had afflicted him night and day for weeks past. For the first time the thought came into Sergeant Platimer's head that there actually might be someone called Miss Cracknell, who lived at 36 Blythe Road, and could help with fairies.

*

Hardy was turning out to be far more formidable than he looked. When he dropped his terrier-like grip on the subject of Doyle's employers, the big Scot was grateful for the chance to regain the initiative.

'The dead man, Elijah Smith, need not be my Eli Smith,' he said.

'I think he was,' said Hardy.

'Thinking is not evidence,' said Doyle.

'No,' said Hardy. 'Evidence would be my seeing that girl Fanny walk past us when we were on our way round to the front of the Royal Opera.'

'What? Why didn't you say?'

'I wasn't sure,' said Hardy. 'She didn't look the same, in the first moment. She looked drunk, or ill. You see it on the streets, women, you know...'

'Yes, all right,' said Doyle.

'And there was someone with her, indistinct. There was a shadow across him. When I looked again, she was almost past and you were already round the corner. I decided I must be mistaken, but given there was someone a few yards away answering to the name Elijah or Eli Smith, it must have been Fanny who passed us.'

'Well, I suppose so,' said Doyle, frowning, 'although there's something not quite right about the reasoning.'

'So,' cut in Hardy cheerfully, throwing a leg over the arm of his chair, then putting the other one beside it and sitting sideways, 'we find that simultaneously present in the same few square yards of London there was the Eli Smith who wrote to you, Fanny, his putative daughter or protegée, and the highly secretive invisible eminence grise by whom you were occasionally employed.'

'You're forgetting the implacable Dorset Bloodhound,' said Doyle sourly.

'Yes,' said Hardy, 'in a way that's the strangest thing of all. Why was I there? I wasn't in the plan.'

'How do you know?'

'Because I am me and I know I wasn't.' Hardy looked at Doyle very directly, unsmiling. 'How about you?'

'I know I wasn't in the plan, because there was no plan!' Doyle had gone very red, right down to his neck and beyond his shirt collar. His big ears, reddest of all, would have passed an inspection as brake lights. Hardy studied him, his lips slightly pursed.

'Hmm,' he said. 'Have a sandwich, they're very good.'

Doyle breathed out loudly and took a sandwich from the tray on the low table, looked at it, took another, and carried them off to the chaise longue like a big sulky lion with a slightly embarrassing kill. He was worried. Hardy was leading them to places where his various lives – public, private and secret – overlapped. The Dorset man was so amazingly quick, so hungry. Unconsciously yielding to his own suggestion, Doyle took a large bite out of a sandwich, thinking about plots. He was amazed that so few of his readers commented on the loose ends and gaping holes in the plots of the Sherlock Holmes stories, that is where there was a plot at all. Thomas Hardy, he knew, was a master, albeit of a rather depressing kind. If there was a plot, especially a dark, complicated one showing human aspiration blighted by fate and the English class system, Hardy would find it. In the present circumstances, that could be a problem.

'Doesn't this mean it's all off anyway?' he said. 'I mean, my enquiries? I don't know about yours... ha ha...'

'Far from it!' exclaimed Hardy, refusing the offer of a laugh at his expense. 'I don't like what I saw last night. I suspect there is something extremely unpleasant going forward.'

These last words were accompanied by a very straight look and Doyle felt a sudden lurch of panic and guilt. How could he have been so stupid, to have brought Hardy, an older man with unknown loyalties, history, energies and insights, into his house and his affairs, at this time. Hardy seemed to sense Doyle's state of mind and his expression softened.

'Look, Doyle, this Eli Smith was a hardened criminal. Sir Philo close-to-the-Prime-Minister Maynebeam says so. What did a man like Smith really want from you? What is his real connection with Fanny, if that is her name? Why does she get on so well with black magicians? Who was that tall fellow in the Wellsian carriage?'

Hardy looked at Doyle quizzically, one tufted eyebrow raised, and said, in dry but not unsympathetic tones, 'This is where you come out with some tremendously revealing fact or insight which I'm too slow or stupid to think of for myself.'

'She went into Kensington Palace,' said Doyle, aware of accepting charity from a sharper mind. 'That surely suggests she's with the right side there, at least.'

Hardy opened his eyes very wide. 'Does it? You hear things, don't you…'

'Do you?' said Doyle. 'I mean, I can't imagine they would involve the Queen in this, whatever this is.'

Hardy did not answer. He was studying Doyle.

'Stop that,' said Doyle sharply, then grinned. 'I refuse to become a character in one of your ruddy novels!'

'No chance,' said Hardy. 'Given it up now.'

'Oh. Of course. Shame you had to…'

'Someone,' said Hardy, low and urgent, 'wanted to pull you into this.'

'I thought you worked out it was her "disprized swain" who wrote the letter.'

'I'm afraid we've got past that game,' said Hardy. 'Show me the letter, please.'

Doyle went slowly to his desk, opened the shallow drawer above the knee-hole and pulled out a sheet of cream-coloured paper, folded twice. He stood there for a long moment, apparently just looking out of the window into the garden, where someone was hanging out washing. Eventually he sighed, handed it to Hardy, at arm's length and sat down again.

Hardy was already reading as he took a pair of gold-rimmed spectacles from his pocket and pushed them onto the bridge of his nose, still engrossed. Doyle smiled a small, sad private smile. He recognized that eager grab of a text, any text, and intense focus on the page. Bad as opium, reading. And writers were generally the most hopeless addicts. Hardy's small blue-grey eyes flicked to and fro, aided by a slight swivel of the head from line to line. I wonder if I do that? thought Doyle.

'Writes funny, this Eli Smith,' said Hardy. 'He can spell some polysyllabic words and not others of equal complexity. His voice says Board School at best but he subordinates like a grammarian. Lays his letter out like a schoolboy and then puts a post-post-scriptum which no schoolmaster drawing breath would countenance for longer than it took to reach for the biggest cane.'

'Biggest cane?' said Doyle.

'Very well resourced, Dorchester Grammar was,' said Hardy absently. 'Rural access scheme.' He narrowed his eyes and looked out of the window as if the Wessex heights lay beyond, unconsciously doing Frustrated Novelist.

'We can't just let this drop,' he said, as if talking to himself.

'So what do we do?' said Doyle. Something had changed. Hardy was now the leader, in charge of doing what you liked.

'We ask ourselves what we might be expected to do,' said Hardy.

'Er... go back to Blythe Road and ask Fanny what's going on?'

'Exactly,' said Hardy, 'so we do something else.'

Doyle said nothing to that, just sat there with an inward look, as if he was thinking about other things entirely. Then with a feline glance. 'I'd have thought you'd be keen to go back.'

There was a long pause. Hardy dropped his eyes then raised them. 'Y'know, Doyle, I'm a national figure too.'

'Of course you are,' said Doyle. 'I know that.'

'Anyway,' said the Dorset man dolefully, 'I don't stand a chance with a woman like that. The desperate, the damaged and the deranged - they're my natural constituency. I have to keep them off with a stick.' Then to and fro went the moustache, whiffle, whiffle. 'What you want,' said Hardy, 'with a good plot, is coincidence. That's the way things happen. It's the unpredictable, the outrageously unlikely, which determines the course of human affairs.'

'Ah, yes, but,' said Doyle, 'that's the thing. The unpredictable. Means you don't get it if you expect it.'

'That's the trick of it, ' said Hardy, 'that's how it works. We're sitting here, talking, as it might be about the case, and not getting very far...'

'Well, we are,' said Doyle, 'I mean aren't.' His eyes, always inclined to droop at the corners, made him look like a confused bloodhound.

'So we're sitting here...'

'Nonplussed?'

'Sounds mathematical, but very well, nonplussed, when a shadow crosses the window, there comes a knock...'

'What, like that?'

'Like what?'

'That knocking at the window,' said Doyle. It came again. A sharp-nosed man with a bush of curly brown hair above each ear and dressed in the uniform of the Post Office slid into view at the french window as if he were on wheels, smiling a wide, closed-lip smile and pointing hopefully at the door handle.

Hardy looked excitedly at Doyle. 'I sense a coincidence,' he said, 'a prickly feeling in the aether, of great weights and counter-weights moving, vast and unseen, while the human sphere trembles in anticipation.'

'It's only Patrick, you know,' said Doyle, 'the postman. He delivers the occasional letter and in return takes enormous liberties and is thoroughly unreliable. Yes, Pat?' Doyle shouted, and beckoned. The postman opened the french window.

'I won't come in,' he said, 'on account of treading grass into the carpet.'

'Very good of you, I'm sure,' said Doyle.

'I thought you'd like to know,' said the postman, 'I've solved the mystery of the letter.'

'What letter?'

'The one you said was a mystery and you'd like to know where it come from. I took the liberty...'

'You took the envelope!' Doyle looked thunderous. 'Which means - you were still here when…' but Hardy extended a restraining hand as if to prevent the big Scotsman from charging.

'Go on,' said Hardy to the postman, 'the letter?'

'Seems to have originated in the EC area of London District but it's an odd postmark. I had to use Old Handling to work it out. Lateral curl suggests a wait overnight in the strong-room the other side of the Newgate boilerhouse, while gum pockle is characteristic of the damp receiving shop opposite the old jail, confirmed by Wally Drake's thumb-sign, him being a snuff-user, which he is collector for Bishops Court, just over from the prison. Ergo and hasta la vista, your letter's origin is right hand side Bishops Court, the left being warehousing or derelict.'

'Brilliant,' said Hardy, 'quite brilliant. Don't you think so, Doyle?'

'What's odd about the postmark?' said Doyle grumpily, because Hardy was stealing the best lines.

'It's a pre-cancel,' said the postman. 'Speeds up the sorting for big companies and the like.'

'But this was a private letter,' said Doyle. 'This is most strange.'

'There is something stranger yet,' said the postman, striking a pose, with Hardy beaming approval and nodding in time to his words like a music-lover following a virtuoso soloist. 'There are pre-cancels for the India trades,' said Patrick, 'there are pre-cancels for the railways, there are pre-cancels for Fortnum and Masons. Our pre-cancel is used by the British Guvmint! Guvmint, Mr Doyle!'

'Government?' said Hardy.

'Our?' said Doyle.

Wednesday afternoon, and the smell of roast lamb and mint sauce filled the Platimer' small terraced house in Wimbledon. Mrs Platimer looked sorrowfully for the last time at their only child's anniversary gift, and hid it under the stairs. The three nicely-painted mallards clinked in their tissue paper as she pushed the box as far as it would go under the debris of twenty summers: a picnic set, folding chairs, two croquet mallets and a box of fireworks left over from the Jubilee – and now a set of china ducks which would never fly forever up their wall. The front door slammed and Mrs Platimer jumped and quickly shut the door to the understairs cupboard. Platimer was in.

On Wednesdays Jim Platimer was allowed two hours at the pub he called the Princerwales. He usually returned in an affectionate and expansive mood, but not tonight. Clump, clump, clump went his boots up the stairs, and after some time, during which Mrs Platimer regarded the ceiling with the face of a da Vinci angel, clump, clump, clump, down they came. Sergeant Platimer was in full uniform.

'Goin straight out again,' he mumbled, as he squeezed past her without meeting her eyes. Mrs Platimer stood her ground, meekly resolute, in the narrow tunnel they liked to say was the hall. Her face was lit gloriously by the coloured glass door-panel which spoke more of their marriage than a wedding ring. 'Jim,' she said, 'I love you.'

Platimer turned reluctantly on the doormat, his mind elsewhere. 'Got to see a woman about a fairy,' he mumbled.

'I know,' said Mrs Platimer.

*

Thomas Hardy noticed things. It made Doyle uncomfortable, although it made the world interesting. It was Hardy who spotted the old black lettering, painted high up on the ancient brickwork of a narrow entry opposite Newgate Prison.

'Bishops Court,' he read. In combination with the smell, the greasy cobbles and soot-blackened bricks, the name appealed both to Hardy's finely-tuned sense of irony and his horrified fascination with squalor. He followed Doyle through the tunnel-like entry, to where the passage opened out into a narrow cobbled space, not much wider than the entry, bounded by a jumble of peeling shop fronts and workshops, some boarded up, as vacant as robbed tombs.

The two authors gazed up at the scarred front of a tenement block on the right of the court. The tall structure seemed to totter, the fourth crusted storey leaning out as if the whole thing were on the point of collapse. The effect was increased by the racing clouds which scudded aslant the prow of the roof-peak where stood a lonely out-of-place stone figure, perhaps a gargoyle that had flown the quarter mile from St Paul's. Lengths of dirty twisted cord hung below many of the upper windows on both sides, and Hardy imagined the washing lines once strung across the court and soapy drips falling like scented rain from clouds of billowing linen. Now it was like a place blasted by a lightning strike that had killed the inhabitants and left everything blackened, empty and still.

'Doesn't look very promising,' said Doyle. 'Don't you think we should just go home and forget about it?' He did not say it very loudly and it is possible that Hardy had not heard him, as he was studying a printed notice roughly nailed to one of the peeling doors.

'According to this, everyone's cleared out,' he said. 'Something to do with the railway, down there.'

At the back of Bishops Court the ground fell steeply away into what had been the valley of the Fleet River, now occupied by a new railway terminus. The hoots and clankings did nothing to reduce the sense of prehistoric dread which hung around the smoke-filled brick canyon. They went and looked, carefully, over the top step of what was once a precipitous flight of stone stairs, now hanging truncated, dangerous and apparently unnoticed high over the sidings, platforms and engine houses below the Holborn Viaduct. Reduced to a grimy gothic backdrop to the steam age, Bishop's Court gave the impression of obstinately clinging to the edge of the recent development by its dirty fingernails, and was filled with the sadness of lost times. The original tenements had been built in the speculation fever of the seventeenth century, when the English upper classes had suddenly discovered the value and uses of money. It was well, even finely constructed but had become grotesque in its decay.

'Is there any point in going in?' said Doyle. 'It's condemned. No one lives here now.'

'There's someone here,' said Hardy.

'How do you know?'

'Trust me,' said Hardy, smiling bright-eyed into Doyle's glum face. 'Come on. I predict we'll find a modern maiden in distress, a country girl brought to town with all the vain hopes of her class, degraded by some toff and forced into selling her fading virtue. Though closely kept under the eye of the heartless old crone, she dreams of being restored to her true love, who will have a strong, sappy name like Bosko Elm. What do you say?'

'Bosko!' Doyle exclaimed, and they both laughed with the painfully suppressed giggles of schoolboys.

'Look,' said Doyle, his darker mood re-asserting itself as he surveyed the forbidding brick frontage, 'You said it yourself - this isn't a game any more. It might be dangerous. You read the report. Eli Smith was a nasty piece of work.'

'He's dead.'

'You said he wasn't.'

'You said he was – and you're the doctor!'

They both considered the next move. Neither wanted to be the first over the threshold. The only available entrance, like the rest of the structure, had outlived its natural span and had become monstrous with time, a carious mouth where once was an elegant welcome.

'It's very dark in there,' said Doyle. 'But faint heart never won fair lady. Come on.' He did not himself feel any physical threat, but this house might well be what they called a knocking shop, a low class brothel. He was wondering what *she* would think; and there was his wife to consider too. Still, you wouldn't take Thomas Hardy on that kind of outing - would you? Doyle suddenly remembered the outraged reviews and comment which Hardy's last novel had provoked, and looked sideways at the little Dorset man. Was there something sinister about the profile, something louche about the moustache?

'Come on,' he said again, 'We've come this far...' and they stepped into the dark together.

It was like going from a sunny morning straight into a coal cellar. Utter darkness. A match rasped and sputtered into brilliant life.

'Good morning, gentlemin.'

They could not see the speaker beyond the dazzle of the leaping match-flame. The voice was female and slightly hoarse, pea-souper fog topped up with gin. Match and voice were at a level suggesting the speaker was seated.

'Seems to be a concierge,' muttered Doyle. Thomas Hardy kept his thoughts to himself; he also kept slightly but definitely just behind Doyle.

'Just a moment dearie,' said the unseen woman. The match dipped, a wick glowed blue then yellow, and the contours of a high vaulted hall or lobby gradually emerged from the dark. A single doorless arch led into further blackness, while a flight of stairs curved with Newtonian precision up to the next floor; but the stair-boards were dirty and strewn with rubbish, the delicate wrought iron banisters corroded and broken. The stairwell loomed, dark and uninviting. Doyle sensed the ghosts of past inhabitants; Hardy saw their dim pale forms flitting up and down the stairs.

Doyle's 'concierge' was blowsy, bottle-nosed and, like the dolphin, with a soft spot for mankind that was unlikely to be gratified except by the curious. She sat behind the open window of a narrow booth like the ticket office in a certain kind of small and select Soho theatre.

'We've come...,' began Doyle, in low confiding tones.

'I know why you've come, dearie,' said the woman in the most suggestively knowing voice that Hardy had ever heard. 'Still,' she said, 'I spose I ought to ask. Do you believe in fairies?'

Doyle looked down at his feet, like a man inspecting his conscience, then brought his pale eyes up straight and level, eyes set rather sadly in his big round honest face, as if real life were a constant disappointment, nobly borne. 'Yes,' he said gruffly, 'I do. Very much in fact.'

'Well, that's all right then,' said the woman briskly. 'Best to do things proper, even though he's gone. Can't hardly believe it.'

'Yes, well,' said Doyle loudly, resorting to his one-size-fits-all professional manner, 'we're here now, and that's the main thing.'

'Yerse, love,' said the frizz-haired concierge, 'and none too soon, hif I may say so. I was just finking of shutting up shop. Nothing's come through on the wire since last night's "Get ready to clear out", so I'm orf, darlin.'

She backed out of her booth, shutting its flimsy door, and came around, carrying a blue canvas bag by its draw-strings. She surprised Doyle by putting a large iron key into his hand. 'That's the final sweep for my bit, and there's the key,' she said. 'You know what to do wiv it after. You won't forget, of course - what am I sayin? You're Cleaners.' And with that she waddled quickly out through the bright doorway, looked each way, and was gone.

'Have you the slightest idea what she was going on about?' said Hardy.

'Not a clue,' said Doyle. 'Seems to think we're domestic servants. Funny about the fairies though.'

'You know,' said Hardy, 'if Fanny is up there, and if we're even half right about her situation, she'll think that we're, you know, customers.'

'Then she'll have a nice surprise then, won't she,' said Doyle impatiently. He wished Hardy would stop making things up and write another novel.

'Fanny is desperate,' said Hardy. 'She's heard us coming. She's up there now, slender shoulders braced against the bed-head, gazing narrow-eyed, like a huntress, at the door.'

'Well we'll quickly put her straight then,' said Doyle, climbing the first five stairs.

'She's got a cross-bow,' Hardy yelped.

'Where? Where,' cried Doyle, ducking.

'Up there, of course,' said Hardy, looking up at Doyle, his eye sockets hollow in the light of the lamp Doyle held above him. 'She no longer cares what happens to her. She's going to restore her honour by killing the next man to walk through the door. Little does she know…'

'Oh for heaven's sake,' said Doyle, and clumped up the stairs like a man dispelling nonsense - or perhaps like someone making sure that any desperate females with crossbows would detect his innocent intentions. Hardy followed, alert, excited and looking ten years younger than when Doyle had encountered him in Kensington Palace's private garden.

At the top of the stairs, Doyle paused, holding the lamp high. It lit up a surprisingly small space at the head of the stairs, no more than a landing, and the staircase went no further. A plain oak-panelled wall faced the top of the stairs and there was a door at ninety degrees to it on either side. 'Here,' said Doyle, 'hold the lamp for a bit, would you?' and he passed it behind him to Hardy.

Cautiously, Doyle pressed an ear to each door in turn. There was not a sound, either behind the doors or in the building. Hardy joined Doyle on the tiny landing and a floorboard creaked, startling him so that the lamplight wavered wildly.

'Hello?' said Doyle, then louder, 'Hello?'

Not a sound. They could hear themselves breathing. Then Hardy spoke up, in his high precise 'Lundun' tones: 'Fanny, we mean you no harm.' No response, not even the thrum of a crossbow string under tension.

Then into the silence broke a sharp metallic scratching. Hardy tried to see what Doyle was doing and the flame in the lamp flickered, making their shadows leap on the walls.

'Hold it still, won't you?'

'Sorry,' said Hardy. 'For a moment, I could have sworn I saw three shadows.'

'Well, hand me the light again, there's a good fellow.'

Hardy gave Doyle the lantern and then set his back against the panelled wall.

'That's right,' said Doyle, 'if anyone jumps out, you can give them a Dorset Hello.'

Hardy said nothing, but the moustache went once each way, whiffle, whiffle, each tip vibrating like a terrier's tail when it sees a rat.

'It's going in all right,' said Doyle, 'but I still can't seem to... ah, that's it.' A tinny snick and the long key turned; but the door stayed firmly shut, as immoveable as if the doorway behind it had been bricked up. He crossed to the other door and inserted the key, which scratched against the black iron face plate for a moment before it found the keyhole. Again the key turned, again came the sound of tumblers rotating, again the door handle was the only thing that moved.

'How odd,' Doyle said. 'Seemed to unlock. No other keyhole. Very odd. She gave us the key. Why do that, unless…'

'Doyle,' murmured Hardy. The oak panel between the two dummy doors had silently opened, revealing a dark space beyond.

They entered the secret room, each in turn having to step over the high threshold and wriggle under the low lintel, even Hardy, who pulled the door to after him but was careful not to latch it shut. When Doyle held up the lantern, its yellow light revealed expensive chaos.

Two big cabin trunks, open and overflowing, occupied most of the floor space in the secret chamber, floor space that is which was not already covered in piles of clothing, books and papers. Doyle poked at the contents of one trunk: 'High-living type, our Fanny,' he said. 'Champagne, tinned salmon, plum pudding. Hard to see why she'd need a dozen different male wigs though. And there's enough bullets in these canisters to fight a small war. So where are the...? Ah, here we are. My God, here we *are*!'

A tall steel cabinet, carelessly unlocked and ajar, contained a whole rack of guns. They looked wickedly efficient, some delicate and walnut-stocked for shooting the pips from playing cards, some with lenses, levers and counterweights for shooting the pips from Archdukes at long range, and one with a barrel like a cannon which looked capable of blowing away an elephant's pips and the elephant.

'I wouldn't like to get on the wrong side of this young woman,' said Doyle, tapping the stock of the big gun thoughtfully with the nail of his index finger.

Hardy was peering up at something carved into the beam above the concealed door. 'Initials,' he said, 'S. H. - your detective gets around, doesn't he?'

Doyle took no notice. He was looking at an untidy pile of documents and other clutter on a spindly-legged writing desk which stood against the wall near the light.

'He's carved a fleur-de-lis too,' said Hardy. 'With a sheath-knife, I'd say. Kind of thing a prisoner would do.'

'Or someone in hiding,' said Doyle absently, inspecting something he had picked up from the desk. 'This room is pure seventeenth century. Those were troubled times.'

'I wonder what S. H. did stand for,' said Hardy. 'And, you know, anyone could call himself Eli Smith.'

'The person who has been using this room is not just anyone,' said Doyle, in a peculiar tone of voice. He was holding a small rectangle of white card. He took it close to the lantern's smoky flame, put on his glasses, read it carefully and handed it without a word to Hardy.

'Sir Philo Maynebeam,' exclaimed Hardy, with a low whistle. 'Now there's a thing.

'Why on earth would a man like Eli Smith have Sir Philo Maynebeam's card?' said Doyle.

Hardy sighed. 'For heaven's sake,' he said, 'can't you see it? You've been set up.'

'Sir Philo Maynebeam,' said Doyle stiffly, 'is a close...'

'...personal friend of Lord Salisbury, a man whom even I have heard called a modern Machiavelli. Look around you,' said Hardy. 'Wigs, guns, tinned food. Maynebeam was up to something, and I'd say he was definitely up to manipulating you. Might this have anything to do with your Empire work?'

'I couldn't say,' said Doyle carelessly, and Hardy pricked up his ears; bad liars recognize each other with the ease of Freemasons. He gazed at Doyle speculatively, as if seeing him for the first time, sniffed, twitched his moustache and turned away. 'What's this?' he said, sweeping a jumble of clothes and – inexplicably – flags from an object in the centre of the floor. It was made with a central plinth and a circular top about five feet in diameter. Unlike the dining table which it generally resembled, its surface was concave, a shallow bowl, with a matte white finish, scuffed, with a brass band running around the top of the flattened perimeter, engraved with points of the compass worn thin and discoloured by use and time.

'I have seen this before, or something like it,' said Doyle distractedly. 'Did you hear something then?'

'Dunno,' said Hardy, the pheasant poaching look back on his face. 'Maybe. Could be anything. Turn that light down.'

'What is it?' said Hardy.

Without the lantern light, the windowless secret room was still not completely dark. There was a soft glow from the round table, a gentle many-coloured radiance as if the shallow bowl contained the ghost of a rainbow.

'There are people moving in it,' he whispered, peering into the bowl. 'What the devil is it?'

'You may have the right word there,' murmured Doyle. He was not looking at the table; he was looking up, as if expecting to see a cloud of demons hovering like gnats over a pond.

'It is a camera obscura, a very old one, I think.'

He reached for a rope which had dangled unnoticed from a large round hole in the high ceiling, and walked around the table-bowl, dragging the rope with him. Within the concave table-top, a misty panorama of rooftop, courtyard and street wheeled with Doyle's movement around the table.

'There will be a concealed mirror, and lenses, on the roof,' said Doyle quietly, as if speaking in church. 'The image is projected down here, to form on this table. It was known to the ancient Greeks and has long been used by artists, but I think this device has a more sinister history. Observe, when I rotate the mirror, it surveys the approaches to Bishops Court.'

Hardy watched the image swing as the secret eye went round, spying on the figures and carriages in the Old Bailey, over a slate sea of rooftops, then to where Bishops Court ended in the high crumbling wall and the doorway where they had looked down on the new railway terminus.

'Nobody could approach this house unobserved while someone watched this device,' said Hardy. 'Not in daylight, at least.'

'You're right,' said Doyle. 'There is a man standing in the entrance to the Court.'

He tugged, carefully, several times on the control rope, coaxing the seventeenth century surveillance device to the limit of its range. In the receiving bowl, the view of the cobbled court trembled and shifted to the near vertical.

'And there,' he said, 'right under the camera - you can see his head and shoulders – someone entering this building.'

This time they both heard it: a tiny wooden give which somehow managed to convey to both men exactly the same image of someone trying to climb the stairs without making any noise. A few seconds later there was a little t-t-t creak as someone eased his weight from one leg to the other outside on the landing.

A listening silence. Then in the dim wavering glow from the camera obscura's softly iridescent bowl, the secret panel could be seen swinging silently open. An indistinct figure stood in the black rectangle of the doorway. A pale hand came feeling around the upright edge, and found a switch neither Doyle nor Hardy had seen, or if they had seen, would have understood.

'Told you,' Hardy said, as electric light flooded the room, because standing in the doorway was Elijah Smith.

He was no longer dressed like a dandified ostler. Top to toe, he was the sleek city gent. His hair was black, not grey, his lean and muscular body was encased in a well cut dark woollen suit and he moved easily, with a predatory poise and focus, like a professional fighter.

'Philo Maynebeam, I presume,' said Hardy.

Conan Doyle's immediate, 'Don't be silly, Hardy,' coincided and clashed with the other man's, 'Oh, very good indeed, Mr Hardy,' producing a long moment of uncertainty. Doyle looked angry and confused. Hardy's face was unreadable.

'You mustn't mind my little deception, Doyle,' said the man in the dark suit, with a confiding little smile and odd writhing gesture of his hand, close to his body as if concealing something in the palm. 'I feel I know you very well, but of course, you only know me through third parties. Philo Maynebeam, at your service. When I say at your service, of course, I don't mean it. You have done well though, bringing Hardy here. It will be so much easier to get rid of the body.'

Maynebeam went very close to Doyle and peered rudely into his face. 'You can't move, or speak,' he said, 'so you may as well stop trying.' Doyle's eyes swivelled sideways to follow Maynebeam as he transferred his mocking attention to Hardy, who was keeping the camera obscura's brass-bound bowl between them.

'Thomas Hardy,' said Maynebeam, 'the great Dorset nuisance. I don't know which of our enemies you're working for, or even if you are, but this is where it ends. Look at my hands - you have no choice - and see, how I make this shape, and then the kernel, pulled through. You feel the tug, don't you, inside? Don't fight it. You find it hard to see now, let go, you are going, going...'

Second succeeded second in the windowless secret chamber. Outside, somewhere in the Old Bailey, a dog was barking. It sounded as if it were under the ground. Suddenly, Philo Maynebeam's pleasant regular features twisted into an ugly shape and he put his head on one side as if listening. Thomas Hardy, with almost imperceptible movements, was sidling around the circumference of the camera table, moving his feet sideways and over each other like a very careful Greek folk dancer.

'It's not working,' snapped Maynebeam, apparently to empty air. His face lost all expression, and his mouth opened as if for the dentist, dribbling a bit. Round the table crept Hardy, bright eyes fixed on Maynebeam. Tss – tss – tss. Personal music players had not been invented, so the simile would not have been available to Hardy, but if you have ever been annoyed by the sounds, like the frenzied stridulations of very small metallic grasshoppers, which escape from someone else's ear-phones, that is what Hardy heard at that moment coming from Maynebeam's wide open mouth. Slowly, slowly, creeping, sidling, around the camera table came Thomas Hardy, always with his blue-grey eyes, the colour of the chilly English sea, on Sir Philo Maynebeam.

Maynebeam suddenly closed his mouth with a snap and wiped the drool off with the back of his hand, frowning with distaste as if it were somebody else's.

'Doyle,' he said, once again in pleasant tones, 'Doyle, yes you can move again, idiot. Doyle, we presume that is the famously large service revolver in your pocket. Take it out and shoot the Thomas Hardy anomaly.'

Doyle let his breath out hoarsely, like the showy mediums of which he disapproved and came to jerky life. He stared stupidly at Maynebeam.

'The gun,' said Maynebeam, articulating loudly and clearly, with exaggerated lip movements. 'Use it, you great Scotch nitwit. Shoot the sport which lacks the thanatogenic key.'

The light of understanding dawned in Doyle's big homely features, but the windows of his soul were still clouded. He thrust his large hairy right hand into the deep side pocket of his Norfolk jacket and brought out his revolver. When he hesitated, the gun held loosely in an undecided fist, Maynebeam's eyes turned up until only the whites were visible, a frightening sight but one which meant that he did not see Thomas Hardy complete his journey around the camera table and take two quick steps towards him.

'Goodbye, Mr Hardy, goodbye,' said Maynebeam with his eyes closed, his whole will directed at some part of Doyle beyond the visible.

Hardy, aware of Doyle bringing the gun up and taking aim, took hold of Maynebeam's lapels as if to help him off with his coat and, as the eyes opened, gave the man a friendly smile. 'Hello!' he said, and his bullet head drew back and then shot forward, hitting Maynebeam with deadly precision at the top of his aristocratically high-bridged nose.

'Welcome to Dorset,' said Hardy.

There was no cry, just a sudden gush of blood and Maynebeam fell to the floor; Doyle simultaneously dropped his gun, which went off, very loudly.

'Tell me I haven't hurt you,' said Doyle to Hardy, agonized, like a wife-beater coming out of an alcoholic frenzy.

'You haven't hurt me,' said Hardy, snapping the electric light off, 'but you have shot Maynebeam. I think this time he is really dead. The other shooting was probably faked with chalk bullets and cochineal blood. No, leave him. Take a look with that thing and see what our friends below are doing.'

Doyle seemed glad to be told what to do. He obediently seized the rope and vigorously rotated the camera obscura. The watchers had gone. There was no sound in the lobby or on the stairs. Hardy crept out and was gone for a few minutes.

'Nobody around,' he said, and switched the light back on. 'Perhaps they thought he'd done the business, when they heard the gun go off. Maybe his fluence was on them and all. Who knows.'

'What are you doing?' said Doyle. 'We should leave, now.'

'Wait a minute,' said Hardy. He was methodically unpinning a large sheet of paper from the wall opposite the door, freeing the corners and then carefully replacing the pins in the way intensely annoying to those who, like Doyle, take the brute force approach to life.

'I don't think...' said Doyle.

'I do,' said Hardy shortly, quickly scanning the desk and stuffing a few selected papers in his pockets. 'Come on. You're right, it is time to go. Someone will come eventually, and find the... oh!'

Maynebeam's body was not there any more and there was a smear of blood on the inner upright edge of the doorway.

'When did he go?' whispered Hardy. Doyle just shook his head, staring at where the body had been, then at the door. He looked smaller, a frightened man.

'How much do you really know about this?' said Hardy.

'Too much,' muttered Doyle, glancing at Hardy then quickly looking away.

It was Hardy who checked the landing and the stairs, not knowing what might be waiting in the dark. Perhaps the body had only pretended to go. Perhaps it was just around the corner, a dead man held on end, with one arm up, ready to strike.

There was nobody there, not in the lobby, no one at all in Bishops Court. Hardy and Doyle walked quickly away, heads down, hands in pockets, as far as St Paul's where they took a cab to Hardy's apartment.

*

'The indeterminacies are multiplying. One becomes two. The words are not contradictory yet, but I feel it, I feel it. There are shapes that do not quite fit. There is a force acting on the Master Sequence. This should be impossible. The Master Sequence creates its own reality. There is nothing outside the Master Sequence, nothing.'

To say that Oberon had summoned the Pook, or Bucca Dhu, and was talking to it would give almost entirely the wrong impression; to say anything else would be no nearer the truth. Oberon, then, had done something as much like summoning his dark fairy servant as makes no difference, and was engaged in something which corresponded almost exactly to conversation. It was one-sided. The King was out of sorts and inclined to go on. Puck, the Pook, the Bucca, let him. It was Oberon's only agent in the material world of mortals, enabled to deal directly with humans by taking small amounts of life energy, unnoticed, like a stealth tax, from every being within a certain radius, the circle increasing according to need. Like many other indispensable employees, the Bucca enjoyed a considerable amount of freedom in interpreting its master's wishes. Now, it waited.

Oberon emerged from deep reflections and focused on his servant again.

'You say you blasted the fairy?'

'Yes, lord.'

'That at least is good. Yeats is under protection and may even survive the Blythe Road incident, but now he will be unfulfilled. With the girl's birth fairy deleted, he will no longer be the image of love in her mind. She will not want him. That timeline is closed. He will never know such love again. He will waste his time trying to recapture what he had, reconstructing half-remembered visions. He may still be a force, but he will not lead his people, and the world, towards peace and understanding. He will not seriously obstruct the Plan.'

Oberon sensed something in the Bucca's silence and asked sharply, 'You did delete her fairy?'

'There was an anomaly, lord. The fairy was still alive when...'

'When what?' said Oberon, secretly amazed: the Bucca Dhu was uncertain!

'The fairy was still functioning when its mortal, Stephanie de Beauharnais, saved the life of her man, the Yeats 500. There was - a transfer, a complex transposition. I felt the words change.'

Oberon said nothing. A human might have been said to be collecting his thoughts. In fact he was bouncing questions to and fro between the beginning and end of time, feeling the resonances build and decay, listening for the shape, looking for the vibration of things to come. What he perceived was worse, to him, than any shape.

Ambiguity

Indeterminacy.

One becoming two.

Direct action is having unintended and dangerous consequences.

Something has to be done.

More direct action is needed.

So the King calculated. He knew there was something wrong with his conclusion, and experienced a sudden sharp longing for the authority of his Queen's insight. He irritably suppressed the feeling.

'What about the female?' he said with deliberate harshness. 'Yeats' woman – her fairy caused the anomaly. There must have been a price.'

The Puck, the Bucca Dhu, grinned. It liked uncertainty no more than its master.

'She is between life and death. I can decide the issue. I can send her to the Dark.'

Coldly, Oberon, the King, regarded his servant.

'Do that,' he said at last. 'These uncertainties must be resolved. How will you...?'

'Does it matter?' said the Bucca Dhu.

Crossings

Yeats woke up in the dark, to the sound of deep, even breathing. He held his breath, and the breathing continued. Consciousness flowed back and his eyes opened on a brightly-lit room. He was lying on a narrow metal bed. Something about the hardness of the bed and a faint odour of boiled cabbage and polish made him think of hospitals and he sat up suddenly. He was at one end of a long narrow attic bedroom; at the other was a bulky dark-suited man sitting by a door, watching him. A very slight division of the man's attention brought Yeats' eyes around; against the opposite wall was a bed, identical to his own, on which lay the South American shaman, Don Eduardo Nejedeka. Without saying a word, the man sitting by the door reached out and operated a bell-push in the wall.

Yeats squinted at the window, where the light seemed wrong. How long had he been asleep?'

'Just eighteen hours.'

It was Crowley, ducking his head under the low lintel as he entered, carrying a mug of tea. Yeats jumped up, and staggered, would have fallen if Crowley had not supported his elbow.

'You let me sleep – you *made* me sleep, while all the time she…'

'Come down,' said Crowley, handing him the tea. 'The Colonel's waiting.'

Colonel Madriver was waiting for them in a first floor room that overlooked a busy intersection below. He looked tired, older than when Yeats had left him at Kensington Palace, almost frail. He might have been any administrator with an in-tray to clear before the weekend. With its utilitarian desk and scattering of ill-assorted threadbare chairs, the office struck Yeats as almost aggressively ordinary, until he noticed a brass-mounted crystal ball on the Colonel's desk. Perhaps it was just a paper-weight.

Crowley received some instructions which Yeats could not hear, and quietly left the room. The poet felt his anger rising. Everything in him strained like a falcon on the wrist to fly to Stephanie's help. He was certain he would find her. He felt she would call to him. Instead he was spoken over like an invalid, left to one side, protected, managed. The anger reached his throat and was ready to ignite.

'Not yet,' said the Colonel, and Yeats almost choked. 'Let it out at the right time.'

Colonel Madriver stood up. He no longer looked frail; the planes and hollows of his face seeming to reveal another man, harsher, even brutal.

'Yes,' he said, 'the time is coming. Events have moved more quickly than we expected. It is time for the Shaman of the Western World to take on the forces of the dark realm.'

Yeats had to restrain an impulse to laugh. 'Me?' he said, 'I haven't done very well so far. It seems even Crowley can hypnotise me.'

'*Even* Crowley?' The Colonel laughed, without humour. 'You mistake your man, I think. In any case, he did exactly the right thing, simply gave your mind a push in the direction it needed to go. You were exhausted. You had been in great danger.'

'And I wanted to run away, is that what you are saying?' said Yeats, the anger rising again.

'No. You wanted to stay. You had taken on an armed assassin, a shot was fired, violence was done, and you wanted to stay.'

'The danger had passed when…'

'I don't mean the gun.'

'Then what?'

'I cannot easily explain. You might say that you have survived an encounter with a powerful magician.'

Now Yeats laughed. 'Oh. I've met a few of those,' he said.

'No, you have not,' said the Colonel. 'Believe me on this.'

Yeats' smile disappeared in the face of the other man's serious intensity. He sighed, and ran a hand down his face. 'You are probably right. I don't care. Where is Stephanie?'

The Colonel took a half-step towards the poet. 'Mrs Toughguid is missing,' he said.

'Couldn't she have just been delayed?'

The Colonel fixed his grey eyes on Yeats. 'Stephanie de Beauharnais would be here by now,' he said, in the clipped and final tones of the military man forced to discuss operational matters with a civilian. 'Trust me on this. Something has happened.'

Yeats moved uneasily, went to the window, crossed to the door, put his hands in his pockets then hunched his shoulders and folded his arms. Colonel Madriver watched him closely and when he came to rest, said:

'You felt worried for her, then obliged to take action, then powerless to help, then guilty and finally embattled and rather defensive.'

When Yeats angrily made to speak, the Colonel smiled his frosty smile and said, 'Forgive my intrusion - she has been making me feel the same way ever since she started to work for us, and it is oddly reassuring to see her having the same effect on another man. She is very strong-minded. In fact I have descended to a rather shameful arrangement with her. Stephanie decides what to do, then I have to dress it up as official policy afterwards. It usually works out. But I am worried about her, this time.'

Yeats' hand was already on the door handle. The Colonel made no move to stop him. 'There's nothing you can do,' he said. 'Where would you start? We've got all our people out there, so you may as well wait here with me. News will come here first, if there is anything to report. Wherever Mrs Toughguid might be, she would tell you now to stay off the streets of London. Sentiment will get you killed.'

He turned away with a world-weary sigh and strolled towards his desk as if to undertake some tedious but necessary paperwork. 'The personal thing, it's the curse of our profession. When she insisted on handling this latest attempt to kill you, I...'

'To kill me?' spluttered Yeats, letting go of the door handle and following the Colonel. 'It was the other man who was shot dead.'

'That other man,' said the Colonel, perching on the corner of his desk, 'has so completely sold himself to the devil that I doubt whether he is fully human now and *can* actually die. He is also director of an assassination cult which has recently made you one of its priorities. Stephanie was there to protect you. It is what she does. Didn't you know?'

Yeats, standing pale and undecided, forced his overloaded memory to recreate the scene outside the Royal Opera House. There had been Stephanie, slim, pink and pretty, flirting with the man in the long riding coat. Then she had whirled Yeats round with that clever shove in the crook of his knee. And then...

'The fair woman,' said Yeats. 'She had a gun.'

'Your assassin,' said the Colonel, much as he might have said *your dance-partner*, Yeats reflected. 'We know about her. Her younger sister died two years ago in police custody. Agitating for female suffrage. It was a very sad case.'

'But why come after me?'

'Ah, the cry of the innocent down the ages,' said the Colonel, going to the window. Yeats then noticed that there were large black-edged golden letters, fat serifed capitals, almost completely covering the glass. He slowly spelt them out backwards for himself - THE IMPERIAL OPTIC COMPANY, LONDON, CAIRO & BOMBAY.

'Very good,' he said.

'That's right,' said the Colonel quietly, inclining his head to see downwards to the foot of the building, 'it's top quality gold leaf – you can actually see through it, but only from this side.'

'Gold to airy thinness beat,' murmured Yeats, intrigued despite his anxiety, joining the Colonel at the window and peering through the big serifed characters. 'Everything looks blue-ish.'

'Gold leaf is transparent, but not to the red end of the spectrum,' said the Colonel. 'Now Yeats, you need to understand that there are some very serious political players who have you in their sights.'

'You mean the British Intelligence Service? I know – they fear my support for Irish independence. Well, I'm not to be put off, you know. If Maud Gonne can...'

'No Yeats, not British Intelligence,' said the Colonel.

'How can you be so sure?'

The colonel turned his small sun and wind-burned face towards the poet. The crows-feet etched on either side of his grey eyes suddenly deepened but the eyes did not reflect the smile. 'Well, for one thing because we *are* British Intelligence,' he said, 'and so are you, since we brought you in. I'm sorry. Angenent said you wouldn't like it.' There was an uncomfortable silence. It lengthened to become an embarrassing silence. The tall Anglo-Irish poet held his dark head very still and continued to gaze expressionlessly through the back-to-front lettering on the window. 'Glas,' he murmured after a while.

'What about the glass?'

'Not glass,' said Yeats, 'glas. The colour of the light which the gold leaf lets through; it's not exactly blue, not quite green – almost glas.'

The Colonel came to squint out through the lettering too, his thinning but well-trimmed hair just level with Yeats' high square shoulder.

'Looks blue to me.'

'If you are the British secret intelligence service,' said Yeats, 'though I find it hard to believe - '

'I'll take it as a compliment,' said the Colonel, still with his attention fixed on the street.

' - well, then you're my enemy.'

'Then so is Stephanie de Beauharnais, who is one of my agents,' said the Colonel sharply. His expression immediately softened and he turned to face Yeats. 'I am sorry,' he said, 'Actually, I sometimes feel I'm working for her. And it's more true to say we are one of several British intelligence services, perhaps the oldest. You know, Yeats, the world is a little like Angenent's microscopic cells – the more closely you look, the more surprises you get and the more you have to re-think your theories. I could add that, just as with scientific enquiry, the closer we get to the truth, the more elusive and strange it becomes. When you approach absolute reality, it is IBI's experience that you find yourself dealing with things that would leave the romancers boggling. Now, come down to the basement – there's a kitchen there, and food, if you trust my cooking. '

'For how long has the intelligence service been interested in magic?' said Yeats. It was now late in the evening and there had been no word about Stephanie. The atmosphere in the spartan office was like that of a railway station waiting room and the two men, sitting either side of the cheerless little fire, each with part of his mind elsewhere, were making conversation much as if that were the case.

'Since the sixteenth century,' said the Colonel. 'IBI stands for Imperial British Intelligencers, the executive arm of the Elizabethan court's inner circle. We have survived for a very long time, in secret of course. By outlasting change, we have retained some practices and ideas which are now generally forgotten or even – I have to say – condemned. Our ancestors didn't think as people do in these industrious Protestant times about magic. If you were able to see what the Armada was getting up to by scrying, well – why not? And no,' he said, seeing Yeats' eyes slide sideways to the crystal ball on the desk, 'nothing there. It's a lost art, I'm afraid. Like their ability to communicate with the Other Side.'

'Wait a minute, wait,' said Yeats, 'are you saying that the secret service was working with the Fairies?'

'That depends which secret service, and also which fairies you mean. The Elizabethans certainly communicated with fairies, lucent or "light" fairies as they called them, from time to time – when they could find them. With King James in power and backed up by Walsingham's intelligence network, they rapidly lost touch – lost *the* touch, you might say. They knew, or suspected, that James' people had some dealings with the dark fairies, but that was that. The Jacobeans pressed their advantage and IBI was cut off from most of its old contacts with the other world.'

'Dark and light fairies? Is that what you meant at Kensington when you said it was a kind of war?' said Yeats. His hand strayed to the pocket where he kept his note book.

'That there are different kinds of Fairies is common knowledge, at least amongst people who look into these things,' said the Colonel, his fierce grey eyes following the movement of Yeats' hand in a way which made the poet pretend he had just been stretching a stiff arm.

'We got Will Shakespeare to put it in a play,' the Colonel continued, 'to see what it flushed out - after all, if we knew at first hand about the reality of the supernatural, then others probably did as well.'

'A play about magic - you mean The Tempest?'

'No.' The Colonel's face set and his eyes narrowed as if he were looking back over three centuries. 'The Tempest was a distress signal for anyone, or anything, that could read it – the loyal Elizabethans were getting pretty desperate by 1610 – and old, of course. The Tempest is a plea for good governance in both worlds, fairy and human. When King James came in, those worlds began to move apart and what came through the gap was a great threat to the human race. No, it is A Midsummer Night's Dream that presents things as we think they are: a dark intelligence and a loving light in recurrent opposition, a male and female beyond human masculine and feminine, a destructive and rapacious will complementing a creative and nurturing instinct – the King and the Queen, Oberon and Titania.'

Yeats kept his head very still. This usually helped when over-excitement threatened his self-possession. So it was all true! More than true. His own Fairy was true of course, true for him; it was another thing to know that a man like the Colonel believed so prosaically in the existence of fairies, and viewed thought-transference and crystal gazing as ordinary professional techniques. Now Yeats saw his daring faith in the unseen and extraordinary as a feeble start, a blinkered conservative stab, a lightly-downed version of the hairy reality: a fairy King and Queen! Then he remembered.

'She appeared to me,' he said.

'What?' said the Colonel sharply.

'The Queen, Titania. She appeared to me at Horton's guest-house. She said something very bad was going to happen.'

'And it's only just occurred to you to tell us! How did you respond?'

'I threw a quince at her.'

'You threw a quince at her. You wouldn't know, of course, but we have been trying to communicate with Titania since 1598. We haven't even found any of her fairies, let alone spoken to their queen.'

It was at this moment that a fairy appeared on the Colonel's shoulder, right beside his razor-trimmed sideburn.

'Perverse narrative logic,' Yeats said to himself.

'I beg your pardon?' said the Colonel, but before Yeats had time to wonder how you tell a military man that you can see his fairy, it had vanished, the street door slammed, there were people in the lobby and then voices on the stairs. Yeats dashed to the landing and leaned over the banister rail. There were two voices audible, one head visible, coming up with a clatter. The voices were excited, talking across each other, but Yeats recognized one.

'Horton?' he called, 'Tom Horton?'

'God, Yeats, is that really you?' came a cry and the dark head tilted back to reveal William Thomas Horton's sharp earnest features. When his friend got to the top of the stairs, Yeats was concerned to read fear and anxiety on the mystical enthusiast's sensitive face.

'We have such a story to tell,' said Horton, gripping the poet's hand like a drowning man. Then Yeats saw that Horton was accompanied by his landlady, Mrs Biggs. She was out of breath and puffing, but not so much so that she could not add her voice to his:

'Such times, Mr Yeats. Who would have thought it?'

'Thought what?' said Yeats, trying not to flinch as Mrs Biggs seemed about to grapple him around the middle like a very small Sumo wrestler. 'Thought what?' he repeated gently.

'Messages, Mr Yeats!' said Mrs Biggs looking up at the underside of the poet's chin. 'Messages from Beyond.'

Yeats felt the familiar cold thrill pass through him again, like the missed step on the stair.

'What messages?' he said, trying to keep his voice steady.

'We wanted to bring them to you,' said Horton, eyes too bright and words falling over themselves, 'at your lodgings in Woburn Buildings, and they tried to stop us.'

'Who?' said the Colonel.

'Demons!' said Horton, and only then did Yeats notice that his friend's hands were shaking. 'Devils, creatures of darkness - we were assailed, Yeats, put to the test, our faith...'

'They are lucky to be alive.'

This new voice came from below. There was a third person coming up the stairs. As his well-brushed head, brown where his father's was grey, came into the landing's light, Yeats realized it was the Colonel's son, Damien.

'The Other Side attacked them as they were approaching Mr Yeats' address,' said Damien. 'It was the most serious, and the most flagrant direct action yet, Sir.' Yeats tried to imagine wanting to call his own father Sir, whether in uniform or not, and failed.

Then Horton and Mrs Biggs, prompting and contradicting each other, one moment laughing helplessly about something incomprehensible to their listeners, the next sobered by a remembered terror, told their story.

Following Yeats' well-meant suggestion, they had been keeping watch in the flowery front parlour while (Yeats saw) Horton had glowed in the oxygen-rich atmosphere of Mrs Biggs' admiration. At the second midnight there had been another Phenomenon, so extraordinary that it had to be communicated to Mr Yeats at once. Whatever had happened had obviously been terrifying, other-wordly and immensely exciting but, it seemed to Yeats, listening on the crowded landing with a patience requiring iron self-control, strangely hard to establish. Mrs Biggs was content to say, 'Go on, you tell,' at the key moment, while Horton seemed less interested in the Phenomenon than in its aftermath, when he and Mrs Biggs had set out to walk the short distance from Bedford Place to Yeats' rooms in Woburn Buildings. As they entered the southern arm of his L-shaped street, something had happened which defeated their joint attempts at description.

'It was...'

'Demons…'

'Voices…'

'I looked at you and I thought I saw…'

'Your hand felt different.'

'We were lost.'

'Couldn't move.'

'Then the blind match seller came.'

'The match-seller?' said the Colonel, glancing at his son, who nodded.

'He did something, and cried out with a great voice,' said Horton, his own voice trembling with mystical passion, 'and it was as if the sun had risen in the night-time.'

'*Then* we could move all right!' said Mrs Biggs. 'How we ran!' She looked at Horton fondly; and he was deadly white.

'Look out, he's going to faint,' cried the Colonel, and Yeats caught Horton as he fell.

The picture came into Yeats' mind of two frightened children, hand in hand, running from a made-up monster that had become too real. They had now all moved into the office, Mrs Biggs sitting comfortably enough in the Colonel's chair but unwilling to speak, the men standing, except Horton, who half-lay in one of the armchairs, his eyes closed and a wet towel across his forehead.

The Colonel whispered something to his son, then raised his voice: 'Mr Horton? Are you well enough to tell us about the message?'

Horton opened his eyes and sat up. The towel slipped down and he threw it aside. He did not answer the Colonel but came right up to Yeats, looking with crazy intensity into his tall friend's face.

'Do you know somebody called Stephanie?' he said.

Yeats mouth dried and he felt faint. 'Yes,' he croaked, then more strongly, 'yes, I do.'

'She is in danger. We received a message.'

'I know, I know! But every moment… Please, just hand me the message,' said Yeats, in agony.

'I'm afraid that's not possible,' said Horton, with the wry twist of the mouth that was his smile. 'The messenger is the message, you see.'

'No,' said Yeats, 'I don't.'

Horton turned round and took his clothes off. To be more accurate, he stripped off his upper half. On his back was the message, line after line of small neat characters, the strokes fine, firm and well-formed after the best copybook practice. It began just above his left shoulderblade, running across the contours of Horton's unexpectedly muscular back, continuing without break or smudge through body-hair and bump, line after line, down the pale tapering torso. The ink was reddish-brown.

'How did you write this' said Yeats to Mrs Biggs.

'I couldn't,' the landlady said, hugging the marvellous secret to herself, 'I didn't.'

'Then who did?' said Yeats.

'No one wrote it,' said Mrs Biggs, her eyes shining. 'It just appeared, didn't it, Tom.'

'Just appeared?' said the Colonel's son.

'Tom?' thought Yeats.

'We could hear them first,' said Horton, 'the spirits, a great host. There was a mighty rushing wind all about the house…'

'But when we went to the door, it was as still as anyfing,' put in Mrs Biggs.

'Then we heard the voices of angels' said Horton, 'and I felt this happening. It was like being sprayed with needles, from the inside.'

'Hold still till I read it,' said Yeats, peering at Horton's back. This is what he saw:

> *For the attention of the Yeats 500 Pollexfen Cross, via the Horton 58 Type Five and Biggs 338 receiver. Message begins. There is a high probability that the Stephanie de Beauharnais 670 Baden cross Bonaparte exogenous cross requires urgent intervention by the Yeats 500 Pollexfen cross if their optimum convergent life-spirals are to be maintained. This communication will not be repeated.*

This brought Yeats down to Horton's waist-band. 'Hang on,' he said, squinting downwards, 'I think there's a PS.'

'Not in front of the lady, perhaps,' murmured the Colonel.

'I shall look the other way,' said Mrs Biggs grandly, and did so, with a frown of righteousness. 'Anyhow, I've seen it already,' she added.

Horton endured the situation with stoic dignity as Yeats delicately revealed more words written under the Brighton mystic's pale skin. They were not exactly a postscript, being in a different hand and style:

my mortal needs you yeats 500 they
have her blythe road risk all your time
now they are coming they are deleting
me they are dTC CCC CAC CGC
CTA CCA CAA CC

'I must go to her,' said Yeats vaguely, already moving towards the stairs.

'Do you understand the messages?' said the Colonel, stepping adroitly in front of the poet so that he had to stop.

'No,' said Yeats, focusing, 'not entirely.'

'You are not concerned that you are acting on a threat and a warning from the fairies which have spontaneously written themselves upon the back and – er – behind of your friend?'

'No, not really.'

'Good,' said the Colonel briskly, standing aside. 'Your future with Imperial British Intelligence is assured, if you survive, of course. Whatever is threatening Stephanie is mainly interested in you, I'm afraid. It is very dangerous. Don Eduardo ...'

'What about Don Eduardo?'

'He has been extremely troubled, said that the wrongness in the land of the gods which brought him here was increasing. He seemed to know at once that something had happened to Stephanie, something on the psychic level. He appeared to think it was his special responsibility to do something about it, almost as if he blamed himself. Seems to have a very high regard and affection for you, may I say. He was convinced if he could talk to the gods, our fairies, he could sort it out. I think he could not believe in inimical extra-naturals. His only experience has been of the gods as benevolent guides and educators of the People. He would not be dissuaded. Frankly, I don't think he quite trusts our abilities. I very much fear though that he is a foreigner in our land of Faerie, just as you would be amongst his Amazonian gods and spirits. His knowledge is great, but I do not think it is the right knowledge.'

'How can you be sure? Have you asked him?'

'I cannot ask him because he cannot speak. Don Eduardo went into the other world last night and remains there. Something is wrong. Very wrong. As you have seen, he is lying upstairs now as if asleep, but it is not sleep. We dare not let a doctor near him, his condition would not be understood and a clumsy attempt to revive him might kill him. We can only wait. We think if you survive, so will he. He practically said as much, before he left us.'

Yeats thought of the wise dark eyes which seemed to be looking out from the dark green shade of an ancient forest, the gentle simplicity of 'I like the gas lamps' and the fragile strength of a native magician, for whom the created world was only good. He thought of Annie Horniman's thin fingers dropping a pinch of mixed herbs on hot coals and intoning the sacred name of Ta-hu-tah seven times through her nose. He thought of himself, of how right he had been, how wrong he had been.

'I will go to Blythe Road,' he said.

'Your enemy is expecting you.'

'Now,' said Yeats.

'Very good,' said the Colonel, and Mrs Biggs agreed, beaming her approval, chin resting on her joined hands, appreciating Yeats as if he were a free show.

'Mr Horton might like to resume his clothing,' said the Colonel.

'What about the message on my back?' said Horton.

'There is no message on your back,' said the Colonel.

As Horton strained to see over his own shoulder and Mrs Biggs came to have a look too, the Colonel clicked his briefcase closed with a brassy snap and said: 'They had no more need of it once it had been read by the intended recipient. The melanin has been reabsorbed.'

'*They* again?' said Yeats. 'Which ones are these? And is Horton right about angels and devils?'

'In a way, I think, yes. We ourselves do not really understand, and our records go back more than three hundred years,' said the Colonel. 'We're opening up the old files again, but it's early days - we've a lot of ground to make up after what was lost or thrown away during the Age of Enlightenment. When science closed its eyes to the extranatural, nearly all intelligent enquiry ceased, in exactly the area that we need it now. Angels and devils may be as accurate as anything else in terms of what you may experience in the next twenty four hours.'

'I must tell you,' said Yeats, quietly, just for the Colonel, 'that I am not doing this for IBI, Britain or its empire.'

The Colonel for a few moments looked up keenly at the tall poet's strong jawline and determinedly set features, then turned away as if the matter was of no consequence.

'Of course not,' he said, 'and we're not a marriage bureau. You'll find Igor outside with the Parker automobile. Crowley will come too. He will ensure you get there at the right time. You are an important man today. Goodbye, Yeats.'

Only when the Colonel said the word *today* did Yeats realize that midnight had come and gone and that dawn was not far off. It was the second of March, 1899.

Goodbye?

*

Stephanie Toughguid, born Stephanie de Beauharnais, one and only true love of W. B. Yeats, sat slumped on the East End pavement, her back against filthy brickwork, the blue lambswool coat turning grey with soot. Her slender stockinged legs were extended carelessly in front of her and one of her shoes was missing. Two men, street urchins grown up and charmlessly vicious, were watching her carefully from across the rubbish-strewn street, like alleycats who have found an escaped canary and are having a problem believing their luck – but only a temporary problem. Stephanie's dark eyes were empty and wandering. If Yeats had seen that dull look he would have gone fighting mad as he had not done since the insults of his first day at an English school; but there was no Yeats, just the perpetual hum of the East End rookeries. The two shabby predators glanced at each other and stepped off the pavement. They knew how it went now.

Halfway across the road they stopped, turned in their tracks and became alley-cats who have come face to face with a tiger. It was not easy, sauntering and running at the same time, but they managed it. A figure had appeared as if from nowhere. It was bulky and darkly-clad, a tall hat and thick cloak making it seem inhumanly large. The dangerous sense of purpose which had seen off the two loiterers did not diminish from closer at hand. There was heavy breathing. There was sweat. The great side-whiskers stooped over the helpless woman and eyes glittered triumphantly in the shade of the hat brim. A hairy hand groped in a capacious side pocket and came out with something that glittered. Stephanie looked up slowly, her hair falling over her face in lank tendrils; she did not otherwise react. Suddenly from behind the great looming shape darted a sharp-faced woman in a long brown coat, with her hair in the kind of bun that can only be called severe, in the same sense as a severe wound or crisis.

'That's not necessary,' said the sharp-faced woman briskly. 'She doesn't want money, she needs taking home. She's no street-girl, surely you can see that. Look at her hands.' She gently pushed the young woman's hair back to look at her face, and drew back in surprise as if she had been stung.

Her companion straightened up and returned the shiny half-crown to his pocket. He stood there, still massive but robbed of the air of menace he had briefly possessed, largely because ducks are not dangerous. Sergeant Platimer stood awaiting orders. He felt he had done his bit. There was no doubt about who was in charge.

Miss Cracknell, who had helped the troubled policeman about the fairies and some other matters too, was looking carefully at the young woman on the pavement. She observed the great splash of brown hair around the pale face, the lips, pale, chapped and parted, and especially the dark eyes, open, unfocused and restlessly moving from side to side, up and down.

'Taken,' she said firmly.

'Does she need the doctor?' said Platimer. He was feeling strangely alone without the voice in his ear, prompting and guiding. It had brought them unerringly, straight to where Stephanie had been left, half-conscious and vulnerable, on the South London pavement.

'No,' said Miss Cracknell. 'I don't think that is what she needs.'

'Not the doctor?' said Sergeant Platimer, surprised but humbly uncertain. Like many uniformed men with authority in their jobs, he rather enjoyed being bossed around by strong-minded ladies, now and again, especially by women like Miss Cracknell, whose figure gave the exciting impression of large natural forces held in check and harnessed for the betterment of mankind. 'Can you do anything for her?'

'I'm not sure,' said Miss Cracknell, bending over the girl, 'maybe not – but I know someone who probably can.'

It had surprised Maud Cracknell that the *she* who needed Platimer's help was the new Golden Dawn girl, because Mrs 'Toogood' could obviously take care of herself. A brief inspection had told the witch what she needed to know. The girl was displaying the classic symptoms of being elf-blasted or fairy-taken, terms misunderstood by the non-magical. In secret witch lore they meant that the victim had been robbed of their birth fairy, their guiding spirit. Fortunately there was at the Golden Dawn a man with the magical knowledge and strength of mind to combat whatever dark power had the young woman in its grip. Miss Cracknell just hoped that Mr William Yeats would get out of bed early enough to attend the Extraordinary General Meeting.

Sergeant Platimer was also surprised. As the big policeman watched Miss Cracknell tending to the girl, something nipped his earlobe and said, 'She needs your help.'

*

Hardy and Doyle had retreated, as fast as a horse tram and suburban train could take them, to Hardy's apartment. Doyle was reluctant to go home and seemed to be in a state of shock. He kept glancing at the older man as if wondering what the Dorset author was thinking. Thomas Hardy at fifty-nine was proving much tougher than anyone could possibly have guessed. Doyle did not understand how Philo Maynebeam could paralyse and kill just by moving his hands in certain ritual ways, but he did know that he was feared by everyone who knew of his existence, even those in government, even, so it was said, the Prime Minister, Lord Salisbury. He had seen Maynebeam direct his deadly malice at Hardy, and he had seen him defeated. Defeated but not destroyed. Philo Maynebeam, whoever or whatever he might be, was still out there somewhere in the darkness.

Now Doyle sat with his shoes and socks off, his hair sticking up in clumps, staring at the wall and fiddling with his gun, after half-heartedly setting about cleaning it then giving up. Hardy was on the floor with the map. He looked like a child playing with a new toy, until the hawklike profile was revealed in a sudden dip of the long head down to read the detail. After a minute or so he looked up, his normally bright eyes sombre.

'This is big, Doyle,' he said. 'It's so big, it's frightening. These people are trying to change the face of the world. Come and see.'

Doyle did not move. He looked depressed and scuffed irritably with a fleshy palm at the knee of one large crossed leg. '...such a bad thing?' he appeared to mutter. Hardy did not seem to hear him and bent his small head with its halo of lively grey hair over the unrolled map again. 'They've changed the names,' he said, running a firm architectural finger from east to west so that the thick paper crackled. 'See here – Ireland is shown as all one country, with an enormous city in the south – makes Dublin look like a village.'

'What about America?' said Doyle, without looking up. His tone was subdued, with none of its usual hearty energy, but still the Dorset man was too engrossed to notice.

'Why, it's not marked as the United States of America at all,' said Hardy. 'The whole continent – South America too – is shown as a British possession, and there's a name, going right down the map, hang on, it's sideways, hard to read... it's...

'Saxonia,' said Doyle, clearly and with a deadly quietness. Hardy at last looked up.

'Don't point that damn gun over here, Doyle,' he said. When Conan Doyle kept the big revolver where it was, Hardy looked beyond it to Doyle's face. Slowly he stood up, the map forgotten.

'Doyle?' said Hardy, as if the man with the gun might be an imposter with a perfect likeness to the creator of Sherlock Holmes.

In fact Doyle had never looked less like himself, so Hardy could be forgiven for clutching at straws. He looked terrible, his face blotched and puffy, his eyes bulging with the effort of betrayal.

'Just... just...,' Doyle said, then, 'Oh, for God's sake...' The big man lowered the gun and launched himself from his chair, one ham-sized fist already arcing like a scythe-point to lay the little novelist out. Hardy watched the fist like someone who knew all about scythes, and leaped inside its arc of travel, driving his small bullet head right into Doyle's surprised face.

'Hello again!' said Hardy sadly, looking down at the groaning bloody-nosed Doyle and drawing back one hobnailed boot. 'You city folk never learn.'

*

'I don't know what's wrong with the wretched thing.'

They had emerged from the basement garage of IBI's London safe house at a sedate five miles an hour, joining the stream of horse-drawn traffic with a lot of exaggerated head turning and fussing over the controls on the part of the bald-headed driver. Yeats remembered Stephanie's cool style of driving with a pang of the heart and he wished that Igor would go faster.

He got his wish. As soon as clear road opened up, Igor's foot went down: one click, two, three and they were moving faster than the thirty miles per hour which had disturbed Yeats on his first experience of the electric car – much faster. If that had been thirty miles per hour, this must be touching sixty.

Instead of turning towards Knightsbridge and the Kensington Road they shot under Marble Arch and through the great gates at Hyde Park Corner without slowing down and veered into the broad avenue of South Drive. And stopped. With Igor's heavy foot still flat to the boards, Mr Parker's automobile had slid gracefully to a halt, near silent as ever apart from the scrunch of tyres, on the tan gravel, pointing up that invitingly straight drive.

The great South Drive of Hyde Park was where London's wealthy and powerful had ridden and driven, to see and be seen, since the time of King Charles I. At this hour it was empty, a wide smooth track, pale in the first light of day, leading directly to Stephanie; and the electric car still sat there and would not go. Igor seemed a lot less confident when he was not encouraging people to behave properly and it was Crowley who was peering into the opened hatch that gave access to the engine space, while Igor sat disconsolately in the driver's seat, leaning on the wheel and staring at nothing in particular. Yeats remained in the back seat, restlessly rapping his knuckles against the polished wooden frame of the open door.

'You know what?' Yeats said suddenly, swinging his long legs out and finding the ground with his size twelve shoes. 'It's not that far. I'll just...'

By the time Igor realized what he meant, Yeats was almost out of sight, running as if for his life across familiar ground, sure of his purpose, sure of his way, sure even of how many paces it took to cross Kensington Gardens.

'Let him go,' said Crowley, putting a restraining hand in Igor's arm. 'The Colonel said let him go.'

*

'Stop him,' said Oberon to the Bucca Dhu. 'I have decided. You have not been efficient and Stephanie de Beauharnais still lives, even though you have sent her to the Dark. You say they are taking her to the Blythe Road temple. This Yeats must not be allowed to reach her. She should be beyond any human help by now, but uncertainties are spawning uncertainties and threatening the Plan. Since the Plan itself guarantees that she will die if Yeats fails to reach Blythe Road, go now and put right your mistake. Prevent him from leaving the Park. The mortal Yeats must not reach his true love, he must not get to Blythe Road tonight. Away, perform my will, and this time avoid error.'

'I go, Lord' said the Bucca Dhu, stung by its master's words, 'and I shall prevent the mortal Yeats from leaving the park.'

You would have to have been a lot less preoccupied than Oberon to have noticed the look in the Bucca Dhu's eye.

*

In the empty grey world just before dawn, putting the pain in his ribs somewhere else until there was time to feel it, Yeats was running through Kensington Palace Gardens, the last stretch before he re-joined the public road that led to Stephanie. From a grove of whispering ash trees something flashed across his path at head height, making him recoil in mid-stride. Bumble-bees again; only it wasn't. This time he had quite clearly seen a humanoid shape at the centre of a blur of rainbow wings, but when he turned his head to follow the motion, there was nothing to be seen but a blackbird tapping for worms on the verge. He looked a little beyond the bird and saw the same boy and girl, identical twins, who had chanted that strange half-familiar rhyme on his previous walk through the Gardens. Now they were kneeling down by a line of evergreen shrubs bordering the path. He was vaguely aware that it was rather early for them to be out. They must live locally, said his mind, determined to make sense of it; perhaps they were embassy children. They did look slightly foreign, with their pale serious faces and raven black hair. Something amongst the close-growing stems was enthralling them. The boy seemed about to poke at whatever it was with a bit of stick, but the girl held his arm by the elbow, stopping him with a look of horrified disapproval.

Yeats looked away. He distrusted children. They reminded him of his father. What was he thinking? He had to get to Blythe Road. He felt faint, appalled that he could so easily be distracted. He made to run on, but the girl was calling after him in the sort of high, clear and annoying voice which could not be ignored.

'Come here,' she said, gesturing urgently. Yeats did not respond, was turning away, when the boy said, very distinctly, without looking up, 'They have taken her.'

'What?' said Yeats. 'What did you say?' but the girl just beckoned. In agony between the urgency of getting to the Blythe Road temple and the growing sensation that this encounter had some meaning for him, Yeats approached; and yet the nearer he drew, the more he felt sure that he was making a mistake. He hoped they hadn't found something horrible, a suicide or something. 'Go on,' said the girl, 'look.'

Yeats peered gingerly into the shadowed ground under the low-growing bushes. The thought came, too late, that it might be some juvenile practical joke. Little creatures were moving. Mice? The movement was too slow, measured. His eyes adjusted. Human figures, none taller than his middle finger, were winding in solemn procession through daffodil shoots and bush stems. The figures shone slightly with their own light, a pale green. Their skin also looked green, and perhaps it was.

Two figures, male and female led the column. She was dressed in filmy robes of rain-washed blue; he was in fiery red and wearing a crown like icicles set in a golden circlet. Behind them came six fairies bearing a seventh, cold and stiff, couched in and partly covered by a great dock leaf. Dozens more followed, two by two, in a courtly train which snaked solemnly through the undergrowth; the scene was accompanied by a high tinkling, on the edge of hearing, like the sound of frost forming.

It is a fairy funeral, thought Yeats, like the one seen by William Blake. He felt warmly fulfilled, silly with gratified desire. The world rang with new ideas. Then a sobering memory came into his mind, of some last words written in haste on his friend's skin: *they are coming, they are deleting me.* He knew beyond any doubt that the small white-haired corpse on the dock leaf bier was that of Stephanie's fairy. He knew, because the face of the fairy was his own face.

He let the leaves fall into place and straightened. 'You saw them too,' he said to the girl, but she was not there. Neither was her twin brother. The sparkly feeling was changing into something else. The sandy paths looked white as if there had been a sudden light fall of snow. Panicking, with a roaring in his ears, he bent down again and pushed the leafy screen aside. No fairy prince and his consort, no mourners, just his own Little Man, the Fairy staring at him from the leaf mould amongst the daffodil stems with a strange expression that Yeats had never seen, never imagined could be on the easy-going Fairy's face: fear.

'Get out, now, go, GO!' screamed the Fairy.

But it was too late. Yeats straightened up, feeling the blood leave his head. This was nothing unusual for someone who had been six feet tall at fourteen; even at thirty-four, standing up suddenly was liable to fill his vision with spots and make his ears sing. Kensington Gardens turned pale and distant, which was normal; but it stayed that way, which was not. He shut his eyes, which usually helped. It did not. After his recent experiences, Yeats recognized the slight nausea, the odd feeling in the back of his nose, an excitement which might turn to fear at any moment – magic was at work, real magic, which could not co-exist with the human world.

This time there was something else, a feeling of being very small and very near to something of unbearable size and mass, as if he were a mite in the dust beneath an enormous door stuck half-open in the silence of a giant's house on an eternal Sunday afternoon. He was being stifled and crushed, shrinking into himself, getting smaller and smaller until he became a cellular atomy in his own body, smaller again until that cell was a whole world to him, smaller and smaller to a state in which the laws of the macroscopic universe meant nothing, smaller and yet smaller until he slipped through the web of Time and floated down as pure spirit in the guise of a pale flickering flame haunting the Emperor's pavement in eternal Byzantium – no, better, haunting, so it was said, the Emperor's golden pavement in eternal...

WHACK! Something had struck his face. Yeats straightened up, too quickly, and had to wait until the white sparks stopped flying and swirling in his vision, like leaping sprites, fire fairies. Fairies. Something had just taken place but he could not, could not call to mind what it was. A warm wind fanned his cheek, not like a smoky London gust at all. No time now. They had Stephanie. He tensed as if to run, relaxed, looked around and sat down in the long damp grass at the side of the path. He rested his chin on his knees and frowned, trying to think. Who was Stephanie? He felt very tired. Regardless of the dewy undergrowth, the mortal Yeats stretched his long limbs out on the ground and went to sleep.

After a moment, several small beings appeared silently from behind dock leaves and daffodil shoots and stood looking at the unconscious poet. None of them even slightly resembled a flower.

WHACK! Yeats had been slapped by his Fairy. Which was impossible. She was standing in front of him, frowning angrily into his face. Also impossible.

'You have grown,' he said stupidly, his voice sounding like someone else's. His ears were ringing; it had been a hefty slap.

'I have not,' said the Fairy. 'It is you that have changed. Something has allowed you to cross over to the Fairy world. We were not ready. You were not ready. If I had not been here to administer the Clout of Greeting...'

'Greeting!' cried Yeats, rubbing his sore face. 'Is that what you call it?'

His Fairy said nothing, just watched him, and waited. Yeats looked down at himself, looked at the Fairy, looked around at the grass stems which towered over his head and...

'I have become a fairy!' he screamed and went on screaming. There followed a few minutes of behaviour which did Yeats no credit at all, a world class panic which his Fairy simply watched with folded arms until the transmogrified poet had run out of verbal and physical resources.

He found that nothing he did had any effect. The new daffodil shoots bore his kicks with insulting indifference. The grass blades ignored his furious attempts to rip them up with the patience of an old dog having its tail pulled by a baby. Only the blackbird looked at him with a bright seeing look in its eye and flew off suddenly when one of his desperate rushes took him too near it.

'Why?' said Yeats, stupidly. He was sitting slumped, exhausted, with his back against a woody stem, long legs stretched on the damp leaf-mould. 'Why here? Why now? I must get to Blythe Road.'

'You have filled a vacancy,' said his Fairy, frowning down at him. 'We think there is some law at work. We think we remember it, at the very beginning. We think the right conditions for its operation have never before existed. '

'What law? What has happened?'

'If a mortal loses its birth fairy, a replacement is gradually called into being. In this case, something has accelerated the process and found an unusual alternative. You have become your true love's fairy.'

'The one I saw, dead, on that bier?'

'I don't know what you saw.'

'But you were standing here!'

'Not a single word of that statement has the same meaning in the fairy world.'

'What, not even the conjunction?'

'Nope!'

The fairy unfolded its slender arms and straightened its baglike hat. Yeats sat up as a strange pang crossed his chest. Could fairies have heart attacks?

'What do I do now?' said Yeats.

'What you were going to do, of course,' said his Fairy calmly. 'Circumstances have changed but you must get to the Golden Dawn's temple in Blythe Road and deal with what you find there. They are saying it is the only way to bring the mortal Stephanie back from where They've taken her.'

'Well,' said Yeats, and his Fairy watched him closely. 'Well,' he said again, 'we'd better be going then.' They set off, Yeats in front, so that he did not see the smile upon his Fairy's face; it was pleased with him.

On they went through the undergrowth and parallel to the paths that he knew so well. William Butler Yeats was now barely longer than his name, and he found it heavy going. After a few minutes' trekking, they had travelled about thirty feet.

'It's no good,' said the poet. He was hot and sweaty and finding it hard to breathe.

'Here,' said the Fairy, 'drink some of this.' It handed a richly embossed leather bottle to Yeats, who took a swig and said, 'What is this? A magical potion?'

'Just water,' said the Fairy. 'You need it. You're dehydrating.'

Yeats tried to laugh and catch his breath at the same time, his face doing what Hardy might have called Crazy Peasant.

'That doesn't make the slightest sense,' he gasped. 'None of this makes the slightest sense. If I can be reduced to this size, and if I am sharing in the mode of life of fairy beings, though I can hardly believe it, then I shouldn't be physically suffering. Ronaldus, in the De Spirituum Natura, says...

...I'm not really out of breath, am I?'

'No,' said the Fairy, smiling, and took its hat off.

'It is only because I thought I was, or should be,' said Yeats. 'And I am not actually thirsty. And I haven't just had a drink of water, have I?'

'No,' said the Fairy.

'And,' said Yeats, gently taking the Fairy by the arm and moving it from the shade of a clump of snowdrops, 'Fairy, you're not a Little Man, are you?

'But you were always my Little Man,' said Yeats crossly.

'While you were a baby. After that... you just didn't notice,' said the Fairy. It would not meet his eyes.

Yeats looked carefully at his Fairy. A pleasant face sprinkled with freckles. A wide mouth. And the long brown hair had always been tucked up into that bag-like hat. No one could blame him, surely? Anyway, he had always been so much bigger than his Fairy. How could he be expected to notice? He looked into the Fairy's dark eyes and saw a great hurt, carried patiently.

'Fairy,' he said, reaching out, 'I...'

'Follow me,' the Fairy cried, ducking away from his touch. She ran off through the wintery stems, her grey bag-hat back on her head, her long hair tucked inside, her long black coat fluttering behind her. Her feet hardly seemed to touch the cold earth and Yeats found when he ran after her that there was no particular reason why they should.

He chased her all the way, over the Serpentine and past the Round Pond, and finally caught her at the great iron gates where he had seen the attack on the Colonel's son. They rested on the gilded scroll-work, thirty feet above the ground. The Fairy was pink-cheeked and out of breath and her eyes were dancing. 'I know you're pretending now,' said

Yeats. 'For, d'ye see, I am not the slightest affected.'

The Fairy laughed and ruffled his hair. 'I am out of breath because I like it, silly Man. And I am only caught when I want to be.' The Fairy gave Yeats a little push over the heart and it was like being kicked by a horse. He fell off the gate and sideslipped like a leaf to the gravel, falling and flying according to whether his insight or intellect dominated.

W. B. Yeats, thirty-four years old and four and a half inches high, stood invisibly amongst the passers-by, his black brows knitted in thought. He was putting together what he had recently learned. People like Bernard Shaw, who disapproved of Yeats' interests and thought him lightweight, never understood or valued the strength of the Anglo-Irish poet's intellect, because it was given over to things they despised. Yeats had a good mind, and now he applied it to fairy physics.

'When I thought I was thirsty, I was. So I am in the state I believe myself to be in,' he said to himself. 'The physical laws still apply, in a way, but I can be anything I wish. To be light, I have to make myself as air, if I want go somewhere fast I have to think what is fast, and be that.' Something else about Yeats – here he was, invisible and too small for a fair fight with a garden gnome, flying around Kensington in pursuit of love – and he was still sane. It came from really believing in magic; it was the non-magical world that he found so difficult.

A few seconds later, a blur travelling at the speed of a stooping hawk arrived at the front door of the greatest magical order of modern times. Unfortunately the over-confident poet had not foreseen the eventual need to travel at the speed of a *stopping* hawk, and the blur flattened itself like a spent bullet against the ornamental brickwork of No. 36.

'I don't think that's very nice,' Yeats said when, after a few confused seconds, he had regained his proper shape and floated to the pavement. His Fairy was rolling on the floor laughing, kicking up her black-stockinged legs. 'Well, it was funny,' she said, standing up. 'You're funny.'

Yeats drew himself up to his full height of four and a half inches. He looked at the Fairy. She dropped her eyes but not quickly enough. 'Fairy...' he said, starting forward, but she had turned and walked straight through the closed door. This gave Yeats a problem.

What could go through a closed door? If he could imagine it, he could do it. Anyway, he had seen the Fairy do it. And now she was on the other side. This made Yeats feel angry and unsure. After all, she was his fairy. A cloud seemed to pass overhead and Yeats shivered even though he was not cold. *They* had made him come to Blythe Road. *They* had Stephanie and *They* would be sure he would come for her. And *They* were probably on the other side of this door, waiting. What had the Fairy been thinking? But of course, she hadn't. She had been laughing at him; his Fairy had seemed happy, for the first time that Yeats could remember. She had always been cross or critical, earnest or ironic. There had always been a sad slant to her smile, he suddenly realized, and a hard edge to her laughter but an edge not meant for him. He had never before seen that wide contented smile on his Fairy's face, never heard that bubbling laugh. Yeats began to panic as he saw a Story taking shape.

Calm down. Think. True sight. The Fairy had said he had the True Sight of the Poet's Eye. Use it. He stared at the door while the back of his fairy neck felt cold. Big shadowy shapes of people billowed past, mooing. He ignored them. He stared at the door. He knew all about the door. Miss Horniman, the tea heiress and committee expert had paid to have it fitted when she fell out with Mathers. She had said it made a statement more in keeping with the dignity and traditions of the Society. The statement made, Yeats reflected, by the triple-ply hardwood and patent steel fittings, was 'This is a very strong door'.

Use True Sight. Yeats stared up at the shiny new blue-painted door, waiting for his gift to kick in. He took in the closed letterbox, the covered keyhole: the door was a wall with hinges. Nothing could pass through steel-reinforced Malayan teak wood, not an ant, not a trickle of water, not even smoke. Nothing could go through such a door. Nothing.

Then he had it: of course! He was misdirecting his True Sight of the Poet's Eye. He was using it on the door. He should have been turning it on the words. If nothing could go through a door like that – then he must become Nothing! Just as he had shot through the air like a diving hawk, he would waft through the door as nothingness personified. He set his mind to the task with all the confidence of his new powers. It was easier this time. The secret was to stand like *that* and narrow your eyes like *this...*

Nothing was beyond him. Perhaps he ought to have thought about that for a moment.

As soon as Yeats had reduced himself to nothing, he knew he might have made a mistake. Even in the most profound darkness you know where you are, even if you don't know where anything else is; but Yeats now found himself without length, breadth and depth. He was the dimensionless point of Geometry. He had willed himself to become Nothing; and was discovering how powerful infinite vacuum energy was. The Blythe Road scene – sky, buildings, trees, pavement and people, was wrapped around him in a bright sphere like a perfectly clear soap bubble.

'Light is bending around me,' he thought.

'You have bent Space, and soon you will do the same to Time, Your Nothingness,' a voice said. 'And then where will you be? Haven't you heard that Nature abhors a vacuum? I do like the word "abhors", so expressive of hatred and social superiority, don't you think?'

As soon as the voice spoke, the colours dimmed in the bubble and the light of day began to fade. It felt cold. Again the voice spoke: 'Who is the Little Man now?' It was a deep grinding voice, like a glacier talking.

Again Yeats felt the inexorable pressure upon his mind and the dry dusty tickle at the back of a nose he no longer had – this could not be happening in a human universe and so magic, strong magic had to be at work.

'Who are you?' he said. He had to reach right down for the words. They had hidden themselves at the base of his non-existent gullet. They did not want to be spoken to the Voice.

'You want my name? Of course. Once you have my name, you can control me – that's how the magic works, isn't it?' The glacier met an extra-hard outcrop of rock. The owner of the Voice was laughing.

'But you will also know, Master Magician, that there are names that kill. The unutterable Names which are too dangerous to be spoken by any less than gods and can only be written, backwards and without the vowels, in water, on water. Would you have me say such a name?'

For Yeats, high on the realization that years of magical study had not been wasted, the answer was simple and clear.

'Yes,' he said, 'please do.'

'You're quite sure,' said the Voice.

'Yes.'

'Actually,' said the Voice, suddenly less gravelly-grand, 'I've got a great many names. Shiva, Arioch, Saturn: in fact you can summon me with almost anything you like, and I'll answer.'

Yeats was remembering his lesson from the Fairy. The way to control a mortal was to encourage him to think he was controlling you. Don't fall for it!

'I know those names,' he said, having to force the words out against the pressure of condensed light inside the bubble which contained him. At the same moment he saw that he was being observed. Outside the bubble and dimly visible through it was the silhouette of a human figure, head inclined, as if pensive or curious. Yeats had the disorientating feeling that the Voice was created by the silent watcher but not coming from it. 'Yes,' Yeats repeated, 'those names are known to me, but I do not think they are your real names, and I do not think they can control you. I think they are your masks.'

'Would you prefer Kether, Ens, Jahbulon?'

'No,' said Yeats, his voice stronger but trembling with the effort. 'Not those. I feel they are also masks. I think I know your true name, because it is what you are. I think you are N…'

Time stopped. The word which Yeats' non-existent mouth tried to utter got stuck on the first syllable, drawing the sound out like the drone that warns everyone in a half-mile radius that a bag-pipe is about to go off. At the same time the crystalline light-bubble encasing him dulled as if it had been turned to jelly. Yeats watched himself being turned into a picture of a man inside a semi-transparent sphere, curled up like a foetus. He was on a page of thick creamy old paper with beautifully uneven edges. Of course that man could not move, he was just an engraved illustration in a book of alchemical symbols. The engraving showed a circle of stars outside his sphere, and beyond the circle, angels. The angel Intelligences looked out at Yeats curiously and he could hear their wings rustle.

'What will you do, little man?' they said.

'Seek help from the master, William Blake,' Yeats said unhesitatingly (it was a good thing he was not the man being turned into an engraving, because if he were he would not be able to say a word by now – he was completely flat)

Detachedly gazing on the engraved man in his bubble, who was now gasping like a fish, Yeats calmly composed his mind in order to work British Magic. 'I summon Master William Blake in the name of

Tharmas and the Water of the Western World, from the darkness of Northern Ulro I call upon Urizen with Air and Swords and passionate Luvah with a burning branch from the East. This trinity I place within a square as I summon him also in the name of our Los, Earth of Paradise, Creator of the Fairies of Albion. To this quadrate I add its own unity to make the secret Quincunx and under the protection of this picture of the tragic division which gives Man life and thought, I summon Blake, Master of Visions, who saw through the qalipoth and tried to teach us better.'

Yeats chanted the formulae of the invocation loudly and with a fine skirling tone, lift of brow and flash of eye. Magical conjuration was like ordering food in a posh restaurant; if you faltered, the very forces you invoked could sense weakness and turn on you.

As soon as he had finished the summoning on 'better', Yeats sensed someone standing just beside and slightly behind him. He could hear breathing, the open-mouthed kind that suggests the breather has a cold, or perhaps is somewhat asthmatic. He must not turn and look. What did one say? Master William Blake sounded like something stencilled on a school trunk, while Mister Blake was just too ordinary. O Blake might embarrass him, while William was too familiar. 'Blake?' said Yeats, looking straight ahead, 'William Blake?'

The loud breathing behind Yeats' right ear was suddenly interrupted by a startled gasp. 'Yeats,' said a voice, 'it's W. B. Yeats again.'

'O Blake,' Yeats began chanting, but without conviction.

'I'm not Blake, for Christ's sake.' Now the breathy voice behind Yeats sounded angry and - with its harmonics of scholarship and intellectual force - unexpectedly familiar.

'You're Ackroyd,' said Yeats, turning round, 'Madame Lauderdale's Red Indian spirit guide.' He saw a middle-aged Englishman in a beige cardigan and baggy blue trousers, with the lineaments of hope and experience competing for dominance in a round indoors face.

'Madame Lauderdale?' said Ackroyd. 'So that's who she is! She's been pestering me in my dreams for months. She was so persistent that eventually I resorted to telling her that all *was* bloody well with Jimmy, just to shut her up. What's going on? Is this some Golden Dawn magical stuff?'

'No,' said Yeats. 'At least - I don't think so. This is to do with Fairies. And spiralling snakes. And a secret which could destroy the world.'

'What secret?' said Ackroyd.

Yeats sketched a shape in the air with his forefinger.

'Well, so?' said Ackroyd.

'Painted on 30,000 year old rock, discovered last year,' said Yeats.

'Ah,' said Ackroyd. Pause. 'The Islamic fundamentalists aren't going to like it.'

'Who are they?' said Yeats. 'Turks? Sudanese?'

Ackroyd's eyes gleamed. 'If this is a dream,' he said, 'it's unusually consistent. That's exactly what you would say. I'm impressed by my own subconscious.'

'To say it is a dream,' said Yeats, in his lecturing manner, 'is not to devalue the experience...'

'Why you, I wonder,' said Ackroyd. 'I wasn't trying for you.'

'Of course not,' replied Yeats. 'It was I who...' Then Ackroyd's words sank in. 'You were summoning? You are a magician?'

Ackroyd thought for a moment before replying. 'Yes, I suppose so, in my own way.'

'Oh,' said Yeats, 'an amateur.'

Ackroyd's round face was briefly lit up by a smile. 'Yes,' he said, 'definitely an amateur.'

'I suppose that explains the error,' said Yeats in the superior tones of someone who has never spent three useless hours chanting necromantic formulae with less to show for it than if he had been trying to borrow money from a cat. 'Whose spirit were you trying to raise?'

'Aleister Crowley's,' said Ackroyd.

Yeats started, brows thunderously drawn. Crowley again!

'He's a character in my next fiction,' said Ackroyd, sensing an atmosphere. 'Can't do his biog of course. He's still too dangerous. So one has to dress it up as post-modern fantasy. And I wouldn't call what I do raising spirits exactly. It is more a suspension of my own self which lets the other personality flow into the space. I suppose it is a kind of summoning.'

'But one does not raise the spirit of a living man,' Yeats said. Ackroyd looked at him, considering. 'Mr Yeats,' he said, with unexpected gentleness, 'think about that.'

The bubble of Nothing which nevertheless contained two men pulsed and swirled. 'Crowley is dead,' said Yeats.

'Yes,' said Peter Ackroyd and watched Yeats' face, and the thought which was forming there, with the tactful sympathy of a man who knows there is nothing we can really do for each other.

'I am dead too,' said Yeats.

'Yes,' said Ackroyd quietly.

'Then,' said Yeats, 'you also are dead, for you too have been summoned.'

'No,' said the spirit of Ackroyd yet-to-come, and the dull light of the Nothing bubble began to show through his corduroy jacket. 'I do not believe I am dead. I am just not alive, not when you are.' Ackroyd's expression sharpened. 'When exactly *are* you? The year!' he said eagerly, but his voice was thinning.

'1899,' Yeats replied, 'beginning of March.'

The writer from the future was now fading fast but Yeats saw his face take on a look of passionate intensity when he said this. Just before Ackroyd disappeared, Yeats could see his mouth opening and shutting rapidly and widely; he was obviously shouting but the words were inaudible and then he was gone. What had he been saying? Time to think about that later. That other man, the one in the alchemical engraving, was looking in a bad way.

Yeats knew really that he was the man in the picture. He also knew that if he knew that he knew, he would begin to believe that he had been magically trapped in an image, and that would be the end of him. So he un-knew it, and the bubble of time and space was held in existence by the power of his will, balancing being and nothingness.

'Impressive, for a mortal,' said the Voice, and then the shape of the dark watcher outside the bubble winked out with the sound of a receding exclamation mark. In one second the sun seemed to rise and Yeats felt a joyful sense of mastery. With the slightest of efforts he lifted the bubble of Nothing and floated it towards the Golden Dawn's front door. The teak and steel offered no more resistance to the Nothing-bubble than sea-mist to an iceberg, and he was quickly through and into the gloom of the stairwell. There the poet reasserted his existence, finding his centre and allowing the Yeatsian ego to inflate to its natural size, which took a little time. Then, with a pop like a gas-jet lighting, Yeats the fairy appeared, and was immediately, furiously, attacked.

Returns

The lower section of an upstairs sash window at 36 Blythe Road slid up an inch and stuck. Somebody on the other side tried to shove it up further, but very carefully. Any upward pressure on the window frame tended to send him back down the steep and rain-slippery dormer roof where he had found a toe-hold. After a pause to let the lactic acid disperse from ageing muscles, cold fingertips again found a purchase, a knee braced itself on the narrow brick sill, and there was another silent eye-popping hernia-risking heave. The winter-swollen wood frame seemed to resist with cruel indifference, then suddenly gave and the window went up with a rush and rumble that sounded titanic in the still small West Kensington hours.

For a full minute nothing else happened; someone was listening, waiting for any reaction. Then a thin green-socked calf and scuffed brown boot were slung over the sill, and a man dressed in a kilt and dark green Highland jacket, and whose foxy head was topped with a feathered tam o'shanter, ducked through the gap. MacGregor Mathers, co-founder and only surviving Chief of the Golden Dawn, had come back to claim his own.

It was a good thing he had known about the window, but it was Crowley who had warned him about the Second Order's meeting: secret and early in the day to defeat intervention, and behind changed locks. Well, he was in, and he was early. He really needed to be. The purpose of the Extraordinary General Meeting was to vote him out.

Mathers was on a make-or-break mission to recapture the Golden Dawn from the upstarts who wanted to steal it from him. He was going to achieve this by magic, Indian magic. Maud Gonne's swami had explained it all to him in Paris. He was to light the Shiva vengeance-candle below ground level in the basement, at exactly nine minutes past nine in the morning. The power of the Hindu god would purge the premises of treachery, easing the path of true adherents of the universal syncretic Way and ridding the Society of the false, the shallow and the hypocritical - starting with Annie Horniman.

When Mathers had mildly questioned the occult basis of the operation, the heavily muffled Swami, who constantly complained about the cold and kept a red-chequered scarf wound around the lower part of his face, explained emphatically, in an almost incomprehensible accent, that the Shiva V-candle had never been known to fail. Mathers was not convinced by this assertion; he was, however, absolutely convinced that he needed W. B. Yeats on his side if he was going to retain the leadership of his own society; and it was made clear to him that he would get Yeats if he did what Maud Gonne wanted. Yeats would support him at the Extraordinary General Meeting, Miss Horniman would be defeated and everyone would come to their senses and recognize Mathers as undisputed leader of the Golden Dawn. And he was to remember, said Maud Gonne, nobody must know about the Shiva candle. 'For your followers to see the light, they must first be kept in the dark.'

'Of course,' he had said with the solemn emphasis befitting the head of the greatest magical order of modern times, 'for is it not said, that all goes by opposites in the Kalipot?'

'You are a real hierophant, Mathers, you know that?' Maud Gonne had said, in her well-bred hoot, with just the hint of a giggle, disconcerting in a woman built like a brick privy, 'and so is Willie. You are definitely a couple of hierophants. Together you will light the sacred flame of Truth under those silly people. Now, you will make sure you set off the candle in the cellar, won't you. It is Earth magic, you see, and the cthonic currents need to be engaged underground. Under the ground, Sammy, in the cellar – got it? At exactly nine minutes past nine on March 2nd, during their silly meeting. I expect that ghastly Farr woman will be presiding. Won't *she* get a surprise!'

Behind the famous apple-blossom complexion and la-di-da accent, Mathers reflected, there was something not quite nice about Maud Gonne.

On the top floor of 36 Blythe Road, Mathers reached outside for his back-pack and hauled it through. He felt for and found the heavy oil-paper wrapped cylinder of the Shiva candle through the canvas of the pack. It was all bollocks of course. He should know. Nevertheless, he had to go through the motions and give Maud and her swami what they wanted. It was worth it, to get his Golden Dawn back.

According to his loyal informant, the Extraordinary General Meeting would not start for two and a half hours. He could roll himself in a blanket till then and doze. He liked the sound of that, and said it aloud. Roll myself in a rough blanket. Roll myself roughly in a blanket. Stay ahead of the game, downwind of the quarry, your hairy knees blending with the heather, that was the Clan MacGregor way. If he remembered that his Highland ancestry was somewhat wishful, he suppressed the thought immediately with the ease of long practice. He would set up his make-do campaign bed in the Vault; as Chief of the Order, it was his right. It was also about the only place in the building where you could lie down out of a draught, apart from Maud Cracknell's room. This made him think about Maud Cracknell, which was another thought he would rather not have.

She had come down from (some whispered been *sent* down from) the Golden Dawn's Edinburgh branch, in mysterious circumstances and with her own independent income and had found a home above the Blythe Road Temple, in an extensive if odd-shaped eyrie under the eaves. She was the sort of person you could imagine needing somewhere handy for broom-based aerial commuting; she was also the kind of person you could imagine quietly watching you in some other shape than her own.

Mathers was attracted to and frightened of Maud Cracknell in about equal measure. He was troubled by her quiet confidence and evident knowledge in the supernatural field. This might seem surprising in the head of a magical society but males have not always appreciated women who make progress in their own profession without proper supervision by a man, and without asking permission.

Miss Cracknell was indeed very attractive and excitingly unworried about what people thought of her (it was how he knew about the broken window catch in her apartment) but instead of putting Mathers more in control, intimacy just made him feel that she was. She kept birds and animals and they were happy and not smelly, unlike Maud Gonne's menagerie; she had big bunches of dried herbs hanging from the rafters (and this in the heart of a city); she had a black cloak; she had a cauldron. She was a witch.

Thus it was that Mathers took great care as he tiptoed down the top-floor passage and past the door to Miss Cracknell's room. There was no light showing under her door and everything was very quiet. He tested every step in case a board was going to creak. Maud Cracknell was not part of the Horniman faction, as far as he knew, but he did not think she would side with him either. She was the sort of person who is on her own side and nobody else's. He had in any case technically – and actually - just broken into her home. Miss Cracknell gave the impression that she would have ways of dealing with burglars.

There was something humpy and black at the end of the darkened passageway which was not helping his nerves. Probably a hat-stand, although he could not remember one there. He felt a strong urge to keep looking over his shoulder. It was easy to imagine getting almost to the head of the stairs and hearing a dry little voice right in your ear, or receiving a light touch on the shoulder, and when you turned you would see a face but it would not be a human face.

Something brushed his ankle and he nearly cried out in fear. It was only one of Maud Cracknell's cats, and it immediately disappeared through a hole cut in her bedroom door. That humpy black thing at the end of the passageway really did look like a person, a small hunched figure silently waiting for him, guarding the stairs. He must get control of his nerves. This was ridiculous.

As he approached, sliding each foot carefully along the carpeting in case of creaks, the black thing looked less and less human. Then it moved and Mathers' heart nearly jumped out of his mouth.

It was a very big black bird sitting silent and motionless on a T-shaped perch. It was watching him with a very knowing look; he could see the tiny amount of moonlight that filtered into the passageway reflected in its eye. Its? Or her? He made to move and the bird opened its dagger-like beak. Mathers froze. The raven closed its beak, staring at him. He slid a foot forward and the bird opened its beak. He stopped, and the beak closed. He moved, the beak opened. Stop, close; move, open; stop, close; move, open... suddenly his nerve broke and Mathers ran for it, clattering down the steep attic stairs pursued by the harsh calls of the raven which sounded far too much like raucous human laughter.

He stumbled in the dark and fell at the foot of the stairs. Blessed relief! He was full length and face down on the familiar dusty carpet of the Temple, his Temple. He lay still for a minute or so, waiting for a door to open upstairs but nothing happened. No one could sleep through that. Maud Cracknell was not at home. *No, but her familiar is,* came the thought

Now to go down to the cellar. There would be a chance of encountering one of the Wilkinson family on the ground floor, but they had always been surprisingly uninterested in what their tenants were doing. Charles, the father, was a builder and carpenter, which had been useful from time to time. His wife Anne was a silent mouselike person, only interested in Edgar her seven year old, and now Frank, her baby, born last year. If anything, Mathers reflected, they did not even exhibit a normal amount of curiosity about the greatest magical society of modern times meeting just above their heads. Odd, really - still, it takes all sorts. Discounting the incurious Wilkinsons, there was nobody to stop him now. In fact, thought Mathers, why was he hurrying? He could do what he liked. He was Adeptus Exemptus; he was the first real person in the List; he was Number 5.

A marvellous idea came to him, a way to enjoy himself, impress the members and restore his authority. He would be discovered in the Vault, a second Rosenkreutz and a Locked Room mystery all in one! Nip down at ten to nine, light the Vengeance candle, and hare back up before all the members arrived. They'd never know in Paris. He would lie down in the pastos, the sacred casket of preservation and renewal. He would have his eyes closed and his arms crossed upon his breast. Or better, he would recline with one leg bent and crossed over the other. When they arrived for their Extraordinary General Meeting, the one they had tried to keep him out of, they would find him in the attitude of the Hanged Man, a living symbol of trials patiently borne, in a locked vault, within a locked building. Ah-hah!

As the women came in, they would twitter and peer at him, and he would open his eyes very suddenly and make them jump. Make the ladies jump. Jump the ladies. Moina, Moina, Moina, he intoned under his breath. He would have to make a noise first, or they would not know he was there. Something ethereal, a keening; Mathers experimented with a few high-pitched squeals and decided groaning would be better – the soul-charged groans of a man who has just materialized and isn't going to talk about it. 'Ooooggghhh!' he went, and liked it; he did another one: 'Oooooooggghhhhh!' This second one was so effective he actually frightened himself and lost his balance in the dark. He decided to open the Vault.

Now the fashion of the Vault of Christian Rosenkreutz at the Isis Urania Temple in Blythe Road was as this: a free-standing seven-sided inner chamber, roofed above and walled around with wooden panels eight feet by five. Each panel was divided into forty squares, each bearing a different symbol. The seven sides were all alike in size and shape and subdivision, and the forty squares on each side bore the same symbols. The symbols on each wall, besides the ten Sephiroth, were these: the four Kerubim, three Alchemical Principles, the three Elements, excluding Earth, the Seven Planets, Twelve Zodiacal Signs and one Wheel of the Spirit. The colouring varied: no two sides were alike in tint, and none of the squares was identical in colour except the single central upper square of each wall, which contained the Wheel of the Spirit. Each of the Seven walls was ruled by a different planet. The subsidiary squares represented the colouring of the combined forces of the planet; the symbol of each square was represented by the ground colour, while the symbol colour contrasted with or complemented that of the ground. These planetary sides were in a special order, neither astronomical nor astrological. The order was Saturn, Jupiter, Mars, Sun, Mercury, Venus, Moon and an initiate was expected to see at a glance that the planets were in the order of the spectral colours of the rainbow because an Adeptus of the Second Order was above all else an expert in the magical use of colour.

Above all else... Mathers paused at the door to the Vault, shook his head as if at an unseen accuser, and let himself in. At least they had not thought to change these locks. All was as it should be: in the centre of the heptagonal chamber stood a cloth-draped altar and beneath it the pastos, a man-long lidded casket. He rolled the altar aside, opened the lid of the coffin-like pastos, slung his pack in to serve as a pillow and got in after it. He lay on his back, hands folded on his stomach, and closed his eyes, just to get into the role. *Sleep.*

He woke with a start. Damn. How long had he been out? It still felt early, but the Vault was completely enclosed and it was too dark even to see his watch. Something had woken him. A sound from the meeting room. There it was again, a heavy tread, a leathery creak, as of someone in new shoes. People arriving already for the EGM. Must be keen. *Very* new shoes. He had not yet lit the Shiva V-candle, but here goes with the ethereal groaning...

'Oooooaaargh!'

Silence. Had he over-done it, scared them off? He drew in his breath to emit a more inviting groan, a come-and-see-the-awakening-magus groan, but before he could let it out - 'Aaaaarr – oooogh!' - a terrible blaring howl came from outside the Vault. It was so loud that it made the thin wooden walls vibrate. Then came a clicking, scratching noise. Someone or something was trying to get into the Vault, pawing at the handle, clumsily, suggesting long claws ill-adapted to round brass doorknobs. Mathers sat up in the pastos as abruptly if it really had some galvanic power. His mind was racing. The Vault, the sacred pastos, the magical images – what might he have called up? Thank God the door was locked!

Then he remembered. Intending to go down to the cellar, he had not locked the Vault door after him before falling asleep. Sooner or later, whatever was trying to get a purchase on the Vault's doorknob would be coming in. Mathers might not in truth have been a descendant of Scottish chieftains but he had some of the Highland character; better to take the initiative. He lifted himself out of the pastos by gripping the two sides in his strong freckly hands, dropped his legs to the floor and with one mighty bound was at the door and flinging it open.

Crowley!

'What the devil did you think you were playing at?'

Mathers had got over the fright but was still angry. Crowley was urbanely amused.

'I could quite reasonably ask you the same question,' he said.

'That business with the Vault door,' said Mathers huffily, aware of his weak position, 'pretending you couldn't get in...'

'I don't know what you're talking about,' said Crowley. 'I did not lay a finger on your Vault, was nowhere near it. I let myself in at the street door, heard a terrible howl and it turns out to be you playing silly buggers.'

Mathers suddenly decided to move closer to the windows, where the primrose rays of the March sunrise fell aslant the red, blue and gold carpet, a cheap copy of a traditional Persian design, with blobby inhuman faces and badly-tied tassels. Crowley followed him.

'They'll be here soon,' he said.

'Probably,' said Mathers, looking out unseeing across an empty Blythe Road. 'There's something I have to do first.'

'I know,' said Crowley.

'Do you?' said Mathers. 'I don't think so.'

'You ought to wait for Yeats,' said Crowley.

Mathers, his pale freckled forehead scored with the worry-lines that had recently taken hold, turned and looked at Crowley for some time before he spoke.

'Perhaps you do know something,' he said. 'But Yeats doesn't need to be there. He just has to know I was. Now, if you would excuse me.'

'No,' said Crowley, blocking Mathers' way to the door that opened onto the stairs. 'Yeats must be present when you light the candle. You must not go down until he arrives.'

'Must not? Since when did you have any authority in this building?'

Crowley's mouth opened, but like a nightmare, went on opening into an unnatural gape, and stayed like that.

'Crowley?' said Mathers. 'Crowley?'

A metallic rasp came from Crowley's open mouth and his tongue went up and down experimentally a few times. His lungs huffed air through his larynx like someone inexpertly working a blacksmith's bellows and saliva dribbled slowly from one side of his mouth. Several dull taps came from Crowley's throat, then a metallic little voice said, 'Is this on?' and laughed, horribly. Crowley's lips and tongue had not moved.

Mathers was staring, white-faced and saying, 'No, no, no,' with a rising inflection well on the way to becoming a scream.

'Stop it!' the thing using Aleister Crowley's body said. 'The Crowley is working for the other side. It was gaining control. I have intervened. Nothing must stop the Plan. I made you sleep, I made you wake: now you must light the Shiva candle in the absence of the Yeats 500 Pollexfen Cross.'

Mathers was trying to remember a formula for banishing demons; he couldn't even remember his own name. His hair was on end, his head shaking so much that his vision was blurring.

'By the sacred name of Ta-hu-tah,' he quavered, 'I command thee to – to - to leave this p-poor wretch whom thou hast in thy possession.'

Again came that horrible laugh, thin and scratchy as one of Mr Edison's recordings.

'I was Thoth, mortal fool!' said the voice, 'and the Crowley is not the only poor wretch I have in my possession.'

Crowley's mouth opened even wider and his larynx clicked a bit. Mathers began to shiver uncontrollably. From the back of Crowley's throat came another voice, thin and distant but perfectly recognizeable to her husband:

'Someone? Please? It is very dark here. I felt something touch my face. Why won't they open the curtains? Sam? Sam?'

'Mina!' cried Mathers. 'I am here. Don't be afraid.'

At that, a truly demonic peal of laughter sounded tinnily from Crowley's gaping mouth.

'Mortal fools!' screeched the voice. 'Don't be afraid! Why not?'

Mathers suddenly felt very calm. He knew now he was dealing with the Devil. The supernatural was real. And it turned out to be unbearable, wicked and wrong, wrong, wrong.

'Do not harm her,' he said, his voice almost under control. 'Release her from wherever you have got her. I will light the magic candle.'

'Don't try to lie to me,' said the voice coming from Crowley's body. 'You don't believe it's a magic candle. I know all about you. Because you know who I really am, don't you?'

'Yes,' said Mathers, his lips moving but almost no sound coming out.

'You know there is only one way out of this, don't you?'

'Yes,' Mathers mumbled, then more loudly, 'yes. Leave her alone. I'm going to do it.'

'Go down,' the scratchy little voice in Crowley's throat said, 'and don't wait for the Yeats. It must be done at exactly nine minutes past the hour.'

Carrying his back-pack, Mathers got up and went straight to the door which gave onto the landing and staircase to the ground floor. His legs were shaking so much he could hardly walk.

He had read that just hearing or seeing a devil could destroy you. There were supposed to be formulae and charms of protection. He himself was an adept, in theory able to summon and dismiss spirits. There had always been dispute concerning good and bad spirits, how you told the difference, whether there could even *be* good ones: it turned out that when you encountered disembodied evil it was so immediately apparent that every cell in your body screamed the truth and all you could do was run, hide or fight; he could neither run, hide or fight because It, in some way, 'had' his wife: he would do what It demanded, although he was sure now something very bad would happen when he did. Only very bad things could possibly result from anything which that voice wanted to happen. He remembered himself saying to a novice, 'Higher order thinking is dangerous for those who lack the deeper knowledge – the concept of evil is especially complicated.' Now he felt ashamed. Evil was simple: evil would step on the face of a child.

He glanced back. Aleister Crowley still stood there, his big athletic body rigidly fixed in the blocking move he had been carrying out when Oberon's dark spirit possessed him. He was paralysed, possessed, except for his eyes, which still retained their personality. The Bucca Dhu was not having it all its own way. 'Wait for Yeats,' croaked Crowley, only it came out as '... ait... aits...,' because he could not move his lips enough.

Mathers turned his back, took a deep breath and reached out for the door handle but before he could touch it, the door was thrown open, sending him staggering back. The Second Order of the Isis-Urania Temple had arrived in full force.

*

Even with the thin leather cushions provided for these meetings, the cold of centuries and the damp of the Hertfordshire clay came up and seeped into your bones like a rising tide of rheumatic aches. Why had they built this place, the Templars? The Twelfth Worthy took an interest in such things, and knew there had been a Knights Templar preceptory at Baldock, twelve miles away: but why this impractically tiny chapel in Royston? And why, given that you wanted a nice little place of worship in a quiet market town, build it deep underground?

The Twelfth Worthy shivered. As all the places filled and the meeting settled, everyone looked towards the First Worthy, who was listening, head inclined towards the man on his right, the Second Worthy. Dapper and well-dressed as ever, the latter had lost some of his easy grace and was moving carefully, as if in pain.

Stray thoughts ran through the Twelfth Worthy's mind. His mask was hurting the bridge of his nose. He wondered if the First Worthy's mask was hurting his nose. He wondered what his wife and friends would think if they could see him now, and immediately blanked out the picture of their baffled or grinning faces: some parts of one's life just did not fit with some other parts, and that was how it was. He inspected the walls, which were the colour of well-smoked kipper. They were covered in mysterious symbols, images cut deep into the stone, as if people of a mystical bent had been using the underground chamber over many, many years – or, the chilling thought came to him, been imprisoned there for a very, very long time.

The Twelfth Worthy shivered again and gathered the skirts of his overcoat around him. In the light of the hanging lantern, with the silent cabal waiting for the Second Worthy to speak, Time seemed less important than Place and the Templars no more than a blink away.

Behind a spy hole about fifteen feet above the Twelfth Worthy's head, someone blinked, and started to listen, very carefully…

Thank you gentlemen, thank you, you have been most patient. I suggest we go straight to the main business if no one has any…

Yes, er, yes, I have something. Is Philo Maynebeam…?

Naming is out of order I think, Seven, as you should know, so if there is nothing else? No, then Two, please?

Thank you, One. Gentlemen, you already know that we have found an answer to the Irish question. The solution will be final. There will be no native Irish left outside selected areas, in which they will be concentrated. Soon after that there will be no native Irish left at all. This obviously raises a question. How is this new policy of genocide to be presented to our European neighbours? With surprising ease, in fact. Our European allies, if not others, will understand and accept the Irish action if it is in response to an atrocity both extreme and threatening, by its nature, to them as well. There will be, in the near future, such an atrocity.

Very soon now the nation and the world will be astonished and horrified by the assassination of the Queen by Irish Nationalists in league with the Boers.

During the past weeks, several of our regiments, mounted, artillery and infantry, have been exercising on Dartmoor. On news of the assassination and while outrage is at its height, several vessels from the Home Fleet will see them across the Irish Sea in transport ships already prepared and lying at Plymouth. Our forces will land in Cork and sweep up through southern Ireland. The Dublin military has already been reinforced, while an army of Loyalist irregulars is waiting in the north.

The native Irish will be driven like game birds, the males shot out of hand, the females and infants corralled and exported for the benefit of the Empire.

Once Ireland is sterilized, we will deal with the Boers in the same fashion. There can be no Irish Nationalists if there is no Irish nation. There will be no Boer freedom-fighters if there is no more freedom and all the fighters are dead.

Any questions? Yes, Seven?

The Irish Republicans are daring but not insane. Why would they commit such an outrage, now, when the public mood is swinging further their way with every election? They are going to get some form of independence anyway. People like William Yeats are making them respectable, even admirable.

We will ignore your flouting of the naming rule, Seven. The Irish enthusiast will be neutralized and there will be no more talk of liberty and legend. For your other point, we control the Irish bombers and run their conspiracies from London, and in any case, the public will have other things to worry about once the deed is done. No, you have been called together to be informed of a greater matter than the bomb plot and destruction of the Irish race in Ireland.

The Irish genocide is an efficient means to an end. Its real purpose is to provoke the United States of America into declaring war on The United Kingdom.

Once war is declared, and our agents in Washington will ensure that it is, the Southern States will secede from the Union. Royalist sympathizers, of whom there are still a great many, aided by the native Americans, will seize power locally and declare for the Crown. We shall be ready to invade in force, from Canada in the north, from the West with the Japanese, and by direct assault on the capital and the East Coast cities. Within a year, we shall rule most of North America.

We shall need administrators, and that, gentlemen, is why you are here – and here, I am afraid, you will remain until the Blythe Road Incident has taken place. Surprise is everything and nothing has been left to chance.

I am sorry, Twelve, you'll just have to hold on.

The person behind the spy hole fitted the last words carefully into the correct memory-places and turned, cautiously, on the uneven flagstones, never replaced or repaired in the last five hundred years. He must report to his superiors at once and then – they would have to decide whether the Knights Templar still existed or not.

*

Madame Lauderdale was dreaming. It was one of her favourites. She was skipping freely through a flowery meadow. She was thin. She was light on her feet. Her auburn hair floated, long and romantic, on the warm wind. A man appeared suddenly, blinking into existence about twenty feet in front of her. She saw at once that it was her spirit guide, Ackroyd.

This time he looked different: he was making an effort. As she came closer, she saw that there were two parallel stripes of red and blue on each of his cheeks and an unconvincing eagle feather jammed behind his ear like a pencil. He was wearing fringed buckskin trews which kept morphing, like a badly-adjusted television receiving two signals at once, into stone-washed jeans with an ironed crease; his expression was that of a man irritably determined to do whatever the job required.

'Listen and hark, white squaw,' Ackroyd intoned loudly while she was still at some distance, 'me have grave tidings which absolutely must be delivered pronto to Mr *W. B. Yeats.*'

Madame Lauderdale stopped skipping. As soon as Ackroyd had appeared the bristly grass-tops had started sticking up her floaty dress and chafing horrible.

'All right,' she said wearily, 'you can drop all that. I know you're not a Red Indian.'

'First American,' said Ackroyd, 'but let it go. There's something I must tell Yeats and I don't know how to reach him, because I don't know how I did it in the first place. He must be warned about Blythe Road. Tell him it was on the morning of the second of March, 1899, at nine minutes past nine.'

'Oh Ackroyd, you're fading,' said Madame Lauderdale.

'No I'm not!' snapped Peter Ackroyd. 'Look, must we stand in this bloody field? Grass always plays hell with my sinuses. Listen, you *must* warn him about the Blythe Road incident. It's where the wickedness started. Victoria assassinated, with Campbell-Bannerman and the others, the reprisals in Ireland, genocide, the war with the States, the re-colonizing of America... you must tell him it's on the second of March, 1899 at nine minutes past nine in the morning, OK?'

Ackroyd tailed off because Madame Lauderdale had stiffened and drooped, no longer the girl of her dreams. In her North London bedroom in 1899 she was waking up, but in the 21st century Ackroyd was not; in his dream, Madame Lauderdale had turned into a scarecrow. A cloud came over the sun and the meadow lost its colour. The scarecrow lifted its drooping head. It did not have a face, just black sacking. Nevertheless it spoke to Ackroyd, who found himself unable to move.

'Did you think I was limited by time?' it said. 'The End is coming. You cannot stop it, you will not stop it, because the End is what you want. I am what you want. I am the Dark, and you know all about that, don't you, Dr Dee?'

Peter Ackroyd woke up with a start, dry-eyed, but with the sensation of having been weeping; as usual he could not remember why. He made coffee and mooched about, watering the pot-plants, then tried to work on his Crowley novel, but was unable to concentrate. There was something he had to do, something he had not done. Every time he came close to remembering, it was as if a dark flag flapped across his inner eye and hid the elusive thought from him. He turned the television on as a last resort; but the news was so frightening that he switched it straight off again.

Sacrifices

As soon as Yeats felt his fairy self pop back into existence on the doormat of 36 Blythe Road, something hit him like a storm of knees and elbows and knocked him down flat on his back. It was his Fairy. She pinned him down, seemingly torn between wanting to punch him, strangle him or hug him. Tears were running down her face and catching in the swaying ends of her long brown hair.

'You idiot, idiot, idiot!' she shouted. 'What did you think you were doing?'

'Getting through the door,' he said, 'like you.'

'All you had to do,' said the Fairy, still kneeling on his chest but calming down, 'was think yourself on the other side.'

'But I saw you go through.'

'Oh you saw me, did you?' said the Fairy, and disappeared. And reappeared. 'You're not seeing anything. That's what mortals do. You're knowing things, which is different. You knew I had gone through the door, so you told yourself a story about what it looked like.'

'Oh,' said Yeats. 'Look, would y'mind getting off my chest? I'm obviously telling myself that I can't breathe.'

The Fairy jumped to her feet, not without a last cross push to assist take-off, and stood, her long black-stockinged legs on either side of the poet's waist, looking down at him. She smiled sadly; a tear-drop still on the end of her nose. 'No,' she said, 'you're telling yourself that you're breathing.'

Yeats got to his feet. The stairwell rose like a wooden Matterhorn, its shadowy summit lost to view. 'Well,' he said, brushing himself down, 'my way seemed to work. I'm through, aren't I?'

For a moment the Fairy seemed about to fly at him again. 'You don't know? You really do not know, do you, what you just got away with.'

'No. What?'

'I don't know either,' said the Fairy, turning away to tuck her hair back into the grey bag-hat, then whipped back at him when he made to speak, 'but I do know that it was really, really dangerous.'

'Why?'

'First, exactly because I don't know what you just did, and I'm the Fairy, see? Secondly, He was there. There are no resources in the language you think I'm speaking to express just what it means, that *He* came to see what *you* were up to. It's like...'

'...God looking in at a boy's window?' said Yeats, remembering Blake's childhood.

The fairy seemed to flicker like a candle flame in a draught as the faint melodic hum of The Others pulsed once, twice, and all expression left her face. 'No,' she said, 'that was not Him.' Behind the statement Yeats sensed the authority of a powerful assembly and lengthy debate. What *were* fairies?

And what was he standing in? The stairwell was filled to the height of a fairy's knees with a heavy vapour, pale gold, pleated and billowed like a river mist at dawn.

'What is it?' he said.

'A super-credulity field.'

It was not Yeats' Fairy who answered. The voice came from someone standing in the shadows at the foot of the stairs; after a moment, its owner waded into view.

It was a female fairy almost as tall as Yeats, with strong features, long golden hair and intensely blue eyes. She was wearing a plain grey jacket, a dark skirt of a sensible length and sturdy ankle boots. Most fairies as depicted by Victorian artists were dressed for nothing more onerous than harassing insects or capering and fluttering, with occasional provocative hovering to demonstrate the properties of short gauze dresses; this fairy was not like that, her eye warned. Definitely.

'You are standing in the surplus magic draining down from the Golden Dawn,' she said.

'What? Are you joking?' blurted Yeats, surprised out of his normal courtesy. After his recent experiences he had come to see the Golden Dawn as a collection of dilettantes who would struggle to compete with a magician at a children's party. He said so.

'You are right,' said the golden-haired fairy, with a bleak look up the darkened stairwell, 'but that's just the point. Even they couldn't ritually invoke Egyptian gods, Cabalistic angels, elemental spirits and cthonic demons without *something* happening. That sort of magic – well, it works, but you have to use it. I'd say it's been accumulating for a long time,' she said, kicking up the golden vapour. 'It would have pooled under the temple first, then risen up through the foundations and basement, an unstable reservoir of magical potential. These people are playing their games on top of a supernatural nuclear bomb.'

'Nuclear bomb?' said Yeats. 'What's that?'

'Don't know,' said the unknown fairy. 'It's your mind we're using – have you been talking to anyone from a future point on your timeline?'

Ackroyd, thought Yeats: *but did he mention a bomb?* Out loud, impressed both by the golden-haired fairy's confident manner and startlingly blue eyes, he said, 'Shouldn't we do something? Clear the area?'

'Mortals will not be affected,' said his own Fairy, coming rather pointedly to stand at his side, 'but it will be very dangerous for any fairy caught in the blast zone. A magical explosion would definitely not kill mortals.'

'No,' said the other fairy, 'it's the dynamite which would do that.'

'What?' said Yeats.

'A hundred crates of dynamite. In the basement. Of this building.'

'But why didn't you tell me that first?'

'Wouldn't have thought I'd have to,' she said. 'It's got your name all over it.'

'The magic candles! Dynamite! Of course - it's for the Republicans! Oh my God! Maud, what have you done?' groaned Yeats, putting his hand over his eyes. 'What are they planning? The Colonel mentioned Victoria coming to Kensington, but surely they wouldn't…'

His hand was gently pulled aside.

'You are right. There is a threat to the mortal Queen. But do not despair,' said his own Fairy, glancing disapprovingly at her colleague, who shrugged and walked away. 'This future is not fixed. Different light paths - lines of possibility - co-exist in space-time. Normally the probabilities collapse into a single path at a steady rate which mortals call Time. But something unusual has happened.' She paused, looking at the other fairy, who was suddenly taking a great interest in adjusting the laces on her boots. Yeats' Fairy sighed and continued.

'Listen, 'she said. 'We – I – want you to know this. Pay attention, you will find it hard to understand. There is a Plan. It has been long in the making. It involves mortals but it is not a human project.'

'Not a human project – those are the Colonel's words!' said Yeats. 'Is this then the Fairy plan to improve the human stock?'

'Yes,' said his Fairy, 'and no. It is *a* fairy plan, but it is not uncontested. The mitochondriarch tried to tell you.'

Yeats lips moved. '...condriarch. My Greek was never much good, but I would guess you mean the Queen, at Horton's guest house.'

'Yes, the Queen, Titania. Direct contact with her was too difficult for your mind.'

'She said it was too hard for *her*,' protested Yeats. His Fairy looked away, frowning, then back.

'Leave that aside for now,' she said. 'The future is shaping. We can expand this moment, but not for ever. You need to know about the Plan. It is meant to accelerate human development,'

'Isn't that a good idea?'

'By mass extermination - of the weak by the strong.'

'Oh.'

For a while Yeats watched the golden-haired fairy reaching up experimentally, like every rock climber in the history of the world, towards the tempting overhang (Grade 3, Challenging) of the bottom stair-tread.

'What can be done about it?' he said.

'The unusual thing which has happened,' said his Fairy, 'is this. The Plan is complex and probably beyond human comprehension but in your world it all comes down to a single stick of dynamite. It was made in Bohemia and sent to Paris disguised as a ceremonial magic candle. Its purpose is to detonate the half ton of dynamite in the packing cases already delivered here, as you know, to the basement beneath us. This stick of dynamite was intercepted as it crossed the German border and a harmless candle, identical in appearance, was secretly put in its place by one of Titania's human agents, the son of the Colonel with whom you have been dealing.

'Damien Madriver?' said Yeats, 'A very capable fellow. Well, that's all right then, isn't it? There will be no real explosion.'

'Unfortunately,' said his Fairy, 'the magic candle was again intercepted en route by the other side and a fresh dynamite version substituted. The Colonel's agents again took action, and before it reached Paris the newly-replaced stick of dynamite disguised as a magic candle disguised as a stick of dynamite was replaced by a magic candle disguised as a stick of dynamite disguised as a magic candle. It is at this point that reality became confused. Two competing timelines somehow sprang into existence simultaneously and remained stable. We think it is something to do with unlawful actions on the Fairy plane of existence. Somehow a courier with the magic candle disguised as dynamite disguised as a magic candle, and another courier with a stick of dynamite disguised as a magic candle disguised as a stick of dynamite both made their deliveries to the Irish Republican Major John MacBride in Paris.'

'Him!' said Yeats. 'I might have known. So he ended up with two magic candles, one real and one faked?'

'No,' said his Fairy. 'I told you it would be difficult for you to accept. There is only the one item, but it will be physically impossible in this universe to determine whether it is a stick of dynamite or a magic candle until nine minutes past nine on the morning of the second of March, 1899. At exactly that time, the Genome predicts a massive explosion at 36 Blythe Road, but what kind, magical or chemical, it cannot see.'

'Let me get this right,' said Yeats. 'This wise gnome, the G-nome as you call it, perhaps counselled by the other gnomes A to F, is predicting that this building will either explode in a magical sense or in a real sense? And it is impossible to know which?'

'Yes,' said the Fairy, after a pause for discussion with the Genome. 'And again no. From a mortal viewpoint, it is absolutely unpredictable. Each event is equally probable, each excludes the other. The space-time paths overlap on the light-cone. However, the event is so finely poised that a single mortal's belief could determine the outcome.' She paused, as if listening. 'Will determine the outcome.'

'Then we must make sure that it is only a magical explosion,' said the fairy Yeats, with an involuntary glance upwards.

'He doesn't know what he is saying,' said his Fairy quickly, cutting across an acrid remark tossed over the other fairy's shoulder. 'Listen,' she said gently to Yeats. 'A magical explosion could be as dangerous for your people as the other kind.'

'My people?'

'The people of the Ireland that you love.'

'How so?'

'The British Queen is protected by a large number of – call them Titania's fairies. Some mortals are so favoured, in some places, at some times. We do not know why. I think not even the Master Sequence knows why. Titania sees furthest, and she may know why. With that protection it is all but impossible for Oberon, his servants or their mortal instruments, to act against your Queen.'

'Why would they want to? Her life, her reign, is near its end. She has little real power.'

'Think,' said his Fairy, looking deep into Yeats' eyes and putting her two cool hands on either side of his face, so that it was hard to think at all. 'What will happen to your country and its people if Victoria is shot dead by an assassin linked to Irish extremists?'

'But you said Victoria is protected, Titania's fairies...'

'If the magical potential trapped in this house is released,' cut in the other fairy, her golden hair flying as she turned to face him, 'it will take every fairy in the vicinity with it, including the royal bodyguard. Anything could have happened to the undefended queen by the time they sequenced themselves again.'

'Sequenced?'

'Pulled themselves together,' she snapped. 'This is wasting time.'

'The Queen will still not be in danger,' said Yeats. 'I happen to know that she is visiting Kensington Palace today. She will be safe there, won't she?'

Yeats' Fairy gently pushed the dark hair back from his forehead with both hands and looked hard into his eyes. 'At nine minutes past nine this morning,' she said, 'Queen Victoria will be in Blythe Road, immediately outside the door which you made such a performance of coming through. Trust us on this. It is the centrepiece of the Master Plan. About that light-path there is no uncertainty.'

Yeats' brows bent into a deep black vee. 'Dynamite ends everything,' he said. 'The other way – there is a chance. If there has to be an explosion, it must be magical. I am sorry. We've got to do something,' he said.

'We can't do anything,' said the golden haired fairy. 'Doing is for mortals. Know any?'

'I take your point,' said Yeats, drawing himself up and looking noble.

'Do you?' she said, in an odd tone of voice. 'Do you, really?'
And she looked him up and down in a way he did not like. His own Fairy frowned disapprovingly.

'I do not wish you to speak to the Yeats like that,' she said.

For a moment the two fairies faced each other, faces blank, as when they conferred with the Others; but the half-heard buzz of the swarm was absent. For what seemed a long time there was no sound, no movement. All sense diminished and the stairwell seemed to fade. Yeats wondered if he was in fact experiencing anything at all. Was it just a dream? Then the world came back and expression returned to the fairies' features. They looked puzzled, even anxious.

'What is happening?' said the blonde fairy.

'We don't know,' said Yeats' Fairy.

'We are modelling scenarios.'

'We are gathering information.'

(tiny pause)

'It has not happened before.'

'We are running model worlds in which it has happened.'

(tiny pause)

'The first two thousand four hundred and fifty models collapse after a million cycles.'

'Therefore the data is corrupt.'

'Therefore there are only two possibilities.'

'One possibility is that we ourselves are being modelled in a sub-world.'

'That is impossible to test and would still lead to the...'

'...other possibility, which is that an Untruth has been perpetrated by the Genome.'

'That is not possible.'

'Yet it is overwhelmingly probable.'

The fairies looked suddenly pathetic. They turned to Yeats. 'You are an anomaly,' they said. 'You must know or represent the answer.'

'Search me!' said Yeats.

'We will,' said the fairies. 'Keep still.'

For about ten seconds each fairy's face went blank, with the unchanging wide-eyed stare of a china doll. Then expression returned and Yeats' Fairy looked away; the other said, with a scowl of contempt:

'You are just a fairy.'

'Now, yes, but...'

'Your mortal self is asleep in the garden,' said Yeats' Fairy, turning to face him. She looked as if she had been crying. 'Here and now, you are a fairy.'

Fairy or not, Yeats was just as persistent: 'You said a mortal will make the difference. Couldn't Mathers...?'

'In MacGregor Mathers' hands, the candle will not be magical. The Genome sees enormous forces being brought to bear on this place. No ordinary mortal will be able to withstand the pressure to see the candle as dynamite. A mortal of superior will and strength is needed, someone with an inviolable sense of self, and an absolute, unshakeable belief in magic.'

The fairy Yeats' face fell. 'Oh. Crowley. Of course.'

'It won't be Crowley,' said the golden-haired fairy.

'You seem very sure about that,' said Yeats, cheering up.

'Yes,' she said, with a proud little smile. 'I am. I know everything about Aleister Crowley that there is to be known.'

Now Yeats understood. This was Crowley's fairy. Somewhere out there would be Crowley's fated true love, blonde, strikingly – ahem - athletic, a touch arrogant, just like this fairy, who was the image of that love in Crowley's heart. He wondered if Crowley would be lucky enough to meet his fairy's mortal counterpart, and the image of a corn-goddess assassin floated into his mind's eye.

'Well,' he said, 'very well, not Crowley if you say so, but we must stop the explosion. My -'

His Fairy's dark eyes were fixed on him.

'The woman I love is in this building,' said Yeats.

And it was true. There was someone he really wanted, someone he was not afraid to claim. Antlers high, pawing the ground and weeing on every available tree, W. B. Yeats had finally joined the human race; but he was currently only four and a half inches tall.

'Can an explosion, I mean a real explosion, be prevented? Can I save her?' he said, gaining energy, 'even as a fairy?'

The two fairies locked eyes for a few moments; this time a hum, varying in pitch like strange music, came from the empty space around and between them. They were consulting the Genome.

It was Crowley's fairy who spoke; Yeats' Fairy folded her arms and turned away.

'Yes, there are futures in which her physical being is maintained for a time, but as for you...'

Yeats found the reticence insulting. Did she think he was such a coward?

'I'll take my chances, thank you very much,' he said, trying for scorn but only making it as far as rudeness. The two fairies, brown-haired and golden, slender and strong, dark-eyed and blue, regarded Yeats with immortal compassion and in unison said, 'Sometimes courage is not enough.'

'Every single one,' said Crowley's fairy, 'of the possible light-cone paths which preserve the life of the mortal Stephanie de Beauharnais requires your extinction. However, there is something which you may not appreciate…'

Cones again, and extinction: dead right, he didn't appreciate it.

Yeats struggled for the mental equilibrium of courageous selfhood, but it was hard. Strange visions crowded and pressed at the borders of his mind. Cones, gyres, funnelling in, winding out, interpenetrating… the vision was so strong this time that little fairy Yeats fell to his knees. He could not support the weight. Everything went black and there was a roaring in his ears. He was so much smaller than everything else, the dusty dry feeling was there again in the back of his nose, he was shrinking, shrinking…

…sinking. The fairies were kind and found the word for him. It was just across an axon in your verbal memory from the shrink cluster, they said, see diminish, laundry, mistake, anxiety and fear of death. Sinking, plumbing, rising down... What is an axon? Axon, tax on, pox on, sirrah, mirror, swan, Coole, calm, connect... An axon is a tendril. Between memory cell and memory cell. Cell, lock, quay, water… they guided him down with gentle hands, deeper into his self and the dryness and dust at the back of his nose went away. As he descended through the levels, there was more light, not less, until Yeats found himself somewhere he recognized: it was the alien schoolroom in which he had first received the vision of the interpenetrating gyres, had seen that a spiral could be a straight line through space-time, that the wand of Asclepius is the answer to everything. But there were two snakes in that vision, and that made it a Caduceus, the wand of Hermes – magical, not medical. 'Yes,' they said, 'and so…?' He had to choose. It all depended how you saw it. One snake or two, one spiral or two. One gyre, one cone, two gyres, two cones …God and the Devil, God or the Devil, being and not being, on kai me on, Hamlet, Shakespeare, fairies, Steph…

Steph, Stephie, Stephanie…

'He's grinning,' said Crowley's fairy. 'He is probably thinking about reproduction. They usually are.'

Yeats woke with his head in his Fairy's lap, her long hair tickling his face, her fingertips rubbing his pointed ears. He smiled up at her. There was something… Something he had to remember.

'Stephanie!' Yeats shouted, leaped to his feet and launched himself at the mountainous staircase, expecting the same easy lift and swoop on the wings of magical imagination which had brought him to Blythe Road. After what seemed a very long time he had to give up. It was like flying against a soundless hurricane. He looked helplessly at his Fairy when she also settled beside him. She was breathing hard and not, apparently, from choice.

'We can't,' she said, looking up and ahead.

Yeats looked up too but all he could see was darkness.

'There's something on the stairs, isn't there?' he said.

Something on the stairs; as soon as he said them, the words made his stomach turn over in fear. He had not known fear like that since childhood. Now it was back, a neighbourhood bully home from holiday. There was something on the stairs. Anybody under ten years old would understand at once what that meant. You could be kept in a state of terrified wakefulness all night long by the thought that there was something on the stairs. While his Little Man had been there, Yeats' childhood had been almost free of night fears; they had struck with a vengeance the night of the day the Fairy left him in the Hammersmith garden, when he had already been past the age to expect or receive much sympathy. 'Don't be silly, there's nothing there.' You wanted to believe it and in the heat and rush of adolescence you could, for a time. Then you grew a little older and found that the whole adult world was secretly telling itself not to worry, that there was nothing there. Don't be silly, think about something nice, like money, sex and power. Yet all the time, It was on the stairs, behind the curtain, round the corner. They knew, the children and the fairies, they knew who the silly ones were. Yeats reached out for his Fairy's hand.

'This fear can only mean one thing,' said Crowley's fairy, annoyingly calm as capable people often are. 'It is here. This must be a crucial moment in the Plan. The Genome is risking a great deal.'

'How so?' said Yeats.

'Every direct intervention alters the probabilities of outcomes, securing some at the expense of multiplying unknowns. He has already damaged the light-cones, creating stable quantum uncertainties at the macro scale.'

'And what is here?' said Yeats quietly, choosing a question to which he might understand the answer.

'The Puck, the Pookah, the Bucca Dhu, the Buggaboo, the Foggy Dew – it is Oberon's agent in the human world. You have studied it, Yeats 500 Pollexfen Cross, now you must fight it.'

'Why can't we fly?' said Yeats, forcing himself to look up into the dark stairwell; his own Fairy slipped free of his hand and stood apart, watching him.

'I have told you. The Puck is the projected will of the Oberon Master Sequence,' said Crowley's fairy. 'If it is the King's wish that we do not ascend, then without our mortals,' she said, with a glance at Yeats' Fairy, 'we can't fly against it.'

'But I'm here!' cried Yeats and then, startled by his own voice, whispered, 'I'm here - I'm a mortal. Why can't...'

The golden-haired fairy looked from Yeats to his fairy. 'He still doesn't realize?' she said.

Yeats' Fairy shook her head, looking with anxious intensity into Yeats' face, dark eyes meeting dark eyes. Again he felt that vertiginous excitement evenly blended with fear. What was it he didn't realize?

'What *can* the Yeats do?' said his Fairy. He had never seen her look like this before; she sounded different, impersonal and distant. It made him afraid. Then it made him lift his head and straighten his back.

'I can climb!' said Yeats.

Crowley's fairy looked at him, sharply.

'Right,' she said. 'Bend over!'

'What?'

The tall fairy grabbed his neck and pushed. 'Make a back,' she said tersely.

'Oh,' said the last hope of the Western World, 'of course,' and did so. Crowley's fairy placed a booted foot between his shoulders. He had braced himself but he felt almost nothing as she sprang lightly from his back to the next stair.

'Now you,' she said, leaning down.

Yeats jumped as she had done, caught the edge of the stair, struggled for a purchase on the riser and was hauled ignominiously over the lip. He did not care; neither did he want to face the thing on the stairs, but it was between him and Stephanie. So he would climb the stairs and face it. Love had made him genuinely careless of himself and he could sift his feelings with no secret fear left rattling on the mesh.

Yeats' Fairy was pulled up and they all stood together, rather closer than necessary, on the first stair. It was absolutely silent and the air was still.

'Let's get it over with,' Yeats suddenly muttered and, breaking away, went right to the edge of the stair-tread and stood on the overhang. The fairies watched the poet turn round with his back to the drop, tilt his head back and peer over their heads into the dark.

'I am not frightened,' said Yeats loudly. 'Whatever is up there, you may think you are powerful because you negate me, but you are mistaken.'

Nothing replied, or perhaps there was a snigger right on the edge of hearing. Behind Yeats, the street door swung ponderously open, slowly, slowly, time operating differently for the enormous shapes that stood ominously silhouetted against the light.

'I have passed the Veil of Paroketh,' said Yeats, unaware of what was happening behind him, his voice growing in power. 'I am an Adept of the Ordo Rosae Rubeae et Aureae Crucis. I know the Secret Wisdom of the Lesser World. I do not fear the Evil Persona below Malkuth, it only makes me stronger. You are trying to use fear to master me, but I have mastered fear. I have become it.' He could see his Fairy looking anxious and saying something but he paid her no attention, concentrating on holding and projecting his power at the thing on the stairs. There was still a flutter of fear in his heart. The thing on the stairs had a leering confidence in itself as a being so evil, so opposite to life and light, that the mere sight of it would strike him dead. He must equal its horror. No, he must out-do it. His voice deepened and he began to chant: 'Whatever you have imagined, so have I. However dark your nature, mine is darker. You may mean mischief, but I am capable of real evil. You threaten me with the unspeakable word, I will speak it.'

'Stop,' cried his Fairy, but Yeats was not listening to her; he was listening to himself. The stairwell was a natural acoustic chamber, giving his voice a dramatic boom, almost gravelly, with a nice rasp in it; but all the time there was something about the thing on the stairs which seemed about to undercut his confidence. Behind him the lobby was filling with cloudy giants.

'I know the slighting words,' chanted the fairy Yeats, 'inscribed on the back of the altar at Lourdes. I am the greatest liar in the universe. I have misled good people. I have...'

'Don't,' shouted his Fairy, and Crowley's fairy started towards him then seemed to stop herself with some effort and stood back with her arms folded. Yeats was too caught up in the size of his voice and the sense of mastery to care. When it came down to it, what were fairies anyway? Little creatures, like ants you could put your boot on. Look at them, down there; and they really were down there. Yeats was growing. The thing on the stairs would have to watch out now. Already Yeats was so big it was like looking down from a high building at the fairies' faces - just two pale dots. One of the dots was moving around agitatedly. The words his Fairy was screaming rose up to him like pond bubbles made by creatures too small to see or care about.

'There's nothing on the stairs. It's just you!'

The voice was annoying: it was life, and life was annoying; the thing on the stairs lifted its foot to crush.

*

In his apartment of theoretical convenience in West Kensington, Thomas Hardy perched on the edge of the optimistic double bed and took stock. With dawn light paling the gas lamp, he had spread out the map from Maynebeam's secret room on the eiderdown beside him and weighted it down at the corners with piles of money which he shook out from his pockets and when that ran out, from various jars and biscuit boxes. The money was mainly gold sovereigns, with a few bright guineas and crowns; there was not much copper coinage in evidence on the bed but previous trouser pocket clearances had left plenty in the waste-bin.

Spectacles on the end of his beaky nose, Hardy pored over the map, and the pencilled notes and diagrams which covered it. He recognized a good plot when he saw one, and this was a belter. He had always pined to be a character in a plot rather than merely its author – and now he was, Conan Doyle had seen to that. He looked down, quite fondly, at his feet, which were propped up on the creator of Sherlock Holmes.

Doyle was bound and gagged and not enjoying it, although it was healthier than the alternative which was having his head kicked in by Hardy's turnip mashers. 'Don't think I dunno how to do it, neither,' Hardy had said, but he had tied him up instead, with the length of clothes line he kept just in case.

Now Hardy grinned and trampled Doyle a bit, nothing malicious. 'You're a deep old file, Doyle,' he said, then frowned. 'Not as deep as some, though. You've been used, left, right and centre. Your chum Maynebeam – if that's his name, which I doubt – used the letter to get you interested in the girl. That led you to the Golden Dawners, as he knew it would. I think you were meant to burst in on their proceedings and embarrass someone, and yourself perhaps – but you followed me instead! I wonder – did Miss so-called Fanny flash me that delightful smile through the carriage window by sheer chance? I know, I know,' he said, as if Doyle could possibly utter a word through his gag, 'it's always happening in my books but, and this is a very important "but", long and painful experience says that it doesn't happen to *me*. I think I knew as much even when I jumped off the train and, now I think about it, she made it suspiciously easy to follow her all the way to that meeting. So was I being used by people who didn't like Maynebeam using you? That *would* be deep, and some.'

He peered at the notes and street-plan on the reverse of the map, his finger tracing a route heavily marked in black ink. 'Something is going to happen here,' he muttered, 'at nine minutes past nine tomorrow. Something so secret it's probably very bad.'

Doyle wagged his head from side to side and mumphed through his gag.

'Not bad?' said Hardy.

He looked more closely, putting his eyes, behind their wire-framed spectacles, right down to the creased surface of the map. His bright eyes moved along the inked route, from Shepherd's Bush to Kensington Palace via Olympia's great exhibition hall, squinting at the written annotations.

'Ye gods and little fishes,' he said, straightening up. 'They're going to assassinate the Queen. And it's happening just down the way, outside that Golden Dawn meeting house. And it's not happening tomorrow,' he said, glancing at the mantelpiece clock and then down at his large silver fob-watch to make sure, 'it's happening this morning, and soon!

You knew, didn't you? It's why you thought about shooting me!'

Doyle had nothing to say about that, even through his gag. He rolled over where he lay, presenting his hunched back. Hardy turned the big crackling paper sheet over, spilling coins everywhere, and looked again at the map of Saxonia covering both Americas in a sullen red, then beyond to India, Australia, South East Asia, the whole of sub-Saharan Africa, to Northern Germany, Northern France... all shaded in the same ominous tint.

'This must not happen,' he said. Hardy hated bullies and the Saxonian Empire was a bully's dream. He sensed something worse: Saxonia was unnatural, a monster. It wasn't meant to be. It must not be. But what could one do?

He might be in a story of his own at last, but if so, he was merely a secondary character, and Hardy knew what *they* were good for: bizarrely ironic deaths – blown off a cliff by a freak gust of wind in mid-marriage proposal, run over by the ambulance wagon – basically, killed by plot

But wait. He could be character *and* author in this plot. There must be another way.

'There is! There is!' shouted the fairies, watching from just the other side of the Veil; but Hardy, almost uniquely amongst mortals, could not be nudged into decisions by fairies, had no fairy of his own to give shape to his desires, to his love.

Conan Doyle definitely had a fairy. She sat on his head, looking out of place indoors and in London. She was long-legged and graceful, with friendly eyes, a determined chin and a mass of long thick wavy hair. Her wings were the pale gold of a summer dawn and her expression suggested she had a big job on her hands.

Doyle's fairy flew with a whirr of wing and swirl of frothy diaphanous skirts to one of Doyle's ears. 'The Hardy must *not* go to the 36 Blythe Road nexus,' she said. Her lips did not appear to move: the Little People were in a hurry. A star appeared in one of Doyle's rolling and bloodshot blue eyes. It grew brighter and bigger. When he blinked, it was still visible through the eyelid. Out of the star came a troop of fairies, two by two, grim and unsmiling, like a marching column appearing over the brow of a hill. They were all male, muscular and moved like special forces occupying hostile ground. Some went to Doyle's gagged mouth, others disappeared behind him. Doyle's birth fairy lifted one lovely arm, waited a moment, then brought it down sharply. Doyle's eyes opened very wide, bulging so much they threatened to pop out of their sockets. His face went red. At the same time, his facial muscles did things of a kind and with a force he would have thought impossible, and the handkerchief gag came loose and fell down to his chin.

'Hardy,' he said hoarsely, turning himself over where he lay, still helplessly tied up, then louder, 'Hardy! You don't understand. The big picture, I mean. I know it looks bad. It's all for the best, you see. You must not interfere.' And, as his fairy said the words into his ear, so Doyle found himself saying, with all the passionate force his large body could generate: *'You must not go to Blythe Road. You must not go now. You must not go with all speed. Your presence alone will obstruct the Plan!'*

The authors stared each other in the eye, Doyle if anything the more startled of the two. 'Well,' said Hardy, 'in that case...'

They were going to murder Victoria. And an image came to his mind, of another woman, and a mild, still-pretty face, nice hair, rather grey now, and a sweetly defeated expression pressed like winter wine from loss and loneliness. 'Emma,' he whispered to himself, 'they're not going to do this.'

Thomas Hardy looked down at Doyle. 'Someone will come and let you go later on,' he said, stooping to replace the gag, taking extra care with the knot. 'Not me, and it won't be the police either – I meant what I said about perlice-men, best avoided in all circumstances. I don't know how much, or why, you're mixed up with these people, but I should keep my head down for a bit, if I were you. Goodnight, Doyle.'

There was no convenient railway link, cabs and all other vehicles were mysteriously absent from the streets of West Kensington that morning, and so it was Hardy's quick countryman's walk, flat, even, unvarying in pace, that carried him towards Blythe Road. About a quarter of a mile away a tall blonde woman was approaching Hardy's destination from the opposite direction, with a light step and fierce purpose in the swing of her hips and shoulders.

Agent 42, Clarissa Jane Laurel, had new instructions, not carried in the pocket of her long winter coat but written in red copperplate letters in the virtual theatre of her mind's eye: *Go to Blythe Road. Target One will be there at nine minutes past nine this morning. Kill her, and your work will be done, your revenge for your sister will be complete and our cause will triumph.*

Oberon relished the movement of Clarissa Jane's body with languid sensuality.

'Isn't she wonderful?' he said. He was always a part of her, of course, as he was of every human being on the planet, but with success so near he was allowing his extended being to realize itself more fully in her, a glowing node in a near infinite network, enjoying the woman's sinuous strength, letting himself flow through her veins, sit in the elastic miracle of her joints, luxuriate in the heat of her belly, triumphing: for the first time ever he was going to win a battle in the long war with the female principle. No matter which path the universe went down at nine minutes past nine that morning, the Oberon Sequence could not lose. Nothing had been left to chance.

'The game is mine,' he said. 'You have been mated.'

'Mmm,' said Titania at his side, rather dutifully, then, 'It doesn't trouble you that we cannot see all the detail in the relevant light cones?'

'Not when simple logic fixes the outcome. You are placing hope in the indeterminacy, but I have cleverly found a way round it. You see, there is either dynamite in that candle, or there isn't. If there is, then the British Queen will be instantly killed in the explosion, along with Yeats and everyone else in the vicinity. If there is no dynamite then Victoria will still be assassinated at the hands of this magnificently vengeful creature and Yeats will survive to be hanged for dynamite treason. Either outcome discredits the moderates, will justify extreme reprisals against the Irish, the Americans will get involved and...

'True,' said Titania. 'Only a fairy could stop you, or a...'

'A fairy!' the King broke in, full of a masculine contempt for weakness and frivolity. 'Why do you use the childish image we ourselves devised in order to communicate with primitive minds? If you mean a parautonomous proxy budded from the Titania sequence, why don't you say so?'

'Whose sequence?' said the Queen, with a shift in electrostatic exchange which equated with wry humour.

'I meant the mitochondriarch, and you know it,' said Oberon

sulkily. 'There has been too much conversation with mortals. It does not change the fact that every one of your "fairies", yes, and mine too, will be blown far and wide if there is an explosion of magical belief rather than dynamite. Robbed of their native intelligences, ordinary mortals will experience a temporary paralysis of the will, but Clarissa Jane Laurel has been long prepared for this moment by my instrument Maynebeam. Her carefully nurtured obsession with revenge for her sister's death will carry her through the hiatus. I cannot see that there will be any other spirits present so tormented that they are capable of independent action. So, you see, even if there is no dynamite blast, Clarissa Jane Laurel will fire the gun, Victoria will still be dead, Yeats executed, moderate opinion silenced, Ireland invaded and America re-colonized. The game is mine.'

A pause, representing precisely the universal masculine insecurity in the face of a knowing silence from the other side of the fireplace or car, then…

'…or a what? You were going to say something,' said Oberon irritably. 'What other than a fairy could stop the assassination of Victoria and the bringing in of the Saxonian Empire?'

'Oh, nothing,' said Titania. 'It is something so rare now that there is no probability for its existence that is distinguishable from zero.'

'What is that? Nothing must be left to chance.'

'Why yes, indeed – that is what I was saying. Nothing has to be left to chance, it is the only way. It cannot be controlled or predicted. The near-zero utterly improbable possibility is that a Changeling could intervene. Changelings need no fairy...'

'...because they are half in our world already, it is known, but there are no more Changelings,' said the King. 'Since Kaspar Hauser…'

'Yes, of course, we know that. Yet Changelings can exist, and you should acknowledge, for it is our strategy and our end, that whatever can exist will exist.'

'Yes, yes,' said the King impatiently, 'but we are not aware of any changelings in the present generations. In the time of Friar Bacon, even John Dee, but after Kaspar Hauser… well, I needn't remind you.'

'No,' said Titania, and she sounded sad, 'you needn't remind me.'

*

Yeats was in several places at once. From a great distance he seemed to see himself, grown much larger, lying down propped on one elbow like a Roman at a feast, in turn watching something very small, him again, with a foot raised to stamp. Wild thoughts possessed him. Cruel passions dried his mouth. His unconscious body stirred, tiny muscular spasms, a twitch of a finger, an irregular breath, reflecting a gigantic battle within the human frame stretched unconscious on the dewy ground.

Then the voice of his Fairy came to him, calm and clear. 'Grow in knowledge. There is no one to fear in the dark. It is your self.'

The voice continued, seeming to come from all directions or perhaps from none, because it was inside him. It no longer sounded like his Fairy. Or rather, it did, and he realized that he had been hearing it all his life, that she had never really been away. She was the voice in his mind that told the truth, knew right from wrong, heard most clearly on waking, before the clamour of the day had drowned her out.

'It's not about power,' said the Voice. 'It's about love. Without love there is nothing.'

Yeats repeated the words. 'Without love there is nothing.' In the gloom of the Blythe Road lobby, happiness filled his heart and suddenly, although there was something on the stairs, there was nothing to fear. 'Without love there is nothing' – and now there *was* love, beyond any doubt.

Four and a half inches high again, he stood tall. He had found strength and gained in wisdom. His Fairy looked at him consideringly. 'Fairy?' said Yeats. There was something different about her, different and yet, like her voice, it had always been there. She was still freckled, brown haired and dark-eyed, yet her slender arms and long legs were suddenly not awkward but graceful, the shapeless grey hat on the back of her head had become a coronet from which a river of braided tresses poured and swayed as she moved and when the shining wings of hair fell forward and shadowed her face and she cast her eyes down so that the lashes made two gentle crescents against the fair skin, then…

'Fairy,' said Yeats in wonder, 'you are…'

'I know,' she said. 'Haven't you worked it out yet? I am, because you are.'

She smiled, he smiled, and the moment was drawing out forever when Crowley's fairy broke in: 'Up! Up!' she cried. 'The Bucca Dhu has been defeated by the Yeats 500, and now that its will has been broken, I can sense that my mortal is in danger.'

They shot up the stairwell like a flight of arrows, led by Crowley's fairy. The second door at the top might have given Yeats ideas, but his Fairy grabbed his wrist before he could think about repeating the experiment with nothingness. His skin tingled where her fingers held it and a thrill went through his arm, but there was no time to think further about it. The door seemed to turn to glass and then to air and suddenly there was the Golden Dawn's meeting room and in the doorway the Chief of the Order, Macgregor Mathers, stumbling back as if he had had the shock of his life.

'He can see us,' said the fairy Yeats in wonder. 'Mathers can see us.'

In fact he could not. As far as MacGregor Mathers was concerned, he opened the door and found Madame Lauderdale on the other side, backed, so it seemed, by the entire membership of the Golden Dawn's Inner Order: they had been the great dim shapes pouring in slow motion up the stairs above and around the fairies. If Mathers was aware of the transmogrified Yeats and his two fairy companions, it was as a fluttering on the edges of his vision, entirely attributable to nervous exhaustion. He was given no time to think about it: led by the iron-grey Madame Lauderdale, the magicians of the Golden Dawn swept their chief with them as they swirled into the room. They had been summoned for Florence Farr's Extraordinary General Meeting, but events had caught up with the agenda. 'That one!' screeched Madame Lauderdale, at the head of the bubbling surge, pointing at Crowley, 'beware that one!'

The fairy Yeats was only distantly aware of the screech, and the person of Madame Lauderdale herself. He found that if he concentrated, he could will her into sharper focus. It made him realize how much effort it took for the fairies, including his own, to deal directly with humans. At the moment, he had no desire to will Madame Lauderdale to be anything at all: where was Stephanie? They had said she would be there, at Blythe Road.

'She will be here,' said his Fairy calmly, appearing at his side, where she hovered easily on shimmering blue-green wings.

'Your wings, Fairy,' said Yeats. 'The colour, it's *glas*. Your wings are the colour of love.'

'Yes, they are, now,' said his Fairy.

'And mine, look,' said the fairy Yeats excitedly, craning his neck around, 'they are the same colour. You said that if ever I saw glas like this...'

'...it would not be with your own eyes, yes, I said that,' said his fairy sadly. 'I did not know what it meant. You have found love. Now – you must endure it.'

His Fairy was not looking at him. He followed her eyes, and saw Crowley. He still stood helpless and open-mouthed, fixed in an attitude of barring someone's way. Nervous magicians had gathered around him, unsure what to do, each accompanied, Yeats now saw, by an equally agitated fairy companion.

'Come on,' said Yeats, wings blurring as he set off to see what had happened. There was no reply and when he looked back, the Fairy was not there. *Endure it.* Yeats put fears aside and flew quickly on, but not as quickly as Crowley's own fairy, who was already at the big young man's side.

Blonde, beautiful and angry, she hovered just above his right shoulder, apparently listening. Then she seemed to reach a decision, pushed her hair back, squared her shoulders and, in mid-air, began to shrug herself out of her clothes. Yeats told himself that it was all right to look, she was a fairy, but it was remarkable how, except for the slightly unconvincing wings, she was essentially a woman in her twenties with a wonderful figure. It was still all right to look. It was about love now, not power, and it was all right to look. She hovered for a moment, naked and radiating light.

'It isn't right!' she shouted at apparently empty air. 'It isn't fair! It is direct action. You will damage him. It is Violating the Code!'

The instant she shouted the last three words, the Golden Dawn fairies froze in mid-air, their eyes all fixed on the same place, just by the Vault, where the air was suddenly no longer empty. A dark figure began to appear, first just an outline, which filled itself in from the edges until it was midnight black right to the centre. The figure was somewhat under adult human size and seemed to be wearing a cloak and broad-brimmed hat which was set at a jaunty angle but the absolute black made any detail uncertain. It turned its featureless face towards them.

Crowley's fairy began to run. As she had nothing to tread on but air, this at first looked odd, but she began to grow with every step, acquiring as she went a few bits of strategically-placed leather and a large sword. She was a warrior, an Amazon, a Valkyrie and Yeats' heart leapt with admiration. Then he saw what she was running towards and his heart sank. The black figure was also growing, rising to the meeting room ceiling like a column of oily black smoke, abandoning its human form.

Crowley's Fairy charged straight for the twisting black column. There were no challenges, no negotiations, she ran straight at the Bucca Dhu, swung the sword – and vanished.

The smoky pillar seemed unaffected, until Yeats realized that he was seeing the far side of the room through it. The Bucca Dhu never exactly left, it simply changed its state, like water evaporating. As its last greying edges evanesced, Crowley stirred, lowered his arms and put a hand to his head, swaying.

'Yeats!' he cried. 'Not here? Mathers!' he croaked, then, recovering himself, more loudly, 'Mathers! Don't go down there without Yeats!'

Macgregor Mathers was at the back of the crowd of members, tip-toeing towards the door, his back-pack slung over his shoulder. He looked back at Crowley over the heads of the initiates. 'I'm sorry,' he said. 'I must... I must just… there's something I have to…'

Crowley lurched forward in an attempt to reach Mathers and with a snarl of frustration fell to his hands and knees. 'The police are on their way,' he gasped, trying to stand up while not one member of the Inner Order moved to help him. 'They know everything.'

'I doubt that,' said Mathers grimly, with the ghost of a smile, 'I doubt that very much.' He squared his shoulders. 'I'm sorry,' he said. It seemed to include the whole room. He put his hand out for the second time that morning and opened the door to the stairs. An enormous policeman, uniformed, caped, helmeted, stood framed in the doorway.

Lovers

It was Sergeant 'Duckman' Platimer, carrying the inert body of Stephanie de Beauharnais Toughguid in his arms. Her head hung back over his arm so that her long hair almost touched the floor. Mathers dithered, unable to affect indifference to this new drama, and also, in any case, to get past the bulky sergeant.

'She's not...?' he said, gently pushing the young woman's hair back from her face with a trembling hand, 'she's not ...'

'No, she isn't,' said Miss Cracknell, appearing from behind Sergeant Platimer. 'But this is as bad as death. It is magical in nature, but beyond me. Is Mr Yeats here?'

'No,' said Annie Horniman, with a quizzical glance at Crowley, who sat slumped against a wall, knees level with his ears like a demoralized grasshopper, 'but he seems to be expected.'

'Take her into the Vault.' Mathers was flushed and panicky, his small pale eyes darting from the door to the vault and down to his wristwatch; but he was concerned for the girl, having now a fairly good idea what was the matter with her. 'Take her to the Vault,' he repeated.

'The Vault?' cried Annie Horniman, regarding the Chief of the Order with amazement. 'Are you serious? It is the sacred vault of Christian Rosenkreutz. And she's not even been inducted yet,' she added.

'It's a small wooden booth which I nailed together myself,' Mathers snapped, 'and I believe I expelled you from the Order.' He pushed past Annie Horniman, clearing the way for Sergeant Platimer to carry the unconscious Stephanie through into the quiet little space and lay her down gently in the sacred pastos, the last resting place and recreative bed of the great Rosenkreutz. Maud Cracknell followed, an enigmatic smile on her strong features and her eyes not looking quite where you would expect.

Inside the Vault, invisible to Sergeant Platimer at least, Yeats' fairy self was hovering by Stephanie's head, and in her dream she sat up in the pastos and looked at him.

'So there you are,' she said with a delighted smile.

'Are you not surprised to see me?' said Yeats, four and a half inches high and wings ablur.

'Surprised?' said Stephanie, and laughed at the idea, her dark eyes half-closing in the way he loved. 'Why would I be surprised to see my Little Man? You have been with me as long as I can remember.'

'No,' said Yeats earnestly, 'you are mistaken, for I am Willie Yeats, d'ye see?'

'Why, now I come to look at you carefully,' said Stephanie (while all the time her body lay unconscious in the coffin-like wooden pastos) you do look a little like poor dear Willie.'

Yeats welcomed the dear but did not appreciate the poor. 'What is poor about me, I'd like to know?' he said.

'Why nothing about *you*, Little Man,' said Stephanie, reaching out her cupped hand and taking him gently within it. 'But William Yeats is lying cold amongst the long grass in the garden. I was not there to protect him. I would like to wake and weep out my grief and shame and loss, but He will not let me.'

'He? Who is that?' said Yeats the Fairy looking around belligerently from the sweet rosy round of Stephanie's palm. 'Who will not let you wake?' Then he saw, at the other end of the pastos, the dark figure, the broad-brimmed hat and featureless face of the Bucca Dhu. It was sitting in a relaxed posture, one arm lying over the back of an invisible chair, one knee drawn up so that the leg made something like a figure four with the other; its head was tilted quizzically on one side. It was clearly watching him with the eyes it did not have.

'I see,' said the fairy Yeats. 'I see.' He sighed and began to remove his clothes.

'What are you doing?' cried Stephanie's spirit, caught between amusement and alarm as more and more of the Yeats fairy's white and rangy raw-boned body was revealed.

'I'm sorry,' he said. 'It's got to be done, and now I have seen how to do it.' Finally naked in Stephanie's hand, he stepped into the empty air beyond, set his fairy muscles and waited like a runner on his marks for the transformative change which had overtaken Aleister Crowley's fairy in similar circumstances. The Bucca Dhu's black blank face stared insolently and Stephanie's mortal body lay still and grew colder.

'Little Man,' whispered Stephanie's spirit, 'though goodness knows I'm not sure now that little is the right word,' she added with a giggle, 'Little Man, what are you doing?'

'You'll see,' said Yeats grimly. He hoped the transformation into his warrior self would happen soon. He had not realized that fairies could get goose-pimples. He made another effort, screwed up his eyes and willed himself to become a giant Celtic fighter. When he opened them he was three feet tall and holding a rush-leaf in his fist. A large sprig of shamrock was tied over his private parts like a limp green sporran. The dreaming Stephanie threw her head back and laughed.

'Oh Little Man, I love you,' she said.

'I love you too,' said Yeats, and ran, brandishing the rush, straight at the sinister silent shape which lounged at the end of Stephanie's coffin.

He expected to strike at it and see it disappear, just as when Crowley's fairy had saved her own human mortal from enslavement to the Black Bucca's will. He expected, like her, to die. Instead, although his legs were galloping and his wings thrashing, he seemed to stand still, while it was the Darkness which moved and reached towards him. And he did not feel dead. He was in an infinite black space, a cavern with no roof, no walls and no floor. The only light was from Yeats himself. He shone like a dust mote in a sunbeam. The Bucca Dhu was gone and there was only, above and below and all around him, the Dark.

And the Dark took him in its finger and thumb. The rush fell from his hand and disintegrated in glimmering dust which drifted away and went out.

'Let's see what you're made of,' said the Dark. It took hold of his life and began to pull it apart.

'Your poetry,' said the Dark. 'Shallow, nauseatingly self-involved, convoluted and false. Lies and rubbish.'

'I know,' said Yeats faintly, but not without a martyr's pride, 'I know.'

'Your Irishness, your great plans, your sentiments, your loyalties, your passions, your intrigues. Lies and rubbish,' said the Dark, and Yeats' politics, like the rush sword, dispersed in an expanding cloud which glowed with a corpse-light for a second and then was nothing. There was now much less of Yeats left behind.

'Your beliefs,' said the Dark. It reached in, there was a deeper pain, and Yeats' Celticism, his mysteries, his magic, his incantations, his systems and his rituals were wrenched into the cruelly cold truth of the

Dark. 'Lies and rubbish,' said the Dark, and Yeats' beliefs became the now familiar expanding cloud of cooling cinders, which rapidly disappeared. The Yeats that was left after this was very small indeed.

'Your loves,' said the Dark, and then there was the worst pain of all. Out of his shrunken self was dragged all that remained. His feelings for Laura, for Florence, for Maud... Here it came, here it came and he could not bear it. Not that one, not her...

'Lies and rubbish!'

The dust of his false loves soon drifted away and the thing that had been W. B. Yeats began to slip into its last long sleep. Where he had been, a brilliant pin-point of light, so bright as to be beyond colour, hung in the void. Nothing sets off a diamond like black velvet, and it did.

'But this *is* love,' said the Dark. 'It is true love. You are not mine. You belong to the other one.'

The voice of W. B. Yeats came sleepily out of the void: 'You should take me. I am no good. My love has always been unreal, willed. I can see that now. Let me sleep.'

'No, Little Man,' said the Dark. 'You must wake up. Wake up. *Wake up!*'

In the garden of his father's house on the Hammersmith Road, twelve year old Willie Yeats stirred in the long damp grass and his dark eyelashes flickered. Something changed in the air around him, like the shimmer of a heat-haze. The garden seemed suddenly full of small presences in constant motion. They spiralled around a common centre in two different directions, making a double gyre or helix. There was a human shape at the centre of the spiral movements. She - and although no detail of face or figure was apparent, it was definitely She – looked down at the sleeping boy and said, 'Sleep. Dream. Do not wake yet.'

W. B. Yeats woke up with a start. He lay there without a thought in his head for a while. It was very restful. Then he began to feel the ground-chill. The grass tickled his cheeks. His back ached. He was forced back into life.

Standing up, he looked around. It was early morning in Kensington

Gardens, the start of a sunny day. He looked guiltily around to see if any keepers were about. There must be a law against dossing in public parks. Something more than his back was bothering him. He ran a hand through his thick black hair. Something more…

'Stephanie!' Stephanie was in danger. Yeats ran like a crazy man, hair streaming, his coat flapping; forty yards and he was slowing; forty nine and he slowed, and stopped. Who was Stephanie? There was no image in his mind to go with the name. Just a feeling. You felt nice just saying the name, so you wanted to say it again, mindlessly, like an idiot striking matches till the box was empty.

Stephanie. Steph – a – nie. A body so graceful it was weightless though long-limbed and capable. A smile, around which a face formed, curved pink lips, freckles, two dark eyes with a mischievous glint. Stephanie. The emptiness which he sensed waiting for him if he could not remember her was terrifying. He made himself reconstruct everything from the Cheshire Cheese on. Slowly, painfully it came back, events falling into line. The drive in the strange carriage. Waking to find her beside him on the couch. The way she saved him from an assassin outside the opera house. The Colonel's voice: 'Stephanie de Beauharnais is missing.' The message on Horton's back: 'she is at Blythe Road'. Yeats began to run, but not towards any of the park gates.

A young man in a black riding-coat and bowler was exercising an enormous bay horse on the Avenue which parallelled the Kensington Road, and it was straight at him that the Anglo-Irish poet dashed.

'Hey there!' shouted Yeats, and the rider reined in his horse, curious and wary: you got all sorts in the Park. Afterwards, that thought was the last thing he remembered.

It was difficult for Yeats to think, clinging on behind the rider of a trotting horse. Stephanie began to escape him again and he had to drag the memories back from where they wanted to go. Even after he had done, it all started leaking away again. He felt that he had lost something, or rather that something had been taken away from him; but the thing that had been taken away was the very thing which could have told him what he had lost. It reminded Yeats painfully of a man who had grown old in his grandfather Pollexfen's employment. The aged man would talk of the sea for a while, then gently and politely ask who Yeats was; after thirty seconds he would make the same request, and then again, and again, always with the same heart-rending humility and gentlemanly self-control.

After his strange sleep in the Gardens, Yeats still knew he loved Stephanie but her image kept slipping away from of his grasp until only her eyes, her dark-bright eyes, remained. It was terrifying, in so final a way that it was strangely exhilarating, like seeing a great wave approaching too fast for any escape, with not even time to flinch. He felt that if he lost his love for Stephanie, his life might just as well be over, and even that thought was exciting because it was a lover's thought, because it made him long to see her, to touch her, hold her and know her reality.

The big brown horse and its owner, with Yeats sitting with awkward determination behind him, stopped at the park gates. Kensington Road stretched away before them and somewhere off its quiet dusty length was the Blythe Road temple of the Golden Dawn, and Stephanie. Running on foot would be too slow, Yeats decided. Everything went white and sparkly for a moment and the black-coated horseman suddenly decided it was a splendid day for galloping down a main road.

Annie Horniman was triumphant. This was her moment, and she was not going to let some foolish girl in a silly faint spoil it.

'As one of the first to be initiated into the mysteries of the Order,' she intoned, with her two spindly arms raised aloft as if invoking the powers of the converted gas fitting at the centre of the ceiling, symbolizing low budgets and the pace of technological change, 'as hierophante I call down upon the Extraordinary General Meeting the justice of Ma'at, and let the truth be the feather in the scale so that we all may be truly On The Right Side!'

'Stuff and nonsense!' came a voice.

'Aieee!' screeched Annie Horniman, with careful attention to the spelling, 'I stand in line of descent from our great founders, and behind them the Secret Chiefs and their intermediary, Sapiens Dominabitur Astris herself, whose given name I so nearly share, the divinely palindromic Anna, Fräulein Sprengel.'

'Stuff and nonsense!' came the voice again. It was Mathers, emerging from the Vault and advancing on Miss Horniman through the frightened members, who parted for him like pack ice in the spring.

'There was no Fräulein Sprengel,' said Mathers curtly, 'The letter was faked.'

The communal gasp from the initiates of the Golden Dawn certainly was not faked. This was heresy. This was treason. This was going to be highly embarrassing if it were true.

'Those rituals you are spouting. I made 'em up, every last one,' said Mathers, shouldering Miss Horniman aside. 'Now, out of my way. I am in touch with real powers that would have you widdling yourself. There's something I have to do.'

Kilt swinging, back-pack clasped to his chest, for the third time that morning Mathers made for the door to the stairs. Before he could get there, it was ripped clean off its hinges and crashed flat to the floor, all but taking Mathers with it. A demon was revealed, a white-faced eye-rolling fury, seven feet tall, with a shock of coal-black hair and the strength of ten. And the demon spoke. And it spoke in the voice of William Butler Yeats:

'WHERE IS SHE?'

Yeats might just as well have been flying as he pounded up the Golden Dawn's steep staircase, for all that he noticed the effort. It was that upward rush which wrenched the door from its hinges when it did not open quickly enough for his frightened rage. MacGregor Mathers was far from being a small man, but Yeats held him at arms length and shook him like a rat. 'Where is she?' he roared again.

'In Paris,' said Mathers, with remarkable self-control, 'Maud's in Paris, Willie.'

'What?' said Yeats, bafflement making his anger lose momentum. Something passed between the two men. Perhaps it was magic, or some animal sense long buried beneath language, but Mathers suddenly understood. 'The girl?' he said. 'She's back there. In the Vault. Miss Cracknell's looking after her.'

Yeats put Mathers down and absent-mindedly set the man's tartan bonnet straight. 'Sorry about the feather,' he muttered, 'only, they said they'd got her, d'ye see?'

Mather's fox-like features softened and a trapped thing looked out of his eyes like someone on Death Row acknowledging a new arrival. 'I know,' he said. 'I know. It's horrible. It's all real, and nothing like we thought. I'm sorry. I'm sorry.'

But Yeats was no longer listening. He left Mathers in the now permanently open doorway at the top of the stairs and went, full of desperate fear and longing, watched all the way by the silent and wondering magicians of the Inner Order, to the Vault.

He found Stephanie lying in the pastos, the painted casket of resurrection and life preserved. She was wearing the long sky-blue coat, now blackened and creased, and her face was pale; she was very still and her eyes were closed. Sergeant Platimer was there too, sitting on the floor, looking vacant and dazed, as if his mind had popped out for a break and left the motor running. Maud Cracknell was sitting on a stool beside the pastos, with a straight back and keen eyes silently watching over the unconscious woman, and holding one of her limp hands; the white witch made no objection when the poet gently took hold of Stephanie's other hand.

He had wanted to reach out and hold her ever since their hands had accidentally come together, when they first met at the Cheshire Cheese. During that night at the palace, it had seemed a privilege beyond his deserving just to lie beside her sleeping form with love roaring silently through his veins. Now that he did touch her, it was without the feelings he had imagined would attend the action. There was just a sickening fear of her stillness and pallor. He had heard of people rubbing wrists to restore life and did so, feeling ineffectual, but Stephanie responded at once, moved her head, her shoulders, eyes still closed but the lids fluttering. Then her eyes opened, unfocused but clear, and she looked up at Yeats with a sweet smile and said, 'Let go of my wrist, now.'

There was a buzz out in the main room. Crowley was unsteadily up on his feet again and lurching around like a mad zombie, trying to direct his feet towards the Vault. He could not move or think properly. Something had been taken; something was gone. For a man used to being physically and mentally in command of himself, it was terrifying.

The Golden Dawn's Inner Order nervously watched his efforts; Crowley damaged was more frightening than Crowley whole. When he had finally navigated himself to the Vault's entrance he paused, the carefully hidden contempt showing in his face at last. His pallid lips moved, uttered some words, and he disappeared.

'What did he say?'

'There's going to be an explosion!'

'What?'

'Crowley is going to destroy the Temple!'

If the door had not already been torn off its hinges by Yeats, then the ensuing stampede of magicians would have done it nicely. They disappeared like magic, except that you could certainly see how it was done. Vases, steles and plaster pedestals reached the end of their trajectories and useful lives, the dust settled and quiet descended on the Isis-Urania Temple of the Golden Dawn.

Crowley entered the seven-sided space within the Vault's painted panels and found a policeman sitting on the floor. Stephanie Toughguid was lying, weak but conscious, in the sacred pastos of Christian Rosenkreutz; Maud Cracknell was looking at Yeats, and Yeats was regarding Stephanie with a sadness so profound that it resembled tranquility. Crowley gazed at the scene with an odd expression. 'Keep away,' he whispered, 'keep out.' No one will ever know why he said this.

'Mathers has gone down,' Crowley said, returning strength filling out his voice. 'He'll kill us all. Yeats, you've got to come with me. This is your moment. It's nearly time. We've got one minute. Come, come now!'

Yeats was slow to respond. He was half-paralysed by Stephanie's changed response to him, even though he understood it. He finally knew why his fairy looked so much like Stephanie, and what it meant when he saw her fairy, the image of himself, pale and still, carried in solemn procession on its bier. He knew there would be another fairy for her, but it would not look like him. Above all he knew that, without the magic of love, for a woman like Stephanie he wasn't anyone, he was nobody, he was nothing; but at least he could be nothing with style.

Stephanie sat up and Maud Cracknell let go of her hand. Yeats looked at her. He was about to do something brave. It was easier when you got used to it. The long-haired young woman looked back at him, holding his gaze, with no particular expression.

'Goodbye,' Yeats said to her. 'Goodbye. You'd better get well away from the building, all of you. Officer, look after them, will you?'

That was the brave bit over; now he just had to go and risk his life and save the world.

They found Mathers in the cellar, sitting gloomily on top of the pyramid of wooden crates. He was hefting the candle, the magic candle given to him by Maud Gonne in Paris, slowly and reflectively, in the palm of his left hand, as if he were conducting a dirge. He swung a leg with the same slow rhythm, bang, bang, bang, like the beat of a state funeral, knocking his steel-tapped heel against the rough wood of the wire-bound packing case on which he was sitting. Crowley stared at the swinging boot as if mesmerized.

'Mathers, old man' he said, his voice carefully controlled. 'I shouldn't do that.'

Mathers' foot ceased its swinging. 'Don't try to stop me,' he said, in a lifeless monotone. 'I've got to do this. Maud Gonne's swami explained everything. Just one candle will purge the Order.'

'Listen to me,' said Crowley, opening his eyes wide so that the whites showed all the way round.

'None of that!' cried Mathers, shielding his own eyes, 'I am an Adeptus Extra-ordinarius of the Secret Conclave of Nid – practise not upon me with your conjuror's tricks!'

'I was going to say,' said Crowley, 'that Imperial British Intelligence knows all about Maud Gonne's swami. His name is Vincent Michael O'Toole and he is a member of the Irish Republican Brotherhood. They have been planning this for a year. It is a plot to assassinate the Queen, who will be passing this building very soon. They have deceived you. Your wife is not in danger. You are holding a stick of dynamite. You are sitting on half a ton of the same explosive.'

Mathers said nothing, just looked straight ahead as if he suddenly found the cellar wall interesting.

'Don't panic,' said Crowley with deliberate calm. 'Just give the stick of dynamite to Yeats.

Mathers swallowed, blinked, sighed and did so. The sound of trotting horses filtered down to them from the street. Someone shouted an order and there were more confused sounds that seemed to come from the rear of the building. Yeats' Fairy appeared on his shoulder, put her two hands on the rim of his ear very gently and whispered to him as lovingly as if a heart could speak: 'I am so sorry.'

Crowley took two or three steps backwards, away from the cellar doorway and the stairs. An inner store-room door burst open and two people rushed out. They were in uniform and had rifles and they aimed the rifles at Yeats. A third man appeared, carrying a camera with tripod and bellows which he quickly and skilfully began to set up. Boots were clattering down the stairs from the ground floor and a strong voice shouted, 'Traitors! Traitors to the Crown! Traitors to the Empire!'

After that, the cellar became very full of people, in a motley mix of army scarlet and green, and police blue. All the while, Yeats and Mathers did not move. Mathers sitting on the crates, half-turned, his foxy face turned in shocked surprise, Yeats standing by Mathers, tall and stooping in his creased green velvet coat, his black hair rather wild, head turned in the same direction and with a similar expression on his white face, holding up the Shiva vengeance candle at arm's length like a truncheon. They looked like characters in a living tableau – 'Discovered, or The Basement Bombers'.

The two soldiers with guns steadily trained on Yeats were joined by two more who aimed their weapons at Mathers; after a few seconds he noticed them and slowly raised his hands. The crowd of officers at the foot of the basement steps parted to allow a second wave of people down. These were in civilian black and came in non-regulation sizes. The smallest of them, Sir Cuthbert Dangermouse, bounced to the fore and snapped his fingers at the waiting photographer. 'Go on,' he said, 'what are you waiting for?'

'Right you are guv,' said the photographer. Squinting down at his view-finder he raised the tee-shaped flash gun. 'Here goes gents, look at me please, three - two…'

'Just a moment!'

Yeats' head turned to see who had spoken. He could not seem to move anything else. A panicky bird was trapped in his chest, his arms and legs had turned to ice, because the voice was that of the Colonel.

It was nine minutes past nine on the second of March 1899. 9+9+2+3+1+8+9+9 = 5+0=5.

Yeats saw it all in a flash of insight which left him sick and empty. Messages from the fairies, instructions from secret masters, for him alone, the saviour of the world – they had told him what he wanted to hear, played upon his secret longings and desires, played him like a stupid vainglorious fish! He would be presented to the world as Yeats, the mad Irish bomber. Frantically he ransacked his memory: had anything supernatural happened that was objectively verifiable? The fairy, the messages, the quincunx - it could all be explained by organized deception compounded by his own will to believe. Perhaps he *was* mad. Either way, it would destroy the campaign for Irish Home

Rule. How could he have been so blind, so gullible?

In a military greatcoat, his grey eyes pale, cold and bright as the rising sun in winter, the Colonel emerged from behind the line of dark-suited government witnesses, and came right up to Mathers and Yeats and the little island of wooden crates. When he was very close to Yeats, so close that those behind him could not see his face, he looked right into the poet's eyes and murmured, with the same tone and depth of feeling as Yeats' Fairy, 'I am so very sorry.' Then his eyes narrowed and he took a smart step back. 'I note with interest,' said the Colonel, 'that there is smoke coming from the stick of dynamite that Mr Yeats is holding. I surmise that Mr Mathers had in fact already lit it. I see him nodding to confirm my theory. I further note that blowing it does not seem to put it out. Nor, I notice, does banging it on the packing cases. Or stamping on it. Yeats… Yeats… YEATS! I think if it was going to go off, it would have …

A few minutes earlier, a body of horsemen, moving at a purposeful clip, had appeared at the end of Blythe Road. Scarlet and silver the Life Guard trotted, the glittering brim of a shiny black crown – the Queen's carriage, open, despite the sharp March morning air. There were two other four-wheelers growling along immediately behind the royal carriage, each full of serious men in top hats. Together the train of speeding carriages and its mounted escort headed for the whale-backed mass of Olympia's Great Hall.

All experience said that the carriage containing that familiar small figure clad in mourning black should be making its way through an avenue of flag-waving subjects, but the only sounds in Blythe Road were a brisk clop-clop of hooves and the rumble of wheels. The spectators were all outside Olympia's Exhibition Hall, expecting the Queen to arrive at the railway station there. In fact the royal party had been advised (by somebody very close to the Prime Minister) to alight at Shepherd's Bush station and then drive the short distance to Olympia in an open carriage, so satisfying both security and decorum by arriving unexpectedly and in the proper style. The unpublicized route would be perfectly safe as long as the royal carriage did not stop for anything.

It stopped. It was always going to stop, but the Plan had not expected it to be at a sharply delivered command from the Queen herself, about halfway along Blythe Road, right outside Number 36, where a big policeman stood supporting a slender young woman with long brown hair and eyes like two smudges of coal in her white face. Perhaps she had fallen over, for her pale blue coat was dirty. The pair seemed to have come from the house, of which the door was open. The cavalry escort halted, keeping formation as tidily as if they had practised for this very thing. Plumes nodded, gloved hands patted the horses strong necks, hooves shuffled and were quiet.

'Steffi!' cried the Queen. Her voice was high, clear and filled with affection, tinged with surprise; she was trying to stand up in the royal carriage. Two officers exchanged a carefully neutral look. 'Steffi,' shouted (and there was no other word for it) the Queen again. Now she was actually waving. One of the two equerries in the third carriage back began thumbing urgently through a thick little pocket-book; the other had his hand over his eyes.

Platimer, confused, tried to salute, stand to attention and support Stephanie all at the same time.

'Stephanie, child, what are you doing here?' said Queen Victoria, loudly and distinctly. The stillness was uncanny. Everybody and everything except that small woman standing in her carriage, seemed frozen. Not a horse twitched its tail or tossed its head. They knew, the horses - something was about to happen.

Enter Thomas Hardy. He rounded the last corner like the people's favourite on Derby Day. At the same moment a woman appeared at the other end of the road. She was tall and blonde and wore a long green winter coat with a black fur collar. She had no hat and her abundant hair flew as she strode at a man's pace but by no means with a man's movements.

Hardy's own steady gait, evolved to eat up country miles, did not falter. Right down the middle of Blythe Road he came, straight toward the mounted troops and the royal carriage. He walked unaffected through the furious malevolence of Oberon's dark fairies. He walked through Titania's royal bodyguard laying down their lives in heroic battle with the Bucca Dhu, summoned in desperation by its master Oberon when he saw what was walking.

Hardy and Clarissa Jane Laurel reached Victoria's carriage at the same moment and the scene was complete. Every cell in every human being present felt a silvery thrill run through its nucleus. Confident in her household guards, each wearing a helmet designed by Prince Albert himself, the Queen gazed with untroubled curiosity at her four oddly-assorted subjects. She smiled inwardly, hearing her husband's voice: as playing cards, they were not a winning hand - the big red-faced policeman, the funny bright-eyed little man with the moustaches, her own dear Steffi - and the other woman, so beautiful and yet so sad, looking up at her as if she had something terribly important to say.

'What is it, my dear?' said Queen Victoria.

Then there was movement. The beautiful blonde woman reached inside her long green coat and when her hand reappeared it was holding a gun. The air, already sparkling, became so thick with exotic energies that it was hard to breathe. Like millions of miniscule bees, buzzing at ultrasonic frequencies, swarming and angry, the fairies fought each other for mastery. The Plan's timeline, counted down minute by minute for the past twenty-two years, enacted by the conspirators of the Saxonian Empire but conceived by a superhuman intelligence, had arrived at zero. It was nine minutes past nine.

The vengeance candle suddenly flared in Yeats' hands, in the basement of the Golden Dawn, just below the royal carriage where Stephanie de Beauharnais, too weak to intervene, was witnessing the assassination of Queen Victoria.

'The trouble with you,' Yeats' father had said to him when he was twelve, 'is that you want to believe the world is full of magic.'

Slowly, silently, inexorably, the misty reservoir of unchanneled credulity beneath the Isis-Urania Temple of the Golden Dawn exploded. The explosion was bigger - much, much bigger - than any fairy had predicted. Catalysed and driven by W. B. Yeats' boundless belief in the supernatural, the circular front of the etheric shock wave expanded, catching and rolling up every single fairy in its path. At the point of contact, for an immeasurable instant, each fairy crossed the Veil and became solidly real and visible in the physical world. Humans stopped what they were doing, eyes widening, mouths opening – then the vision was gone, mouths were closed, eyes were rubbed and it had not happened. On and on went the magical blast wave, escaping the city at last to race across the southern counties and beyond, north, east and west, taking with it all the silent ones, the good neighbours, the fair folk: all, all seized and whirled – not to destruction, but to a fragmentation and scattering that would take time, time on the human scale, to reverse. Think of ten thousand candles reflected in a still pool, then imagine a splash at the pool's centre, and the radiating ripples dashing those reflections to pieces; so it was with England's fairies.

Amongst the first to be so scattered were the dark fairies who had sat, whispering, on the shoulders of the troops of the Royal Guard and their commander, convincing them that they were serving their country by betraying its Queen; but it also blew away Titania's fairy bodyguard, who attended in their flowery thousands on the mortal Queen and preserved her from harm. This tactical sacrifice was the Fairy King's master stroke. Nothing now seemed to stand between Queen Victoria and her assassin, who was taking aim.

Just under their feet, in the Blythe Road Temple basement, there was a scene of noisy chaos. When important officials find they are standing beside half a ton of dynamite and a lit fuse, it is at once apparent that there are heights to which they do not wish to rise. The stairway was a mass of kicking legs and waving arms; one almost spherical under-secretary had thought it was smart idea to escape up the chimney and was thoroughly jammed. The Colonel and Sir Cuthbert looked at each other, briefly of one mind. Yeats, still holding the smouldering remains of the Shiva Candle, his hair on end and face sooty, had not moved; Mathers had sat down morosely on a packing case, chin on hand; the soldiers dutifully continued to point rifles each of which aimed slightly off its target.

Sir Cuthbert Dangermouse looked at his watch, then at the Colonel. 'I hope you know what you're doing,' he said quietly. 'As things stand, nothing will save them from hanging - and as for Ireland...'

'I'm sure it will be all right,' said the Colonel. 'I have it on good authority that nothing has been left to chance.'

Clarissa Jane Laurel, Agent 42, took a deep breath. This was it. The moment when she would be revenged on the ruling class which had foully murdered her sister – in the name of law, in the name of order, in the name of freedom! She had not managed to kill any of *them* yet, only her own secret master; always some wretched complication or, worse, some weak compunction, a small clear voice which spoke of love. You could almost think something had been protecting her from herself. Whatever it was, it had gone; she had felt it go just a moment before, like a leaf blown away in the wind. Now there would be no mistake. The way was clear, just as they had said it would be. This time.

She was so close to the carriage that she could smell its new varnish, laid on thick as glass, so close that she could read the expression in the eyes of the eighty year old monarch. It surprised her. All she could see there was love, and pain long-borne. Victoria's eyes said, 'Send me to him, if that is Your will.'

Agent 42's determination and old hatred both wavered. She collected herself, took aim, and the sun seemed to suffer a sudden eclipse: Sergeant Platimer had put himself in the way.

'Now then young lady,' he said kindly, 'you don't want to do that.'

'Actually,' she said, stepping back, 'I do. Now, duck!'

'What?' said the Sergeant.

'Duck,' she said.

'Duck man!' bellowed the cavalry escort's commander. The pressure of the dark will had suddenly lifted, leaving him confused and impatient of any gap in the action which might be filled by thought.

'Duck man!' screamed his junior officers, obedient and terrified.

'Duckman? Duckman? What, you an' all?' roared Platimer. Eighteen square feet of policeman continued to fill Agent 42's sights, with no suggestion of a duck. A great fat-fingered hand was reaching forward for the gun. For a vital second she hesitated. Shooting Sergeant Platimer would in theory be taking revenge on the people who had killed her sister, but in practice it felt like shooting everyone's dad. And you could not shoot a big man who bit his nails. But you could shoot a policeman.

In that moment she became aware that someone was standing beside her. They had said there would be no one else there. They had taken care of everything, they said. No one had taken care of her sister.

Clarissa Jane's eyes flickered, the gun barrel wobbled and she turned to look. She saw a rather small man with a large moustache and humorously observant eyes. Something wounded but untamed and infinitely caring spoke to her from behind those eyes, and everything changed. Crowley's fairy had sacrificed herself, extending her mortal's life but casting the destiny of his one true love, Clarissa Jane Laurel, adrift on the seas of chance; the miserable assassin's own birth fairy, tall, clever, wilful and self-assured, Crowley in miniature, had just been blasted into northern France. By fairy law, until it found its way back, Thomas Hardy was going to be a very happy man.

'Hello,' he said, 'have you ever been to Dorset?' and everything went black.

This had nothing to do with Hardy's forehead: Sergeant Platimer, having taken the gun from Clarissa Jane's unresisting hand, and appalled at his own courage, had fainted and fallen on top of her.

There was a moment in which the Universe seemed to pause, gather itself and set out on a new path. The memories of all the humans involved in the Blythe Road incident simultaneously decided that nothing had happened. The cavalry troop, loyal guardians of the royal personage, looked to their order. A dashing officer of the Guard, gorgeous in scarlet and gold, white horse-hair crest nodding, handed Stephanie to a seat beside her second cousin twice removed, Victoria, Queen and Empress. The officer backed carefully down to the pavement, feeling his way with his mirror-shiny boots, folded up the carriage step, saluted smartly with a white-gauntleted hand and said, 'With your permission, Ma'am?'

The aged Queen of England, fussing over her young cousin, flapped her own small hand at him in assent.

'Move on!' said the officer in command, 'Move on!' repeated his lieutenant, and the carriages, the cavalry guard, the blonde woman with the – ahem – striking figure, the spry old gent with the lively eye and the big policeman, shaky but smiling, all did just that.

'Did I know Thomas Hardy was a changeling?' Oberon was being careful to keep his temper.

'You knew,' said Titania, 'because you are the King and you know everything, but you did not notice because you are not interested in babies.'

'Show me.'

'Come.'

There was a tiny adjustment and the two figures, slowly circling around a common centre, moved a little way back down the timeline and a very short distance through space. They were in the attic above a small upper room in an overcrowded cottage. The plaster and lathes of the room's ceiling were completely transparent to their mode of seeing.

In the bedroom a woman was giving birth and it was not going well. The child was early and the doctor, a man with mutton-chop whiskers, puffing and blowing with the self-importance of the frightened professional, was out of his depth. The tiny baby slipped out all at once, its old, old features ominously composed, still and calm as an eastern sage in deep contemplation. Its eyes were shut; it did not seem to be breathing. Goody Lovage, the village midwife, wanted to massage it and hold it, skin to skin in the old style but the doctor was embarrassed and harshly ordered her to behave decently and get rid of it. The baby was placed on the sideboard like an unwanted dish. Attention in the poky little bedroom was all on the mother – the human attention, that is: the watchers up by the rafters were looking down at the baby.

Two fairies in drab overalls appeared from the cracked plaster of the wall. One was carrying a tiny clipboard. He had an almost invisible pencil stuck behind one pointed ear. Oberon cocked a quizzical eyebrow at Titania.

'Whose imagination is this?'

'The midwife's,' said Titania, smiling fondly; Goody Lovage had been a favourite of hers, with gentle hands and firm views on bringing new life into the world and where possible protecting the mothers from the cruel ignorance of men.

Now the two worker-fairies were carrying away a small fairy body, feet first, arms dangling. As they disappeared back through the wall, another little being, fairy-sized but subtly different, emerged from a point further along, moving in a way that could only be called furtive. It was naked but its skin was the colour and texture of autumn leaves, its hair was a shock of twiggy strands and its eyes were an owl's eyes. It looked a great deal less human than the fairies did.

The owl-eyed sprite stepped cautiously into the dim lamplight, sauntered over to the still form of the infant, looked innocently around and gave the baby a powerful kick in the chest. Immediately a change came over the tiny body on the sideboard. It was like a squall passing over open water, a ruffle, a flurry of energy and a change of colour. The little rib-cage trembled and lifted and the baby took a faltering breath. The midwife noticed at once, made to speak, thought better of it, and went straight to the baby; the doctor, fussing and tutting ineffectually over the mother, who had fallen into a pallid sleep, had seen nothing yet.

The slowly circling watchers under the rafters, suspended full length in mid-air like mediaeval Christmas angels with their toes pointing downwards, spoke as one, the male and female voices harmonizing into one note that made the cottage's ancient frame resonate to superhuman frequencies which the mortals sensed but were too busy to consider.

'Why?'

The personage who had all this time been lounging on the cobwebby cross beams, as long from head to toe as the cottage was wide, green-skinned and leaf-clad, shrugged its two bushy shoulders.

'Don't ask me,' it seemed to say, jerking a thumb at the midwife, 'I'm with her.'

'So,' said the half of the circling pair that mortals knew as Oberon, 'This Thomas Hardy is a changeling – of sorts.'

'Not like Kaspar Hauser though,' said Titania soothingly as the scene began to fade and they let themselves drift on the ever-flowing tide of time back to the five dimensional crossroads which humans call the present, where Clarissa Jane Laurel and Thomas Hardy, walked away, arm in arm, towards Olympia.

'The Green Man was there at his birth,' said Titania musingly.

'He is not completely human. The Hardy is a changeling, but not of our making. He is unpredictable. We do not know what will happen.'

'Yes. Isn't it wonderful!' said Queen Titania.

'No. He has spoiled the Plan,' the King said.

The two circling figures began to follow new paths, the circles first elongating to form ellipses, then moving along an axis defined by their common centre. The circles had become spirals, gyres, each greatest where the other was least, each defining the other, always opposed, always dependent. The spiralling quickened, became a vibration, and the two figures became one.

'No one can spoil the Plan,' said the Secret Masters to themselves, 'the Plan is what happens.'

'Set and match, I think,' whispered the Queen.

*

Stephanie Toughguid remembered Yeats as someone she had protected, a civilian. There might even have been something – a flirtation – you get bored on these assignments. Why see him again?

He saw her again. Not at the Golden Dawn. She never came back after the Blythe Road incident. Not many members noticed or cared; there were other, more significant absences. Mathers had returned to his Paris stronghold and Crowley was said to be with him. Several notable initiates, including Miss Horniman, the tea-heiress and crystal-gazer, were no longer seen at the weekly meetings. The members looked increasingly for direction to Mr Yeats, who let it be known that the events of March 2nd were best not discussed. In case anyone felt differently, there was a discreet visit from a short and charming civil servant with golden curls and shoulders like a wrestler, explaining and excusing the basement raid. Too much security, he said. Over-reaction. Hoped the members understood. Better not to talk about it. In fact, it would almost be – no, he could safely say, ha ha, it *would* be illegal to talk about it.

He saw her at an exhibition of some rather ugly bronze figures, in a smart Oxford Street gallery. Annie Horniman was helping the artist to whom, as usual, it would mean so much if Mr W. B. Yeats were at the opening.

After a sleepless night, Yeats had guiltily pushed Miss Horniman into inviting Stephanie. He was immediately tormented by doubt and fear. The reason for the invitation would be transparent. Would she come? What would it mean if she did? How could he bear it if she did not?

She was standing by herself in a corner, slender and straight, self-possessed, watching the roomful of chattering poseurs and half-smiling, Yeats knew, because she was aware of the men who eyed her and wanted her. Should he approach her? Once he would have thought the world turned on such a decision, but he had learned that courage was only the beginning; courage allows things to happen, but after that it is the unseen hand which shapes life and cares nothing for individuals.

Courage is not always enough.

Dublin, October 1899. She looked lovely that evening at the gallery, but somehow changed, in a way which made my heart shrink like a tropical plant in a frost. She looked now like any other woman, any of the innumerable women, that is, who didn't want me. The dancing spark in her elfin eyes was no longer dancing for me. Neither of us spoke. I needed to break the silence, especially when she slightly lowered her head and smiled, looking steadily into my eyes in the way that made my heart beat like a hammer in my chest. I wanted to say Stephanie, I love you, I love you... What I actually said was 'Good evening' and the words did not come out properly as something seemed to have gone wrong with my voice.

Was I in town for long? No, I was going to Dublin tomorrow. She had liked The Wind in the Reeds. I did not want her to like the Wind in the Reeds because it had not been written for her. Awkward silence. Then worse: she wanted to thank me for what I had done, and was doing, for poetry and for theatre. She wanted to thank me for that, and I wanted to thank her for once looking at me as if I were a desirable man, for saying 'yes' with her beautiful dark eyes, for letting me be close to her scented warmth, and all I said, stiffly, even angrily, was that I simply did what came to me, and my projects were a professional duty. More silence, more awkward than ever. I had to force words out as if the act of speaking were something I had learned that morning: might we meet when I came back from Dublin?

'Oh I will not be in London after this weekend. I am going to Jamaica. My husband has a plantation there and he needs me with him.'

I need you too, I wanted to say, doesn't that matter? But I didn't, of course. Because I truly loved Stephanie I did not want to plead, to push, to persuade in order to have things my way; I did not want to be the kind of man who selfishly interfered in a life. That's what I told myself, then. So, witty and quick-thinking as ever, I just said, 'Oh.'

And that was that. Almost.

As soon as his key touched the lock, the door opened. For a moment, his foolish heart leapt, but it was only the housekeeper, Mrs Old, standing in the shade of the front hall.

'Mr Yeats, there was a letter for you, dear. I told her you weren't here.'

'Told who – er – whom?'

'The young lady who brought it. Looked like she was going

somewhere. All dressed up, hat and veil, carriage with all boxes and such. Rather a hoity-toity miss, I thought, behind that veil. "Make sure Mr Yeats receives this letter," without never a please nor thank you. But she decided not to leave it when I... I told her you were in Paris.'

The quiet of the afternoon took a long deep breath and let it out. The plane tree leaves, autumn yellow, stirred and were still.

'Why did you say that, Mrs Old,' said Yeats, putting on the mask of careful calm, 'when you knew I was in Dublin?'

Mrs Old looked as if she were going to cry. She put her hand up to her face. 'I don't know,' she said, 'I don't know.' Then she did cry.

Yeats looked at her, asking himself, not for the first time in his life, how he could have been so unobservant.

'Never mind,' he said, more to himself than his housekeeper. 'It could have been anybody. The letter could have been anything.'

'Pardon?' said Mrs Old, who had also been lost in her own thoughts.

'Nothing,' said Yeats. 'Good night.'

He put a foot heavily on the first of the stairs which now only led back to his own life. Why did they do things like that? Push you away and then leave you wondering. What if? Did she? Should I have? He willed such questions out of his mind and began to climb, counting. He had done the stairs before, but never the ones that creaked.

The High King of Ireland nods at his Fool over the dying flame of the Samhain fire. As one man they stand up, waving. 'Has he seen us?' they say. 'He seemed to turn at the last minute. I think he might have seen us. I think he might have waved.'

But W. B. Yeats is already below the skyline, descending the further slope into the twentieth century.

For he gave all his heart and lost.

Printed in Great Britain
by Amazon.co.uk, Ltd.,
Marston Gate.